A Sagebrush Soul

A Biographical Novel of Mark Twain

John Isaac Jones

Table of Contents

1
Halley's I

The year 1835 had not been kind to John Marshall Clemens. Two years earlier, he had loaded up his worldly possessions and moved his wife and two children from Fentress County, Tennessee to Florida, Missouri in hopes of finding a better life. Friends had said land was cheap in Florida, locals were friendly and, although there were already two lawyers in the town, it should provide enough legal work for a third attorney to earn a living wage. So, Clemens took their advice and, upon arrival, bought twenty acres of land with a five-room house and a barn, opened a law office and dug out a place for himself and his family in the rolling hills of northeastern Missouri.

Once settled, however, his expectations did not materialize as planned. First, there were repairs to be made to the house, then there were fees to practice law in the county, and finally, he had to pay $350 in back taxes on the property. In 1833, his first year in Florida, Missouri, he handled twelve legal cases and earned a paltry $420 after expenses, just enough to scrape by. The following year, 1834, proved to be even worse. That year, he handled a total of five cases—two divorces, a murder case and two bankruptcies—for a total of $380. Now, in early 1835, his family was barely making ends meet and the financial hole he had been digging was becoming deeper and deeper. In early January, he was forced to borrow $5,000 against his home and land to stay financially afloat.

***

Finally, in early March, Clemens saw a glimmer of salvation when two freed slaves suddenly appeared in his life. One Saturday afternoon, he was returning from town in the family buckboard when he saw a wagon stopped in front of his home. One of the rear wheels was off the wagon and a middle-aged black couple were sitting idly on the side of the road. Clemens turned the buckboard onto the dirt road leading to his home, then got out. A tall, fortyish man with a gaunt face and a balding head, he approached the black couple.

"What's the problem?" he asked.

"Wheel broke off and I don't have a spare one," the black man said. He was in his early forties, coal black in color, with a solemn face and a stubble of salt-and-pepper beard.

"Why aren't you on a plantation?" Clemens asked.

"Our master freed us. He said we could leave the plantation and do as we liked. We been traveling almost two weeks looking for a place to light."

"You are without a home?"

"Yes, sir! Just me and her and this mule."

"Will the mule plow?"

"Yes. And he's a young mule."

Clemens studied the couple for a moment.

"I believe I have an extra wagon wheel in the barn."

"I have no money to pay you," the black man said, "but I can do some work."

"You know how to plant and grow cotton?"

"Been doing it all my life."

"What's your name?"

"Hezekiah. This here is my wife Delrina."

The black woman nodded politely. In her late thirties, she had a puffy face, bulky hips and bosom, and a white head rag knotted around her head.

An hour later, Clemens had retrieved a wagon wheel from the barn, then, working with Hezekiah, they managed to mount it securely on the wagon.

"Much obliged to you," Hezekiah said. "Now what can I do for you?"

Clemens came straight to the point.

"I have ten acres of land sitting idle back there," he said, pointing to the acreage behind his home. "I want to plant it in cotton. You already own a mule. I'll buy the seed, fertilizer and the necessary plows. I will be expecting you to do the work and I'll share profits 50-50. Is that a fair offer?"

"Yes, sir!"

"I'll clean out a space in the tool shed for you and your wife to sleep. You and her can eat off the family table. Is that agreeable?"

"Yes, sir!"

"Can your wife work?"

"Delrina is a mite lame," he said. "When she was four years old back in North Carolina, a bear dragged her into the woods and gnawed off a good part of her right leg. Now she gets around on a wooden peg."

"A peg?"

"Her moves are slow, but she's a good cook and knows how to care for white children."

"Well, I have two children to be cared for," Clemens said. "So, I shall be expecting assistance from both of you."

"Yes, sir!" Hezekiah said. "We'll start tomorrow."

* * *

That night, Clemens told his wife Jane about the deal he had struck.

"Our only salvation is this cotton crop," he said. "If we don't bring it in, we're in deep financial trouble."

"How much longer can we forestall this?" Jane said. "For more than two years now, we have been living hand to mouth."

"What would you have me do?"

"Our predicament won't improve until we leave this town," she said. "There are not enough people here to support another attorney."

"Perhaps you're right," he said. "Where would you have us go?"

"Hannibal!" Jane said quickly. "An abundance of people. An abundance of opportunity. I received a post from Lydia Foster this past week. She informed me that, since the family

3

moved to Hannibal, her husband is getting more blacksmith work than ever before."

John was hesitant.

"I'm convinced we should wait a bit longer."

"More waiting is not the answer. We have to move with due speed. And soon."

"Why should we do that?" he replied.

"I'm with child again."

He turned to her.

"Are you certain?"

"I'm certain."

"If it's a male child," John said, "I want to name him Samuel, after my father."

"If it's a girl," Jane said, "we'll name her Abigail after my aunt on my mother's side."

"Done!"

***

Born of Cornish-American parents in 1798, John Clemens grew up in Kentucky, where his family owned both land and slaves. Named after U.S. Chief Justice John Marshall, he took a job at age 11 as a clerk at an iron mine, then undertook the study of law and became a licensed lawyer at the age of 21. In May of 1823, he married Jane Lampton, the oldest of seven children who grew up on her family's cotton farm in Adair County, Kentucky. She was a devout Baptist while John was an agnostic freethinker. In her youth, Jane was known far and wide for her resourcefulness and story-telling abilities. In the fall of 1825, Clemens moved his growing family from Kentucky to Fentress County, Tennessee, where he practiced law, operated a general store, and served as a county commissioner. In 1832, when the Tennessee state legislature moved the Fentress county seat to another town, John's legal work dried up to almost nothing and he made the decision to move to Florida, Missouri.

***

The following morning, Clemens and Hezekiah went into town to prepare for their great endeavor. At the local mercantile store, they bought three plows, cotton seed and fertilizer. Clemens paid for it all. That afternoon, Hezekiah had his mule hitched to the new turning plow and was breaking open the virgin earth behind the Clemens home for a cotton crop.

Over the next two weeks, Hezekiah turned and harrowed the entire ten acres. Two days later, he was using a borrowed planter to put the cotton seeds and fertilizer in the ground and, by late May, the crop had been planted.

"The crop is in the ground," Hezekiah said. "All we got to do now is watch it grow."

Meanwhile, his wife Delrina, after only a few short months, proved to be a boon for the Clemens family. She had assumed most of the cooking and cleaning duties in the household. She got along well with the children and she always seemed to have an effective home remedy for childhood illnesses, such as the croup, sore throats, and cuts and bruises. John felt that bringing the two former slaves into the family was a wise decision.

***

Over the next few months, Clemens and Hezekiah kept a close watch on the progress of their cotton crop. On the first day of July, the plants were almost two feet high and the wide expanse of land behind the Clemens home was now a sea of deep green with thousands of strong, healthy cotton plants. On that day, John and Hezekiah were strolling through the fields.

"We going to have a good crop," Hezekiah said.

By mid-August, the plants were knee high and the sprawling sea of green was now dotted with millions upon millions of little white cotton flowers.

"High cotton is such a pretty sight," Hezekiah said. "We going to see fiber here in the next week or two."

By early September, the cotton fibers were bursting out of their bolls with puffs of fluffy white cotton.

"When can you start picking?" Clemens asked.

"Probably another two weeks."

"How much time you need to pick it?"

"Five or six weeks," he said. "Now, I'll be expecting you to help me some with the picking."

"I can't pick cotton," Clemens said.

"You can unload the bags while I fill them up."

"I can do that," Clemens said. "Can Delrina pick cotton?"

"To pick cotton, you have to bend over," Hezekiah said. "If she tries to bend over on that peg leg, she'll fall on her face."

***

Meanwhile, over the next two months, Jane's belly was growing larger and larger with her third child. In early September, she was in her sixth month.

"Delrina has been a Godsend," she told her husband. "Her movements are slow, but she can do a heap of work. Because of her, this pregnancy has been easier than all the others."

"It pleases me to hear that," Clemens said.

***

In late October, Hezekiah started picking cotton and Clemens closed his law office and went into the field to help. Hezekiah was a master at picking cotton. His hands were a blur moving through the cotton plants; his fingers seemed to know exactly where to move next and, the instant he had one hand full of cotton, the other was right behind it with another handful. Once a 100-pound sack was filled, Clemens would drag it to the end of the row and dump it in the wagon. Once the picking was finished for the day, they would go to the cotton dealer in town, sell it, and collect the money. At the end of October, Clemens shared the proceeds of that month's picking. He handed Hezekiah his share of $212.

Hezekiah looked at the wad of cash in his hand. He seemed amazed.

"I never had so much money in all my life," he said. "Now I can buy me some new shoes and some new dresses for

Delrina."

***

By mid-November, more than five acres of the cotton crop had been picked. Hezekiah, who was now working for himself rather than a plantation owner, was relentless in picking the cotton. Then, one day in late November, Clemens took a murder case in town and told Hezekiah he would be absent from the fields for a few days. On the same day, he asked Hezekiah to forego the cotton picking and take the wagon into town to buy household supplies from the local mercantile store.

So, that morning, Hezekiah took the wagon and Jane's grocery list into town. John had credit with the establishment, so whatever supplies Hezekiah bought were to be added to John's bill. Upon arrival at the mercantile store, Hezekiah gave the list to the proprietor and, after some thirty minutes, a pile of supplies, flour, bacon, rice, beans, lard, coffee and other items were all stacked together at the front of the store. The proprietor asked Hezekiah to load the flour last because the 100-pound bags were too heavy for him to lift. Finally, all of the supplies, including the flour, were loaded into the wagon, then Hezekiah took the reins and headed back to the Clemens homestead.

***

That afternoon, when the local sheriff appeared at the Clemens home, Jane answered the door.

"Where's the darkie you sent into town this morning to buy supplies?" he said.

"Why do you ask?"

"He stole a 100-pound sack of flour," the sheriff said. "One sack went on the bill, but he took two."

"There must be some mistake," Jane said. "Hezekiah wouldn't steal."

"I've got to take him in," the sheriff said. "Where is he?"

"He's picking cotton in the field behind the house."

***

Later that afternoon, when John arrived back at home in the buckboard, Jane told him Hezekiah had been arrested. Instantly, he turned the buckboard around and headed back into town to the city jail to talk to Hezekiah.

"Why did you take an extra bag of flour?" John asked.

"I thought you were paying for two," Hezekiah said, "so I took two bags. I didn't mean to steal nothing."

Ten minutes later, John was down the street at the mercantile store. He told the proprietor he would be happy to pay for the extra bag of flour.

"It's the principle of the thing," the proprietor said. "I can't have no darkies coming into my establishment and walking off with an extra bag of flour."

"He thought we were paying for two bags," Clemens said, "so he took two bags."

"I'm sorry, John," the proprietor said. "You know how darkies will steal from white folks. I've got to protect my business."

Twenty minutes later, Clemens was at the city jail.

"He is charged with grand theft," the sheriff said. "The law says he has to stay in jail until his trial."

"What about bail?"

"There is no bail for freed slaves in the state of Missouri," he said. "They must remain incarcerated until a judge hears the case."

John shook his head impatiently.

"Look!" he said. "I need Hezekiah in the field to finish picking a cotton crop."

"I'm sorry," the sheriff said. "You're going to have to wait until his trial."

"When is his trial?"

The sheriff turned and looked at a calendar.

"The circuit solicitor won't pass through here again until December 13."

"I can't wait that long," John said.

Back at the jail, Clemens told Hezekiah the sad news.

"What about our cotton crop?" Hezekiah said. "You going to have to get it picked and in the shed before the end of November. If you don't, that cotton will rot in the boll when the winter rains come."

Clemens took a deep breath.

"Let me see what I can do."

***

That night, at the dinner table, Clemens told his wife their dilemma.

"We've still got four acres of cotton to be picked," he said. "And only a week to get it done. I guess me and Orion can do it."

John looked across the table at his oldest child. Orion, at age 11, was a strong, sturdy child with a handsome face, a shock of unruly black hair and intelligent eyes.

"You know how to pick cotton?"

"I've seen it done," Orion said. "I could learn."

"The murder trial I'm handling will be finished tomorrow," the father said. "The following day, we'll try our hand at picking cotton."

***

Two days later, Clemens and Orion were in the field picking cotton. They worked from early morning until dark, dragging the cotton sacks down the rows, watching the sharp hulls of the bolls closely so they didn't cut their fingers. By the end of the day, they had picked just over 100 pounds of cotton.

At the dinner table that night, Jane, who was raised on a cotton farm, mocked their efforts.

"Only 100 pounds?" she said. "Why, I used to pick that much cotton before lunchtime."

"We did the best we could," John said.

"Tomorrow, I'll go pick cotton with you," she said. "The three of us, if we work at it, should get it done in four or five days."

Delrina spoke up.

"Mrs. Clemens!" she said. "You can't go picking no cotton in your condition."

"Don't venture to tell me my abilities, Delrina," Jane said. "I was picking cotton for my father in Kentucky when I was ten years old."

"You're heavy with child," Delrina said. "Only two more months."

"When I had Pamela," she said. "I worked right up until two hours before she was born. The work didn't bother me then. Why should it bother me now?"

"Perhaps Delrina is right," John said finally. "It might be best if you let me and Orion pick the cotton."

"I reckon I know my abilities better than either of you," Jane said. "Tomorrow, we'll arise early and go to the field. If we persevere, we should have all four acres picked in four or five days."

***

Early the following day, Jane, her husband, and their son Orion were in the field picking cotton. Jane, like Hezekiah, was an expert. On the first day, the three of them picked just over one acre with Jane accumulating more cotton in her bag than the other two combined.

That night, at the dinner table, John asked about her health.

"I'm fine," she said. "I had forgotten what a good cotton picker I was. We should finish that field in the next few days."

***

Over the next three days, the three managed to pick the remainder of the cotton crop. On the afternoon of the third day, they started picking on the final row.

"One more row," Jane said. "Thank God! I knew we could do it."

Two hours later, the sun was setting as John, his wife and their son finished the final row. Then, with Jane in front and John and Orion dragging the two bulky cotton sacks behind them, they started for the wagon. Once the wagon was out of the field and into the front yard, Jane started to get out. As she stepped to the ground, she suddenly stopped.

"What's wrong?" John said.

"I'm going to faint."

Jane put her hand to her head, then her face grimaced in pain and she collapsed on the ground.

"Oh, my God!" said John.

He knelt beside her.

"Orion! Go into the house and fetch Delrina."

Orion turned and ran into the house.

Moments later, Delrina appeared.

"Mr. Clemens! What's happened?"

"Jane has collapsed."

"Oh Lord!" Delrina said. "I was afraid of this."

Moments later, John pulled his wife to her feet, then, with him on one side and Delrina on the other, they started across the yard to the house.

When they entered the sitting room, Pamela, aged eight, was playing on the floor. Upon seeing their father and Delrina helping their mother, she became frightened.

"What happened to Mother?" Pamela said.

"We don't know," John said.

Pamela started to cry as she watched her mother being helped into the bedroom. Moments later, John and Delrina had Jane in bed as Orion looked on. She lay quiet for a few moments, then suddenly opened her eyes.

"I'm going to give birth very soon," she said.

"I was afraid of that," John said.

He turned to Orion.

"Help Delrina with your mother!" he said. "I'm going to fetch the doctor. I'll return as soon as possible."

Moments later, John was out the door.

Delrina turned to Jane.

"Let's go ahead and get your clothes off," she said, handing Jane a clean sheet. "You can cover yourself with this."

Moments later, Jane was lying naked under the sheet, the bulge in her midsection looming largely.

Delrina turned to Orion.

"Start a fire in the cook stove and put some water on to

boil," she said.

"Yes, ma'am!"

Delrina pulled back the sheet and examined Jane.

"You're opening up," she said. "You're going to have this baby any minute."

Suddenly, Jane's face grimaced in pain.

"Oh, God!" Jane said. "My water is breaking!"

She screamed, and her body convulsed violently.

"Hold my arms!" Delrina said, standing behind her.

Jane grasped each of the black woman's arms tightly.

"Now take a deep breath and push!" Delrina said.

Jane's body lurched forward.

"Ooooh! Ooooh!"

"Push! Push!"

Jane took another deep breath.

"OHHHHHH!" she said as she strained with all her might.

"Push! Push harder!"

"Oh!" Jane said, her back arching upward. "Oh, God! Here it comes!"

Suddenly, the walls of the wood cabin reverberated with the screams of a woman giving birth. It was a sound as old as humankind.

"Push! Push! Just a little more!"

Jane let out another series of screams; then, just as suddenly as the screams started, they stopped.

"It's a boy," Delrina said, picking up the newborn. Then, holding his feet, she slapped the newborn's bottom. No response. She slapped the baby's bottom again. Again, no response.

"Poor little thing ain't breathing," Delrina said.

"Oh, God! No!" Jane said. "Is he stillborn?"

"Looks that way," Delrina said. "Do you have an old shoebox?"

"Up in the closet," she said. "What are you about to do?"

"I've seen my older sister do this. I hope it works."

Delrina hobbled to the closet and pulled down an old shoebox. After dumping the contents on the floor, she placed the newborn inside, then started making her way to the kitchen.

"Orion!" Delrina said. "You got a fire started?"

"Yes, ma'am!"

Then, as Jane watched from the bedroom, Delrina limped into the kitchen to the cook stove. While holding the newborn in the shoebox in one hand, she reached her other hand inside the oven to check the heat. Then, satisfied with the temperature, she placed the shoebox with the newborn into the oven, closed the door, then watched through the glass window in the door.

Several seconds passed. As she watched, she prayed.

"Oh, Lord! Please do this! I'm begging you to let this little boychild live. Please hear my prayers!"

For several more seconds, she continued to gaze into the oven. Then, suddenly, a big smile flashed across her face.

"He's moving! He's moving!" she shouted. "Thanks be to God!"

Then she opened the oven door and withdrew the shoebox.

Suddenly, the walls of the cabin reverberated with a new sound, the cries of a newborn infant.

"Thanks be to God!" Delrina said again.

"Glory be!" Jane said. "Let me have him!"

"Let me clean him up first."

Moments later, Delrina handed the wailing newborn to his mother and the infant was quietly nursing at his mother's breast.

"You saved him, Delrina," Jane said.

"I didn't do it. God did it!"

***

An hour later, John returned to the family home with Dr. Jeremiah Goodnight.

"Premature children tend to be sickly," he said. "Their bones break easily, they don't eat well and they often suffer from breathing problems."

"We'll do the best we can with him," Jane said.

Later that night, a warm November evening, John and Jane were sitting quietly on the front porch of their home. Orion and Pamela were in bed and the newborn was nursing quietly at his mother's breast.

"I've got another mortgage payment coming up next month," he said. "I'm going to have to scramble to make the payment."

"When we got married," Jane said. "We agreed that the children and the house would be my domain and earning the money and managing it would be yours."

"That's right."

"I must say that you have not managed your domain well of late."

"I know full well my shortcomings."

"The longer we just sit here," she said, "the worse it will become."

"Can we drop this subject? Please!"

Jane knew better than to reply to that tone.

For several moments, the husband and wife were quiet again.

"What about a middle name for Samuel?" Jane said finally.

"I like Langhorne."

"Langhorne? After your brother that murdered his neighbor?"

"It wasn't murder. He killed the other man in self-defense."

A pause.

"So, his full name will be Samuel Langhorne Clemens?" Jane said.

"Yes. We'll call him Sam."

For several moments, they were quiet again.

Suddenly, Jane peered up to see a dazzling streak of yellow light flash across the night sky.

"Look!" Jane said, pointing into the night sky. "It's Halley's comet. It passes earth every seventy-five years."

"A beautiful sight," John said as he watched the blazing star and its bright tail flash across the heavens. "I hope it's a sign of good fortune. A sign of better things to come."

2
Orion

Hezekiah was in the Florida city jail until December 14. The circuit solicitor, the state prosecutor who traveled the county trying cases, arrived on December 13, and Hezekiah's case was scheduled the following morning. After hearing both sides, he ruled the incident a misunderstanding and decreed that, if John would pay for the extra sack of flour, Hezekiah could go free. Once John showed proof that the extra sack of flour had been paid for, Hezekiah was released and John was there to take him home.

That afternoon, when the buckboard pulled up in front of the Clemenses' house, Delrina burst out the front door, then hobbled across the yard on her peg leg to greet her husband.

"Oh, Hezekiah!" she said. "God has answered my prayers."

Then, as he stepped off the buckboard, she folded him into her arms and kissed him.

"I've missed you!" he said.

***

The following morning, John settled up with Hezekiah.

"All of the cotton has been picked and sold to the local warehouse," he said. "You've got $845 coming to you."

John counted out the cash money and handed it to Hezekiah.

"Much obliged!" the black man said, taking the money and putting it in his pocket.

"That cotton crop saved me this year," John said. "I hope we can make another one next year."

Hezekiah studied John for a long moment, then spoke.

"There is something I have to tell you."

"What might that be?"

"While I was in jail, I met another freed slave who was looking for somebody to go in with him on five acres of land out at Goshen. He says if I could come up with $1000, I could be half owner."

John wasn't prepared for that revelation.

"So, what are you going to do?"

"I'm going to take this money," he said, patting the wad of cash in his pocket. "I'm going to put it together with what you gave me back in October and I'm going in with him to buy that piece of land."

"Have I not always shown fairness and honesty with you?" John said.

"You have, and I'm obliged," Hezekiah said, "but this is the chance me and Delrina have been waiting for. Delrina has always wanted her own house with a vegetable garden and some chickens."

Hezekiah could see John was crestfallen.

"I'm sorry," he said. "I have to do this for Delrina."

John could see there was nothing to be done.

"As you wish," he said finally.

***

Early the next morning, a Sunday, Hezekiah had his wagon loaded with his and Delrina's personal belongings. After saying their good-byes, John and Jane watched as the rickety old wagon trundled down the pathway to the main road then disappeared out of sight.

"There goes our last hope," John said. "I don't know what we're going to do now."

"God will find a way," Jane said.

"Is God going to give us $5,000 to pay off the bank loan?"

"He works in mysterious ways."

John shook his head.

"Without another cotton crop, I don't see how we're going to make it."

"Oh, ye of little faith."

***

The following morning, John left the house as usual to go to his office in town. That night, he did not return at the usual hour. Normally, Jane would have dinner ready at seven and John would arrive shortly afterward so the entire family could eat together. When he didn't arrive by 7:30, the rest of the family went ahead and had dinner. Just after 8:30 p.m., Jane heard the buckboard pull up in the front yard, then she waited for her husband to come into the house. After waiting several minutes, John didn't appear, so she went outside to investigate. There, keeled over on his side in the front seat of the buckboard, she found her husband, dog-drunk and sound asleep.

"John! John!" she said, reaching up and shaking him. No response.

Moments later, she was back in the house.

"Orion!" she said. "Go outside and help your father."

"Is he…?"

Jane put her finger to her lips to cut him short.

"Just go out there and help him."

Moments later, Orion was outside.

At the buckboard, he reached up and shook his father.

"Father! Father!"

No response.

"Come on!" Orion said.

Then, as he pulled his father up to a sitting position, John awoke from his drunken stupor.

"Huh!" he said. "Orion, is that you?"

"It's me, Father," the son said. "Let me help you into the house."

John rose unsteadily to his feet, then, with Orion's help, he made it to the ground. Then, with one arm over Orion's shoulder, they slowly made it across the yard and into the house. In the sitting room, Pamela looked up to see Orion and their father.

"What's wrong with Father?" Pamela asked.

"He's sick," Jane said.

"I'm not sick. I'm drunk," John said.

Jane turned to Orion.

"Take him into the bedroom."

Orion helped his father into the bedroom, removed his clothes and put him into bed.

***

The following morning, when John wasn't up at his regular time, Jane went into the bedroom to check on him.

"Don't bother me," he said. "I want to sleep."

"Are you going to the office today?"

"Let me sleep!" he said.

Around noon, he got out of bed, had breakfast, dressed and took the buckboard into town. That night, when he arrived back at home, he was drunk again and passed out in the buckboard seat. Once again, Orion helped him into the house and into bed.

***

Over the next three days, John stayed in bed all day, only getting up to eat. On the morning of the third day, after they had breakfast, Jane confronted her husband.

"What in God's name has happened to you?"

"I don't want to live this life any longer," he said.

"What do you mean? You can't just give up. We've got three children to raise."

John shook his head, then stared blankly at her.

"You made a mistake by moving to Florida," Jane said. "Why can't you accept it, learn from it and move on?"

"It's much deeper than that."

"What else is there?"

"Hezekiah deserted me. We've got a $5,000 bank loan hanging over our heads. I'm not getting any new cases. I shouldn't have allowed you to go into that cottonfield while you were carrying Samuel. Should I continue?"

"We did what we had to do," Jane said. "What's done is done. Now let's pick up and go on."

John shook his head in indecision.

"I'm going back to bed," he said. "Leave me alone."

"What are we going to do until then?"

"I don't know."

Once John was back in the bedroom, Jane went to Orion.

"Go into town and get Dr. Goodnight."

Two hours later, when Orion arrived back at the homestead with the family physician, Jane explained her husband's behavior over the past few days.

"Something terrible has befallen him," she said. "He seems to have no desire for anything. It's as if he doesn't want to live anymore."

"Let me go in and talk to him," Dr. Goodnight said.

"I'll go with you."

"I want to talk to him alone."

"As you wish."

An hour later, Dr. Goodnight emerged from the bedroom. Jane was waiting.

"He has a severe case of melancholia," the doctor said. "He no longer wants to face the world and all of the problems it presents. His demons have consumed him."

"What can be done?"

"Nothing. The drinking only feeds it. If he continues in this state, you can have him committed to the state asylum in Springfield."

"Oh, I could not bear that. The shame and disgrace would be too burdensome for the family."

"Then I'm afraid you'll have to maintain him at home."

"Oh, God!" Jane said. "What did I do to deserve this?"

"It's more common than you think," Dr. Goodnight said.

After the doctor left, Jane went to Orion, who was reading in the sitting room.

"Your father is useless to us," Jane told Orion. "We're going to have to make it on our own."

"Maybe I can get a job," he said.

"Who is going to hire an eleven-year-old?"

She paused.

"Let's go into town and see how much money is in the bank. Then we will proceed from there."

***

Over the next few days, Jane took charge of the family finances. There was over $2,600 in the family bank account.

"We've got some breathing room with that cash," Jane said. "But we're going to have to watch every penny. We must eliminate all expenses that are not absolutely necessary. I shall close John's law office. I want you to clean out a stall in the barn so we can get a cow. This spring, we'll plant a vegetable garden. If we are diligent and watch our pennies, we can overcome this."

***

There was no Christmas, not even a tree, in the Clemens home that year. Jane was guarding every penny and spent money only on essentials: food, wood and coal for cooking and warmth, and a winter coat for Pamela. Although the children questioned the absence of a Christmas celebration, there was nothing to be done. Maintenance of the family was more important than holiday cheer.

***

The following spring, Jane and Orion bought a cow and calf and, after the mother showed her son how to milk, the family had a gallon of fresh milk every night for the dinner table. In late April, Jane and Orion planted a vegetable garden and, that fall, they harvested and dried a wide variety of vegetables. This included fifteen pounds of green beans, ten pounds of tomatoes, two large bags of dried apples and more than twenty pounds of squash. For the root cellar, they stored away fifty pounds of white potatoes and more than twenty pounds of carrots. At Thanksgiving, the calf was slaughtered and the meat was smoked and hung to dry in the family smokehouse. The family was squeezing by financially.

***

In late November of 1837, little Samuel turned two. As the doctor had predicted, he was a sickly child. His movements were feeble, he was not a good eater, and he seemed to always be tired and quick to get sick. In early December, he caught the croup and was near death for three days. He was gasping for breath, refused to take food and had a high fever. When Dr. Goodnight arrived at the Clemens home, he had sad news.

"I fear to tell you he won't make it through the night," he said. "His lungs are too infected. His fever is too high."

All that night, Jane and Orion kept shifts at Samuel's bedside. Orion waited for a break in his temperature while Jane prayed, asking God to spare her son's life.

"Oh, God! Please don't take my little Samuel," she prayed. "I'm asking You to keep him safe and allow me to see him grown to manhood."

The following morning at daybreak, by some sheer miracle, the child's fever broke and he was breathing normally again. Orion, who had been sleeping at his bedside, immediately awakened Jane.

"Mother! Mother!" he said. "Samuel has taken a turn for the better."

Immediately, the mother arose from her bed and went to the child.

"Thanks be to God!" she said. "He has answered my prayers."

"Mother!" Orion said. "What can we do to help Samuel? There must be something we can do to improve his health."

"I don't know what it could be," she said. "He shows no promise and the doctor has no answers, but I'm trying my best to raise him."

***

Ten months passed. One night in early February, Jane was in the kitchen washing the dinner dishes while Orion was playing with two-year-old Samuel in the living room.

"Mother!' he called. "Come and see this!"

Jane, wiping her hands on her apron, appeared in the doorway.

"What is it?"

"Watch!" Orion said.

Samuel was sitting on the floor entertaining himself by stacking, then restacking several old magazines atop one another. Once Samuel had the magazines stacked in a neat pile, Orion arose from his seat and moved the stack several feet away. Instantly, Samuel's face screwed up in annoyance. Then, he stood up, took several halting steps to the magazines, then sat down beside the stack again.

Orion burst out in joyful laughter. Then Jane, giggling with delight, stepped forward and moved the magazines away from the child. Again, the two-year-old stood up, took several unsteady steps to the magazines, then plopped to the floor on his bottom again.

"He's walking!" Jane said.

Orion shook his head with pure amazement.

"Now that he is walking, perhaps his health will start to improve," Orion said.

***

The following Saturday morning while Orion was in town, he met an old friend who wanted to get rid of a dog, a black-and-tan hound.

"I'll take him," Orion said. "My younger brother will love it."

When he arrived back at home, Orion took Samuel into the field behind the house to play with the animal. Orion would throw a stick, then watch as the dog retrieved it.

"Now, you throw the stick," Orion said.

Samuel looked at the stick, then at Orion, and started walking back to the house.

"Samuel! Come back! Let's play with the dog."

The child continued walking back to the house as if he hadn't heard.

When Orion returned to the house, he found his mother in

the sitting room mending an old dress.

"Samuel shows no interest in anything," Orion said.

"He doesn't feel well," Jane said. "It's difficult to take an interest when you don't feel well."

***

In early July, when the weather warmed, it was Orion's habit to take Pamela to the swimming hole on the small creek behind the house to frolic in the water. One Saturday morning, he took Samuel to the swimming hole for the first time. Upon arrival, Pamela, at age ten, wasted no time wading out into the shallow water. Then Orion took Samuel's hand and led him to the water. The moment the two-year-old's toe touched the cold water, he began to cry, pulled his hand out of Orion's and quickly dashed back to shore.

That night, Orion told his mother what had happened.

"I tried to be as gentle as I knew how," Orion said, "but he wouldn't hear of it."

"When you don't feel well, you're forever in a foul mood."

"There has got to be something we can do," Orion said.

"I wish I knew what it was."

***

Another year passed. Samuel would soon be four years old and, all the while, Orion was seeking a solution to his health problems. Pamela was now in sixth grade and proving to be an excellent student. Meanwhile, John continued in his state of obliviousness to the world around him. Some days, he would sleep until noon, then get up to eat and spend the rest of the day sitting on the front porch doing nothing. After the evening meal, he would sit quietly on the porch listening to the sounds of the night until bed time, then the cycle would repeat itself. When other family members spoke to him, he smiled and didn't reply. The family no longer had a father.

***

Then, in August of 1839, the family had a stroke of good fortune. Orion, who was now fourteen, was in town one Saturday at the mercantile store when the proprietor showed him a small hand-cranked printing press in the storage room. The store owner said he bought the press to print advertisements for his business, but could never find the time to actually do the printing. When Orion asked the proprietor if he wanted to sell it, the man said he wanted $50. That night, Orion told his mother.

"What would you do with it?" Jane asked.

"I could print advertisements for local businesses," Orion said. "I could notify their customers of sales and new items."

"Does he have everything you would need?"

"Oh, yes," Orion replied. "He already has ink and paper. The press is old but still useable."

That afternoon, Jane and Orion went to the bank in town, where she withdrew $50 and handed it to Orion. Then they went to the mercantile store, bought the press and other supplies, and returned home.

The following day, Orion set up the press in the barn, printed out dummy advertisements for the local mercantile store, then returned to town and showed them to the proprietor.

"Impressive!" the proprietor said. "How much would it cost if I had you print real advertisements for me?"

"Twenty-five cents each," Orion said. "If you want me to pass them around town and post them on the city bulletin board, they will be another ten cents each."

The proprietor took a deep breath.

"I want ten like this," the man said, showing Orion one of the dummy ads.

"Delivered or undelivered?" Orion said.

"Delivered!" the proprietor said. "Let me get you a list of my sale items this week."

***

Two days later, when Orion returned with the sheet ads, the store owner was impressed.

"Well done!" he said. "These will help sales."

Once Orion had collected the five dollars, he gave three of the sheets to the store owner, then passed out the others to passersby in town and posted the final two on the community bulletin board in the town square. Then he went to other businesses—a harness shop, a bakery, a law firm, an insurance agency and a brewery—to sell more ads. At the end of the day, he had forty-two new advertisements to print.

When he told his mother that night, she was elated.

"Oh, Orion! I fear that I would be lost without you."

Over the next two months, Orion's printing business took off with leaps and bounds. By the end of July, he was printing fifty to sixty ads a week for local businesses. For the first time in three years, Jane and Orion had some relief from their financial woes.

***

Meanwhile, little Samuel's health continued to show no improvement.

Then, during the summer of 1839, when he was four months shy of his fourth birthday, a miracle happened.

In late August, Orion was at a harness maker's shop in Goshen, Missouri, a small community near Florida. While he waited for a buckboard harness to be made, Orion watched the shop owner's son playing on a stack of saddles in the corner of the shop.

"Ezekiel!" the father said, upon seeing the child. "Get down! You're going to fall and hurt yourself."

No sooner were the words out of the father's mouth than the stack of saddles tipped over, and the child, along with the saddles, came crashing to the floor. The child, unhurt, got up and dusted himself off.

"Go to the house!" the angry father shouted.

The child looked at his father dejectedly, then turned and started walking to the family home nearby.

"Frisky child!" Orion said.

"He hasn't always been so feisty," the father said.

"How do you mean?"

"He was born two months early, and for the first two years, he was sick every day."

"What happened?"

"We have an old slave woman living with us that said he should be drinking water from the sulfur spring every day."

"Sulfur spring?"

"There's a sulfur spring back in the woods behind our house. It's got a God-awful smell, but it made a healthy child out of my Ezekiel."

"How did it happen?" Orion said.

"My wife told the slave woman, if she thought it would help, to start giving Ezekiel some of the sulfur water every day. She did and, two weeks later, he was a healthy child for the first time in his life."

"Interesting story," Orion said.

By now, the new harness was made. Orion paid for it, took it in hand, then started back to the buckboard. Once the new harness was safely inside, he got into the driver's seat and slapped the reins. The horse took about twenty steps, then Orion jerked on the reins.

"Whoa!"

He got down from the buckboard seat, went back into the harness shop and asked the owner if he could speak to the slave who knew about the sulfur spring.

"Her name is Calpurnia," the man said. "Go on up to the house and talk to her."

Orion returned to the buckboard and took a water jug, which was kept under the seat of the buckboard for drinking water. Then he turned and walked up the hill to the harness maker's home and told his wife he had permission to talk to Calpurnia. The wife called the old slave woman. She was in her late sixties, gray-headed, bent over, and had only a few teeth.

Orion asked her to take him to the sulfur spring.

After walking some two hundred yards back into the woods, they came upon a pool of clear water pouring out of the hillside. The edges of the pool were encrusted with stacks upon stacks of white and tan alkaline salts, and the place smelled of rotten eggs. Orion, water jug in hand, made his way to the edge of the water and filled the container.

"Have him drink a glass of that every day," Calpurnia said. "That's what I did for Ezekiel, and it helped him a heap."

***

That night, Orion told his mother the story the old slave woman had related to him and showed her the gallon jug of sulfur water. She held the glass jug up to the light to inspect it.

"I want to taste it first," she said.

She took a sip.

"Tastes salty," she said. "Maybe it will help him. It's certainly worth an attempt."

Over the next week, Jane had Samuel drink a glass of the sulfur water every day. Although the three-year-old grimaced at the taste, Jane forced him to take it down. After only a few days, they noticed a marked improvement.

"Glory be to god!" Jane said. "The sulfur water is helping him."

At the end of the first week, Samuel was a new child. He was running around the house excitedly, asking Orion to come out and play, aggravating his sister Pamela and arguing with her about who got the pulley bone at the dinner table.

"It's a miracle," Jane said. "An absolute miracle."

***

In late November of 1839, Samuel Langhorne Clemens turned four years old. Now, rather than being the sickly runt of the family, he became its mischief maker. The day after Thanksgiving, a neighbor, Mrs. Gertrude Grayson, appeared on their front porch at the Clemens home. Jane answered the door.

"Mrs. Clemens, I fear to tell you, but your child Samuel stole three apples from my tree yesterday."

"How do you know it was Samuel?" the mother asked.

"I saw him with my own eyes."

"I'll talk to him. Do I owe you anything?"

"No. Just be certain that it doesn't happen again."

Instantly, Jane went to the back yard of the house where Samuel and Pamela were playing hopscotch. She went straight to her son.

"Did you take some apples from Mrs. Grayson's tree yesterday?"

"No, ma'am."

"She says you climbed the tree and took three apples."

"It wasn't me," he said.

"It was you!" Pamela said. "I saw you hiding behind the barn to eat them."

"You fibbed to me," Jane said. "Now you're going to get a whipping."

"No!" he cried.

"Come with me!" Jane said.

Then, holding the child's ear, she led him into the house.

Moments later, the mother and son were in the sitting room and Jane had the four-year-old bent over her knee. Then she proceeded to slap his bottom side five times with a razor strap.

"Ow! Ow! Ow!" little Samuel cried.

Once the final blow was administered, she removed him from her knee and turned him to face her.

"Now go to your room and stay there for the rest of the day."

Samuel, crying and distraught, turned and went into his bedroom. An hour later, once he had stopped crying, he climbed out of the bedroom window and went to play at the creek.

***

That night, after the family had dinner, the mother and children were in the sitting room. Pamela was on the settee studying her lessons when she noticed Samuel standing behind her.

"What are you doing?" she asked.

"Nothing!" he replied innocently.

Pamela, calmer now, returned to her books.

Suddenly, Samuel reached into his pocket, withdrew a

small frog and slipped it down the back of Pamela's dress. Instantly, Pamela screamed and began dancing around the room trying to remove the frog.

"What's wrong?" Jane said.

"Samuel put something down my back."

The frog fell out of the bottom of Pamela's dress.

Jane peered angrily at Samuel.

"All right, young man," she said. "You're due for another whipping."

***

In the wintertime, Jane kept a chamber pot in the children's bedroom because it was too cold for them to go out at night to the outhouse. Late one night, half-asleep, Samuel got up to use it and, once finished, he accidentally knocked it over and the human waste spilled on the bedroom floor. The next morning, when Jane entered the children's bedroom, she instantly smelled the foul odor.

"Who turned over the pee pot?" she said.

"I didn't do it!" said Sam.

"Yes, you did!" Pamela said. "I saw you when you did it."

Jane peered angrily at Samuel.

"Prepare yourself for another whipping," she said.

As she led Samuel into the sitting room to administer the blows, she looked to the heavens for assistance.

"Oh, dear God! This is three whippings in two weeks," she said. "What sort of child have you given me? This child was born to be hanged!"

***

Two weeks later, on a Saturday, Orion was in town to buy supplies. Once he had bought everything he needed, he noticed a stack of newspapers on the counter. He picked up one.

"That's the *Hannibal Journal*," the proprietor said. "It's three days old, but it tells you what's happening in the world outside of Florida."

Orion bought a copy.

Back at home, he and Jane went through the publication.

"Mother! Look at this!" Orion said. "There are jobs galore in Hannibal. If we were there, I could get a job with the newspaper."

Jane pored over the newspaper pages.

"It would be a big move to pick up and leave Florida."

"It would be worth it," Orion said. "There is so much more opportunity."

"Let me think about it."

That night, Orion was sound asleep when Jane came into his room and woke him up.

"Mother! What's the matter?"

"I've decided we're moving to Hannibal," she said. "It's something we should have done long ago."

***

The following morning, Jane and Orion started making plans.

"We can't get all of our belongings into the buckboard," Jane said. "So, we're going to have to buy a wagon and a horse."

"A mule would cost less," Orion said.

"Let's sell the cow and buy a mule and a wagon. I will put the house up for sale. You start packing. We're going to need some rope to tie the mattresses and furniture on a wagon. I want to be in Hannibal two weeks from today."

An hour later, she was on the front porch telling her husband about her new plans.

"I'm not going," he said.

"Then me and the children will leave without you. You have been totally useless as a father and husband for the past three years."

"I'm not going," he said again.

"Suit yourself!"

***

Six days later, on a Sunday morning, Jane and Orion had

the new wagon and the family buckboard loaded with all of their worldly possessions. Furniture, pots and pans, clothing, gardening tools, eating utensils, house decorations and all of the other equipment needed for the family's daily living had been prepared for transport. Jane brought the children out of the house and ordered them to take seats, Pamela in the buckboard with Jane and Samuel in the wagon with Orion. Once the children were onboard, Jane turned to Orion.

"We're ready," she said.

Then, before she stepped on the buckboard, she turned to her husband, who was sitting on the front porch.

"Me and the kids are leaving," she said.

"I'm not going."

"We're taking your clothes," Jane said. "Will one shirt and one pair of trousers be enough?"

"I'll be fine."

"Good luck!" Jane said.

Wasting no time, Jane mounted the buckboard steps and got into the driver's seat. For a moment, she looked back at her husband, then slapped the reins. The buckboard and wagon started moving slowly out of the yard.

The wagon, with Orion at the reins, was right behind her.

For a long moment, John peered after the vehicles. Suddenly, upon seeing his family leaving him, he arose from his chair, jumped off the porch and went racing across the yard.

"Wait! Wait! I want to go!"

3
Tom and Huck

In the mid-1840s, Hannibal, Missouri was a bustling port town nestled along the western shore of the Mississippi River some one hundred miles northwest of St. Louis. Founded in 1819 by Moses Bates, the settlement flourished rapidly as a principal docking port for paddle wheelers, flatboats and packet steamers traveling the upper Mississippi River. Early industries that contributed to the city's growth included pork packing, soap and candle making, coopering and lumber milling. As railroad transportation became less prominent with the river traffic, other businesses took its place, including button making, shoe manufacturing and cement production. By 1845, Hannibal had achieved city status and, in 1850, the U.S. Census put its population at 7,652 souls, which made it the second largest city and the third largest commercial center in Missouri.

***

When the Clemens family first arrived in Hannibal in late 1839, Jane rented a small house on the outskirts of town. Only days after the family moved in, Orion set up his little printing press and was soon cranking out advertisements for local businesses. This meant the family had instant income. Pamela, at age twelve, was enrolled at Lewis and Clark Elementary, and John, now seeing economic opportunities on every hand, suddenly decided he wanted to live again. In November of 1840, with Jane's and Orion's help, he opened a new law office on Hill Street and started taking cases. That same year, Jane gave birth to a fourth child, a son named Henry, which would be her last. In the spring of 1841, the old home and property in Florida was sold, and John and Jane bought a new home in downtown Hannibal at 120 Main Street.

***

Now, in mid-May of 1847, the Clemens family had been settled in Hannibal for eight years. John had become head of the household again, had a thriving legal practice and had been elected Justice of the Peace. Jane stayed busy keeping house and playing mother to seven-year-old Henry. Orion, at age 22, had abandoned his printing business and, after only two years, had become an assistant editor at the local newspaper, the Hannibal Journal. Pamela, at age 19, met a music teacher through her school and learned to play both the piano and guitar and was giving music lessons. Meanwhile, Samuel, soon to be twelve, had just finished the fifth grade at Lewis and Clark and was out of school for the summer.

The Clemens family home, located at the north end of Main Street, was little more than a stone's throw from the docks. While the steamboats were tied up on the south end of the wharf, the north end had been reserved for storing equipment and supplies needed to support them. This included huge piles of coal and wood for fuel, all sorts of blocks and tackles needed to hoist the heavy cargoes on and off the boats and empty hogsheads, large, wooden barrels used to store and transport pork, tobacco, rice and wheat.

Some nights, Sam would wander away from the family home down to the docks to watch the steamships passing in the night. One night, as he stood alone on the pier, he watched as a young boy slipped into one of the empty barrels. At the time, Sam wondered what the boy was doing. Curious, Sam ventured down to the docks the following morning, and there he found the youngster sound asleep in one of the barrels.

"Hello!" Sam said.

The boy awoke with a start.

"Huh?" he said, waking up. "Who might you be?"

"I live in the house across the street. Say, why are you

sleeping in a hogshead?"

"I reckon I ain't got a home," the boy said, rubbing his eyes.

"No home?"

"My mother croaked when I was a lad of seven," he said. "My father turned into the town drunk, and now I sleep where I can find a hole."

"You wander about the streets all day?"

"Pretty much. I stick my head in the school house when the truant man finds me."

"How old are you?" Sam asked.

"Soon to be thirteen."

"You got a year on me," Sam said.

Sam looked the other boy up and down. An alert, sturdy lad, he had a pleasant face, a shock of brown hair and was wearing castoff, ill-fitting adult clothes. There was a hole in the shoulder of the dirty white shirt he was wearing, and the bottoms of his trousers, which had only one suspender, had been rolled up so he could walk.

"Say!" the boy said. "Might you spare a quarter so I can get some ham biscuits for breakfast?"

Sam fished through his pocket and produced a quarter.

"Much obliged."

"What might your name be?" Sam asked.

"Tom Blankenship. What's yours?"

"Sam Clemens."

From that moment forward, the two boys were the best of friends and, during the summer of 1847, they were inseparable. They fished and swam at Bear Creek. They spent endless hours exploring Wheeler's Cave, the mysterious, reportedly endless cavern nearby and, when newly-arrived paddle wheelers docked at the wharf, they watched with great interest as passengers made their entrances and exits and workmen unloaded the massive cargoes of lumber, coal, hay and machinery. Most of their time that summer was spent roaming the streets of Hannibal.

***

One Saturday morning in early June, Sam met Tom at the wharf and, for over an hour, the two boys roamed the docks, admiring the mighty steamships, talking to flatboat workers and watching packet ships steam up and down the river. Finally, bored with the docks, they turned and started down Hill Street through a residential neighborhood.

After they had walked some six blocks, Sam suddenly stopped. At the house in front of them, they saw a young girl playing with a dog in the front yard. She had long, yellow hair, which had been braided into pigtails, and was wearing a white summer frock with embroidered pantalettes. Sam was enthralled.

"Who might she be?" Sam said.

"Laura Hawkins," Tom said. "Her father is Judge Hawkins."

"She's mighty pretty," Sam said.

Finally, he ventured a greeting.

"Hello!" he said.

For a moment, the young girl turned her attention from the dog and glanced at the two boys. Then, without responding, she returned to the dog.

"Hello!" Sam said again.

"She don't give a whit for you," Tom said. "Come along! Let's go fishing."

Sam, still peering at the girl, didn't hear.

"My name is Samuel," he said. "What's yours?"

Finally, the little girl turned and smiled.

"My name is Laura," she said. "This is my dog Caesar."

"Hello, Caesar," Sam said. "He's a pretty dog."

"He can fetch a stick," the little girl said. "Would you like to see?"

"Oh, yes!" Sam said.

Suddenly, the girl's father, a tall, dignified man with a solemn face and a white mane, stepped out on the porch.

"Laura!" he said. "Come into the house this instant."

"But, Father!"

"Do as I say," the man said.

Without another word, the girl gathered the dog into her arms and disappeared into the house.

The man turned his attention to Sam and Tom.

"What are you two boys doing loitering in front of my home?"

"We were admiring your house, sir," Sam said.

"Hogwash! You were attempting to win the attention of my daughter. I don't permit my daughter to consort with riff-raff."

"Riff-raff?" Tom said.

"You two are street urchins!" he said. "Look at you! Dirty clothes. Bare-footed. Unbathed. Not fit for my daughter."

Sam looked to Tom for an answer. He had none.

"Remove yourself from these premises," the older man ordered.

For a moment, the two boys hesitated.

"Now!" the man said. "Move along or I'll fetch the sheriff."

Dejectedly, Sam turned to Tom, then they started walking back up the street.

"What's a street urchin?" Sam said.

"I don't know," Tom said with a shrug. "Come along! Let's go to Wheeler's Cave and go swimming."

Ten minutes later, the two boys were walking up Sixth Street past rows of quiet residential homes when Tom suddenly stopped. At one of the homes, cooling in an open window, he saw three freshly-baked cherry pies.

"Look yonder!" he said. "Widow Grierson has baked some fine cherry pies. Come along; let's see if we can get some."

The two boys strode across the front yard and Tom knocked on the door. Widow Grierson, an elderly woman in her sixties with white hair and wearing a regency cap and a Mother Hubbard outfit, answered.

"Pray tell, what I might do for you boys?"

"We're mighty hungry,' Tom said. "We was wondering if you could spare a mite crust of bread."

The old woman looked the boys up and down.

"Since when was the last time you boys eat?"

"Two or three days," Tom said. "We had a stale chunk of cornbread and a hambone. We sucked all of the marrow out of the hambone."

A shocked expression crossed the old woman's face.

"Sucked out the marrow?" she said. "Oh, you poor darlings! Come in and let me feed you."

Ten minutes later, the boys were seated at her table eating roast turkey, green beans, mashed potatoes and biscuits. Once that was finished, Tom turned to her.

"Would you happen to have any dessert? Maybe some cherry pie?"

"I certainly do."

She served each of them a huge piece of warm cherry pie with a large dollop of vanilla whipping cream. Five minutes later, the desserts were finished.

"Ahhh!" Tom said. "My belly is full once more. I reckon we'll be going now. Much obliged for the vittles."

"If you boys feel hungry, you can come to my table and I'll feed you. I can't bear to see children go hungry."

Twenty minutes later, the two boys were walking along Sixth Street again toward Hannibal's downtown area. Ahead of them, they could see the Yellow Dog Saloon, the town's most notorious tavern. Several men were loitering out front. As they approached, Tom suddenly stopped.

"Yonder is my pap," Tom said. "I don't want him to lay eyes on me."

Instantly, Tom moved to the other side of Sam, hoping to hide and, as they neared the tavern, he turned his face downward to appear as inconspicuous as possible. As they strode past, Tom heard someone called his name.

"Tom! Tommy boy," the voice called.

Tom, caught red-handed, stopped. Seated on the ground with his back resting against the tavern wall, was his father, Woodson Blankenship. He was drunk, unshaven and dressed in dirty, ill-fitting clothes.

"Howdy, Pap!" Tom said.

"Might you spare a quarter that I could use to buy a drink?"

"Not a penny."

The father turned to Sam.

"And you, young fellow, might you spare a quarter?"

"Flat broke!" Sam said.

"Perhaps you might borrow a quarter," Woodson said.

Sam ignored the statement, then turned and peered at the other two men loitering in front of the tavern. One was a short man in his late thirties with long black hair, a scraggly beard and wearing a three-cornered hat. Nearby, apparently his friend, was another man, tall with graying hair and a big black patch over his right eye. Upon noticing Sam staring at him, the short man sneered.

"What you gawking at, you little whippersnapper?" he said.

Quickly, he stepped forward, grabbed a handful of Sam's shirt and pulled Sam's face close to his. Then, with the other hand, he reached into his back pocket and flashed a large knife.

"Cast your eyes on this!" he said, waving the blade in front of Sam's face. "Are you wanting me to cut out yo' gizzard and feed it to the buzzards?"

Sam's eyes followed the shiny blade.

"No, sir!" he said. "I'm in sore need of my gizzard."

Suddenly, the tall man with the eye patch spoke up.

"Go ahead! Cut him!" he said with an angry sneer. "I ain't seen no blood today."

"Please, sir!" Sam said. "I didn't mean no harm."

With that, the short man with the knife appeared calmer. He released Sam's shirt.

"You sniveling little pup! You two best get out of my sight."

Slowly, Tom and Sam backed away, then, once at a safe distance, they launched into a full run toward the docks. Finally, when they reached Third Street, they stopped.

"Gosh almighty! That was close!" Sam said. "Who might those two be?"

"The short one is called Griege the Pirate and the taller one is One-eyed Bill," Tom said. "Griege the Pirate just got freed from the state pen for killing a man down in St. Louis."

"I'll be steering clear of those two," Sam said.

"Come along!" Tom said. "Let's go talk to Injun Joe."

Five minutes later, the two boys were at the Hannibal Cigar Emporium on Main Street sitting on the ground in front of

Injun Joe, a native Chippewa Indian who had been hired to sit on a tree stump in front of the tobacco shop and tell stories. In his early fifties, Injun Joe had a grave face, shoulder-length graying hair and a medicine hat with a silver band. In the past, Sam and Tom had listened to his yarns about the first buffalo he had killed, his boyhood days exploring Wheeler's Cave and falling in love with Sally Two Tree. Sam and Tom waited as the old Indian took a puff from a long peace pipe, exhaled the smoke, then peered off serenely into the distance.

"Since many moons, my people live peacefully on these lands and fed their families by killing buffalo. Then, the railroads and white eyes came and killed the buffalo that had fed and clothed my people. During cold winters, the old people and babies starve. Mothers cry loudly when they bury their little papooses in cold ground to send them to Happy Hunting Ground. My people have to eat rats to continue their lives."

Injun Joe looked down at Sam.

"You ever eat rat?"

"Never!" Sam said.

"Me neither!" said Tom.

Injun Joe got up from his seat.

"Might you be leaving?" asked Sam.

"No more stories," he said. "My work finished today. If you like more stories, you come back tomorrow."

The two boys watched as Injun Joe took his peace pipe in hand, arose from the oak stump, threw a dapple-colored blanket over his shoulder, then sauntered off up the street.

"You reckon Injun Joe hates white people because they killed all the buffalo?"

"No notion," Sam said. "I reckon I wouldn't care to eat rats."

***

Twenty minutes later, the two boys were walking down Main Street. At the corner of Sixth Street and Main, they stopped in front of Holloway's Produce Company.

"Say, put your eyes on those red apples," Tom said. "Go over to the counter and win the clerk's attention. When his eyes are averted, I'll fetch a couple and meet you down Sixth Street."

Sam went to the counter and began asking the clerk questions about the cantaloupes. Once Tom saw the clerk's attention was diverted, he grabbed two apples. At the very instant he pocketed the apples, the clerk looked up and saw him.

"You there!" the clerk yelled. "Are you pilfering the apples?"

Moments later, Sam and Tom were running down Sixth Street, the clerk right behind them. After they had run several blocks, they ducked into the alley behind the Yellow Dog Saloon and hid under the back porch. They waited. Soon, they saw the clerk stop and peer down the alleyway. Then, seeing nothing, he turned and dashed down Sixth Street.

"Whew! That was close," Sam said.

Seconds later, as they started to crawl out from their hiding place, they heard someone come out of the tavern and onto the porch above them. It was Griege the Pirate and One-eyed Bill.

Tom put his finger to his lips for Sam to remain quiet. Above them, they could hear the two men talking.

"Here lays the plan," Griege said. "Tonight, after dark, we will conceal ourselves in the bushes behind Widow Grierson's house. Mostly likely, she'll be slumbering, so we can go through her belongings without disturbing her."

"Suppose she comes awake?"

"Then I reckon I'll give her a thump on the head with my pistol. She's just an old woman and she'll go out like a candlelight. We'll be wanting silverware, jewelry and anything more we can sell to the pawn broker."

Moments later, the two boys heard the two men's feet shuffle across the wood floor above them as they went back into the saloon. All was quiet again.

"Did you hear Griege's words?" Sam said. "They're about to rob Widow Grierson's house tonight."

"Let's go tell her," Tom said.

Fifteen minutes later, the two boys were at Widow Grierson's house and told her about Griege and One-eyed Bill's plans.

"Well," she said. "We'll just see about that. I'll fetch Sheriff Cunningham and he'll be waiting."

***

Just after nightfall that evening, Sam and Tom were hiding in the bushes at the front of Widow Grierson's house. The house was dark, as if all of the occupants were asleep. After they waited for almost an hour, they saw two shadowy figures slip into the front yard, force open a front window, then go inside. After waiting another ten minutes, lights suddenly popped on in the house, the front door opened, and out came Widow Grierson and Sheriff Cunningham leading Griege the Pirate and One-eyed Bill, both in handcuffs.

Widow Grierson went to the bushes where Sam and Tom were hiding.

"You boys can come out now."

Hesitantly, the two boys emerged.

Widow Grierson turned to the sheriff.

"These two boys are heroes," she said. "They saved me from robbery and possible death."

"Well done," the sheriff said. "You two have saved the day."

Griege the Pirate, shaking his handcuffed wrist, glared angrily at the two boys.

"So, it was you two whippersnappers that overheard my plan," he said. "I'll have you for this."

"You won't be having nobody," Sheriff Cunningham said. "You're going back to the state pen."

***

That night, when Sam went home for dinner, Jane was in the kitchen preparing the evening meal.

"Didn't I see you in town today with that no-count Tom Blankenship?"

"He's my friend."

"His father is the town drunk."

"It's not Tom's fault if his father can't stay away from

drink."

"He's a vile influence on you. The clerk at Holland's produce said he stole three apples today."

"Mother, Tom would never commit such an act."

"That boy is going to land you in a heap of trouble."

"Mother, you're getting yourself into a stir over nothing."

***

The following morning, a Sunday, Jane rousted Sam out of bed early to go to church. As always, he hated these "church Sundays." Jane forced him to wash behind his ears, comb his hair and dress up in an ill-fitting church coat. Even worse, he had to wear under-sized leather shoes that pinched his toes. After Jane had listened to all of his complaints, she pulled him by the ear to the carriage where Orion was waiting to take the family to the church house. Once at church, Sam endured an hour of Sunday school lessons, then, in the main church building, he took a seat in the back pews to make it appear he would be present for the sermon. Once the preaching began, however, he darted out the side door and went to play in the cemetery.

Outside, as he wandered up the road to the cemetery, he met, of all people, Laura Hawkins. He hadn't seen her since school let out the previous May.

"Hi!" he said. "Why aren't you in church?"

"I'm not feeling well," she said. "My mother said I could come outside for some fresh air."

"Come on!" Sam said. "Let's go play among the tombstones."

Moments later, the two were wandering about the cemetery, examining the headstones.

"Look at this one!" Sam said. "This man was born in 1708 and died in 1762. He was really old."

Laura stopped in front of another headstone.

"This little girl only lived seven years," she said.

She read the inscription.

"'Mother and Father, don't weep for me, for I am waiting in heaven for thee.'"

"So sad," she said.

They stopped and seated themselves on a large flat headstone.

Both were quiet for a moment.

"Samuel," Laura said. "What do you want to be when you grow up?"

"A riverboat captain," Sam said. "I'll operate steamers all up and down the Mississippi from Cairo, Illinois all the way down to New Orleans."

"My father says you'll never amount to anything," she said. "He says you and your friend Tom are street urchins, bound to spend your days up to no good."

"Your father doesn't truly know me," Sam said. "Someday, when I'm a big riverboat pilot, he'll change his tune."

"You are a good student in school," Laura said. "I can say that for you."

"Someday, your father will see who I really am."

They were quiet for a moment.

After several seconds, Sam looked wistfully at her.

"Laura?" he said.

"Yes?"

"Have you ever been engaged?"

"Never."

"Would you like to be?"

"Oh, Samuel!" she said. "You're so sweet."

"Would you like to be engaged to me?"

She blushed.

He waited.

"Yes!" she said finally.

"If we're going to be engaged, we have to kiss. An engagement is not official without a kiss."

Sam moved closer to her, closed his eyes and puckered his lips. Laura did likewise.

Suddenly, before their lips could touch, the church bell began to ring, sending notification that the sermon had ended and services were over.

Quickly, Laura broke the reverie and jumped off the headstone.

"Come on!" she said. "Church is over. We need to get

back."

***

Two days later, Sam and Tom were back at the swimming hole on Bear Creek, directly in front of Wheeler's Cave. For more than two hours, the boys had been swimming, then stopped to rest and dry out under an oak tree.

"Let's go exploring in the cave," Tom said.

"What if we got lost?"

"You can't get lost," Tom said. "Injun Joe reckons there is a back exit."

"Naw," Sam said. "It goes on forever and ever under the ground with no way out."

"Injun Joe said he knows how to go all the way through and come out on the other end."

"You joshing me?" Sam said.

"It's the truth. Let's go ask him."

Fifteen minutes later, the boys were back at the cigar store.

"I remember," the old Indian said. "Cave has three forks. Right at the first, right at the second and left at the last to back door."

Tom turned to Sam.

"Right, right, then left. Can you remember that?"

"Reckon I can," Sam said.

"Remember the turns or be lost forever," Injun Joe warned.

Later that afternoon, the boys were back at Wheeler's Cave.

"We'll need a torch," Tom said. "You got some matches?"

"Always," Sam said.

Moments later, using his trusty Barlow, Sam cut a pine knot from a dead tree, peeled away the bark and set it aflame.

"Come along!" Tom said.

"Suppose we get lost?" Sam said.

"How might we be lost? We'll just follow our tracks back to the entrance."

In a few minutes, the two boys, with Tom in the lead, were

inside the bowels of the cave. The light from the torch cast long shadows across the cave walls. In many places, the passages, rife with stalactites and stalagmites, were narrow, and the boys had to duck down to pass through.

"Look!" Tom said, pointing to several drawings of buffalo on the cave wall. "Those were made by Indians many years ago. It might have been Injun Joe's relatives."

They negotiated a sharp turn in the cave, then came up a point where they had to make a choice.

"This is the first fork," Tom said. "Injun Joe says you go to the right."

After taking the designated passage, they arrived at a second fork.

"We go right again," Tom said.

For another fifteen minutes, the two boys wandered through the passages, but found only darkness and more stalactites. Tom suddenly stopped.

"We took a wrong turn," he said. "Let's go back."

Several moments later, they were back at the second fork, then took the passage to the left.

After they had trekked some forty feet down the new passage, Tom saw daylight.

"Look!" he said. "There it is. There's the back door."

Once outside the cave, the boys were bathed in bright sunlight.

"We did it!" Tom said. "Right. Left. Left. Injun Joe had it wrong."

Now, outside the cave, the two boys found themselves surrounded by deep woods.

"Where might we be?" Sam said.

Somewhere nearby, they could hear the sound of rushing water.

"That's the creek over there," Sam said. "Let's just follow it back to the front door of the cave."

They turned and started along a narrow rabbit trail back to Bear Creek. Suddenly, from the thick undergrowth along the trail, they heard a voice.

"Howdy!" the voice said.

Sam and Tom turned.

There in the middle of the trail was a huge black man, with ragged clothes and pleading eyes, standing in the middle of the trail. For a long moment, the two boys stared at the black man.

"Who are you?" Tom said.

"Name of Jim," the black man said.

"Why aren't you on a plantation?" Sam asked.

"I ran away," Jim said. "I couldn't do the hard work no more and I was beaten by my master so many times, I'd rather die than be a slave."

"My heart aches for you," said Sam.

"Mine too," said Tom.

"I sure would be obliged if you two white boys could get me some food. I haven't eaten in three days."

Tom looked at Sam.

"You go to your house and see what you can find," Tom said. "I'll get some fruit and meet you back at the front of the cave."

Ten minutes later, Sam was at the family home. When he entered, he saw his mother sitting at the kitchen table peeling apples. Sam went straight to the cook stove and took half a pone of cornbread, wrapped it in a newspaper, then started for the door.

"Where you going with that pone of cornbread?" Jane asked.

"I'm going fishing," Sam said. "I get hungry sometimes when I'm fishing."

"Have you been consorting with that no-count Tom Blankenship?"

"Oh, no, Mother! I haven't seen him in days."

***

Fifteen minutes later, Sam was back at Wheeler's Cave. Tom was waiting. He had two apples and a cantaloupe. The two boys started back up the wooded trail. Several minutes later, they were back in the deep woods near the cave exit. When Jim saw the food, a big smile crossed his face.

"God bless you white boys," he said.

He took the pone of cornbread and devoured it quickly. Moments later, he was gnawing through the apples and the cantaloupe. When he finished the cantaloupe, Sam asked about his escape plans.

"I don't rightly know," Jim said. "I've been a few steps ahead of the slave catchers for three days now. If I could just get over to Shuck Island, I'd be in Illinois, and then I'd be a free man."

"We could build a raft," Tom said. "It would take a couple days, but it would get you over to the island."

"We would need tools and rope to build a raft," Jim said.

"I could get tools and rope," Sam said.

"Where?" Jim asked.

"From the work shed at my house."

"I'm obliged to you boys for trying to help me," Jim said, "but first, I got to have some more food."

"Tomorrow, we'll bring more food and tools to build a raft," Sam said. "You stay right here. We'll meet you here again tomorrow."

"You not going to turn me in, are you?" Jim asked.

"We're not going to turn you in," Tom said. "You just be here tomorrow."

***

The following morning, Sam, carrying another pone of cornbread, a chopping axe and a length of rope, met Tom at Wheeler's Cave. Tom had brought two more apples and another cantaloupe. Once Jim had eaten, the three set about building a raft. Over the next two hours, Jim had chopped down several sapling trees and Tom and Sam were lashing them together to make a raft. Nearby, Jim was felling another sapling.

"I'm going to lift this log," Tom said. "When I get it high enough, swing the rope up and loop it twice around."

Sam performed as instructed. Moments later, Tom dropped the log into place and Sam secured it to the other logs with the rope.

Suddenly, the stillness of the woods was interrupted by a

voice.

"Hold it right there!"

Two men, with guns drawn, stepped out of the underground.

"Slave catchers!" Jim said.

Instantly, Jim turned to run. As he did, one of the slave catchers fired a warning shot.

Jim stopped instantly.

"I could have killed you," said the first slave catcher, "but you're worth more to me alive than dead."

His eyes fell on the half-made raft.

"You boys were helping this runaway build a raft," he said. "Don't you know you can go to prison for helping a runaway?"

"Oh, no!" Tom said. "The raft was for us."

The man laughed.

"Do you think we're blind?"

Then he turned to the other slave catcher.

"Charley! Put chains on that slave."

"No!" Jim said. "Don't take me back! Please don't take me back!"

Moments later, Jim had a chain around his neck.

"Oh, woe is me!" he said. "Now I'm in for more floggings and more hard work."

"Come along!" said the first slave catcher. "You're worth $100 to me."

"Where are we going?" Jim asked

"You're going back to the plantation. These two here will be turned over to the sheriff."

***

Late that afternoon, Sheriff Cunningham, with Samuel in tow, appeared at the Clemens family home. Jane answered the door.

"Sheriff Cunningham!" she said. "Is Sam in trouble?"

"Him and another boy was building a raft to help a runaway slave escape over to Illinois. You know he could go to prison for that."

"Who was the other boy?"

"Tom Blankenship!"

Jane glared at Sam angrily.

"When boys come out of the state pen," the sheriff continued, "they're worse than they were when they went in. I don't want to see that happen to your son."

"Neither do I."

"Mrs. Clemens, it is your duty to show some authority over this boy," he said. "If you don't, then next time, I'll have to turn him over to the courts."

"I'll see that this matter is accomplished," Jane said. "I'm grateful for your kind attitude."

***

That night, when Orion arrived at the Clemens home, Jane told him what had happened.

"You're going to have to do something with Samuel," she said. "If you don't keep him away from Tom Blankenship, he's going to end up in prison."

"What would you have me do?"

"Drive it into his head that it is forbidden for him to consort with this no-count Tom Blankenship. Find some occupation for him. His idle time is too plentiful. Find him some sort of job. Lay down the law. You're the only one he'll listen to."

"I'll have a talk with him. Where is he now?"

"On the front porch."

***

Ten minutes later, Orion was on the front porch with Sam.

"Why were you and the other boy helping a runaway slave?" Orion said.

"It was the right thing to do."

"Did you consider that you could be sent to the state penitentiary for aiding a runaway slave?"

Sam shook his head.

"Why are you shaking your head?"

"It seemed not to matter."

"Five years in the state pen could ruin your entire life."

Sam looked up sheepishly at his older brother.

"Now wouldn't that be a fine howdy-do?"

Sam felt absolutely terrible that he had disappointed his brother. He cowered away as Orion stood over him.

"Now listen to me and listen good," Orion said. "As of today, you will no longer associate with this Tom Blankenship character."

"But he's my best friend."

"No matter! He's leading you down the wrong road."

Sam's face was still downcast.

Orion reached down, grabbed Sam's chin and harshly pulled his face to his own.

"Look into my face when I'm talking to you," Orion said.

Sam eyes were now staring straight into Orion's.

"Do you understand?" Orion said.

Sam didn't answer. Orion squeezed Sam's chin in his hand.

"Ow!" Sam said. "You're hurting my chin."

"I MEAN to hurt your chin," Orion said. "Do you understand?"

Sam looked into his brother's eyes.

"Yes, sir!" he said. "I understand."

***

After that day, Samuel Langhorne Clemens would never see Tom Blankenship again, but his memories of the summer of 1847 would be forever etched in his mind. He would never forget the footloose, fancy-free youngster who slept in barrels, stole fruit for food, lied at every turn and lived off the mercies of the world. His memories of their days roaming the streets, exploring Wheeler's Cave, listening to Injun Joe's yarns and trying to help a runaway slave would play a major role in Sam's later years.

4
Laura

A year passed. On the morning of September 3, 1848, Samuel Langhorne Clemens, two months shy of his thirteenth birthday, walked the eight blocks from the family home on Main Street to the Lewis and Clark School on Eighth Street for the first day of the seventh grade. The schoolhouse, a white, six-room wooden structure, stood in the middle of an open field at the corner of Eighth and Oak streets in downtown Hannibal. As Sam took a seat in the classroom, his eyes scanned the premises for Laura Hawkins. She hadn't attended Lewis and Clark the previous year and Sam later learned that her father had enrolled her in a private school in St. Louis. Despite this knowledge, Sam had hoped with all his heart she would return to Lewis and Clark for the new school year.

The classroom was a large, high-ceilinged room with the pungent smell of burned coal hanging in the air. In front, behind the teacher's desk, hung a large picture of Lewis and Clark, looking very brave and resourceful, peering into the distance. Along the walls on either side were strung small placards displaying the printed letters of the alphabet. In the corner, near the pot-bellied stove, sat a stool with a dunce cap, and hanging at the edge of the blackboard was a cane for whippings.

Promptly at 8 a.m., Miss Agnes Strickland, the teacher, entered the classroom ringing a small bell, indicating all students should be at their desks. A smallish, plain-looking woman in her late thirties, Miss Strickland wore glasses and her dark hair was done up in a bun.

The class grew quiet.

"Welcome to another year at Lewis and Clark," she began. "During this new term, the rules remain the same. All students are to be present at their desks promptly at 8 a.m.; home lessons are to be completed fully and on time; any disruptions will be punished with the cane. Is that understood?"

"Yes, Miss Strickland," the class said in unison.

"Today, we will begin with a composition…"

She stopped.

At the back of the classroom, a late student entered and slipped into a seat.

Miss Strickland's eyes fell on the errant student.

"All students are required to be at their desks when the final bell rings," she said.

"Yes, ma'am," the late student replied.

"What is your name?" the instructor said.

"Laura. Laura Hawkins."

As the words were spoken, Sam turned instantly. For Sam, it was like a miracle. There, sitting three rows away at the end of the line of desks, sat the girl of his dreams. Dressed in a pale blue summer frock, her yellow hair was plaited into long pigtails and she wore black buckle-up shoes. Sam was delighted.

***

In the first portion of the day's class, Miss Strickland ordered the class to write a short composition about their favorite memory of summer. Sam put pencil to paper and began scribbling.

My favorite recollection of summer past was discovering the back exit to Wheeler's Cave with my friend Tom Blankenship. Long we had heard the cave had a back entrance, but out of fear of becoming lost, my friend and I had not attempted such a daring feat. Then, after Injun Joe said he knew the exit from childhood, we gathered our courage and, with some light assistance from a pine torch, we determined to attempt it. Injun Joe allowed that the escape route had three forks and the adventurer should take the passage to the right at the first two forks and left at the third. Although we took two wrong turns, we diligently pushed on until we saw the bright light of the back exit and happily claimed our prize.

Once the students had completed the compositions, they were presented to Miss Strickland. When she saw Sam's offering, she read it to the class.

"Very clever, Samuel," she said. "You have a natural inclination for words."

After lunch, Miss Strickland selected eight students, including Sam and Laura, to participate in a spelling bee. The selectees left their desks and stood in front of the class while Miss Strickland presented the words. Once the event started, five of the students fell off quickly and the contest came down to Nell Hughes, Sam and Laura.

"Nell!" Miss Strickland said. "Spell the word 'unnecessary'."

Nell pondered for a moment.

"U-n-n-e-c-a-s-s-a-r-y."

"Incorrect. Take your seat."

The teacher turned to Laura.

"Your word is 'unnecessary'."

"U-n-n-e-c-e-s-s-a-r-y."

"Very good!" the teacher said.

She turned to Sam.

"Samuel, your word is 'increased.'"

"I-n-c-r-e-a-s-e-d."

"Perfect!" Miss Strickland said.

Over the next few minutes, both Sam and Laura correctly spelled the words "windowless," "compromise" and "wholesome." Then Laura stumbled.

"Laura, spell the word 'incredulous'."

"I-n-c-r-e-d-u-l-u-s."

"Incorrect."

She turned to Sam.

"Samuel, your word is 'incredulous'."

"I-n-c-r-e-d-u-l-o-u-s."

"Well done!" she said. "Samuel Clemens is the winner of

the spelling bee."

The other class members applauded.

As Sam started back to his desk, he glanced at Laura. She glared at him; there was livid anger in her eyes.

***

That night, after dinner at the Clemens home, Sam and Orion were seated at the family table talking while Jane washed dishes. Orion turned to Sam.

"What plans do you have for Saturday next?" he asked.

"No plans," Sam said. "What do you have in mind?"

"I want you to accompany me to the *Journal* offices."

"Done!" Sam said.

A pause, then Jane spoke up.

"I've been asking you two to whitewash the outside of the back fence for over two weeks. Is it ever going to be done?"

"Mother, my time has been filled with school," Sam said.

"The back fence will be whitewashed at some point," Orion said. "Saturday next, I want Sam to go to the *Journal* offices with me."

"Very well," Jane said.

***

Over the next two months, despite his best efforts, Laura rejected each and every one of Sam's overtures. She was angry that Sam had beaten her in the spelling bee. One day, when he took a seat at the desk beside her, she immediately moved away. Another day at lunch, when he offered her half of his ham sandwich, she totally ignored him. Several times, as students were walking home after class, Sam sidled up to her and asked to carry her books. Each time, he got an emphatic "no."

Then, one day in early November, she had a change of heart.

All that morning, a winter rain had been pouring down and, at recess, students were forced to remain inside. During such times, students would amuse themselves with indoor games.

Usually, the girls would play the game of graces or charades while the boys would entertain themselves with dominoes or checkers. Graces was a game played by tossing a wooden, ribbon-covered hoop back and forth between two players, each of which would try to catch it on a dowel-like stick. Laura and another student were playing the game behind the classroom coal heater, when Laura, lunging to catch the hoop, accidentally turned over the coal scuttle, scattering the black lumps of coal across the floor. Only seconds later, Miss Strickland returned to the classroom and the students immediately scrambled into their seats.

Once the class was seated, Miss Strickland immediately noticed the spilled coal on the floor.

"Whoever turned over the coal scuttle is due for a caning," she said.

"It was Laura!" said another student.

The teacher's eyes fell on Laura.

"It wasn't me," Laura said.

The class grew quiet as Miss Strickland peered at Laura. Suddenly, Sam spoke up.

"I did it," he said.

Miss Strickland turned and glared at him.

"Samuel! Go to the cloak room!" she said, indicating he was about to be caned.

***

That afternoon, when class was dismissed and students were leaving the school, Laura took it upon herself to approach Sam.

"I'm grateful for your noble deed today," she said. "Would you like to carry my books?"

"Well.... Yes! I would like that!" he said.

Sam took Laura's books and, over the next twenty minutes, they walked the eight blocks to Hill Street.

"You were Sir Galahad today," she said as they walked. "Saving the princess from the fearsome dragon."

"All I did was take your caning."

"Oh no! It was much more than that," she said. "You

showed your fierce love for the fair maiden by slaying the evil dragon."

"It was nothing," Sam said.

A long pause.

Finally, Laura spoke.

"Do you think you would like to marry me some day?"

Sam's eyes lit up.

"Oh, yes! I would love that."

"Oh, Sam!" Laura said. "That would be so grand. We would have a beautiful home and little children and be in love forever."

"What about your father?" Sam said. "He would never approve. He thinks I'm a street boy."

Laura stopped to ponder his words.

"That could be a problem."

Moments later, they had reached the corner of Sixth and Hill Streets. Laura stopped.

"You may return my books now."

"We haven't arrived at your house yet."

"If my father sees me with you," Laura said. "He will have a conniption."

Sam handed her the books.

"Would you like to meet me at Harrington's Ice Cream Parlor on Saturday afternoon?" he said.

"What time?"

"Three."

"I would like that."

***

That night, after dinner, Orion made a firm decision about the whitewashing project.

"No further procrastination!" he said. "Tomorrow, we shall arise early, I'll fetch the brushes and the whitewash, and we'll paint the back fence."

"Fine with me," Sam said.

The next morning, Orion and Sam gathered the brushes and two buckets of whitewash and went to the back fence. The outside of the back fence at the Clemenses' home fronted on First Street. The inside had been whitewashed several times over the years, but the outside had gone without whitewash since the first day the family moved in.

Before beginning, Sam and Orion viewed the project for a long moment.

"In truth, I have no interest in this," Orion said.

"Neither do I," Sam replied.

"We promised Mother," Orion said, "so we are obligated to do it. You start on one end, I'll begin on the other. We'll meet in the middle."

Moments later, the two brothers were busy applying whitewash. As Sam pulled the brush up and down the wooden boards, he saw Robert Overby, a neighborhood boy, coming down the street.

"What are you doing, Sam?"

"Whitewashing," Sam said. "I've been waiting all week to do this."

"What?"

"There is a passel of joy in each brush stroke," Sam said, adding new whitewash, then stroking the brush up and down. "See how smoothly the whitewash soaks into the chinks?"

"Yeah!" Robert said. "Can I try my hand?"

"What will you give me?"

"My blue log roller," Robert said, reaching into his pocket and producing a large blue marble.

"Very well," Sam said, taking the marble and handing the brush to Robert.

Moments later, Robert was happily applying whitewash to the fence.

"Boy, oh boy! I like whitewashing," he said.

As Sam watched, he noticed another neighborhood boy, William Olson, approaching.

"William!" Robert called. "Look at me! I'm whitewashing!"

For a moment, William studied Robert stroking the brush up and down the fence boards.

"Can I do it?" William said. "It looks like a passel of fun."

"No! I want to do it."

William turned to Sam.

"Will you allow me to whitewash?" William said.

"Come along!" Sam said.

The two boys hurried to the other end of the fence.

"Orion!" Sam said. "William wants to try his hand at whitewashing."

"Very well," Orion said, handing his brush to William. "Just remember to make smooth, even strokes."

Moments later, William was happily applying the white wash.

"This is such fun," he said.

For several minutes, Sam and Orion watched as the two neighborhood boys painted the fence. Then they turned to see Thaddeus Morrison coming down the street, his eyes fixed on William and Robert whitewashing the fence.

"What y'all doing?" he asked.

"We're whitewashing," Robert replied. "A fine way to spend the day."

"Can I do it?"

"You have to ask Samuel," Robert said.

Sam, who had heard the conversation, turned to Orion.

"Do we have another brush?"

"Certainly!"

Instantly, Orion returned to the house. Moments later, he was back with another brush and handed it to Thaddeus, who began smearing the whitewash on the fence.

Two hours later, the back fence at the Clemenses' home had a new coat of whitewash. Once finished, the other boys returned the brushes.

"That was fun," said Robert. "If you need any more whitewashing, just let me know."

"Me too," said William.

"And me!" said Thaddeus. "See y'all later."

For a moment, Sam and Orion watched as the three boys, happy with their accomplishments, sauntered back up the street to their homes. Then, instinctively, they turned to admire the newly whitewashed fence. They smiled at one another, then burst out in raucous laughter.

***

Five months passed. During that time, Sam and Laura's relationship flourished. In class, they sat side by side. They spent lunches together, swapping food and chatting. After school each day, Sam carried her books and walked with her to the corner of Sixth Street and Hill. On Saturdays, she would meet him at Harrington's for ice cream and, afterward, they would take long walks along the wharf, admiring the ships.

One afternoon, they were wandering among the steamboats when they came upon the steamship *Big Missouri*, the newest and mightiest paddle wheeler of the day.

"Look at this one!" Laura said.

"That's the *Big Missouri*," Sam said. "The biggest paddle-wheel on the river. She's 180 feet long, carries up to 222 tons of cargo and can carry 250 passengers. Someday, I'll be a pilot and I'll guide one of those up and down the river."

"Sounds like a dangerous occupation," Laura said.

"So it is," Sam said. "Boilers can explode. A snag in the river could tear a hole in the bottom and sink the vessel."

"If we were married, you would be gone most of the time."

"I would see you when the ship landed back in Hannibal."

"Yes, but the nights would be so lonely."

A pause.

Sam looked along the wharf for a private spot.

"Let's step over here a moment," he said, taking her hand and leading her behind a stack of lifeboats. "There's something I want to show you."

Once they were safely out of sight, Sam turned to her.

His eyes met hers and he kissed her softly on the lips.

For a long moment, he held the kiss, then broke it.

"I liked that," Laura said. "Can we do it again?"

Sam kissed her again.

"Someday, we'll be married." he said.

"First, you must convince my father you are worthy."

"That day shall come to pass," Sam said.

"I hope so," she said.

A pause.

"School ends next week," Laura said. "Will you be

attending the school picnic?"

"We'll attend together."

***

On Monday night of the following week, John Marshall Clemens was late once again for the family dinner table. Some thirty minutes after the other members of the family had finished their dinner, they heard the buckboard roll up in the front yard. Several minutes later, after he did not appear in the house, Orion and Sam went outside. There they found their father lying down in the seat of the buckboard.

"Come along," Orion said. "We'll help you inside."

Moments later, Sam and Orion helped their father into the house and into the bed. When they emerged from the bedroom, Jane was there.

"I hope he's not taking another powder," she said.

"He's not intoxicated," Orion said. "He's ill. Desperately ill."

Moments later, Jane was in the bedroom inquiring about his health.

"It's my eyes," he said. "My vision is going blurry and I have this insufferable rash on my back."

"Will you be all right tonight?"

"Let me get some sleep," he said. "Maybe I'll feel better tomorrow."

***

The following morning, John was unable to get out of bed and Jane sent Orion to get Dr. Tom Morgan, the family doctor in Hannibal. Upon arrival, he questioned Jane about her husband's health, then went into the bedroom. Thirty minutes later, he returned.

"Your husband is very ill," he said

"What sort of ailment does he have?"

"I'm not certain," Dr. Morgan said. "He should be admitted to the hospital. There I can better diagnose him."

The following morning, Jane packed a suitcase for a

hospital visit, then Sam and Orion delivered their father to the Hannibal hospital.

***

A week later, on a Friday afternoon, the school picnic was held at Pilgrim's Rest Baptist Church at Bear Creek. During the first part of the school day, students had tests, then they were all loaded into two wagons and delivered to the church picnic grounds. During the first part of the picnic, food and drink was served inside the church, then there were games, including pick up the handkerchief and dodge ball. After thirty minutes of dodge ball, Sam and Laura came off the field to rest.

"Let's go down to the swimming hole," Sam said. "Just you and me."

"What would we do down there?'

"We could be alone."

Laura smiled.

Instantly, Sam jumped up and offered his hand.

"Come on!" he said.

Sam pulled her to her feet, then together they went striding down the wooded trail to the swimming hole. Upon arrival, Sam pointed out a grassy knoll under an oak tree.

"Let's have a seat over here," Sam said, taking a seat in the designated area.

Laura took a seat beside him, and they looked around.

"What's in that cave?" she said.

"Darkness and skunk water."

"Have you ever been in there?"

"Many times," Sam said.

Laura lay back in the grass under the oak tree.

As she did, Sam leaned his body over hers and slipped his hand into her bosom. She didn't deny him.

For several moments, he fondled her breasts and kissed her.

"I love you," Sam said.

"And I love you," Laura replied.

Now, Sam's raw passion started to take over. His hand slipped down to her thigh. Quickly, she grasped his hand.

"No! That is forbidden!" Laura said. "You can kiss me and

frolic with my lilies, but you must never put your hand down there. You can't do that until we're married. Do you understand?"

Sam, the wind taken out of his sails, pulled back.

"I understand," he said.

Then Sam jumped to his feet.

"Come on! Let's go exploring in the cave."

"We can't go in there. We might get lost."

"We can't get lost. I know how to reach the back exit."

Interested, Laura got up and went to the mouth of the cave and peered inside.

"How will we be able to see?"

"I'll make a torch," Sam said. "I always have my Barlow and some matches."

Moments later, Sam had fashioned a torch out of the limb of a cedar tree. Once it was ready, he lit it. Then, taking Laura's hand, they started into the cave.

"Oh!" Laura said.

Sam turned to see what the problem was.

"I've snagged my petticoat on that thorn bush."

"Here! Let me get it," Sam said.

He tore away the ripped portion of the undergarment, leaving a small scrap in the thorn bush.

"There!" he said. "You're free now! Come on!"

Moments later, Sam and Laura were inside the cave.

"Look at all these twists and turns," Laura said as they made their way through the cave. "Are you sure you know your way through here?"

"Oh, yes!" Sam said. "Just follow me."

Ten minutes later, they had reached the first fork.

"We go to the right here," Sam said, confidently leading the way. After another ten minutes, however, he stopped abruptly, seeming undecided.

"What's wrong?" Laura said.

"The second fork should be right along here, but I don't see it."

"Are we lost?"

"I'm not certain," Sam said. "Let's go a little further. We should see the second fork up here somewhere."

"If you say so," Laura said.

After another twenty minutes, Sam stopped again.

"What's wrong?"

"I'm not sure if we've passed the second fork or haven't arrived at it yet."

"What are we going to do?"

"I'm not sure. Give me time to think."

"I'm tired," Laura said. "I can't go any further."

Laura sat down on the cave floor.

"What are we going to do?" she said.

"I don't know," Sam said.

"I'm tired. I'm going to rest," she said.

Sam folded her into his arms and they lay down together on the cave floor.

"Are we going to die here?" she said.

"No. I'll figure something out."

A pause as Sam held her tightly.

"I shall always love you," he said.

"And I shall always love you."

"Let's rest for a while." he said. "Maybe if I can sleep, I can get my bearings."

Moments later, they were sound asleep in one another's arms.

***

They slept for an hour, then awoke in total darkness. Sam fumbled for matches to relight the torch. Seconds later, the cave walls were bright with light.

"Come along," Sam said, pulling Laura to her feet. "Let us try once more. I'm sure Injun Joe said it was right, right, then left. Maybe I got the forks mixed up."

They trudged down the cave passageways. Then, as they rounded a turn, they saw a light and heard the sound of voices.

"Sam! Laura!" the voices called. Instantly, Sam recognized the voice as Injun Joe's. Then in a nearby passage, they saw a flicker of light.

"Injun Joe! Injun Joe!" Sam called. "We're over here."

"Where are you?" Injun Joe said.

"Here! Here!" Sam replied.

Now the light moved closer and, moments later, Injun Joe appeared, holding a torch. Behind him was Jane, Judge Hawkins, Miss Strickland and several townspeople.

"Thanks be to God!" Jane said.

Judge Hawkins stepped forward and hugged Laura.

"I'm so happy you're safe."

"Oh, Father! I'm sorry to have worried you so."

Injun Joe turned to Sam.

"We thought you were a goner," he said.

"What steered you to us?" Sam asked.

"Your composition of last fall," Miss Strickland said. "When we found a piece of Laura's garment at the cave entrance, we knew you were lost in this cave. I also knew Injun Joe was the person who could find you."

"I know this cave like the back of my hand," Injun Joe said. "Everyone come along now. Let's get back into town."

***

Two nights later, Sam and the other members of the Clemens family were having dinner. Orion, who was late as usual, went straight to Sam when he arrived at the table.

"Your little yellow-haired girlfriend came in the newspaper office today."

"What did she want?"

"She asked me to give you this note," he said, handing Sam a small scrap of paper.

Sam took the note and opened it.

"On Saturday next, I shall be leaving Hannibal to go to St. Louis and attend the Presbyterian boarding school for girls. I wanted to say good-bye. Can you meet me at pier number 14 at 2 p.m.?"

***

The following Saturday, Sam was at pier 14 at the appointed time. When he arrived, he saw Laura and her parents waiting to board a steamship. When Laura saw him, she stepped away from her parents and went to Sam.

"Hello, Sam," she said.

"Hello!"

"I'm not sure if I'll ever see you again," she said. "I shall be gone for at least three years."

"I'm sorry to hear that," he said. "Will you write me?"

"I'm afraid not. My father would not approve. You're the reason he wants to send me away. He said getting lost in the cave was the last straw."

Sam didn't reply at first.

"Will you hold me in your heart?" he said finally.

"I shall," she said. "You are my true love."

"And you are mine."

A long pause. Sam didn't dare to make any show of affection with her father so near.

"Good-bye!" Laura said.

"Good-bye."

Sam watched sadly as Laura rejoined her parents, then boarded the steamship. Once passengers were loaded, he watched as the ship's captain blew the whistle and the mighty steamer slowly pulled away from the harbor. As it did, Sam's eyes began to fill with tears.

***

When Sam arrived back at home later that afternoon, Orion had sad news.

"Father died at the hospital this morning," he said.

Sam looked at his brother. He seemed unmoved.

"I'm sorry to hear that," Sam said.

"Don't you have any tears?"

"I never knew him," Sam said.

"He was your father."

"You were the closest thing to a father I ever had," Sam said. "You were the only one who had time for me."

Orion looked at his brother.

"Perhaps you're right," he said. "The funeral is day after tomorrow."

"What was the cause of death?"

65

"No one seems to know," Orion said. "I've asked for an autopsy."

***

The following afternoon, Sam and Orion were at the Marion County Coroner's office in Hannibal. The coroner, a short man in his early forties with a balding head and mustache, led them to the corpse room.

When they arrived, the coroner pulled the sheet back to reveal the deceased. Sam was still unmoved at the sight of his dead father.

"You have conducted a full autopsy of the remains?" Orion asked.

"I have."

"And your findings?"

"The cause of death was an advanced case of syphilis."

Shocked, both Orion and Sam peered at one another for a long moment.

"Are you certain?" Orion said.

"I'm certain."

For a long moment, the coroner waited.

"Anything further?" he asked.

"No. That's all," Orion said. "I'm obliged for your accommodation."

***

Ten minutes later, Sam and Orion were walking down the street outside the coroner's office.

"Now that Father has passed," Orion said, "the time has come for you to take gainful employment and help with family expenses. I want you to go to work at the *Journal*."

"What shall my work be?"

"You'll be a printer's Devil."

5
Printer's Devil

In the late spring of 1848, Joseph L. Arment, a German immigrant and St. Louis businessman, arrived in Hannibal to visit his sister. While strolling the city streets, he caught sight of a For Sale sign in the window of the *Hannibal Gazette*, the town's lone newspaper. While his sister waited, he went inside to inquire. Two days later, he purchased the paper and moved his family and four slaves from St. Louis to Hannibal. Immediately, Arment changed the newspaper's name to the *Hannibal Journal*, revamped the advertising pages, purchased a new Church printing press and, in early September of 1848, promoted Orion to managing editor. By the early spring of 1849, the publication was a thriving enterprise. Published daily, it had 4,800 subscribers, five employees, a modern press and was hailed as the "most trusted publication on the upper Mississippi."

***

On the morning of May 13, 1849, Orion took thirteen-year-old Sam into the *Journal* offices and introduced him to the publisher. Arment, a short-statured, balding man in his late forties with glasses and a bushy mustache, was reading a page proof.

"Joseph, this is my brother Samuel," Orion said. "I propose that he become the new typesetting apprentice."

Arment produced his trademark scowl, pushed his glasses up on his nose, then looked Sam up and down.

"He seems rather small," he said.

"He'll grow larger as he gets older," Orion said.

Arment turned to Sam.

"Can you spell?

"Yes, sir."

"Spell the word unscrupulous."

"U-n-s-c-r-u-p-u-l-o-u-s."

"Spell prognostication."

"P-r-o-g-n-o-s-t-i-c-a-t-i-o-n."

"Do you know how to mix printer's ink?"

"No, sir, but I am capable of learning."

Arment paused, glanced at Orion, then took a deep breath.

"I reckon you'll do," he said.

Then he turned back to Sam.

"Now, you must understand I don't contend with any manner of tomfoolery. Be to work on time. Follow instructions. Get along with other employees. And keep your nose clean."

"Yes, sir!"

"The pay is $2 a week."

"That's agreeable."

Arment turned back to Orion.

"Put him to work under Wales."

***

Wales McCormick, the journeyman typesetter at the *Journal*, was a tall, handsome, dandified twenty-year-old and the publisher's nephew. That morning, he and Sam sat down in front of the type compositor for the first time and Wales began the task of teaching his pupil to set type.

"The war in Mexico is winding down," he said. "A treaty has been signed, but there is still sporadic fighting near the towns of Cerro Gordo and Chapultapec. If nothing else happens, it will be the main story on the front page today."

At the *Journal*, news pages were built by picking individual letters from a case of metal typefaces which had been sorted alphabetically. Using "the stick," a long handheld metal tray, letters were formed into words and words into lines, which were then placed onto the press bed. Once pages were built, viscous ink was slathered over the typefaces, then sheets of papers were fed into the rollers, which pressed the typefaces against the paper to make a printed page. The most tedious part of the job was breaking down the lines of type into individual letters once an issue had been printed. Each line of letters had to be broken up, soaked in cleaning fluid to remove dried ink, then returned, one letter a time, into the case of typefaces.

As Wales picked the letters from the case, he regaled his young pupil with stories about his amorous conquests.

"You should have seen her," Wales said as he worked. "Her lilies were sumptuous white melons. Once I glimpsed them, I was overtaken with this sudden madness to have my way with her."

As he gathered letters on the stick, Sam was watching his every move.

"You have an error," he said. "The word apprehensive has two Ps."

Wales stopped and reread the line of type.

He smiled.

"Clever little devil!"

Once the war story was safely built into the press's letter bed, Wales began building another story about an ongoing murder trial in Hannibal's City court. The moment he was working again, Wales launched into another yarn.

"She was a mulatto girl, perhaps fifteen or sixteen, the daughter of one of Uncle Joseph's slaves. When I made love to her, she squealed like a hungry piglet at feeding time."

Each morning, after the day's news pages had been built, Sam had a wide assortment of other duties. He swept the floor, brewed coffee, built and fed fires on cold days, ran personal errands for the publisher, made deliveries to newsstands, hauled paper stock out of the storage shed and mixed ink in large wooden barrels. After lunch each day, he would go to the local telegraph office to retrieve the latest dispatches about the Mexican War, new congressional legislation and women's suffrage. Many afternoons, he would be waiting at the wharf for the packet ships to arrive, bringing copies of newspapers from New Orleans, St. Louis and Cairo, Illinois. The stories, if deemed newsworthy, would be rewritten and printed in the

Journal. In short, Sam's duties included whatever task the publisher deemed necessary at the time.

***

A year passed. During that time, Sam became a master typesetter and learned every detail of press operation. He trained his hands to work in tandem with his mind, composing words, sentences and paragraphs to translate the handwritten pages of raw copy into clean, legible type. He learned, when mixing ink, to not put in all of the powder into the container at once, but rather enter half, mix the batch, then wait a day before mixing in the other half. This gave the final product a smoother texture, which flowed more evenly across the press rollers. He developed a keen eye for spelling mistakes, uncapitalized letters, broken paragraph indentations, mismatched fonts and uneven printing. Once, after Arment had approved a final proof for publication, Sam pointed out that the masthead date was wrong. Arment, failing to acknowledge the mistake, ordered Wales to make the correction. All that time, Sam listened to Wales's stories about his romantic interludes, the mulatto girl, the minister's wife, the dance hall girl, the woman at the bakery shop and on and on.

***

Two days later, when Sam appeared at work, Wales pulled him aside.

"I've got something I want to show you," he said, withdrawing a white card from his pocket.

"What is that?" Sam asked, examining the card.

"My union card," Wales said. "As a member of the National Typographers Union, I can go to work at any major newspaper in the nation. New York, Chicago, Philadelphia… anywhere that is an affiliate of the typographer's union."

"You mean you could travel wherever you like and find work?"

"That's right," Wales said. "All you have to do is show them this card."

"How can I get one?"

"How old are you?"

"Fourteen."

"You're not old enough. You have to be at least sixteen to join the union."

"I could lie and tell them I was sixteen."

Wales laughed.

"Do you want to do that?"

"Absolutely," Sam said.

"This afternoon, we'll go down to the union hall and I'll vouch for you being sixteen."

"Much obliged," Sam said.

***

One morning in early June of 1850, an early morning fire erupted at the Hannibal wharf. The fire, of unknown origin, started in a warehouse filled with more than 500 bales of cotton and quickly spread to an adjacent facility housing some 700 hogsheads of tobacco. Immediately, steamboats docked near the conflagration were moved to a safe distance and resecured, then workmen began removing as much stored cotton and tobacco as possible before the fire destroyed it. Despite their best efforts, the raging fire consumed most of the cotton and more than half of the tobacco before firemen could bring it under control. Meanwhile, a huge crowd of townspeople were gathered to witness the fire's destruction.

At mid-morning of that day, Arment, Orion and Wales left the office and went to the wharf to witness the conflagration, leaving Sam alone to finish his work.

"When you're finished, be certain the front door is secured," Orion said. "We shall return later this afternoon. The fire will be the big story in tomorrow's paper."

Once he was alone in the office, Sam finished building the day's pages, then, noticing the paper stock was low, he went to the storage shed behind the office to retrieve more paper. At the moment he reentered the offices through the back door, his hands were filled with large bundles of paper stock, so he went inside with his load, vowing to return later and close the rear door. Unfortunately, he forgot and, when he left the office that afternoon, he locked the front door as instructed, but failed to return to the rear of the building and close the back door.

***

Just after 4 p.m., Orion and Arment returned to their workplace and, as Orion was unlocking the front door, he glanced into the office and saw a cow peering through the front window at him. The animal, a big brindle creature, had wandered into the office through the open back door and had been rummaging aimlessly through the premises for almost two hours. A stack of page proofs had been knocked off Orion's desk, there were several fresh cow patties littering the floor, and the animal had bumped into the wood stove and disjoined the flue pipe, but the creature's most grievous sin was that it had eaten one of the cloth ink rollers on the printing press.

"Great God!" Arment said, upon discovering the mangled roller. "I'm out of business until I can get a new roller. A new roller must be ordered from New York and that can take ten days. That means we can't publish again until then."

Arment, livid anger in his face, turned to Orion.

"Your brother is no longer employed at the *Journal.*"

"What madness is this?" Orion said. "It was an innocent mistake."

"Your brother's innocent mistake is going to cost me the printing of two, perhaps three issues. That's several hundred dollars. Inform your brother he's terminated. I wish to never again see him in this office."

***

That night, at the family dinner table, Orion told Sam the bad news. He was surprised when the fourteen-year-old didn't seem to be overly concerned.

"In truth, it is a blessing," Sam said. "I have now learned a trade, a splendid one, and I am free to travel and practice my trade wherever I wish."

"What is your meaning?" Orion asked.

Sam reached into his pocket and produced his National Typesetters Association union card.

"This is my passport to finding work in any newspaper that's a union affiliate. I intend to travel, be a typesetter, and see the world and all that it offers."

Jane peered at him.

"Do you reckon you can care for yourself?" she said. "Who will wash your clothes and cook your meals?"

"Mother!" Sam said. "I'll soon be fifteen years old."

Jane still wasn't satisfied.

"I trust that you realize the gravity of what you are about to undertake."

"Mother, rest assured that I do."

"When do you plan to begin?" Orion asked.

"Next week."

***

On Wednesday morning of the following week, Sam was prepared for his great adventure. With suitcase in hand, he said goodbye to his mother and Orion, then took a cab carriage to the wharf. There he purchased a ticket to St. Louis on the mighty steamship *Louisiana Queen*. After a four-hour journey, he arrived late that afternoon and took lodging at a local hotel. The following morning, he went scouring the streets for work at one of the city's four newspapers.

When he began his search, Sam concluded that the only logical method for finding newspaper employment would be to go to the newspaper office, then into the saloon nearest the office. After arriving at the offices of the *St. Louis Chronicle*, he stopped and peered up and down the street. There, directly across the street, was Ryan's Tavern. Immediately, Sam went inside and began asking questions.

"The *Chronicle* is fully staffed at the moment," said one patron. "The one that's hiring is the *Missourian* down on DeLancey Street."

An hour later, Sam was in the offices of the *Missourian* speaking with the editor, a red-faced, jowly man. Sam produced his union card and reported his work experience at the *Hannibal Journal*. The editor asked about the type of press the *Journal* used and the corresponding typesetting mechanisms. Once Sam explained, the editor seemed satisfied.

"Currently, we have four typesetters and each of them are working overtime," he said. "Can you report for work in the morning at seven?"

"I shall be here."

***

In the 1850s, the *Missourian* was the largest newspaper in St. Louis. Printed daily, it boasted a circulation of over 10,000 subscribers, had twenty-three employees and a modern, steam-powered type-revolving press where the type was placed on the circumference of a cylinder that rotated about a horizontal axis and could print up to 10,000 sheets per hour. Each unit of type was held in a long, narrow box that was released by a keyboard strike, which sent it sliding down an inclined channel to a point where it was assembled into lines. These lines were then stacked together to create columns, which were then moved to the press. The task required sure fingers and a comprehensive knowledge of spelling, capitalization and punctuation. After only a month, Sam mastered the entire typesetting operation.

On afternoons and weekends, Sam entertained himself sight-seeing and wandering along the city's wharf. This last pastime held a special fascination for him. By the late 1840s, St. Louis had become a major commercial center, not only because it was the doorway to the Oregon and California trails, but as a supply point for the Mississippi River. The depth and smoothness of the water surrounding the harbor had made it popular as the most navigable port on the river. As a result, famous paddle wheelers such as the *New Orleans*, the *Vesuvius* and the *Natchez* transformed St. Louis into a booming port town and it was common to see more than 150 steamboats docked at one time.

Sam spent his nights in the St. Louis City library. The first night, Sam roamed leisurely through the stacks determining subjects of interest. The second night, he made a reading list and a schedule. For the month of December, he chose the works of Dickens and put five books, *A Tale of Two Cities, Oliver Twist, The Old Curiosity Shop, Great Expectations* and *David Copperfield,* on his list. Sam was enthralled with Dickens. The following month, for January 1851, he chose the works of Victor Hugo and Alexandre Dumas. In February, he turned to the works of Daniel Defoe, James Fenimore Cooper and Washington Irving. Over the following months, he read books about the French Revolution, the Spanish Inquisition, Joan of Arc, the history of Rome and the Revolutionary War. By early summer, he had read a total of 51 books.

Meanwhile, his employment at the *Missourian* filled his days. He arrived promptly in the composing room at 7 a.m. each morning and, for the next eight hours, save for lunch, he built news pages. Here, unlike at the *Hannibal Journal*, once columns of type were built, they were collected by pressmen who put the columns on the press bed. Once editors recognized how clean Sam's lines were, he was often asked to fill in as a proof-reader at overtime pay. Meanwhile, his bank account was growing. By Thanksgiving of 1850, since he had no expenses other than lodging and meals, he had saved $63.

***

Another year passed. One night in early December of 1851 in the city library, Sam came upon a small volume titled *Notes from the Constitutional Convention* by James Madison. It was a narrative detailing the organization of the convention, the infighting among delegates and the haggling that finally led to the drafting and ratification of the U.S. Constitution. As he read, Sam had visions of Independence Hall, Benjamin Franklin, Thomas Jefferson, George Washington and Alexander Hamilton. When he left the library that night, his heart was set on going to Philadelphia.

The following morning, Sam notified the *Missourian* editor he would be leaving the newspaper's employ at the end of the week. The editor offered to raise his salary by another $5 a week, but Sam refused.

***

By the 1840s, the spirit of freedom that had grown out of the Revolutionary War had sparked a cultural movement in Philadelphia, which earned it the nickname the Athens of America. During those years, Philadelphia became a thriving, pulsating beehive of artistic creativity as architects, painters, sculptors, authors, and craftsmen of all types arrived from other states and England to make their mark. Public art galleries, a natural history museum, a public library, as well as numerous theaters and concert halls, offered instant culture and artistic expression to all who sought it. Buildings, including Congress Hall, Independence Hall, Christ Church, the State House, the Philadelphia Museum of Art, and the Bank of Pennsylvania sprang up throughout the city to celebrate the architectural glory of ancient Greece. In April of 1843, British-born architect Henry Latrobe told members of the city's Benjamin Franklin Intellectual Society that "Philadelphia is the most cultured city in America. Its public library is open eight hours a day."

***

The train journey from St. Louis to Philadelphia required a full two days and, when Sam arrived on December 6, 1851, he found lodging, then took to the streets to find employment. As before, to discover new employment, he used the same tactic he had used in St. Louis: go to the newspaper office, then into the nearest saloon and start asking questions. This time, Sam went to three separate taverns before finally finding work at the *American Advocate*, one of the city's smaller dailies, which focused heavily on politics, local news and social affairs.

That same night, he went to the Philadelphia City library on Penn Street for the first time. Although books could not be borrowed, it was a veritable treasure trove of literacy when compared to the St. Louis library. As he wandered among the stacks, the first book to catch his eye was the *Autobiography of Benjamin Franklin*. Once he sat down and began reading, he was enthralled by the scope of Franklin's life and the practical wisdom he offered. When the library closed that night, he had read almost half the book and, when he returned to his hotel room, he took pencil and paper in hand and sat down at the hotel desk to begin a personal journal.

March 23, 1852 While perusing Benjamin Franklin's autobiography this night, I encountered a nugget of wisdom which I shall take to heart. Franklin proposes every thinking man worth his salt should maintain a personal diary, a record of his daily activities, cogitations, musings and whatever else he may deem worthy of mention. It is a personal history, a record of one's self-progression from day to day and year to year. With these words, I hereby initiate my own personal journal, a record of my life which will be offered up as honestly and completely as I can abide.

***

Over the first few months, when Sam wasn't in the library, he spent his afternoons and weekends sight-seeing. First, there was the President's House. Before the White House, The President's House was home to presidents George Washington and John Adams when Philadelphia was the capital of the United States from 1790 to 1800. Next came Independence Hall and Congress Hall, where the Declaration of Independence and the U.S. Constitution were conceived, drawn up and ratified. Then came Benjamin Franklin's grave at Christ Church, the Liberty Bell, the State House, the Philadelphia Museum of Art and Mother Bethel Cemetery, the burial ground at the north end of the city where more than 5,000 slaves had been interred.

July 14, 1852 My knowledge of early American history has exploded tenfold since I arrived in Philadelphia. All of the famous American who were little more than tiresome names before, Washington, Jefferson, Adams, Madison and Monroe, have now fallen into their proper historical context. My knowledge of our nation's founding, the intellectual underpinnings of the Constitution and the Declaration of Independence has afforded me a greater understanding and appreciation of our nation and its greatness.

November 4, 1852 *The plentitude of Greek architecture in Philadelphia has turned my attention to the Greek civilization and the works of its greatest philosophers. Over the past week, I have been perusing the works of Aristotle, Plato and Diogenes. Aristotle displays the analytical mind of a scientist while Plato was a pure thinker. Over 2,000 years ago, Plato espoused the essential principles of all future political systems in his volume* The Republic. *Together, with his sidekick Aristotle, they defined political perspectives for the remainder of human history. Name tags have changed over the centuries, but the essential political perspectives remain the same. In England, they are referred to as Whigs and Tories. In France, they are Republican and Socialist. In my native land, the tags are Democratic and Republican.*

***

February 3, 1853 *This night, while browsing the stacks, I was gladdened to find a small volume titled* The Social Contract *by French Philosopher Jean-Jacques Rousseau. From the moment I began reading, I was enthralled. For the first time, I was reading the cogitations of a philosopher who believed in the goodness, rather that the evil, of mankind. A thinker who believed, if man were left alone in nature, he would master himself. Rousseau believed that civilization and its trappings breeds corruption in humankind. Once I finished the book, I asked the librarian if there was another volume by Rousseau available. After checking her list, she said* The Social Contract *was the only volume the library owned.*

***

March 2, 1853 *My term of employment at the* Advocate *has now reached fourteen months. I have mastered their typesetting operation; I have seen with my own eyes every worthwhile historical monument the city has to offer and the number of books I have perused, ranging across a wide variety of subjects, has now reached 113. At this juncture, I must conclude that I have exhausted myself with the sights, the history, the architecture, the culture, the food and the people of Philadelphia. I now have only one more city to peruse before I return to Hannibal. That is New York.*

***

A week later, Sam resigned from his employment at the *American Advocate* and boarded a train for an overnight trip to New York. Upon arrival, he took lodging at a boarding house, and the following morning, he was on the streets seeking employment. First, he went to the offices of the *New York Tribune* at Printing House Square in lower Manhattan, then to the nearby Polite Gentleman saloon. There he began questioning patrons about employment.

"They're full up with typesetters at the *Tribune*," said one patron. "There is a small magazine at Broadway and 42nd Street that is looking for new hires. That will be your best bet."

"What's the magazine name?"

"*The Sporting Gentleman*," the patron replied.

***

An hour later, Sam arrived at the offices of *The Sporting Gentleman*. The editor, a smallish man in his late thirties with glasses, breezed through Sam's application form.

"We print stories about sports of interest to men," he said. "Fly fishing, sailing, mountain climbing, skiing and such. The typesetting operation here isn't that much different from that of newspapers. Any questions?"

"No!" Sam said.

"Can you report to work tomorrow at seven?"

***

So, Sam, for the very first time, began setting type for a

magazine. Since it was published monthly, the routine and the rhythm of the work was totally different from that of a newspaper. Rather than the frenzied pace of rushing about to set type for a daily printing deadline, it was more leisurely, more relaxed. After he had been there a week, one of the proofreaders suddenly quit and he started reading proofs two nights a week for extra money.

The first night Sam entered the John Jacob Astor Library at LaFayette Square in lower Manhattan, it was like a dream come true. Not only did it house more books than the library in Philadelphia, but offered a much broader variety. There was a complete set of Shakespeare's plays, a copy of Marcus Aurelius's *Meditations* and Plutarch's *Parallel Lives*. Best of all, they had a copy of Rousseau's *The French Revolution*.

During his time off, when he wasn't in the library, Sam spent his time sight-seeing. One Saturday, he walked the entire distance from lower Manhattan up to 42nd Street, which, at the time, was essentially the end of the city's development. On June 2, 1853, Sam attended the opening of the Crystal Palace, an exhibition building constructed for the Exhibition of the Industry of All Nations and heard President Franklin Pierce deliver the dedication. While touring the exhibition, he fell upon an exhibit of steamboats and how they had revolutionized both travel and the transport of goods around the world. When he left the exhibition that afternoon, his thoughts were on his childhood days in Hannibal.

* * *

August 12, 1853 *Last night, I dreamed I was seated at the dinner table at the Clemens family home. Mother, Orion, Pamela and Henry were all present and a sumptuous fare of fried chicken, green beans, mashed potatoes and hot biscuits awaited us. Orion and I discussed newspapers, Pamela spoke of her new music students. Henry, at age twelve, expressed his enthusiasm in finding a job. It was such a comforting feeling to be near the warmth of my family once again. Somehow, I no longer wish to be a carefree rover, absorbing the world and its various offerings at my leisure. I yearn to see my mother's* *smile and to hear the comforting sound of Orion's voice. During my days as a traveling typesetter, I have saved $336.*

***

Three days later, Sam resigned his position at *The Sporting Gentleman* and boarded a train bound for St. Louis. From there, his plans were to take a steamboat to Hannibal.

August 17, 1853 *The past four years has been the hour of my self-education. Now, on my return to Hannibal, I sense a new wholesome fullness within myself. Travel is fatal to prejudice, bigotry, and narrow-mindedness, and many people need it sorely on those accounts. Broad, wholesome, charitable views of men cannot be acquired by vegetating in one little corner of the earth all one's lifetime. Further, reading, travel's first cousin, has broadened me, persuaded me to see the world with new eyes and evaluate my fellow human beings in a completely different perspective. I now know who Hammurabi, Diogenes, Sophocles and Belshazzar were; I understand how a bicameral legislature works, the origins of the French Revolution and how Oliver Cromwell became Lord Protector of England in the 17th Century. When, where and how I will use all of this new knowledge, I have no clue. Strangely, I have not exhibited an interest in the fairer sex during my wanderings and self-education. In my heart, I am still engaged to Laura Hawkins.*

6
Laura Redux

On the morning of August 23, 1853, the mighty steamboat, the *Natchez II*, arrived in Hannibal from St. Louis. Once Sam strode down the gangplank, the soon-to-be eighteen-year-old started walking up Main Street to the Clemens home. As he approached, suitcase in hand, he saw his mother sitting on the front porch snapping green beans. For a moment, she casually glanced up from her work, then, after a double-take, her eyes firmly fixed on her son. Right away, she set aside the pan of snapped beans and ran down the steps and across the yard.

"Sam!" she said, embracing him and pecking him on the cheek. "I'm so happy to see you."

"I'm glad to be home," he said.

***

That night, just like in his dream, Jane served up a meal of fried chicken, green beans, mashed potatoes and gravy and hot biscuits. Oldest brother Orion was now the owner of the *Hannibal Journal*, having bought out all interest after Arment suddenly died in the fall of 1851. Further, he reported that Wales, the dandified typesetter at the *Journal* who trained Sam, had been shot to death by a jealous husband in the fall of 1851. That same year, Pamela, at age 24, had married William Moffett, a St. Louis businessman, and was now living there. Meanwhile, Henry, Sam's youngest sibling at age 13, was still living at home. Finally, everyone wanted to hear about Sam and his wanderings, and he happily obliged.

Later that night, after dinner was finished and all of the

others were in bed, Orion and Sam slipped out to the back porch to smoke.

"There's a civil war coming!" Orion began. "It's not a question of if, but when. Some slave states are already threatening to secede. Others want to keep the Union together. In all the states, battle lines are being drawn. Where do you stand on slavery?"

"I'm opposed to it," Sam said. "It's unjust to chain your fellow human beings and force them to work against their will."

"Then you're with me and the *Journal*," Orion said. "This past year, I have established the *Journal* as a staunch abolitionist publication. It has caused me some grief, but I expected it."

"What sort of grief?"

"Three weeks ago, after I published excerpts from Frederick Douglass' anti-slavery pamphlets, the office was attacked," Orion said. "Somebody tried to burn it down in the middle of the night. Fortunately, an alert policeman spotted the blaze early and there was only minor damage."

"Any idea who started it?"

"Both the sheriff and I suspect it was Horace Cobb, a local plantation owner and leader of pro-slavery forces in Marion County, but we have no evidence."

A pause.

"What are your plans?" Orion said.

"I have none."

"Can you come to work for me at the *Journal*? I need another reporter and I want you to teach Henry to set type."

"How much is the pay?"

"Fifteen dollars a week."

"That's fair pay."

"Do you plan on staying here?"

"I'm going to get a room at Flannigan's boarding house."

"Why? Mother will be glad to have you here."

"I like my privacy."

***

The following morning, Sam rented a room at a boarding house near the Clemenses' home. Over the next few weeks, he settled into his new duties at the *Journal*. Since Orion had purchased the publication, it had become one of the most highly-respected newspapers in Missouri with more than 4,500 daily subscribers and seven employees, and gained a reputation as "Missouri's honest newspaper." In his new role, Sam spent his mornings teaching younger brother Henry to set type. A thin, wiry thirteen-year-old, Henry was an eager pupil, but a poor speller, so Sam bought him a dictionary and gave him impromptu spelling lessons.

"As a typesetter, you pick the letters for the words just like you were writing," Sam told his brother. "In fact, typesetting is composition's first cousin."

Meanwhile, as a reporter, Sam was already becoming controversial. In late March, after he wrote an expose about a Hannibal City Councilman named Hiram Vandiver who received favorable tax breaks after a land deal, the man came to the Hannibal office with a gun looking for Sam. Sam happened to be out of the office at the time and Orion told Vandiver Sam wouldn't be back in the office until the following morning. That afternoon, after Vandiver left, Orion had Sheriff Cunningham arrest him.

***

A month passed. One afternoon in mid-September, Sam returned to the office after covering a tornado which had destroyed several buildings on the south side of town. The moment he entered the office, Orion went to him.

"Remember the little blonde-headed girlfriend you had before you went wandering?"

"Laura Hawkins?" Sam replied.

"That's her. She is my new secretary," Orion said. "She reports to work tomorrow."

***

The next morning when Sam arrived for work, he found

Laura Hawkins sitting at a desk outside Orion's office. At eighteen, she was tall, thin, fashionably dressed and in the full flower of maidenhood. The moment Sam laid eyes on her, all the old feelings of romantic affection flooded over him.

"Laura!" he said, trying to act surprised. "You're an employee of the *Journal* now?"

"I most certainly am," she said.

"Where have you been the past four years?"

"I completed my studies at the Presbyterian School for Girls."

"Is anyone courting you?"

"Not at the moment."

"Would you like to have dinner on Friday night at Killian's?"

"I'm committed on Friday night, but I'm available on Saturday."

"We have a date," Sam said.

***

The following Saturday night, Sam met Laura at Killian's Dining Emporium. When he first saw her, dressed in a long, flowing dress with her blonde hair knotted in a bun at the back of her head, his heart swelled with pride. She was lovelier than ever. Once they were seated and ordered food, the conversation turned quickly to their relationship.

"Oh, Sam," she said. "I'm so happy to see you again. So many times, you have been in my mind since we last met."

"I've missed you too," he said. "I went traveling for four years, but, during all that time, you were always in my heart."

"Are we still engaged?"

"Of course," he said.

"What are we going to do about my father?" she said. "He will never approve of you."

"We'll cross that bridge when we come to it," Sam said.

"I'll leave that task to you."

After dinner, they bought a bottle of wine, left the restaurant and returned to Sam's quarters at the boarding house. While they sipped wine, they sat on the settee and Sam showed her souvenirs of his travels. There were photos of the Crystal Palace in New York, pictures of Independence Hall in Philadelphia, a signed copy of Benjamin Franklin's *Poor Richard's Almanac,* and a dog-eared copy of the *New York Tribune*.

"I'd love to travel like that," Laura said. "And see the world and all that it contains, but today's society does not allow a woman to travel alone in such a manner."

"Perhaps someday we could do it together."

"Oh, Sam," she said. "I love you."

"And I love you."

Sam moved closer to her and took her into his arms. Their eyes met, and moments later, they were passionately kissing. Sam, his lust out of control, put his hand into her bosom. She didn't move to stop him. Now both were breathing hard and Sam's hand slipped down to her thigh. For a moment, she didn't resist, then suddenly realizing the gravity of the moment, she pulled his hand back.

"No!" she said. "We can't do that until we're married. That's the rule. You know that."

Upset, she quickly sat up on the settee and began to straighten herself.

"It's time for me to go!" she said.

"Would you like another glass of wine?"

"No, it's time to go."

***

Fifteen minutes later, they were in a cab carriage en route to the Hawkins' home on Hill Street. As always, Sam stopped the carriage a block away from the home so they would not be seen together. When Laura stood up to get out, she turned to him for a good night kiss. Sam kissed her lightly on the lips.

"When can I see you again?" he said.

"I'll see you in the office Monday morning."

Laura started to exit the carriage, then stopped.

"When are we going to get married?" she said.

Sam didn't answer at first.

"One of these days…"

"What does that mean?"

"I'm not ready to be a husband yet," he said. "At some juncture, we'll be married but not just yet.'

"I'm not going to wait forever," she said.

Then, as if she were miffed, she exited the carriage and started up the walkway.

"Good night!" Sam said.

She didn't look back.

***

Twenty minutes later, the cab carriage pulled up in front of the Clemenses' home on Main Street. Sam got out. The house was in total darkness; it was after 10 p.m. and the family was in bed. As he started to the door, he heard Orion's voice. Then he peered into the darkness of the front porch and saw Orion sitting in the swing.

"Come up and join me," Orion said. "How was the date with the yellow-haired girlfriend?"

"Interesting," Sam said.

"Did you get into her bloomers?"

"I won't discuss that."

Orion laughed.

"You can go with me to Mollies Follies one night," Orion said. "Lots of action over there."

"No interest."

"Suit yourself."

A long pause.

"I wanted to tell you Henry will never make it as a typesetter," Sam said finally. "He's an atrocious speller."

"I feared that," Orion said.

"How much education did he get?"

"He finished the sixth grade at Lewis and Clark."

"He's not the sharpest knife in the drawer," Sam said. "He has no literacy skills."

"I'm aware he's not very bright. I'll put him on deliveries. It's the simplest job in the company. Maybe he'll be all right with that."

***

By early November of 1853, the race for the Missouri governorship was in full swing. Although Missouri had joined the Union as a slave state, there was a strong abolitionist faction among the citizenry. As a result, all observers were expecting the upcoming governor's contest to be a firestorm. In the race, Sterling price, a plantation owner and staunch pro-slavery advocate from St. Louis, was the Democratic candidate. His opponent, James Winston, an attorney and fiery abolitionist from Wentzville, was running on the Whig ticket.

On the night of November 11, 1853, a crowd of more than 500 people, a volatile mix of both pro-slavers and abolitionists, were congregated in the Hannibal town square for a debate between the two candidates. On the podium were the two candidates along with Orion, who was to introduce abolitionist Winston, and Horace Cobb, a local plantation owner who was to introduce Price, the pro-slavery candidate. Also in attendance, standing at the edge of the podium, was Sheriff James Cunningham and two deputies.

Once Orion introduced Winston, the candidate took to the dais and began to rail about the evils of slavery.

"Slavery is dead," Winston said to a round of loud applause. "The practice of subjugating the black man to the will of the white man is immoral, unfair and a mortal sin. The state of Missouri can no longer abide the practice."

"Lies!" shouted one member of the audience.

"Mangy dog!" shouted another.

"Son of a whore!" shouted still another.

Over the next twenty minutes, Winston railed against the evils of slavery, citing the cruelty of breaking up slave families, the unmerciful whipping of runaway slaves and the buying and selling of Negroes "as if they were cattle."

Finally, Winston was finished and, amid a loud chorus of name-calling and insults, returned to his seat on the podium.

Moments later, Horace Cobb, a tall, thirtyish, poorly-dressed man with a scraggly beard, took to the dais and introduced Price, the pro-slavery candidate.

"The abolitionists are attempting to destroy a way of life we have cultivated for the past eighty years," Price began. "They wish to not only destroy our history and our culture, but our very livelihood. We shall not allow that to occur."

Suddenly, a rotten tomato flew out of the crowd and hit Price in the face.

The candidate raked his hand across his face to wipe away the red, gooey mess.

"Who threw that?" he shouted.

"I did!" said a tall man wearing a farmer's flop hat.

"Let's kill him!" shouted another abolitionist.

Immediately, the political rally descended into chaos. Participants on both sides began throwing rotten eggs, old shoes and bricks at the podium. Fist fights broke out at ground level and on the podium. Wooden benches, provided as seating, suddenly became weapons and some participants were wildly swinging the heavy timbers at one another. After several men mounted the stage and attacked Orion, Sam quickly joined into the fray, pulling one man off Orion, then, with a single blow, knocked the other off the podium. Once Orion was back on his feet, another combatant mounted the stage and came at Sam swinging an antislavery placard. Sam ducked the blow, then turned back to deliver a hard right hand to the man's face. As he did, a brick suddenly hit Sam in the head and he collapsed on the podium.

Orion rushed to his brother.

"Sam! Sam!" Orion said, kneeling over his brother. "Are you all right?"

Sam raised himself to a sitting position.

Suddenly, a shot rang out.

Instantly, the sound of the shot caught the attention of the attendees, and they turned to see Sheriff Cunningham had fired a single shot into the air. The crowd was quieter now.

"That's enough!" the sheriff shouted. "The political rally is at an end! It's time for everybody to go home."

One attendee, blood streaming down the side of his face, turned to confront the sheriff.

"What are you going to do?" he shouted. "Just you and two little deputies?"

"I'm not alone," the sheriff said.

"Ha!" said another man. "What do you mean?"

Calmly, Sheriff Cunningham pointed into the shadows beyond the podium. The crowd turned to where the sheriff indicated. There, standing quietly in the shadows and pointing their rifles at the crowd, was a contingent of the Missouri state militia.

"All I've got to do is give the command," the sheriff said.

Instantly, the mood of the crowd changed.

"The political rally is at an end," Sheriff Cunningham said. "Everybody go home before somebody gets killed."

Slowly, reluctantly, the crowd began to disperse.

On the podium, Orion was trying to attend to Sam's head wound. With a ripped portion of his shirt, he tied it around Sam's head to staunch the bleeding.

"Come on!" he said. "Let's go to the office."

Ten minutes later, Orion and Sam arrived at the *Journal* offices. As they approached, they saw Laura standing in front of the locked building. The moment she saw Sam, she rushed forward.

"Oh, Sam!" she said. "You're hurt."

"It's just a cut."

Laura examined Sam's wound.

"You're going to need medical attention," she said.

"I'll be all right," Sam said. "I just need to have the wound cleaned."

"There are no medical supplies at the office," Orion said.

"I have iodine and bandages in my room," Sam said.

"Come along," Laura said. "I'll take care of it."

Back at Sam's room, Laura cleaned his head wound, applied iodine and bandaged it.

"Now you'll be fine," she said. "Get a good night's rest."

"You're so good to me," he said.

"That's because I love you."

"And I love you," she replied. "When are you going to make me your wife?"

"I'm not sure," Sam said. "At some point…."

Laura, seemingly miffed at his reply, didn't answer at first. "Good night!" she said finally.

"Good night!"

Soon after Laura left, Sam was sound asleep.

***

Two nights later, Sam and Laura had dinner at Killian's again, then, after buying two extra bottles of wine, they returned to his quarters. There, for almost an hour, Sam regaled Laura with stories about his travels while they drank the first bottle of wine. After making their way halfway through the second bottle, they threw caution to the wind and, after some furious kissing and fondling, they ended up naked in Sam's bed.

***

The following morning, when Laura woke up and found herself naked in Sam's bed, she was beside herself.

"Oh my God!" Laura said. "What happened last night?"

"I'm not certain," Sam said. "Both of us were very intoxicated."

"In our drunkenness, we had carnal intercourse. In the eyes of God, that's a mortal sin outside of marriage."

Sam shook his head innocently.

"What if I'm with child?" Laura said. "My family would never survive the scandal."

"You're becoming agitated over nothing," Sam said.

Laura calmed down.

"Perhaps you're right," she said. "My womanly time is at the end of the month. Then we shall know whether I am with child."

***

Three weeks passed. On the morning of December 6, Sam and Laura left the office and had lunch at Killian's Restaurant again. Once seated, Sam ordered the roast chicken plate lunch while Laura had a ham and cheese sandwich. Once the food was served, they began to eat quietly. Finally, Laura spoke.

"I have some news."

"What might that be?"

"My womanly time for the month of November started this morning. I'm not with child."

"It pleases me to hear that," Sam said. "I was sorely worried."

They ate quietly for another moment.

"We can't be doing that again until we're husband and wife," Laura said finally. "When are you going to marry me?"

"I informed you earlier that I'm not ready to be married."

"You've known me for over ten years," she said. "When do you feel you'll be ready?"

"I'm not sure," he said.

Another long silence.

"I want to be married and have a home and children," she said finally. "If you are unable to commit to me, I want to find a man who wants to be my husband."

"What does that mean?"

"I want to end our romance so I can be free to find someone else."

Sam turned suddenly to her, a shocked look on his face.

"You're going to terminate our relationship if I don't marry you?"

"That is correct," she said.

"That means you won't see me again?"

"Yes."

Sam peered at her.

"You're downright serious, aren't you?"

"I sure am!"

Sam threw up his hands and shrugged.

"Then so be it," he said. "We've reached an impasse. You want a husband and I want my freedom."

"Looks that way," she said.

"So, you're saying good-bye?"

"That I am."

"Then do as you wish."

Sam watched as Laura pushed her chair back, took her

purse and stood up.

"Tell your brother I won't be back to work. Can you do that?"

"I shall."

"Good-bye, Sam!"

Without another word, she stepped away from the table, then strode out of the restaurant. For a moment, Sam watched through the window as she disappeared down the street.

***

Thirty minutes later, Sam was back at the newspaper office telling Orion what had happened.

"Once you get into her bloomers," Orion said, "she starts making demands."

"I didn't know what to say," Sam said. "I love her, but I can't be chained to a woman and a home at this point in my life."

"You made the right decision," Orion said. "In the years ahead, you'll see the truth of that."

"I'm not a person who relishes disappointing others."

"It's natural to feel guilty about an incident like that," Orion said. "You did what you had to do. You had to protect yourself."

Sam bowed his head.

"My heart has been broken," he said.

"Forget her!" Orion said. "The best way to do that is to throw yourself into your work. I have a new series of articles I want you to write."

Sam perked up.

"What might that be?" he said.

"A series of articles about steamships. Riverboats have been the heart and soul of Hannibal since its beginnings. I want you to write humorous sketches about riverboats. The lives of people that run them, passengers, crewmen, pilots and the river's sense of romance. It will get your mind off of Laura Hawkins."

"When do you want me to start?"

"Next week," Orion said.

***

Two days later, Sam was on the riverboat, the *Mississippi Queen,* interviewing Horace Bixby about his career as a riverboat pilot. Bixby, in his early fifties, was a medium height man with a lean, wind-burned face and a well-trimmed gray mustache. As a steamboat pilot for more than fifteen years, he was not only a legend, but one of the most respected steamboat men on the river. As Sam listened to Bixby recall his years on the river, learning its twists and turns, the accidents and near-accidents as well as the colorful people he had known, Sam had a personal realization. Suddenly, he remembered his boyhood days with Tom Blankenship when they would admire the steamboats coursing gloriously up and down the river and dream of the day when they would pilot one themselves. Now, out of the blue, for whatever reason, the opportunity to fulfill that dream was being dropped in his lap.

Once the interview was finished, Sam changed the subject.

"How do you become a riverboat pilot?" he asked.

"First, you apply to be a cub with the Steamboat Inspection Service," Bixby replied. "Then you must find a pilot who will take you on as an apprentice. That's the hardest part."

"Have you ever trained a cub pilot?"

"Oh, yes," he said. "Many, down through the years, but now I'm getting old. I don't have the patience I had as a younger man."

"Would you consider training me as a cub pilot?"

Bixby, surprised at the words, turned quickly to him.

"You seem to be very happy being a newspaper man."

"I enjoy being a newsman, but I've always dreamed of being a riverboat pilot."

Bixby laughed.

"Lots of boys up and down this river have that same dream."

A long pause.

"If you'll train me, I'll give you the first $500 of my salary," Sam said finally.

"That's a handsome offer."

"I'm willing to sacrifice to make my dreams come true."

Another long pause.

"If you'll go to the Steamboat Inspection Service in Hannibal and bring me back an approved application, I'll take your offer."

"Splendid!" Sam said.

***

The following morning, Sam was in the *Journal* office bright and early and wrote up the article about his interview with Bixby. Once complete, he took it to Orion, who read the piece.

"Good job, Sam! Exactly what I wanted."

A long pause, then Sam spoke up.

"I have another matter I wish to discuss with you," he said.

"What might that be?"

"I want to change careers."

"What are your plans?"

"I wish to become a riverboat pilot."

Sam explained his conversation with Bixby and the deal they had struck.

Orion laughed.

"You're the wild one in the family, Sam," he said. "Life to you is just one big adventure. I never know what insane mission you're going to undertake next."

"I want to try it," Sam said. "At least for a while. I'll be back once I get tired of it."

Orion laughed again.

"You'll always have a job at the *Journal*."

"Much obliged," Sam said. "How's Henry doing with deliveries?"

Orion shrugged.

"Totally incpt," he said. "Yesterday, he delivered one bundle to the wrong place. Two other bundles he left outside the business office and they were ruined in the rain."

"What are we going to do?"

"I'm not certain," Orion said. "We must find something for him."

7

Henry

Three years passed. The year was 1857 and, all across America, the flames of civil war were being fanned. James Buchanan, a Pennsylvania moderate, had been elected the 15th president and pledged to bring peace to a rapidly-dividing nation; in the ongoing Kansas/Missouri border war, pro-slavery forces captured and burned down the abolitionist town of Lawrence, Kansas with the loss of 160 lives; in the halls of Congress, Sen. Preston Brooks of South Carolina beat Sen. Charles Sumner of Massachusetts with a cane after he gave a speech attacking Southerners; several deep southern states, including South Carolina and Georgia, were threatening to secede, all the while trying to convince neighboring states like Kentucky, North Carolina and Tennessee to follow suit. The War between the States was becoming a stark inevitability.

Meanwhile, in early December of that year, twenty-two-year-old Samuel Langhorne Clemens was living out his dream of being a riverboat pilot. Six months earlier, after a grueling two-year apprenticeship, Sam received his official pilot's license from the Steamboat Inspection Service and was feeling quite flush with his new salary of $250 a month, a princely sum for the time. First, he replenished his entire wardrobe: two new suits, new shoes, underwear, shirts and ties. Next, he purchased his first top hat and an expensive gold watch and chain for the vest pocket of his new suits. Finally, he opened a savings account at a local bank and invested $500 in Missouri Consolidated, a new steamboat company on the river.

Sam was not above showing off his new-found wealth.

December 14, 1857 *The City of Memphis is the largest boat on the river and the hardest to pilot, and consequently, I have received an enviable reputation for that very reason. The young pilots, who used to tell me patronizingly that I could never learn the river, cannot keep from showing a bit of their chagrin upon seeing me now so far ahead of them. And when I go to the union hall to pay my dues, I rather like to let the damn scoundrels get a glimpse of a crisp one-hundred-dollar bill peeping out from among notes of smaller dimensions whose faces I do not exhibit.*

January 4, 1858 *I love the riverboat pilot's profession more than any I have ever followed and I take a measureless pride in it. The reason is plain: a pilot is the only unfettered and entirely independent human being that lives on this earth. Kings are little more than the hampered servants of parliament and people; parliaments sit in chains forged by their constituency; the editor of a newspaper cannot be truly independent, but must work with one hand tied behind him by party and patrons, and be content to utter only one-half or two-thirds of his mind; no clergyman is a free man and may speak the whole truth, regardless of his parish's opinions. In truth, every man, woman and child has a master and worries and frets in servitude, but the Mississippi riverboat pilot has none. The moment the boat is underway in the river, she is under the sole and unquestioned control of the pilot. He can do with her exactly as he pleases, run her when and whether he chooses and tie her up to the bank wherever his judgement deems best.*

***

Further, he loved the sheer complexity of being a riverboat pilot.

January 14, 1858 *A riverboat pilot must commit to memory every landmark along the twelve hundred mile route from St. Louis to New Orleans and back again. He is also required to anticipate the force of the current going upstream and downstream; know the difference between the riffles on the water's surface caused by the wind and those created by dangerous reefs; be able to find the safest channel both in dangerously low water and during the spring "rise" when the whole stream sometimes seems choked with trees from the constantly changing banks; make mental notes of the changing of every crucial spot where the leadsman drops his knotted rope line into the water and sing out his measurements: "quarter twain," "half twain" and the most pleasant sound of all to a pilot, "mark twain," meaning two fathoms or a depth of twelve feet, which is safe water.*

***

In his new riverboat profession, Sam's life had become an endless string of trips from St. Louis to New Orleans and back again piloting various steamboats transporting passengers, goods and mail up and down the Mississippi River. As a result, St. Louis had become his new home base and, during layovers between piloting trips, he was a frequent visitor at the home of his sister, Pamela Clemens Moffett. Over the past six years, Pamela and her husband William had been operating the River Queen Hotel near the St. Louis docks, and Sam, while a guest at the hotel, frequently joined the family for evening meals at the Moffett home. During the visits, Sam enjoyed spending time with their daughter Annie Moffett, his one and only niece. The four-year-old, knowing her Uncle Sam was bringing her gifts and stories from his travels, squealed with delight each time he paid a visit.

***

One Saturday in early June of 1858, Clemens had completed a run from New Orleans to St. Louis aboard the *John J. Roe*. It had been a grueling, four-day journey with a near-grounding near Greenville, Mississippi, and Sam was glad for it to be over. Once he exited the ship, he went straight to the River Queen Hotel to relax and get a good night's sleep. When he arrived, William Moffett, his brother-in-law, had some family news.

"Your mother is residing with us now," he said.

Sam peered at him.

"Mother is here? In St. Louis?"

"Correct!" William said. "She can't wait to see you."

That night, Sam had dinner and a happy reunion with his mother Jane at the Moffett home. It was the first time in almost two years he had seen her. After the evening meal, Sam and his mother slipped out to the back porch for a private conversation.

"Why did you decide to move to St. Louis?" Sam began.

"I'm fifty-two years old and I'm alone," she said. "My children have been flung to the four corners of the earth and I need family to help care for me in my old age."

"What about the old family home?"

"Orion and Henry are still living there," she said. "Both continue to work at the newspaper."

A pause.

"How's Henry doing?"

"Not well," she said. "He doesn't like the newspaper business. You know, he has problems reading and writing."

"He is a terrible speller. I could see that when I was trying to teach him to set type."

"There's something wrong with his eyes," she said. "When he reads a word, he doesn't see it exactly as it lays. If he sees the word 'J-a-n-e,' he sees something else. Either 'J-e-a-n' or 'J-a-e-n.'"

"Does he need glasses?"

"No!" she said. "It's something in his eyes. He's trying to get away from working at the newspaper, but he can't find anything else."

A long pause.

"He has no confidence in himself," Jane continued. "You and Orion are not afraid to put yourself out there in the world. Henry doesn't have that trait."

"I know he is meek," Sam said. "It's a chore for him to assert himself."

"Do you think you could help find him some sort of different work?" Jane said. "Maybe some sort of menial job on a steamship?"

Sam pondered for a moment.

"Let me see what I can do."

***

Two days later, Sam was serving as pilot aboard the SS *Pennsylvania,* one of the largest and most famous ships on the river, as it made its regular run between St. Louis to New Orleans. The ship's captain was William Brown, an early fifties, heavy-set man who Sam later described as "an ignorant, stingy, snarling, fault-finding, mote-magnifying tyrant." Once the trip was underway and Sam and Brown were alone in the pilothouse, Sam asked the burning question.

"Do you have any open positions in the crew?"

"What sort of open position?" Brown replied with a scowl.

"A beginner's position," Sam said. "Perhaps a mud clerk or a freight clerk."

"Who are you asking for?"

"My brother. He wants to work on a steamboat."

"I have nothing!" Brown said with a scowl. "Your brother is like every other snot-nosed kid on this river. They have big dreams of working on a riverboat, but their abilities fall far short of what the job requires."

"You have no knowledge of my brother," Sam said. "He's hard-working and dedicated to whatever task he undertakes."

"You say that because he's your brother."

Sam turned from him. His first instinct was to take a swing at his captain, but instantly, he thought the better of it.

"Perhaps you're right, sir."

"I KNOW I'm right!"

***

On the afternoon of the following day, the SS *Pennsylvania* docked in New Orleans. During a four-hour layover, the ship's passengers, freight and mail were unloaded, more passengers and freight were placed into the holds, and the mighty steamship was ready to head back north to St. Louis. As the ship pulled away from the levee, its freight clerk, a young blonde-haired boy in his twenties, rushed out to the dock yelling and frantically waving his arms for the ship to stop.

"The freight clerk missed the boat," Sam said to his captain. "Are you going to go back and get him?"

"Serves him right," Brown said.

"How will he return to St. Louis?"

"The best way he can," Brown said with a big laugh.

Ten minutes later, as the vessel slipped into the river's main current, Sam watched as the panicked youngster, still frantically waving and yelling, disappeared from view.

***

Two days later, when the SS *Pennsylvania* arrived back in St. Louis, Sam was preparing to leave the ship and go to the River Queen Hotel. As he started down the gangplank, suitcase in hand, Captain Brown called to him.

"Clemens!"

Sam turned to him.

"What did you say your brother's name was?"

"Henry! Henry Clemens!"

"When we leave again on Tuesday, have him here and he can assume the duties of freight clerk."

"Yes, sir!" Sam replied.

That night, Sam told his mother of the arrangements he had made with Captain Brown.

"Have him to get on the next boat from Hannibal," he said. "He has to be in St. Louis by Tuesday afternoon."

"Glory be! I'll send a telegram this afternoon," Jane said.

***

That night, while asleep at the River Queen Hotel, Sam had a vivid nightmare. In the dream, he saw Henry's corpse, laid out in a metal coffin in the parlor of the Moffetts' home. A bouquet of white flowers with a single red bloom lay over Henry's chest and all the family members were gathered around the casket weeping. Standing over the coffin was a solemn-faced minister dressed in black reading the final words. Suddenly, Sam awoke. When he did, he was happy to realize it was only a dream. As he drifted off back to sleep, he wondered if it was an omen.

***

The following Tuesday morning when Henry arrived in St Louis, Sam and Jane greeted him at the docks. He hadn't changed much in the past two years. Although he was almost eighteen years old, he still had the thin, wiry frame and the innocent look of a teenager. When Sam boarded the SS *Pennsylvania* that afternoon, Henry was at his side.

"The captain is a tyrant," Sam warned as they strode up the gangplank. "He is mean, vicious and unyielding. Whatever cruel comment he might make to you, overlook it and do your job."

"I promise," Henry said.

Once they were on board, Sam introduced Henry to the captain, then proceeded to show his brother the details of the position. The job of the freight clerk was to notify the captain when freight was to be dropped at an upcoming port. When a trip began, the freight clerk was given a manifest of all freight to be delivered at each port. Once the ship left one port and headed to the next, it was the freight clerk's duty to call out to the captain that freight was to be dropped at the next port. The job paid $5 a day, which included meals and lodging aboard the vessel.

Over the first two days, Henry performed well. At Natchez, Mississippi, Henry made the freight call a bit early, but Captain Brown didn't complain. The following day, as the SS *Pennsylvania* neared Baton Rouge, Louisiana, Henry made a freight call. Despite the call, the ship failed to slow down and make the stop. As the ship passed the Baton Rouge Harbor, Sam turned to the captain.

"We had a freight drop at Baton Rouge," he said. "We missed it."

"I didn't hear a freight call," Brown said. "If I had, I would have ordered a stop."

Now the steamboat had to turn around and go back to Baton Rouge and make the drop. This meant more than an hour had been lost on the ship's schedule. Once the drop was completed, the SS *Pennsylvania* headed south again and Captain Brown instructed Sam to call Henry to the pilothouse. When Henry appeared, the captain was livid.

"Why didn't you give a freight call at Baton Rouge?" he said.

"I gave a call," Henry said.

"You did not!" Brown said. "If you had, I would have heard it."

"But I did, sir!"

"You lying little whelp!" Brown yelled, then he turned and slapped Henry across the face with his open palm. Henry, on the verge of tears, pulled back, holding his red cheek.

Instantly, in a fiery rage, Sam picked up a stool, knocked Brown down with a single blow, then jumped on top of him with both fists flying. When the first mate saw the fight, he rushed forward and pulled Sam off the captain. The captain arose from the desk, bruises on his face and his nose bleeding. Once peace was restored, both men resettled themselves to continue the journey.

***

Upon arrival in New Orleans, Sam wanted to forget the incident. Brown didn't. Once the boat was unloaded, Brown went straight to the local Maritime Union Hall, reported the incident and informed officials he would never work with Sam Clemens again. Two hours later, union officials were on board the SS *Pennsylvania* and informed Sam of Brown's decision. This meant Sam would not be on the return trip aboard the SS *Pennsylvania* to St. Louis.

The following morning, the SS *Pennsylvania*, with Henry on board as freight clerk and Brown as the ship's captain, pulled up anchor at New Orleans and headed north again to St. Louis. Later that afternoon, union hall officials reassigned Sam to the *A.T. Lacey*. As the *Lacey* pulled away from the New Orleans levee and headed north to St. Louis, Sam was happy with the reassignment. Having worked with the captain before, Sam knew him to be a fair and honest gentleman.

***

On the afternoon of the following day, as the *A.T. Lacey* passed close to shore at Greenville, Mississippi, a voice called out to the steamship's crew.

"Terrible news! The SS *Pennsylvania* has blown up just below Memphis at Ship Island," the voice called. "One hundred and fifty lives have been lost."

As Sam heard the words, his heart flew into his mouth. He feared Henry was among those who were lost. Wild with fear and anxiety, Sam hung on to every scrap of news as the *Lacey* sped upriver.

Late that afternoon, when the *A.T. Lacey* pulled into Memphis, Sam told the captain his brother was aboard the SS *Pennsylvania* and explained he wanted to be off-duty so he could check on his brother. The captain approved his absence, noting that another pilot could work a double shift.

At the Memphis emergency hospital, Sam found Henry lying unconscious on a thin mattress among the other victims. Instantly, Sam burst into tears when he saw the dark liver coloration of Henry's face and hands, marks left by scalding hot water on human flesh. For several moments, Sam took a seat beside his brother and wept uncontrollably.

Suddenly, Sam turned to look up as someone touched his shoulder. It was Tom Dempsey, a man Sam remembered as second mate on the SS *Pennsylvania*.

"Your brother was a hero," Dempsey said. "At the initial explosion, Henry was blown clear of the wreckage, but instead of swimming to shore, he swam back to the ship to help rescue others. When he reached the ship, the second boiler exploded and the hot steam scalded his body and seared his lungs."

***

For four days, Sam remained at Henry's bedside as the brother lingered between life and death. Henry's case was hopeless, but nursing attendants didn't have the heart to tell Sam. They cried for Sam in his grief and brought him flowers daily. One young doctor, perhaps out of pity, told Sam that his brother might pull through. Clinging to hope, Sam remained at Henry's bedside. On the morning of June 21, 1858, six days after the accident, Henry died in his sleep, never having regained consciousness. He was three weeks shy of his eighteenth birthday.

At the funeral home, where most victims were being buried in coffins of unpainted wood, Sam was told Henry's case had aroused so much sympathy that hospital workers had collected a total of sixty dollars to buy something more durable. When Sam saw Henry in the metal coffin he would be buried in, with a cluster of red roses and a single red rose on his chest, he knew his dream had become all too true.

***

Four days after his death, Henry was buried in the cemetery at Pilgrim's Rest Church in Hannibal alongside his father John. After the funeral service, Sam, Orion and Jane were striding back down the hillside to their waiting carriage.

"If I had not won the job for him on the *Pennsylvania*," Sam said, "he would still be alive today."

"Don't blame yourself!" Jane said. "It was God's will that you obtained the job for him. It was God's will that he died in the explosion. God controls these matters, not men, so don't be blaming yourself."

***

That night, after Henry's funeral, all of the family gathered at the Moffett home for dinner. At the table, each family member remembered Henry in their own way. Orion recalled the day he bought Henry two new shirts for his tenth birthday. Jane remembered the time Henry had cried when he killed a small bird with a home-made bow and arrow. Sam recalled the smile that broke across Henry's face when he announced that he was going to work on the SS *Pennsylvania*. Once dinner and recollections were finished, Sam and Orion slipped out of the house and went for a walk along the St. Louis docks.

"After what happened to Henry," Sam said, "I'm disheartened at being a steamboat pilot."

"You ready to go back to work for the *Journal*?"

"That I am."

"Do you want to return to Hannibal with me?"

"Give me a few days to clear up some matters with the Maritime Union and I'll be back in Hannibal next Monday."

"Those are the sweetest words I've heard today," Orion said.

8
1860 Presidential Election

So, Samuel Langhorne Clemens returned to writing, his first love, and over the next seventeen months, he plied his trade by covering stories on a host of far-ranging subjects. These included an Indian massacre near Goshen, a raid by slavers in the Kansas/Missouri border war, which left more than sixty people dead, a catastrophic cotton house fire in nearby Wentzville, which took eleven lives, and a gruesome story about a crewman on the steamboat *A.T. Lacey* who accidentally hanged himself while trying to repair the vessel's smokestack. As the need arose, Sam also spent time performing editorial duties including checking page proofs, composing lines of type, writing editorials and assisting Orion with the creation and placement of advertisements.

***

In mid-May of 1860, the Republican national convention was held in Chicago to nominate the party's candidates for the upcoming November election. When the convention opened, the leading nominees were Sen. William Seward of New York, former representative Abraham Lincoln of Illinois, former representative Edward Bates of Missouri and Sen. Simon Cameron of Pennsylvania. In the first ballot, Seward led all the voting but fell short of a majority, while Lincoln finished in a strong second place. On the second ballot, Cameron's delegates switched to Lincoln, which left Lincoln essentially tied with Seward. On the third ballot, Lincoln clinched the nomination after consolidating support from more delegates who had backed candidates other than Seward. Finally, Sen. Hannibal Hamlin, a popular moderate from Maine, was selected as Lincoln's running mate.

Once the convention was over, losing candidate Edward Bates, a well-known attorney and political figure in St. Louis, returned to Missouri and launched a statewide campaign to drum up support for the Lincoln ticket. Well aware that the *Journal* was a staunch abolitionist publication, one of the first stops Bates made was in Hannibal to befriend Orion and seek support for his cause.

***

On the morning of June 3, 1860, when Bates arrived in Hannibal, Orion and Sam were waiting to greet him at the docks. Bates, a heavy-set, fiftyish man with a broad face and a well-trimmed white beard, offered a glad hand when he stepped off the steamboat. Later, at the *Journal* offices, Bates carefully laid out his plans and expectations for the upcoming presidential election.

"It's going to be a historic election," he said. "If Lincoln doesn't win, I fear to say our nation is going to descend into chaos. That's why I'll be depending on the fair-minded people of Missouri like yourself to help me promote the Lincoln cause."

"You have my full support," Orion said. "The *Journal* will endorse Lincoln on every front. Not only will you have the paper's editorial support, my brother and I will personally assist in coordinating political events in Hannibal throughout the campaign."

"That's music to my ears," Bates said. "In all likelihood, Mr. Lincoln himself will be making an appearance in Hannibal toward the end of the campaign."

Over the next three hours, Bates, Orion and Sam laid out plans for the forthcoming presidential campaign in Hannibal. Bates would ship pro-Lincoln placards and handbills from St. Louis to Hannibal for display in public places. The *Journal* would advertise for and keep tabs on local volunteers who wanted to contribute to the Republican cause. Finally, Orion agreed to run political advertisements in the *Journal* promoting Lincoln at a fifty percent discount. That afternoon, when Bates boarded the steamship to return to St. Louis, the three men had a plan in place to get Abraham Lincoln elected in the upcoming presidential election.

***

The following morning, in a front-page editorial, the *Hannibal Journal* declared its support for Lincoln in the strongest of terms. The article concluded:

"The hour has arrived for fair-minded men to rise up and make their voices heard above the evils of slavery and its incalculable costs in human lives and suffering. Republican candidate Abraham Lincoln, like the Biblical Moses, is the only personage qualified to lead our nation out of this quagmire and make the Union whole once again."

***

That afternoon, Orion and Sam were in the *Journal* office poring over a stack of ad page proofs for errors. After they had been through most of the pile, Orion suddenly looked up from their work.

"Take the looking glass and see who's available at Mollie's Follies," he said.

Sam turned from the proofs, picked up the telescope on Orion's desk, then, after going to the window, trained it on the balcony of Hannibal's house of ill-repute, which was less than a block away.

Sam didn't answer right away.

"Who's out there?" he said impatiently.

"Only one woman."

"What color is her hair?"

"Red."

"Red?" Orion said. "There are no redheads at Mollie's."

"There is now!"

Orion arose from the desk.

"Let me see!"

Then he took the glass and trained it on the whorehouse balcony.

"Holy Christ!" Orion said. "That's Fannie Mae! She hasn't been there in over a year."

Orion immediately turned and took his coat.

"Finish these proofs," he said. "I'll be back in an hour."

"Where are you going?"

"I can't miss an opportunity with Fannie Mae."

Once Orion had his coat on, he turned back to Sam.

"Can you loan me $5?"

"You're the owner of a newspaper," Sam said. "You can't raise $5 in cash?"

"I've got debts to pay," Orion said impatiently. "Come now! Give me $5."

Sam reached in his pocket, pulled out a roll and handed Orion a five.

"I'll pay you back!" Orion said.

Then he sat down at the desk again and withdrew a small bottle of turmeric powder. As Sam watched, Orion mixed a teaspoonful of the powder into a glass of water and drank it down.

"What's that for?" Sam asked.

"So I won't catch anything."

***

Two nights later, Sam and Orion were in attendance at a social gathering at Hannibal City Hall to honor Mayor James Brady. All of the city's primary movers and shakers—politicians, businessmen and community leaders—were there to make their presence felt. As the two brothers sat quietly waiting for the event to begin, a pretty dark-haired woman, mid-twenties with a pleasant smile, was moving through the crowd passing out program sheets. Once Sam and Orion received programs, Orion's eyes followed her swaying hips as she continued around the room.

"Who is that woman?" he said.

"That's Mary Stotts," Sam said. "I attended Lewis and

Clark Elementary with her many years ago."

"Is she married?" Orion asked.

"Not that I'm aware," Sam said.

Instantly, Orion got up from his seat and followed the woman around the room until she had passed out the sheets. Once she was finished, Orion approached her and showed her the flyer he had received.

"If I may say so," he said, "as editor of the local newspaper, I must point out that the word 'society' is spelled wrong in your hand-out."

The woman took the printed sheet and examined it.

"Where?"

"Here!" Orion said, pointing to the error.

As the woman examined the word, Orion's eyes were gazing at her bulging breasts.

"I'm terribly sorry," she said. "I must speak to the printer about this."

Orion smiled and changed the subject.

"My brother says he attended Lewis and Clark Elementary with you."

"Who is your brother?"

"Sam Clemens."

"Oh yes," she said. "I remember Samuel."

A pause.

"May I ask a personal question?"

"So long as it's not overly personal."

"Are you a married woman?"

"No!"

"Are you engaged?"

"I am not."

"I would love to have the pleasure of your company one evening for dinner."

"I'm agreeable to that, but you must obtain my father's permission."

"How can I do that?"

"Go to Stotts' Haberdashery on Third Street and ask him."

***

The following morning, Orion was at the designated location and introduced himself to the proprietor.

"Oh yes, I know who you are," Stotts said. "You're the editor of the *Hannibal Journal*."

"I would like to court your daughter Mary," Orion said.

"I'm in agreement so long as you promise to treat her with dignity and respect."

"It shall be done," Orion said.

***

Over the next two weeks, Orion began his courtship of Mary Eleanor Stotts. Rather than having lunch at the office each day, Orion began meeting her at various restaurants in Hannibal or having picnics in the public square. In the office, between editorial duties, Sam would catch Orion writing long love letters to her. Orion's evenings were spent at either the Stotts home or on dinner dates. At the end of the second week, Sam pulled his brother aside.

"Looks like you've fallen head over heels for Mary Stotts," he said.

"I'm in love. I'm going to propose tomorrow night."

"Are you certain you aren't rushing into things?"

"I'm certain. If she accepts, I want you to be the best man at my wedding."

"As you wish," Sam said.

***

Two weeks later, Orion and Mary Stotts were married in a public ceremony at the Pilgrim's Rest Church at Bear Creek. Attendees included community leaders, politicians, *Journal* employees, friends, relatives and other well-wishers. Sam, looking very uncomfortable in an ill-fitting jacket, stood by quietly as the vows were read and the old women sniffled into their handkerchiefs and commented about what a beautiful couple they were. Once the ceremony was finished, well-wishers stood on the church house steps and threw handfuls of rice as the happy couple boarded a cab carriage which would take them to the docks, then to St. Louis for a four-day honeymoon. Before leaving, Orion told Sam he was to make all major decisions at the *Journal* until his return.

***

When Orion and his new bride returned from the honeymoon, they took up residence in the old Clemens home on Main Street. Once moved in, Orion and Sam shifted the furniture around to Mary's satisfaction. The new bride created flower beds at the front of the house and planted zinnias, pansies and roses. Since there had been little or no cooking in the house since Jane went to St, Louis, Mary bought new pots and pans and began cooking hot meals for Orion and Sam each night. The new bride was quickly turning the old homestead into a traditional household once again.

***

Three months passed. Now, in late September of 1860, anticipation over the upcoming presidential election was swelling throughout the nation and, in Hannibal, it was at a fever pitch since candidate Lincoln himself was due to make a personal appearance there later that month. On the first day of October, Edward Bates was back in Hannibal to meet the Clemens brothers and make plans for Lincoln's appearance.

"Mr. Lincoln will address the crowd from the deck of the riverboat *Mississippi Queen* on the afternoon of October 30," Bates said. "We must notify voters and have them at the docks in a timely fashion so they can hear his speech."

"Handbills have already been printed and volunteers are passing them out as we speak," Orion said.

"Don't pass out the flyers too early," Bates said. "Save most of them for a final push during the last two days before the appearance."

"It shall be done," Orion said. "What about security?"

"Mr. Lincoln will have his own security personnel," Bates said. "Some will be at his side, others will be hidden within the crowd."

"What about Sheriff Cunningham?" Orion said.

"He won't be here on the day of Lincoln's appearance," Bates said. "He's in St. Louis that week testifying in a murder trial."

A long pause, then Bates turned to a box of campaign buttons he had brought to the newspaper office.

"On the day of Mr. Lincoln's appearance, pass out these buttons to all of his supporters so they can wear them proudly," he said, taking one of the buttons, then handing it to Orion.

Orion examined the button. It was a round metal piece with a pin on the back to attach to clothing and featured the faces of Lincoln and his running mate Hamlin.

"You must keep Mr. Lincoln's name and likeness in front of the voters up until the day of the election," Bates said.

"It shall be done," Orion said.

***

Three weeks passed. One afternoon, when Orion and Sam returned to the *Journal* offices after lunch, the first thing Orion did was take the telescope from his desk and train it on the balcony at Mollie's.

Sam was flabbergasted.

"What are you doing?"

"I'm checking out the girls."

"You're a married man!" Sam said. "What about your marriage vows? What about love, honor and faithfulness?"

Orion slowly took down the telescope and studied his brother.

"I love my wife," he said finally. "But I am also a discriminating man who likes some spice in his life."

With that, he returned the telescope to his desk, then mixed a teaspoon of turmeric in a glass of water and drank it down. Next, he grabbed his coat and started for the office door.

"I'll be back in an hour."

At the office door, he stopped.

"Can I borrow $5?"

"I gave you $5 last time."

"I need another $5."

Sam smiled, pulled out his roll and handed a fiver to his older brother.

"I'll pay you back," he said.

Sam nodded.

Orion started out the door, then abruptly stopped and looked back at Sam.

"If you wish, you can accompany me," he said.

Sam shook his head.

"I have no interest."

"Suit yourself!"

***

On the afternoon of October 30, 1860, when the *Mississippi Queen* docked at Hannibal harbor, more than 3,000 people, including Orion and Sam, were gathered to hear candidate Abraham Lincoln deliver his campaign speech. Across the top of the ship, strung between the smokestacks, was a huge red, white and blue banner, which read: "The Union shall be preserved!" Once the vessel was tied up, a band began playing "God Bless America." As the assembled crowd sang along, a group of eight to ten dignitaries gathered on the ship's main deck to face the crowd. These included Edward Bates, Missouri Governor Claiborne Fox Jackson, Hannibal Mayor James Brady and presidential candidate Abraham Lincoln. Once the song was finished and the crowd grew quiet, Bates stepped to the railing to address the crowd.

"Today, I stand before you to introduce the one and only man who can save our nation from being torn apart. This man represents integrity, experience and the courage to stand up for decency and justice for all people. I now present you with the next President of the United States, Mr. Abraham Lincoln."

With that, Bates backed away from the railing, then Lincoln, tall, wiry, lean of jaw and wearing his signature top hat, stepped forward to a round of tumultuous applause. Moments later, the crowd was quiet and Lincoln began to speak.

"Our nation stands on the brink of a precipice," Lincoln began. "Today, we are faced with a national crisis like no other in…"

Lincoln stopped speaking as a tomato flew past his head. Suddenly, a mob of some twenty to thirty men who had been hiding within the crowd stepped forward and began throwing rotten fruit, old shoes and stones at the candidate. Instantly, Orion recognized the leader of the mob as Horace Cobb.

"Slavers!" he shouted. "Let's get them!"

"Let's kill them!" said one man.

"We'll hang them!" said another.

A group of pro-Lincoln supporters, led by Orion, converged angrily on the pro-slavery mob. At first, the slavers tried to stand their ground but, seeing they were outnumbered, they began to retreat south on Main Street. By then, Orion and his allies had overwhelmed the group and had Cobb on the ground, kicking him and beating him about the head with their fists. By now, other slavers, seeing their leader was receiving the beating of his life, rushed back and pulled Cobb away from his tormentors. As Orion watched Cobb being dragged away by other slavers, he turned back to the assembled crowd.

"Now, we shall hear Mr. Lincoln speak," he shouted.

Instantly, a roar of applause arose from the crowd. Moments later, Lincoln returned to the railing and began to speak again. First, he warned against the evils of slavery, the dangers of dividing the nation and the "growing animosity which was pitting neighbor against neighbor, brother against brother, and father against son." Toward the end of the speech, he quoted the Declaration of Independence and the famous line "all men are created equal. Does this principle of equality not apply to Negroes?" Finally, Lincoln concluded by saying, if elected, he would "preserve the union and keep the states together at all costs."

When he stepped away from the railing, the crowd roared with applause and loud shouts of "Lincoln! Lincoln! Lincoln!"

Later that afternoon, when the *Mississippi Queen* was ready to depart Hannibal for Lincoln's next campaign stop, Bates had some final words for Orion.

"You have performed admirably well in support of Mr. Lincoln and the Republican Party during this election campaign," Bates said. "If Lincoln wins, I intend to speak to the appropriate people about the rewards for your efforts."

"Rewards?" Orion said. "What manner of rewards are you referring to?"

Bates raised his hand reassuringly.

"Let us wait until the election is finished, then we shall discuss it."

The following morning, the *Hannibal Journal* carried a glowing front-page editorial about the success of Lincoln's Hannibal stop.

"Never has a political candidate been greeted in our city with such resounding enthusiasm. Each time Mr. Lincoln made a new point, the crowd cheered him on with great, then even greater applause. Mr. Lincoln has pledged to save our union and this publication has full confidence that Mr. Lincoln will fulfill his promise."

***

A week passed. On November 6, 1860, the United States held its 19th quadrennial presidential election and, once all the votes were counted, Abraham Lincoln, the former congressman from Illinois, turned out to be the clear winner. The Republican ticket had won a national popular plurality, a popular majority in the North where states already had abolished slavery, and a national electoral majority comprising only Northern electoral votes. Only days after the election, Lincoln began naming the members of his cabinet. His secretary of state was William Seward and his attorney general none other than Edward Bates.

***

Two weeks after the election, Orion received a letter from Bates congratulating him on their success in the recent election.

November 20, 1860

My Dear Orion:

The Republican party in Missouri plans to hold victory celebrations commemorating the recent election of Mr. Lincoln as our new president.

This event will represent a golden opportunity to garner further support for Mr. Lincoln and raise political donations for the state's Republican party. Presently, victory marches are planned in St. Louis, St. Joseph, Hannibal and Kansas City. The Hannibal event is scheduled for the night of December 14, 1860.

Your publication should begin carrying notifications of the event starting the week before the actual event. I shall depend on you to have all of the announcement placards and handbills printed and distributed. All printing expenses should be billed to the Missouri Republication Party here in St. Louis.

At the moment, I am uncertain of my presence for the event. However, rest assured you shall have unlimited support from other devoted party members in Hannibal, including Mayor James Brady and Sheriff Cunningham.

Yours truly,
Edward Bates

***

On the night of December 14, Orion and Sam had fulfilled all their duties regarding preparations for the event. Advertisements for the event had been printed in the *Journal*, volunteers had been notified and placards printed and passed out. Before they left the family home that night, Orion came out of his bedroom with a .45 caliber pistol and a cartridge belt strapped on his side.

"What do you plan to do with that?" Sam asked.

"I have a sneaky suspicion that I'm going to have it out with Horace Cobb tonight."

"How do you know he will even be present?"

"Rest assured he will be there," Orion said. "He despises me too much to let an opportunity like this pass."

***

Just after 7 p.m. that night, an uproarious crowd of more than a thousand Lincoln supporters were gathered at the north end of Main Street. Many were volunteers who had worked in the local campaign; others were staunch Republicans who wanted to further the abolitionist cause; still others were simply curiosity seekers looking for some excitement. Once the parade began, Orion, with his pistol on his hip, and Sam were at the forefront carrying a banner that read: "Lincoln forever!" As the group marched down Main Street, small groups of bystanders dotted the sidewalk, shouting their praise and enthusiasm.

Once they had traveled the five blocks to Hill Street, the demonstration appeared to be proceeding peacefully. Then, as the marchers approached Ninth Street, they saw torches and a barricade of old wagons and furniture blocking the street ahead of them. Upon seeing it, Orion signaled a halt.

Suddenly, when the marchers stopped, shots rang out. One of the marchers at the front of the group dropped. A woman screamed, then more shots were fired and pandemonium ensued. Quickly, the marchers dispersed, taking cover in the alleys between the buildings along the route. Orion drew his pistol, then, as the two brothers raced for cover, more shots rang out and Sam suddenly felt a burning sensation in his shoulder.

Moments later, they were safely behind one of the store buildings.

"I've been shot," Sam said.

Orion turned to his brother.

"You're bleeding," he said. "Tear away part of your shirt and stop the blood."

Sam did as instructed. Although he was holding the ripped shirt firmly to the wound, blood was continuing to flow.

"We've got to get you to a doctor," Orion said.

Suddenly, the shooting from the barricade stopped. By now, Hannibal's Main Street was empty, save for scattered placards. Other marchers had dragged the bodies of their wounded comrades to safety.

"Come out and fight, Clemens!" said a voice from behind

the barricade.

"That's Horace Cobb!" Orion said. "I recognize his voice."

"What are we going to do?"

"Let's take the alley back to Hill Street," Orion said. "Then we'll go back up Second Street to Dr. Johnson's Office. It's next door to the sheriff's office."

***

Moments later, Orion and Sam, holding his bleeding shoulder, were running through Hannibal's back alleys to Dr. Johnson's office. Once they reached Second Street, Orion peered across the street at Dr. Johnson's office. Then he turned and peered south along Main Street. As he did, he saw Cobb and another man coming up the street toward them.

"Holy Christ!" Orion said. "It's Cobb! The son-of-a-whore followed us. We're going to have to make a run for it."

For a moment, they waited. Down the street, they could hear footsteps coming toward them.

"Ready?" Orion asked.

"I'm ready," Sam said, grasping his shoulder.

"Come on!" Orion said.

Quickly, the two brothers stepped out of the alleyway into the street.

Instantly, Cobb recognized him.

"Aha! Now you're mine!" he said, raising his pistol.

Before Cobb could fire, Orion fired off three rounds. For a moment, Cobb staggered, his pistol fired into the ground, and he fell dead in the middle of the street.

***

Ten minutes later, Orion and Sam were in Dr. Johnson's office.

"That's a nasty wound," the doctor said as he plucked the piece of lead from Sam's shoulder. "Another inch and it would have hit a main artery and you wouldn't be here."

"I'm glad we made it in time," Orion said.

Once the doctor had Sam all bandaged up, they were ready

to leave.

"That will be $6 for my services," the doctor said.

Sam looked at Orion.

"Don't look to me," Orion said. "It was your injury."

Sam reached into his pocket, withdrew $6 from a roll and handed it to the doctor.

When they stepped back out on the street, a sheriff's deputy was there to meet them.

"I saw what happened when you shot Horace Cobb," the deputy said. "As far as I'm concerned, it was self-defense. If anyone questions you, I'm your witness."

"I shall remember that!" Orion said. "Much obliged!"

***

Ten minutes later, Sam, holding his bandaged shoulder, and Orion were walking back up Main Street to the Clemens home. After they had walked some fifty yards, Sam noticed a huge plume of smoke coming from the other side of town.

"Look!" he said, pointing. "That's coming from the newspaper office."

Orion looked up.

"You're right! Those bastards have set the *Journal* office on fire. Come on!"

Five minutes later, Sam and Orion were standing in front of the *Journal* building watching a raging fire consume it. Already the office's reception area and press room were totally engulfed in flames. Sam's desk was smoldering ashes and now the blaze was quickly making its way to the storage room where the ink and cleaning materials were stored.

For a long moment, Orion and Sam watched silently as the flames consumed the building. Suddenly, Orion began to laugh.

Sam turned to him.

"Why do you find this so comical? he asked.

"It's probably the best thing," he said. "The best way for me to get out of the newspaper business."

"What is your meaning?"

"The business has been on the verge of bankruptcy for the

past two years," he said. "Expenses getting higher and higher and revenue remaining the same. It's all for the best."

"Didn't you have insurance?"

"It expired last year."

Sam shook his head.

"What are you going to do?" he asked.

Orion laughed, stood up, stretched his arms, then turned back to Sam.

"I'm going to get drunk," he said.

Sam laughed.

"I shall get drunk with you."

The Clemens brothers spent the rest of that evening at the Yellow Dog saloon drinking whiskey shots and beer. When the establishment closed at midnight, Orion and Sam, still nursing his injured shoulder, went staggering up the street singing "Sweet Molly Malone."

When they reached the front steps of the old Clemens home, they were arm-in-arm, still singing the chorus of the song.

"As she rolled her wheelbarrow through the streets broad and narrow crying 'cockles and mussels, alive, alive, oh!' Alive, alive, oh...."

***

Four months passed. On the morning of March 6, 1861, Orion and Sam were having a breakfast of scrambled eggs, ham, biscuits and coffee at the Clemens home. Both of them loved Mary's breakfasts. As they ate, there was a knock at the door; Mary answered it, then returned moments later with a telegram for Orion. Curiously, Orion stopped eating and opened the message.

At the top, the caption read: "From the office of U.S. Secretary of State William H. Seward.

March 5, 1861
To the Honorable Orion Clemens:
This is to inform you that, upon the recommendation of

U.S. Attorney General Edward Bates, you have been named secretary of the Territory of Nevada.

To assume your duties, you must report to Governor James W. Nye at Carson City on or before April 15, 1861.

You shall be expected to pay for your transportation to Carson City. Upon arrival, these expenditures will be reimbursed from state coffers. The salary is $1800 a year.

Signed,

William H. Seward

After reading the message, Orion turned to Sam.

"Read this!"

Sam took the telegram and read it.

"If you have to arrive by April 15," Sam said, "You only have one week to prepare. It's a three-week journey across the plains."

For a long moment, Orion didn't reply.

"I fear there is one small problem," he said finally.

"What might that be?"

"I don't have money to pay for the journey."

"If you'll allow me to accompany you, I'll loan you the money."

"You can be my secretary," Orion said. "The secretary to the secretary."

Sam laughed.

"Done," he said.

***

That night, Orion spoke with his wife Mary about his new plans and the changes in their family arrangements.

"I cannot let such an opportunity pass," he said. "I want you to remain in Hannibal with your parents while I'm gone. Once I'm established out there, I'll send for you and we'll start our new lives together again."

"As you wish," Mary said. "I shall be well cared for at my parents' while you're becoming reestablished. You know I shall always love you."

9
Across the Plains

A week passed. On the afternoon of March 13, 1861, Sam and his older brother Orion checked into the Whiskey Mansion Hotel on the outskirts of St. Joseph, Missouri. Their sleep that night was fitful at best as they anticipated the great adventure that awaited them. Bright and early the next morning, they loaded their belongings, checked out of the hotel and took a cab carriage to the Overland Stagecoach office on Third Street.

As they rode, Orion turned to Sam.

"How much money do you have?" he said.

"Two hundred and eighty-six dollars in cash and a ten-dollar bill sewed into the lining of my coat."

"Why would you do that?"

"In case we get robbed."

Orion laughed.

"No need to worry about that. Those things only happen in western novels."

"You never know."

Upon arrival at the stage office, Orion paid the carriage driver, then they unloaded their luggage and went inside. The clerk was a red-faced, middle-aged man with a pronounced paunch, a jowly face and glasses.

"Carson City, Nevada?" he said. "The price will be $150 each and you are only allowed fifty pounds of luggage between the two of you. Excess baggage costs fifty cents a pound. Place your bags on the platform."

Sam hefted the four bags onto the scales.

The clerk pushed his glasses up on his nose and read the dial.

"That's eighty-four pounds. You're going to have to lighten the load down to fifty."

Quickly, both brothers began rummaging through their baggage and picking out only essentials. Of the four suits he had packed, Sam removed two. Then he took out a pair of work boots, a wool coat, three shirts, a copy of *The Diary of Samuel Pepys* and a strap for sharpening his razor. He withdrew a seven-shot Allen pistol, which he stuck in his belt.

Meanwhile, Orion had finished removing his non-essentials. Beside the suitcase was several pairs of trousers, a smoothing iron, an extra pair of shoes and a bowie knife. His Colt revolver was in his waistband. Once finished, he put the bags back on the scales.

"Now you're got sixty-three pounds."

Sam peered at his brother.

"What do you have in there?"

Sam opened Orion's suitcases. Inside, he found a five-volume set of law books and a large unabridged dictionary.

"Why do you need these? They weigh a ton."

"I'll need those to discharge my duties as secretary."

Sam turned back to the clerk.

"We'll pay the excess."

"That will be $4.50," the clerk said.

Sam paid the money and the clerk provided each of them a voucher for passage.

"We want to ship our excess belongings back to St. Louis," Sam said.

"Do you have a shipping box?"

"No."

The clerk provided a shipping crate, then Sam packed the extraneous items inside, scribbled the St. Louis address of his sister Pamela on the package then returned it to the clerk.

"That's another $2," the clerk said.

Sam paid the requested amount.

"Looks like you're ready," the clerk said. "The coach will be leaving in thirty minutes."

Outside the office, Sam saw a bright red stagecoach with yellow wheels proudly bearing the name Overland Stage and Pike's Peak Express #16. Two workmen were hitching up a team of six sturdy horses and sorting out the six sets of reins used to control the animals. Clemens watched as the conductor, the man responsible for passengers, placed their baggage in the coach's rear storage boot. Atop the carriage, Clemens could see mailbags piled high, and inside, the conductor was rearranging the mailbags to make seats for three passengers, Sam, Orion and a uniformed soldier on his way to Fort Kearney, Nebraska. Finally, all passengers were seated, the driver and the conductor were in place and the journey was ready to begin.

Once the stagecoach pulled away from the St. Joseph station, Sam wasted no time recording the journey's start.

March 14, 1861 *We jumped into the stage, the driver cracked the whip and we howled away and left "the states" behind. There was a freshness and breeziness and a sudden exhilarating sense of emancipation that almost made us feel that the years we had spent in the close, hot city, toiling and slaving, had been wasted and thrown away. We were on our way.*

***

March 15, 1861 *The first day was a sprint across the northeastern corner of Kansas Territory, where the stage passed through the stations of Rock Creek, St. Mary's, Kiowa, Rabbit Gulch and Simpson's Junction. At each station, a fresh team of six horses were exchanged for tired ones and, while waiting, passengers could enjoy a short respite from the carriage's constant rocking motion. In some stations, passengers could refresh themselves or buy food and drink while waiting for the horses to be swapped. Stations were usually managed by a couple or a general store owner. In some cases, the stations were simply ranches which provided fresh horses and little else. Many of the stops along the stage route had been established originally to provide fresh horses for the Pony Express.*

***

On the morning of the second day, still in Kansas, the stagecoach received a new driver and new conductor at the Wilson's Pass station. The stop had a small general store and Sam replenished his and Orion's stock of ham, strawberry jam, boiled eggs and white bread. When Sam told the proprietor he was headed to Nevada territory, the man warned, "That's lawless country. Keep your money and your gun close at hand."

***

March 18, 1861 *Transport by stagecoach must be the most uncomfortable, God-forsaken, unforgiving, troublesome mode of travel known to man. The constant bouncing and quaking motion will shake a man's insides into scrambled eggs. The only respite from this constant torture was the brief stops to change horses. It travels both day and night, so there is no hope of restful slumber. The only way I can get cool enough to sleep at night is to ride on top in my underwear. The constant dust, the infernal heat and the dreary odor of sweaty horses never disappears. Such is life among the mailbags.*

***

In the early morning hours of the fourth day, Overland Stage #16 bowled into Nebraska territory at the Platte River. Its three passengers were sound asleep when, suddenly, the vehicle jerked to a complete stop. Instantly, this brought the passengers wide awake.

Moments later, the conductor pulled back the curtain and, with his face close to his lantern, he thrust his head inside.

"All right, gents," he said. "Time to get out for a spell."

"What's the problem? Sam asked.

"Thoroughbrace is broke."

The Clemens brothers and the soldier climbed out of the carriage into a drizzling rain to assess the situation.

"On which part of this vehicle is the thoroughbrace located?" Sam asked.

The conductor pointed to the massive system of belts and springs that comprised the cradle upon which the stagecoach rocked.

Sam, taking a closer look, could see one corner of the coach had broken free of the suspension system.

"How did it happen?" Sam said.

"How? It happened by trying to make one coach carry three days' mail. That's how it happened. We're uncommon lucky, because it's so dark, we could have gone another ten miles unbeknownst that the thoroughbrace was broken."

Over the next twenty minutes, passengers and crew unloaded the mailbags by the roadside until the carriage was empty. Once the conductor had mended the thoroughbrace, he began reloading the mailbags. This time, no mail was placed top side, and the rear boot was filled to the brim. The conductor then bent all the seatbacks down flat and filled the coach half full of mailbags from end to end.

"Now we're not going to have seats," Sam said.

"Soon enough, you will appreciate me," the conductor said. "I'm obliged to accomplish this to protect the thoroughbrace. A bed is better than seats."

Thirty minutes later, the reloading had been finished and a huge pyramid of mailbags remained on the roadside.

As the passengers started to reenter the carriage, Sam turned to the conductor.

"What about the extra mailbags?"

"I'll send a guard from the next station to pick them up," the conductor said.

***

That night, to pass the time, Sam and Orion chatted with Jack Slade, the soldier and fellow passenger bound for Fort Kearney. Slade was a tall, thin, serious man with a black hat, sharp face and a thick mustache. He said he had grown up in Western Montana where, since there were no laws or lawmen, he was part of a vigilante committee charged with ridding the countryside of its criminals.

"There was more than thirty of us vigilantes that caught up

with Jules Murdoch, the most hated thief and assassin in those parts, and his gang at Coldwater Creek," Slade said. "There must have been six or seven of them. They were sleeping when we jumped them early one morning. Immediately, two of them went for their irons and we shot them outright. The others drowsed themselves awake, then we tied 'em up like young calves and started looking for a hanging tree. Moses Kimball, the vigilante leader whose wife and child had been killed by Jules, said he wanted to hang all of them quick except for his despised enemy Jules. 'Then we'll have our way with the old boy,' he said. So, we hung the first four without further ado, then each vigilante who had a grudge against Jules got their turn. Several men used him for target practice, one nipping his flesh here and there, another clipping off some fingers and still another blew his nose away, leaving his face a bleeding, ragged mush. Finally, Jules begged to be killed outright, so Moses walked up close, uttered a batch of uncomplimentary words, then dispatched him. Before we buried him, Moses cut off his ears and put them in his vest pocket. I heard later that Moses had a watch fob made of Jules' right ear."

Later that night, as Overland Stage #16 rumbled across the wilds of eastern Nebraska territory, the passengers realized the wisdom of the conductor's method. For the first time, they could recline on a flat surface of mailbags to sleep. It was the soundest night of sleep they had had during the entire journey.

***

March 20, 1861 *Our fellow passenger and former vigilante Jack Slade left our midst at Fort Kearney this afternoon. He shook our hands, shouldered a large rucksack, then waved good-bye and started up the street. As I watched him disappear around the corner of a harness shop, I remembered his story. As for myself, I'm not certain my conscience could bear the thought that I had been a member of a party that had lynched four men and tortured a fifth to death. On the other hand, these pioneers must necessarily have some means of maintaining peace and order in their lives.*

***

March 22, 1861 *Now that we have journeyed deep into the deserts of Nebraska Territory, my eyes are catching sight of small forests of sagebrush along the route. Imagine a venerable live oak tree reduced to a small shrub two feet high with rough bark, thin V-shaped leaves and twisted boughs. It is an imposing monarch of the forest in exquisite miniature. Its foliage is grayish-green and gives that peculiar tint to the desert and mountains surrounding it. The sagebrush grows from six to seven feet apart all over the mountains and deserts of the far west, clear to the borders of California. There is not a tree of any kind in these deserts and, for hundreds of miles, there is no vegetation except the noble sagebrush.*

***

Late that afternoon, Overland Stage #16 was rolling across central Nebraska Territory toward Platte Valley. At one point, upon approaching a steep rise, the driver, seeing the horses were straining far beyond their abilities, ordered the passengers to get out and push. Finally, after almost an hour of strenuous human and animal labor, the vehicle was on level earth once more and the passengers reboarded.

March 23, 1861 *As we neared the top of the rise, we heard a sudden rumbling sound. It was a constant roar like a waterfall, and the nearer we approached the top, the louder the rumbling became. Finally, when we reached the top, our vehicle started downward into the Platte Valley and, only then, did we realize the origins of the rumbling. At that moment, I gasped in awe at the majestic spectacle looming below me. There, grazing lazily about the valley floor, was a buffalo herd at least five to six miles wide. Never have I seen such a wonderous sight. Their number must have been in the tens of thousands and, from all appearances, this lush valley was their domicile. At first appearance, the buffalo, save for the large hump which abruptly arises from its shoulders and descends midway of its backbone, has the general characteristics of a domesticated bull. Long strands of winter fur dangle from its chin and underside. This regal creature is around seven feet long, again like a domesticated bull, and stands about six feet tall at the shoulder. As splendid an animal as I have ever envisaged. For as long as I breathe, I shall not disremember the exquisite beauty of the buffalo herd.*

***

Two days later, the ninth day of the journey, Overland Stage #16 crossed into Wyoming Territory and passed through a string of way stations: Independence, Devil's Forge and Apache Junction. At Fort Laramie, while the horses were changed, the Clemens brothers enjoyed antelope steak sandwiches and, once they were rolling again, they caught their first sight of the Rocky Mountains. Twelve miles further on, they took on a new passenger, a smallish, wiry woman in her early thirties with a plain, unkempt appearance and an overall rough-hewn look.

March 25, 1861 *Our new fellow traveler was not a talkative woman. She would sit there in the gathering twilight and fasten her steadfast eyes on a mosquito rooting into her arm, then slowly, she would raise her other hand till she had the range, then she would launch a slap that would have jolted a cow; after that, she would sit and contemplate the corpse with tranquil satisfaction, for she never missed her mosquito; she was a dead shot at short range. She never removed a carcass but left them there for bait. I sat by this grim sphynx and watched her kill thirty or forty mosquitoes, all the while waiting for her to say something, but she never did. So, I decided to open the conversation.*

"The mosquitoes are pretty bad around here, madam," I said.

"You bet!"

"What did I understand you to say, madam?"

"You BET!" she said again in a much louder voice.

Then she cheered up, faced around to us and began to

131

speak: "Danged if I didn't think you fellers were deaf and dumb. Here I've sat, and sat and sat, busting mosquitoes and wondering what was ailing y'all. I thought you was sick or crazy, or something, and then by and by, I begin to reckon you was a passel of sickly fools that couldn't think of nothing to say."

Suddenly, the sphynx was a sphynx no more! The fountains of her great depth were broken open, and she rained the nine parts of speech forty days and forty nights, metaphorically speaking, and buried us under a desolating deluge of trivial gossip. Oh, how we suffered! She went on, hour after hour, till I was sorry I ever opened the mosquito question. She didn't stop until Orion and I told her we were going up top for some fresh air.

***

Early the following morning, Overland Stage #16 was rolling across Central Wyoming through the foothills of the Rocky Mountains. At the Big Sandy station, the Clemens brothers got out to stretch their legs and get coffee and sweet cakes. Once the horses were exchanged and passengers were ready to reload, the conductor had some words for his charges.

"Two weeks ago, just a mite west of Silver Hill station, a stagecoach was attacked by White Wolf and his band of renegades. The conductor and two passengers were killed."

"Are you saying we could be attacked by Indians?" Sam said.

"That's what I'm saying," he said.

The conductor turned to the woman.

"Ma'am! Do you know how you use a rifle?"

The woman seemed insulted.

"I'll have you know I can blow out a squirrel's eye at thirty yards."

"Well, you might possibly be forced to use those skills. If we get attacked, we got an extra Winchester up here."

"Don't be skittish," she said. "I tried to make it plain that I know how to shoot."

The conductor turned to Sam and Orion.

"You gents got weapons?"

Sam withdrew the seven-shot Allen pistol and displayed it.

The conductor turned to Orion.

Orion put his hand on the Colt six-shooter at his side.

"We'll have to hold a close vigil for the next ten to fifteen miles."

***

Three hours later, Overland Stage #16 pulled into Silver Hill station without incident. While waiting, Sam bought more boiled eggs, ham, bread and a jar of pickled peaches at the small general store. As they reboarded, he showed his prize to Orion.

"Can't wait to taste these," he said. "These are like the ones Mother used to make back in Hannibal."

An hour later, as the stagecoach rolled quietly along through a sprawling landscape of desolate sand, huge piles of boulders and sagebrush. Suddenly, the quiet was shattered with the crack of a rifle and a shout from the conductor.

"Indians!" he shouted.

Sam pulled back the curtain to reveal a band of mounted, war-painted Indians, some eight to ten strong, charging straight toward them. Instantly, the driver cracked his whip and the stagecoach lurched forward. Now the stagecoach was racing along at top speed and two of the Indians were riding alongside the stagecoach.

Suddenly, one of the Indians sent an arrow swishing through one stagecoach window and out the other. Seconds later, another arrow whizzed through the window and buried itself above Sam's head into the glass jar of peaches. The syrupy liquid inside the jar spilled out and ran down on Sam's back.

"Those bastards," Sam said, drawing his pistol.

In no time, the second Indian, who had been riding stride for stride beside the stagecoach, leapt from his horse, grasped one of the stagecoach's side rails and was hanging on to the flying coach. Then, tomahawk raised, he stuck his head through the window and Sam fired a shot directly into his face.

For a moment, his face was a mess of blood and ragged flesh, then, with a loud scream, he fell away from the stagecoach.

All the while, Orion was firing his Colt through the window. Over the next few minutes, both brothers fired away at their attackers, but the short-barreled pistols were not very effective at hitting moving targets. Orion turned to Sam.

"My gun is empty," he said. "My extra rounds are in my suitcase in the rear."

"Same here," Sam said. "Looks like we going to die."

Both brothers lowered their heads helplessly and hugged the mailbags on the stagecoach floor for protection.

Suddenly, the woman shouted to the conductor.

"Hand me down that Winchester!"

Seconds later, as three more Indians surrounded the flying stagecoach, the woman grasped the rifle. Quickly, she threw a cartridge in the chamber, took a position behind the stagecoach door, and, using the window as a rest, she began firing in quick succession. Before each shot, she waited until the tip of the barrel perfectly matched the movement of the horse, then she would fire.

Blam! Blam! Blam! Blam! Blam!

With five shots, five Indians flew from their ponies into the desert sand. With that, one of the Indians, apparently their leader, motioned a retreat. Suddenly, the sound of loud whoops, galloping horse hooves and the swishing of arrows disappeared as the remaining attackers retreated hastily back into the desert.

"Damn! Some powerful fine shooting, ma'am," said the conductor. "We owe our lives to you."

"It weren't nothing," she said.

"Is anybody hurt?" the conductor said.

"Nothing wrong here," said the woman.

"Same here," Orion said.

"Only casualty was my jar of pickled peaches," said Sam.

"We're dab-burned lucky to be alive," the conductor said. "Thanks to God for the woman."

***

Later that afternoon, when the stage pulled into Cottonwood station, the woman started to say her farewell.

"I'll getting off up here," she said. "Now if you fellers want to get out at Cottonwood and lay by a couple days, I'll be along sometime tonight, and, if I can do you any good, all you got to do is just holler. I got lots of fine skills beside knowing my way around a rifle."

Orion glanced at Sam and winked knowingly.

Moments later, before she started out of the stagecoach, she turned for one final word.

"Y'all boys remember that I saved yo' necks from those Indians."

"We'll remember," Sam said. "We're much obliged to you."

Then the woman, suitcase in hand, turned abruptly and stepped out of the stagecoach. The Clemens brothers remained in the stagecoach cabin while the horses were swapped.

"I don't think we'll be laying by at Cottonwood," Sam said.

Orion laughed.

***

March 27, 1861 *This morning, about thirty miles west of Cottonwood station, we overtook a Mormon emigrant train of thirty-three wagons bound for Utah's great Salt Lake; tramping wearily along and driving their herd of loose cows, were dozens of coarse-clad and sad-looking men, women and children, who had walked as they were walking now, day after day for eight lingering weeks, and in that time had encompassed the distance our stage had come in eight days and three hours—seven hundred and ninety-eight miles! They were dusty and uncombed, hatless, bonnet-less and ragged, and they did look so tired! I am forever complaining about the misery of stagecoach travel, but now I felt my fortunes were infinitely greater than that of these poor creatures.*

***

March 28, 1861 *Today, at midmorning, we whirled gaily*

along through the renowned South Pass, the lowest point in the Continental Divide. We were perched upon the extreme summit of the Rocky Mountains, toward which we had been climbing, patiently climbing, ceaselessly climbing, for days and nights together--and around us was gathered a convention of Nature's kings that stood ten, twelve, and even 13,000 feet high--grand old fellows who would have to stoop to see Mount Washington. We were in such an airy elevation above the creeping populations of the earth, that now and then when the obstructing crags stood out of the way, it seemed that we could look around and contemplate the whole great globe, with its dissolving views of mountains, seas and continents stretching away through the mystery of the summer haze.

***

March 29, 1861 *While traversing the South Pass, the conductor stopped our vehicle so as to refill our water barrel with fresh, cold liquid from a trout stream. As we waited, I noticed a wagon-train resting in one of the high meadows and my eyes scanned its members. One of the woefully dusty horsemen in charge of the expedition I recognized as John Winehouse. Of all persons in the world to meet on top of the Rocky Mountains thousands of miles from home, he was the last one I should have expected. We were schoolboys together and warm friends years ago in Hannibal, but a boyish prank of mine had disrupted this friendship. The act of which I speak was this. I had been accustomed to occasionally visit an editor whose room was on the third floor of the same building where the* Hannibal Journal *was housed. One day, this editor gave me a ripe watermelon, which I made preparations to devour on the spot, but chancing to look out of the window, I saw John standing directly under it and an irresistible desire came upon me to drop the melon on his head, which I immediately did. I was the loser, for it spoiled the melon, and John never forgave me. I leapt out of the stagehouse and approached him. We recognized each other simultaneously, and hands were grasped as warmly as if no coldness had ever existed. All animosities were buried and the simple fact of meeting a familiar face in that isolated spot so far from home was sufficient to make us forget all things but happy ones. After some ten minutes of pleasantries, we parted again with sincere "good-byes" and "God bless you" from both.*

***

March 30, 1861 *Over the past two days, our conveyance has been climbing the long, treacherous shoulders of the Rocky Mountains. Today, it started its descent down the western slopes toward Salt Lake City, leaving behind the snowy Wind River Mountains and Uinta Mountains and its magnificent scenes of snow-covered mountains and clear blue lakes. Occasionally, passengers caught sight of massive clumps of white skeletons, mules, oxen and horses, remnants of earlier emigrations. Here and there were up-ended boards or small piles of stones which marked the resting-place of human remains.*

***

March 31, 1861 *Early this morning, we entered Utah territory at Hanging Rock station. At the small general store, we purchased strong coffee and mutton stew, then ventured back outside and watched as the workmen swapped the horses. Suddenly, a workman pointed along the trail and shouted: "Pony Express coming!" All necks stretched into the direction he pointed and we witnessed a "pony rider" – the fleet messenger who sped across the continent from St. Joe to Sacramento, carrying letters nineteen hundred miles in eight days! Like a circus acrobat, he leapt, mailbag at his shoulder, from one pony, then sprinted to the next animal, made a leap onto its back then streaked back out on the trail faster than a jackrabbit. He rode a splendid horse born to be a racer and fed and lodged like a gentleman; the rider's dress was thin and closely fitted; he wore a tight-fitting waist jacket and a skull cap and tucked his pantaloons into his boot-tops like a race-rider. He carried no arms; nothing that was not absolutely necessary for the postage on his literary freight was worth five dollars a letter.*

***

On the afternoon of April 1, the 15th day of the journey, Overland Stage #16 rolled into the Salt Lake City station. With 17,000 people, Salt Lake was the most populous settlement the travelers had seen since St. Joseph, Missouri. Settled originally in 1847 by Brigham Young and his Mormon followers, Salt Lake City was a thriving beehive of 18,000 souls and featured a wide variety of businesses, including a pie shop. Once the horses were changed, the stagecoach had a new passenger. He was a well-dressed, medium height man in his early thirties with glasses, a well-trimmed mustache and a solemn expression. He gave his name as Austin Garfield Johnson and claimed to have been an administrative assistant to Brigham Young.

That night, as the stagecoach rolled down the western foothills of the Rocky Mountains, Sam, interested in knowing more about the Mormons, chatted with the new passenger.

"You worked for the king himself?" he asked.

"For almost six years."

"Why did you leave?"

"There was a dispute about some church money I spent on draperies for the grand tabernacle. One of the apostles charged me with dishonesty, saying I had put some of the church's money in my own pocket. Then, several days later, the supreme council voted me out of the church. Now I'm going to Reese River, Nevada, to live with my mother."

The two men rode quietly for several minutes.

"This Brigham Young feller," Sam said finally. "What sort of man is he?"

"He is king, the lion of the Lord. Like Moses and the children of Israel, he brought his people across the desert to the Salt Lake Valley. Further, like Moses, he dispenses the law at will, and rest assured, his dictates are followed to the letter."

"What's this about all these wives he's got?"

"The King entertains a harem of fifty, sometimes up to fifty-five wives. Some have grown old and gone out of active service but are comfortably housed and cared for in the hennery—or the Lion House—as it is strangely named. Each wife has living quarters with her children. As of last August, the King had a total of fifty-two children. He had four special beds constructed so that all of his children could sleep in one room, fifteen per bed. Over the years, I had the several opportunities to break bread with the family. Before anyone lifts a fork, one of the wives calls the roll to insure all wives and children are present. During one meal, Mr. Young confided to me that one of his children, three-year-old toddler Jacob, was an especially gifted child. Then he decided to fetch little Jacob to demonstrate his special talents. So, he arose from the table and began searching through his brood for the aforementioned 'Jacob.' After an hour of searching through the faces of his fifty-two children, he was wholly unable to locate the child. Finally, he gave up and, with a sigh, said: 'I thought I would know the little cub again, but I don't.'"

***

The following morning, Overland Stage #16 and its weary passengers entered Nevada territory at Mule's Breath station. Once the horses were changed, the vehicle struck out across the treacherous wastelands of Eastern Nevada Territory through the piles of massive boulders, the seemingly endless sand and the sagebrush.

April 3, 1861 *Oh, the Great American Desert—forty memorable miles of bottomless sand into which the coach wheels sank from six inches to a foot. We worked our passage most of the way across. That is to say, we got out and walked. It was a dreary pull, and a long and thirsty one, for we had no water. From one extremity of this desert to the other, the road was white with the bones of oxen and horses. It would hardly be an exaggeration to say that we could have walked the forty miles and set our feet on a bone at every step! The desert was one prodigious graveyard. The log-chains, wagon wheels and rotting wrecks of vehicles were almost as thick as the bones. I think we saw enough log chains rusting there in the desert to reach across any state in the Union.*

***

The following morning, Overland Stage #16 arrived at Reese River station in the heart of Nevada Territory. As the stagecoach approached the tiny desert settlement, its passengers witnessed telegraph constructors setting poles and stringing wire. This was the latest, easternmost extension of the new telegraph service, which had begun in San Francisco and would ultimately stretch across the entire United States. As the stagecoach pulled into the station, Orion shouted to the conductor.

"I want to send a telegraph while the horses are exchanged," he said.

"Make haste," the conductor replied. "I can't linger."

Once the vehicle had stopped, Orion and Sam got out and, after a brief questioning of the station master about the location of the telegraph office, the two brothers streaked up the street to send their message. Once inside, the telegraph operator warned that the charge was five cents a word and Orion quickly set about composing his message.

> *April 4, 1861*
> *To his Excellency Governor James W. Nye:*
> *Esteemed sir:*
> *Good tidings from Reese River, Nevada.*
> *My journey across the frontier is near its end.*
> *In two days, I shall arrive in Carson City to begin my service as your secretary.*
> *Best regards,*
> *Orion Clemens*

Once the fee was paid, the two brothers raced back up the street to the stagecoach office. Workmen were completing the task of swapping the horses when they arrived. Moments later, the passengers were reloaded and Overland Stage #16 was rolling across the barren wastelands of central Nevada.

***

April 5, 1861 *At mid-morning today, our conveyance pulled into the Limestone Creek station, the vehicle's final stop before Carson City. There we took on two new passengers. One was a woman in her mid-twenties wearing a baby-blue dress and a white bonnet who announced she was going to Sacramento to be married. The second new passenger was a reserved man, medium height, thirtyish, with a long black beard who gave his name as Thaddeus Winslow. He claimed he was going to Carson City to attend his mother's funeral. Very quickly, I noted that he didn't own a suitcase and I could see the handle of a Colt revolver protruding from his waistband which he kept close at hand. Somehow, from the first, I didn't trust this Mr. Thaddeus Winslow.*

Two hours later, Overland Stage #16 was passing up a sharp rise in the road when it suddenly ground to a stop. Wondering what the problem was, Sam stuck his head out the window and, at the top of the hill, he saw four riders with masks over their faces and guns drawn. Instantly, the driver on top went for his Winchester, but one of the masked riders fired first.

"I'm wounded!" said the driver.

Now, inside the stagecoach cabin, Thaddeus Winslow pulled his Colt pistol and took charge.

"Don't nobody move," he said. "This is a robbery!"

Quickly, he snatched Sam's Allen pistol from his belt, then pointed his weapon at Orion.

"Hand over that pistol!"

Orion, watching his every move, handed over his weapon.

Then the robber turned to the woman, pointing to her personal bag.

"You got a gun in there?"

"No!" she said.

"Give me that!" he said, snatching the purse from her hand and dumping the contents on the stagecoach floor. There were several personal items, some letters, a beautification kit, a set of keys and a shiny silver brooch. The robber picked up the brooch and inspected it.

"Please! My mother gave me that!"

"Shut your trap," the lead robber snapped as he tucked it into his pocket.

Then he turned to the others.

"Hands up and everybody out!"

Moments later, the conductor, the driver, Sam, Orion and the bride-to-be were standing outside the stagecoach as the bandit leader went from one to the other. From Sam, he took $63 cash, a gold ring and four cigars. After rifling through Orion's pockets, he took $53 cash and a pocket knife. The conductor gave up $16 and another gold watch. All he took from the wounded stage driver was a black slab of chewing tobacco.

Once finished with the passengers, the bandit leader started pulling suitcases out of the rear boot and rifling through them. From Orion's suitcase, he took the extra suit of clothing and a straight razor. He happily eyed the razor.

"I been needing one of these," he said.

Finally, he rifled through Sam's suitcase, took a pair of boots and the extra suit, then, finding nothing else he considered of value, he turned to his comrades.

"Charley, pull out that lead horse and shoot the others," the leader said. "That way, if these folks want to go somewhere, they'll be walking."

One of the masked men dismounted, then unhitched the lead horse and led it to one of his fellow robbers. Then he withdrew his weapon, walked to the front of the team and took careful aim at one of the other horses.

"No! No!" shouted the driver. "You can't kill my charges!"

Suddenly, in livid anger, the driver, who was holding his injured arm, lurched toward the shooter. Once he was at arm's length, the shooter slapped the driver full in the face with the barrel of the pistol. Instantly, the driver fell to the ground, then the shooter, going from one animal to another, shot each member of the remaining team.

Moments later, the bandit leader, with his minions and the stagecoach's lead horse trailing behind him, rode off into the desolation of sand and sagebrush.

Sam and Orion gathered their scattered personal belongings and crammed them back into the suitcases. Then, suitcase in hand, Sam turned to the others.

"What do we do now?"

"It's three miles to Carson City," the conductor said. "Looks like we'll be walking."

He turned to the driver.

"What about your wound?"

"It's only a flesh wound," he said. "I'll have the doctor look at it when we get to Carson City."

"Ma'am!" the conductor said. "Are you capable of walking to Carson City?"

"Do I have a choice?"

"When we get into town, I can send a buckboard back out for you."

"I'll walk," she said. "I'm afraid the robbers will return."

Over the next two hours, the weary passengers of Overland Stage #16 plodded through the sand and sagebrush, finally stumbling into Carson City at sundown. The conductor and the driver headed to the doctor, the bride-to-be went to the stagecoach office, and Sam and Orion stood in the middle of Main Street.

"What do we do now?" Orion said unnecessarily.

"Remember, I have a ten-dollar bill sewn inside the lining of my coat."

"Thank God!" Orion said. "We are saved. At minimum, we can get food and lodging for tonight. Tomorrow, I'll ask the governor for an advance on my pay."

10
Mark Twain

The following morning, after spending the night in a cheap hotel, the Clemens brothers arrived at the governor's office in the Nevada State House. When they appeared before the governor's assistant, both men had a rough, unkempt appearance since they were wearing the same rumpled clothes they had been wearing the past three weeks. The governor's assistant, a well-dressed, dark-haired woman in her late twenties, appeared suspicious.

"May I assist you?"

"I wish to see Governor Nye," Orion said.

"Who might you be?"

"My name is Orion Clemens. I'm his new secretary."

The assistant curiously looked the brothers up and down.

"You are certain you're in the correct office?" she said.

"We're certain," Sam said.

Still not satisfied, she opened a desk drawer, withdrew a letter and read it.

"Orion Clemens!" she said. "That's the correct name."

Then she rose from her desk and strode into the nearby governor's office. A short while later, she reappeared.

"You may go in."

Gov. James W. Nye, a big, gruff-looking man in his early fifties, was smoking a cigar and was seated behind an expensive-looking oak desk. He looked up from the desk when the two brothers presented themselves.

"Which of you is Orion?" he began.

"That would be me," Orion said.

"Who might this be?"

"My brother Samuel."

The governor looked them up and down.

"Why would you present yourself in such a disheveled fashion?"

"We were robbed on the Overland Stage yesterday," Orion said. "Our valuables as well as our additional clothing was stolen."

The governor shook his head disapprovingly then peered at the two brothers for a long moment.

"This is a fine kettle of fish," he said finally. "My new secretary arrives for his first day of service and every inch of him looks like a street vagrant."

"The bandits took our belongings."

"What would you have me do?"

"I need an advance on my salary so I can present myself as a civilized man. Further, my brother and I must find lodging and board."

The governor smirked, shook his head with disapproval again, then reached into the desk and withdrew a book of blank bank drafts. Seconds later, he was scribbling.

"Here is $50," he said. "Take this to the Washoe Basin bank across the street. I expect you in this office early tomorrow. Further, I demand that you present yourself with dignity."

"I shall do as you wish," Orion said. "Until tomorrow."

Later that morning, the Clemens brothers brought new clothes and took lodging at a good hotel.

***

At the Nevada State House the following morning, Orion was assigned an office just down the hall from the governor. As secretary, he was the second most powerful politician in the territory and, in the governor's absence, he had the authority to act in the governor's stead. His duties included making recommendations to the state legislature, lobbying for bills which were favorable to the governor's office and creating public notices which would make the actions of the governor's office appear without fault to the voting public. His years of experience as a reporter/editor with the Missouri state legislature had prepared him well for the role.

Once settled into his new office, Orion was ordered into the governor's office for a briefing. When it was over, he was dispatched to address the Nevada local Ranchers Association that afternoon about water rights in the Washoe Valley.

"Tomorrow," the governor said, "I want you to inspect tax records for the past year and determine why there was a shortfall of revenues into territorial coffers in July and August. Once that is finished, I want you to organize a local agency for Indian Affairs. Rest assured that I intend to keep you busy."

***

During the first week, Orion, busy with his own assignments, had no secretarial duties for Sam. As a result, Sam dawdled about the hotel, roamed the streets, visited Washoe Lake, helped members of a wagon train repair a broken axle, listened to miners' tales of great riches won, then lost, and otherwise idled away his time waiting for his brother to assign him some work.

On Sunday, at the end of their first week in Nevada, Sam wrote a letter to his mother in St. Louis.

April 12, 1861
Dearest Mother:
Orion and I are now ensconced in our new sagebrush lives here in the great state of Nevada. Carson City lies in the middle of a desert of the purest, most unadulterated, most inhospitable sand, an infernal soil in which nothing but sagebrush dares to grow.

Sage is the ugliest plant ever conceived and, when crushed, the leaves emit an odor which is neither magnolia nor polecat, but a pleasant compromise.

Yesterday, I overheard a man say Carson City was "the most God-forsaken country under the sun." That comprehensive conception I fully subscribe to.

"This country is fabulously rich in gold, silver, copper,

lead, coal, iron, quicksilver as well as thieves, murderers, desperadoes, lawyers, Christians, Indians, Chinamen, Spaniards, gamblers, sharpers, coyotes, poets, preachers and jackass rabbits."

Despite the plethora of colorful, often dangerous personages we must rub elbows with, we have determined to make this location our home and so it shall be.

I trust you and other family members are faring well.

All my love,

Samuel

That afternoon, when Orion arrived back at the hotel, Sam asked again if he had duties for him.

"Nothing yet. I'll let you know."

"I need some activity," Sam said. "I'm afflicted with a severe case of butterfly idleness."

***

That night, as the Clemens brothers returned to their hotel after dinner, they came upon a crowd of townspeople watching a gunfight on the main street. A drunken miner, angry after losing his shirt in a card game, first shot holes in the saloon ceiling, then staggered out into the street, firing wildly into the air. There, the city marshal, his weapon drawn, confronted him.

"Drop that pistol, James!" the marshal shouted.

"Not on your life, you scum-sucking pig," the miner replied.

"Lay down that six-shooter!"

"I'm not giving up nothing," the miner said again, pausing to spit.

Then, apparently thinking he could use the spitting motion as a distraction, the miner wheeled around and fired.

Instantly, the marshal grabbed his midsection, then squeezed off two rounds. The drunken miner pitched forward into the dirt street, mortally wounded. The onlookers watched as the marshal fell to his knees, then, still holding his midsection, slumped to the ground.

"Get the doctor!" someone said.

Moments later, as the Clemens brothers watched, several townspeople rushed forward to help the marshal.

***

The following morning, after Orion left the hotel for work, Sam had a breakfast of scrambled eggs, ham hock, grits and hot biscuits in the hotel restaurant. When he exited the restaurant and entered the lobby, he asked the clerk about news of the marshal.

"No news," the clerk said. "Ask the young gentleman over there. He's a reporter."

The clerk pointed out a well-dressed, dark-haired young man reading a newspaper in the lobby.

Sam strode across the lobby.

"Pardon me!" Clemens said. "The clerk allowed that you might have some news about the marshal."

The young man looked up from the newspaper, pushed his glasses up on his nose, then turned to Sam.

"I spoke with the doctor this morning," he said. "The marshal will be back on duty within a few days."

"That's good news," Sam said. "The clerk tells me you're a reporter."

"I am employed by the *Territorial Enterprise* in Virginia City, the largest paper in the territory."

"Where is Virginia City?"

The young man seemed insulted.

"Sir, you do not know Virginia City? Why, man, Virginia City is the home of the Comstock lode, the largest vein of silver ore ever discovered."

"Excuse my ignorance."

"Why do you ask?"

"I'm a reporter myself."

"You have experience?"

"Five years with the *Hannibal Journal* in Missouri."

"Impressive. Looking for work?"

"Absolutely."

"At the moment, there is an editorial position available at the *Enterprise*."

Sam studied the young man.

"Where is Virginia City?"

"Fifteen miles north. If you're interested in the position, you can ride back with me this afternoon. I've got a buckboard."

"I would love that," Sam said. "Much obliged to you."

The young man stood up and offered his hand.

"My name is True Williams."

Sam shook his hand.

"My name is Sam Clemens," he said. "Pleased to meet you."

***

Late that afternoon, Sam and True, after a grueling three-hour jaunt across the desert, pulled into Virginia City. Upon arrival, True stopped the buckboard in front of a three-story brick building at the corner of A Street and Sutton Avenue. High overhead, a sign read: "The *Territorial Enterprise*: Nevada's Finest Newspaper."

Once inside the office, Sam looked around at the cluttered desks, the haggard reporters, the stacks of old newspapers, the compositors and the stacks of unread proofs. Instantly, he felt right at home. True led him to a corner office, then asked him to wait outside.

"Let me have a word with Mr. Goodman before you enter," he said.

As Sam waited, he could see the two men talking and gesturing through the office's glass window. Moments later, True emerged, then he motioned for Sam to go in.

Joseph Goodman was a stocky, well-dressed, fortyish man with a pleasant face and a well-trimmed mustache. After introductions, Sam took a seat across from the editor.

"True has informed me that you have experience as a reporter."

Sam explained his years with the *Hannibal Journal*.

"I need someone to cover vice, the mines, ghost stories, social functions, Indian massacres, gunfights and other various intrigues. I want a reporter with sharp eyes and a keen ear for stirring news."

"I can fulfill all of those requirements."

"This fall, when the territorial legislature reconvenes," he continued, "you'll be expected to cover the proceedings."

"I've had experience covering politics," Sam replied. "How much is the pay?"

"Thirty-five dollars a week."

"That sum is satisfactory. What about travel?"

"We have three company buckboards and five able horses at the stables across the street. Can you start work tomorrow?"

"I shall be here."

When Sam emerged from the office, True offered his hand.

"Congratulations!" he said. "You're going to need lodging. Come with me and I'll introduce you to the owner at my boarding house."

***

That afternoon, Sam took a room at the same boarding house where True resided. Once the room was rented, he sent a letter to Orion notifying him he had taken a job in Virginia City and would return that weekend to retrieve his belongings. In the late spring of 1861, Virginia City, Nevada was a wide-open boomtown, home to a dozen breweries, saloons at every corner, three bawdy houses, two jails, three billiard parlors and a single church. Money and silver mine stock certificates were as plentiful as dust. Some saloon patrons paid their bar bills with stock certificates and many miners, hoping to arouse interest in their claims, would outright give certificates away. In the saloons, there were stories of wealthy miners losing $10,000 on a single hand of cards. Flush times were rampant in Virginia City.

***

Sam's first assignment was to write a story about the mysterious ghost which had been haunting Simpson's Tavern, a popular saloon on Eureka Street. Goodman said several patrons had reported seeing the fearful apparition of a young boy, weeping and clad in yellow and blue, loitering in front of the bar after closing time. He said, in the story, he wanted first-hand quotes from witnesses. That afternoon, Sam interviewed two bartenders, several regular customers and a long-time barmaid, then returned to the office to compose his story.

Late that afternoon, he presented it to Goodman. It read: *Are we to be scared to death every time we venture down Eureka Street? Have the ghosts of the dead returned to haunt patrons of Simpson's Tavern, who, upon exiting the establishment after a night of frivolity, are accosted by the fearful apparition of a weeping, blue and yellow-clad young boy? These claims are arising from the lips of numerous personages who frequent that establishment.*

Barmaid Amanda Hildebrand claimed: "I bore witness to the pitiful soul last night at the closing hour. Suddenly, he appeared to my visage from out of the mist. Never have I witnessed a countenance so woeful and agitated. I was almost frightened out of my bloomers."

Miner Clemson Beauregard corroborated this account. "I espied him in broad daylight on Thursday last sitting near the tavern entrance. He was placidly reclining against his board near the doorway, with his blue coat, and his yellow pants, and his high boots, and his fancy hat, just lifted from his head. I'm obliged to say he appeared a rather engaging youth."

Harness maker Josh Foreman retorted: "I'm not one to be conjuring up specters, but upon witnessing the melancholy lad, I high-tailed it down Eureka Street." When questioned, another patron projected the fearful visage was born from "imbibing too much John Barleycorn." Our readers are welcome to arrive at their own conclusions.

"Worthwhile piece," Goodman said. "I appreciate the tone of light frivolity. Provide me with more of the same."

***

Over the next few months. Sam threw himself into his work. He frequented saloons, theaters, billiard rooms, bawdy houses, police stations, mining camps and social functions seeking information. He wrote stories about mine cave-ins,

151

poked fun at local politicians, was judge at a prize fight, faced down the madam of a brothel who disagreed with the obituary he had written about one of her girls, wrote exposes about corruption in the legislature and covered no less than six gunfights and four Indian massacres. Meanwhile, his nights were spent drinking, smoking, and playing cards and billiards into the wee hours with other reporters.

His favorite haunt was Willard's Billiards, a combination saloon and pool parlor on Eureka Street. It was the regular watering hole for local newsmen, and many nights, Sam would remain in the establishment drinking beer and playing billiards until closing time. One night, while Sam waited for a table, another patron, a sun-burned young man with blonde hair and beard, a slouch hat and miner's clothing, asked Sam to partner with him at eight-ball doubles. Sam agreed.

"I'm Steve Gillis," he said. "Pleased to meet you."

Their opponents were James Laird, owner of the *Virginia Daily Union*, the *Enterprise*'s cross-town rival, and one of his reporters. After playing six games, in which each team won three each, the contest came down to a single contest. In the seventh game, Clemens ran five balls and prepared to shoot the eight ball to win the game.

Sam took careful aim, stroked the cue ball and shot the eight ball into the side pocket.

"Bad hit!" Laird shouted. "You hit the four ball before you made the eight ball. You lose!"

"No!" Gillis said. "If the cue ball had struck the four ball first, he could not have made the eight ball."

"Cheater!" Laird said, turning from the table and hanging up his cue.

"Where are you going?" Sam said. "You owe me and my partner $5."

Angrily, Laird turned to face him.

"Would you like to wrest it from me?" he said.

Sam, thinking the better of it, backed away.

"It's not worth going to jail for $5," he said.

"Further, it's not worth handing over $5 to a couple of cheats," Laird said.

Then he turned and started for the door.

"Come back here!" Sam said.

By then, Laird and his reporter were already out the door.

"Let them go," Gillis said. "I never cared for him anyway. Come now, let's have a beer."

Moments later, Sam and Gillis were seated at the bar. Gillis said he had grown up in Oklahoma and had been in Virginia City for almost two years.

"I staked a claim at Piute Pass," he said. "I been working it for almost a year now. It turns up some ore. Enough to keep me in food and beer. Ever thought about mining?"

"I have, but I've got ink in my blood," Sam said. "Newspapering is what I love. I'd rather write stories about mining than actually do it."

***

Over the course of the year 1861, Sam made a name for himself in Virginia City with an outpouring of colorful stories, satirical sketches and "stirring" news. The truth seemed to hold little importance for him, and Sam, by his very nature, never let the facts stand in the way of an entertaining story.

One of his most controversial pieces, printed in the September 4, 1861, bore the headline: "A Profound Sensation." It read:

"A petrified man was found last week in the mountains south of Gravelly Ford. Every limb and feature of the stony mummy was perfect, excepting the left leg, which had evidently been a wooden one during the lifetime of the owner - which lifetime, by the way, came to a close about a century ago, in the opinion of a local savant who has examined the defunct carcass.

The body was in a sitting posture, leaning against a huge mass of outcroppings; the attitude was pensive, the right thumb resting against the side of the nose; the left thumb partially supported the chin, the fore-finger pressing the inner corner of the left eye and drawing it partly open; the right eye was closed, and the fingers of the right hand spread wide apart.

This strange freak of nature created a profound sensation in the vicinity, and our informant states that by request, Justice

Sewell of Humboldt City, at once proceeded to the spot and held an inquest on the body. The verdict of the jury was that "the deceased came to his death from protracted exposure to the elements."

The people of the neighborhood volunteered to bury the poor unfortunate, but it was discovered, when they attempted to remove him, that the water which had dripped upon him for ages from the crag above had coursed down his back and deposited a limestone sediment under him, which had glued him to the bedrock upon which he sat."
Mark Twain

Sam's article, printed at the top of the front page, was an immediate sensation. The entire issue sold out before day's end. Taken as fact, it was reprinted by other newspapers, including the *Carson Daily Appeal*, the *Gold Hill News* and the *San Francisco Bulletin*. Despite Sam's retraction the following day, his critics held it against him. Many *Enterprise* subscribers canceled their subscriptions and turned to its cross-town rival, the *Union*. The newspapers that had reprinted it were outraged, with the *Bulletin* demanding that the reporter be fired.

The following morning, Sam appeared in Goodman's office.

"A whirlwind of controversy has arisen over my petrified man story," he said. "I am hereby offering my resignation if you so desire."

"Oh no!" Goodman said with a laugh. "A magnificent piece. In fact, I want more of the same."

***

One night the following week, Sam was back in Willard's Billiard parlor. Gillis was waiting and they quickly paired off as partners for eight ball. As they waited for a table, Laird walked in. The moment he saw Sam, he wasted no time going on the attack.

"Clemens!" he said. "Your petrified man story is total hogwash. More outright lies."

"You fool!" Sam said. "Can you explain why circulation at the *Enterprise* is twice that of the poor rag you put your name on?"

"The *Daily Union* wouldn't dare print such worthless garbage," Laird said. "Reporters like you give newspapers a bad name."

Sam turned angrily to him.

"One of these days, you're going to get me to bust your block."

Laird walked over and stood directly in front of Sam.

"When is the block busting going to begin?"

Instantly, Sam stood up and the two men faced off to fight.

"Hold it!" shouted Willard, the proprietor. "If you two want to fight, you'll have to take it outside. Go on! Leave my establishment!"

Gillis turned to Sam.

"Don't get involved in this," he said. "You'll tear up your clothes and you'll get your face bruised and bloodied."

"I must stand up for myself."

"It's not worth it," Gillis said, pulling Sam away from the confrontation.

For a moment, Sam glared at Gillis, then gathered himself.

"Maybe you're right," he said.

"Come on outside and fight," Laird shouted. "I can whip you with one hand tied behind my back."

Sam, calmer now, laughed at his words, then turned, and he and Gillis went out the back door.

***

In the late spring of 1862, another one of Clemens' articles launched a new firestorm of controversy. It bore the headline "Bloody Massacre near Carson."

"On Wednesday last, one Phillip Hopkins, a resident of Ormsby County and deranged after learning he had lost his life's holdings in the Spring Valley Water Company swindle, massacred his family, a loving wife and nine innocent children. About ten o'clock on Thursday evening, Hopkins rode into

Carson on horseback with his throat cut from ear to ear, bearing in his hand a red-haired scalp from which the warm, smoking blood was still dripping, then fell in a dying condition in front of the Magnolia Saloon. With no time to spare, Sheriff Goshen mounted and rode down to the Hopkins' residence, an old log house just at the edge of the great pine forest near Carson. There the sheriff found the scalp-less corpse of Mrs. Hopkins lying across the threshold, her head split wide open and her right hand almost severed from the wrist. Near her lay the ax with which the murderous deed had been committed. In one bedroom, six of the children were found, one in bed and the others scattered about the floor. Their brains had evidently been dashed out with a club, and every mark about them seemed to have been made with a blunt instrument. The children must have struggled hard for their lives, as articles of clothing and broken furniture were strewn in the utmost confusion. Julia and Emma, aged respectively fourteen and seventeen, were found in the kitchen, their throats sliced ear to ear. The eldest girl, Mary, must have taken refuge in the garret, as her body was found there, frightfully mutilated, a bowie knife still sticking in her side. The bloody bodies of the other two girls, Martha and Jane, were discovered in the back yard of the home."

Mark Twain

This was only the second time Sam had used the Mark Twain byline.

The very same day the massacre story hit the street, the entire issue sold out before nightfall. The following morning, Goodman called Sam into his office.

"Readers are clamoring for more of these Mark Twain pieces," Goodman said. "Circulation has shot through the roof over your most recent one. Look at these letters."

He pointed to a huge stack of letters on his desk. He picked one.

"Listen to this! 'This Mark Twain has brought new life to the *Territorial Enterprise*. Not only is his writing substantial and magnificently worded, but he has a biting wit which inspires both mirth and a new respect for unveiled truths.'

"Here's another!" Goodman said. "'Mark Twain is a breath of fresh air to your publication. For too long now, the paper has been printing the same monotonous, ill-conceived columns without redeeming value. This Mark Twain is bringing vibrant new life to your publication.'"

Goodman turned from the letters.

"It pleases me to bring in new readers," Sam said.

"I'm raising your salary to forty dollars a week," Goodman continued. "But I want you to ascribe this pen name, Mark Twain, to all your future articles. It has a certain quaint ring to it."

"That's agreeable."

"By the by," Goodman continued, "what is the origin of the term 'Mark Twain'?"

"Mark twain is riverboat parlance for two fathoms, or twelve feet of water. Should a steamboat captain ask about water depth and the first mate replies, 'Mark twain!' That means the vessel is in safe water, that the water depth is two fathoms or twelve feet deep. Each fathom equals six feet."

Goodman paused for a moment, waiting for the thought to register.

"Splendid!" he said finally. "I cannot envision a more perfect pen name."

***

A year passed and, during that time, Sam was cranking out three to four "Mark Twain" pieces a week on subjects ranging from stubborn mules and ghostly stagecoaches to corrupt politicians and long-winded speakers. By the spring of 1864, stories by Mark Twain began to be regularly reprinted in California and Nevada newspapers and occasionally in the East. The story of the petrified man appeared in the *Atlantic Monthly* in New York City and brought Clemens a warm letter from its editor, William Dean Howells.

May 4, 1864
My Dear Twain:

With great gusto did I peruse your composition about the petrified man who thumbed his nose at the world. There is a liveliness and imagination contained therein which is normally not observed in Eastern publications.

The aforementioned piece garnered a warm reception from Atlantic Monthly *readers and, in all earnestness, I am requesting that you forward me similar compositions for publication in the* Atlantic Monthly.

For each such composition I receive, I will remit to you a sum of $100.

Entrusting you to vibrant health and good fortune.
Yours truly,
William Dean Howells

Inside the envelope, Sam found a bank draft for $100.

June 13, 1864 *Flush times are in flower for this no-count, unwashed country boy from Hannibal, Missouri. In consideration of still another raise at the* Enterprise, *adding to that my correspondent income, I find myself bathing in new-found wealth. As of yesterday, more than $1000 is registered in my name in the Washoe Basin Bank. With such lofty wealth, I could well afford an excursion to Europe, if I so desired, but what reason would I require to go loafing when I'm indulging in such wonderous frivolity? One thousand dollars is the single largest amount of money ever ascribed in my name.*

***

In late August of 1864, still another of Sam's "Mark Twain" stories aroused an uproar. The headline for the piece read: "Scene at Rawhide Ranch."

"Two miners, hard-nosed, weather-beaten veterans of the excavation trade and bent on purchasing a claim, escaped near calamity on Thursday last while investigating an abandoned mine shaft at Rawhide Ranch. It seems bold adventurers, Bill Clotfelter and Johnny Styles, were being lowered into the shaft in a bucket tied to the rope which was powered by 'Old

Cotton,' an old gray horse with a tendency to indulge in profound meditation at the most inconvenient of times. Whilst being lowered, the bucket abruptly broke free, leaving the pair clinging by the rope and peering into the eyes of death eighty feet below. 'Help! Help! We are dying!' the pair shouted upward, hoping to be heard by either the old horse or a good Samaritan. For nigh on thirty minutes, the pair clung to the rope, looking into one another's faces and making pleas to anyone who might hear them. Finally, Old Cotton, considering that his meditation had grown tiring, decided to return to active duty and pulled the pair to the top of the shaft. The following morning, the two purchased the mine.... and Old Cotton."

Mark Twain

***

On the night of the day the article was published, Sam was back at Willard's pool parlor partnered with Steve Gillis in a game of eight ball. At the table next to theirs, Laird was playing pool with one of his reporters.

"Twain!" Laird said. "I witnessed your new fiction in today's *Enterprise*."

"What is your meaning?"

"'Help! Help! We're dying!' That's my meaning! How could you possibly have known what the miners were uttering as they dangled from the rope?"

"It was a quote from the miner who related the story," Sam lied.

"Help! Help! We're dying!" Laird said again. "Help! Help! We're dying!"

His mockery brought a loud laugh from his playing partner.

"Never have I seen such reckless disregard for the truth," Laird continued.

Sam glared at him.

"You wouldn't know the truth if it jumped up your blasphemous rear end," he said.

Laird, livid anger in his eyes, laid aside his pool cue.

"You son of a whore!" he said.

Suddenly, at the words, Sam turned to face Laird.

"I could kill you over words like that."

Laird laughed.

"How do you propose to do that?" he said.

"I hereby challenge you to a duel."

"Accepted!" Laird shot back. "When and where?"

"Tomorrow morning at eight behind the livery stable on Eureka Street."

"Done!" Laird said.

With that, he retrieved his hat and stalked out.

"You're going to need a second," said Gillis. "I've had experience."

"It shall be you!" Sam said.

***

That afternoon, Goodman called Sam into his office.

"I heard you're engaging in a duel with James Laird tomorrow morning."

"That's the plan."

"What if he kills you?"

"So be it."

"I shall lose the best reporter I've ever had."

"I intend to defend my personal honor."

"Are you aware that dueling is illegal in Nevada?"

"No matter!"

"The penalty is a year in jail."

Sam shrugged.

Goodman hesitated before he spoke again.

"There is no reasoning with you, is there?" he said finally.

"Not in this!"

Goodman studied Sam for a long moment.

"At what hour will the event take place?"

"Eight a.m. tomorrow. Behind the livery stables on Eureka Street."

***

That night, back at the pool hall, Sam chatted with Gillis

while they waited for a table.

"I'm leaving Virginia City next week," Steve said.

"Where you headed?"

"Jackass Hill in Tuolumne County, California. My friend Ben Coon has staked a claim on a gold mine and is looking for partners. I joined up with him. Would you be interested in partnering with us?"

"What's the price of a partnership?"

"One hundred fifty dollars. Ben has a wagon, two mules, picks, shovels and some old sluice boxes. I have tents, beds, a stove and house-keeping supplies. We've got everything we'll need but grub."

"I'm not interested," Sam said. "I already have a substantial position at the *Enterprise*."

"If you encounter anyone who might be interested," Gillis said, "pass me the word."

***

The following morning, just before eight, Sam and Gillis were at the picketing area at the rear of the Eureka Street livery stable. When they arrived, they saw Laird, his second and several other men who had gathered to witness the event.

When Laird's second saw Sam and Gillis, he came over and presented a brace of dueling pistols.

"These are the weapons," he said. "Choose the one you prefer."

Both men examined the pistols.

"The one on the left is an Union Army pistol and they tend to shoot to the right," Gillis said. "Take the other."

Clemens took the pistol Gillis designated.

"The weapon is loaded and ready to fire," said Laird's second, then he stepped away.

"Gentlemen!" the second called out "Take your positions!"

Seconds later, Sam and Laird were standing with their backs to one another in the middle of the livery stable picketing lot, their weapons pointing into the air.

Laird's second continued his instructions.

"Each of you will now take ten steps forward, then turn and

fire at will."

With that, both Sam and Laird started walking forward. On the tenth step, both men turned and pointed their weapons.

Laird fired first.

Blam!

The lead bullet whizzed by Sam's head.

He hesitated.

"Fire!" Gillis yelled. "Fire!"

Sam hesitated further.

"Shoot him!" Gillis said.

Sam lowered his pistol.

"I can't shoot a man in cold blood," he said.

"He would have killed you," Gillis said.

"No matter!" Sam said. "Such is beyond my principles."

At the instant Sam lowered his weapon, Laird threw his pistol down, then turned and ran off up the street.

Gillis laughed and hugged Sam.

"You stood your ground," he said. "I'll give you that."

***

Early the following morning, Sam was awakened by a knock on his door. It was Goodman.

"The marshal arrested Laird yesterday afternoon for dueling. He'll be coming for you next. Maybe you should lay low for a while and let this blow over. I don't want to lose my best reporter."

"What should I do?"

"I own a cabin at Piute Pass. You could go there and hide out for a few days."

"Where is the cabin?"

Goodman provided the cabin's location.

"Can I use one of the company's horses?"

"Certainly."

***

An hour later, suitcase in hand, Sam, ever watchful for the city marshal, was at the *Enterprise* livery stables. Quickly, he picked a horse, then sped off up a back street. Twenty minutes later, upon arrival at Piute Pass, he galloped straight to the mining camp where Gillis had a claim. Upon arrival, he dismounted and went from tent to tent until he found one with the name Gillis.

"Steve!" he called. "Steve Gillis!"

Seconds later, Gillis appeared from behind the flap in long johns, rubbing his eyes.

"Sam! What are you doing here?"

"Is the offer still open for a partner in the California gold mine?"

"Sure is. We'll need to talk to Ben."

Moments later, Gillis was fully clothed, and he and Sam were walking among the miners' tents. Finally, seated in front of a fire with a pot of coffee brewing, they saw Ben Coon. Ben Coon was a stocky man, late fifties with a sunburned face, a flop hat turned up in front, a full white beard, red suspenders and a flannel shirt.

"Morning, Steve!" he said.

"Morning!" Gillis said. "This is Sam Clemens. He wants to partner in the claim at Jackass Hill."

The old miner looked Sam up and down.

"He looks kind of soft to me," he said. "Ever done any mining?"

"I have not."

"Mining is back-breaking work," he said. "Using a pick and shovel day after day will make a young man old."

"I feel I'm up for it."

The old man studied Sam.

"Did Steve tell you it's $150 to buy in?"

"He did."

The old miner grew quiet again.

"Sam's a good man," Gillis interjected. "I've been knowing him nigh on three years. If he tells you something, you can bet your last dollar it will get done."

Ben Coon inhaled.

"All right, you can come in, but if you start slacking and expecting me and Steve to do all the work, you won't be around long."

"I'll perform as promised."

The old miner turned, then spat a splat of tobacco juice on the ground.

"All right. I reckon you're worth a try. Where's your money?"

Sam handed him $150.

Ben took the money, folded it and stuck it in the pocket of his flannel shirt.

"We leave in the morning at sunrise."

11
Calaveras County

The following morning at daybreak, Sam, Steve and Ben Coon, riding in a wagon loaded with mining equipment, were headed south from Piute Pass to Virginia City. Behind them trailed an extra mule and the horse Sam had borrowed from Goodman the previous day. That afternoon, when the wagon rolled into town, Clemens was safely hidden under the mining equipment. While Ben and Sam waited, ever watchful for the city marshal, Gillis returned the borrowed horse to the *Enterprise* livery stable. Thirty minutes later, the adventurers were out of the Virginia City town limits. That afternoon, the wagon pulled into Carson City and Clemens went straight to the Washoe Basin Bank on Main Street. There, he withdrew $1,400 in savings and closed the account. An hour later, the wagon was headed due west toward California.

***

The journey from Carson City to Jackass Hill required a total of eight days. First, they crossed the desert wastelands south of Carson City, then started upward into the high, green foothills of the Sierra Nevada into California, past dense forests of redwoods, cottonwoods and box elders, then through the deep canyons and towering peaks of Yosemite Valley. They traveled from sunrise to sunset; Ben said traveling at night was too dangerous because, in the darkness, the mules could stumble or step into a hole and break a leg. Nights were spent camped out alongside the trail.

***

August 19, 1864 *On the journey to Jackass hill, I perceived an entirely new appreciation for sagebrush. When a party camps, the first thing to be done is to cut sagebrush; and in a few minutes, there is an opulent pile of it ready for use. A hole a foot wide, two feet deep, and two feet long, is dug, and sage brush chopped up and burned in it till it is full to the brim with glowing coals. Then the cooking begins, and there is no smoke, and consequently, no swearing. Such a fire will keep all night, with very little replenishing, and it makes a very sociable campfire, one around which the most impossible reminiscences sound plausible, instructive, and profoundly entertaining.*

***

On the late morning of the eighth day, the wagon pulled into the rolling, grassy meadows of Tuolumne County, California. There, after another two hours along a rocky, uneven trail strewn with boulders, they arrived at Jackass Hill, so named for the numerous jackasses whose pack trains stopped there overnight on their way to and from various points in the gold fields. Some said as many as two hundred of the beasts had been picketed there at the same time, making their presence known for miles around with their incessant braying.

Upon arrival, Sam got out of the wagon to survey the countryside. From the top of the hill, looking southward along the Tuolumne River, he could see miners' cabins and tents dotting the banks, each structure indicating a claim. Some men were in the shallows of the river using a screen, one man on either side, sifting through the river sediment. Others were involved in sluice mining where an oblong box was placed in the river so that its flow washed over the freshly dug earth and revealed flakes of gold among its gradients. Still others were squatted at the river's edge, swirling sediment and earth around in a tin pan, the original method of gold mining known as panning.

Thirty minutes later, the wagon was slogging along the muddy trail at the river's edge. Finally, it stopped in front of a cottonwood tree, which had a white sign nailed to it. Ben searched through his belongings, withdrew a piece of paper, then went to the tree.

"Claim number 114," he said, checking the number on the claim certificate. "This is us. All right, boys, let's get started."

***

By nightfall, the adventurers had the wagon unloaded, two tents erected, the mules pastured and their equipment unpacked.

"Looks like we're ready for tomorrow," Ben said. "Come on, let's go meet the other miners."

Moments later, they were walking back along the trail at the river's edge toward a brilliant glow of light at the bottom of the hill. There, in a circle of sagebrush some thirty feet across, they could see a group of ten to fifteen other miners sitting around a campfire. As they appeared in the campfire's light, a smallish man in his forties with a thick beard, torn pants and a flop hat stood up.

"Looks like we got some new boys," he said to the other miners.

Then he stepped forward and offered his hand to Ben.

"Howdy," he said. "My name is Wilson Mitchell, but folks around here call me 'Scratchy.'"

"Pleased to meet you," Ben said, shaking his hand. "This is Steve Gillis and Sam Clemens."

Scratchy shook hands with each of the newcomers.

"You boys have a seat and jaw with us for a spell," he said.

Ben, Steve and Sam took places around the campfire, then the other miners came forward, one at a time, to greet them. There was "Texas Bob" Ferguson, "Arky" Wilkerson, Howard Willingham and "Three-finger" Brown. The last miner to introduce himself was a short-statured man in his twenties with a boyish face, a shock of black hair and clean-shaven except for a drooping mustache. He said his name was Bret Harte.

Once the newcomers were seated, Scratchy threw new sagebrush logs on the fire, then turned to Howard Willingham, a tall, solemn-faced man with a bushy beard and a sweat-stained felt hat.

"Howard, tell us a story," he said. "Tell us about one of your hunting trips."

The other miners grew quiet, then Howard began to speak.

"One day back home in Kentucky, I got my double-barreled shotgun and my horse and we headed to the woods to go hunting. Oh, my, it was nasty hot weather. It was so hot that, as I was riding across a cornfield, the popcorn started popping off the stalk until the popcorn was three feet deep on the ground. My poor horse thought it was snowing, so he froze to death then and there. Well, then I had to walk. So, I kept going till I come up on this creek. Well, sir, I looked up the creek one way and I saw 10,000 ducks coming. I looked down the creek and I saw 12,000 geese heading for me. On the other side of the creek, I saw at least a thousand bullfrogs, then I looked down at my feet and saw a rattlesnake ready to strike. I thought, well, I guess I better save my life and kill that venomous devil. So, I pulled down on both barrels. One barrel went up the creek and killed all 10,000 geese, the other barrel went down the creek and killed all those ducks, the blast from the gun killed all those bullfrogs and the ramrod from the gun went down the snake's throat and choked it to death. I tell you, boys, it was the best hunting trip I ever had."

For a moment, quietness prevailed among the group. Finally, Arky Wilkerson spoke up.

"Are you reckoning we're going to believe that?" he said. "Why, I never seen a shotgun that had a ramrod."

"Gospel truth!" said Howard.

"I believe it," said Scratchy. "Went on a hunting trip myself like that one time."

"You tell us a story, Scratchy," said Three-finger Brown. "You always got good stories about miners."

"Well, I have to say I've done some excavating in my day. Four years ago, me and a passel of other miners were working claims over in Stanislaus County that was going nowhere. Every man there was busting their back, but nobody was finding gold. At the camp, there was seventeen miners and one woman, a half-breed Indian named Cherokee Sal. Well, all the men had partaken of Cherokee Sal's body at one time or another for a fee, so, when she got pregnant, none of the miners knew who the father was, but every one of them knew the child could be theirs. So, after Sal had her baby, everything suddenly changed. Miners started hitting bonanzas here and there and everywhere. Some miners were turning up ore worth $5,000 a day and every miner there believed the birth of Sal's boy child had brought the change in fortune, so they named the child 'The Luck.' After that, the miners worshipped that boy and treated him like a king."

Quietness prevailed once more.

"Whatever happened to the child?" Bret Harte asked.

"I never knew exactly," Scratchy said. "Last I heard, the other miners divided up their pokes with Sal and she took 'The Luck' and went to San Francisco."

Over the next two hours, several other miners told stories. Three-finger Brown related the story of a woman he knew in Sacramento and, every time he was with her, he was mesmerized by her blue eyes. Another miner told the story of Portuguese Joe, a miner from Australia, who made $100,000 at Angels Camp, and left another $50,000 buried in tin cans.

"Old Joe would fill a sardine can with gold nuggets, bury it, then forget where he buried it. Some say he left more gold buried in sardine cans than he took with him."

The group grew quiet again. Now there was only the sound of a screech owl somewhere in a nearby tree and the popping sound of the fire.

"Well, it's time for me to get some shut-eye," Scratchy said.

"Can you do one rendition of 'My Old Kentucky Home'?" Howard said.

Scratchy reached behind him and withdrew a guitar. Then, as he strummed the tune, all of the miners joined in to sing.

"Oh, the sun shines bright on my old Kentucky home; 'tis summer, the old folks are gay, well, the corn top's ripe, and the meadows in the bloom, while the birds make music all day."

Then, as they launched into the chorus: "Weep no more, my lady. Oh, weep no more, today," the lonely miners' eyes filled with tears of longing as they remembered olden places and times when their hearts were young and free, a time when there were no picks, no shovels, no sluice boxes and no wheelbarrows.

***

Sam spent the next week working sluice boxes. A sluice box was a rectangular wooden contraption with a small metal screen, which served as a porous bottom. First, the box was filled almost to the brim with fresh earth and placed in the river. Then, as the water washed over the edges of the box, the "shaker," who was Sam, would swirl the muddy mixture round and round and the flakes of gold, since they were heavier, were captured by the metal screen. Clemens' job was to dig fresh earth out of the hillside with a pick, then shovel it into a wheelbarrow, and finally roll it to the river where he would process it in a sluice box. Meanwhile, Ben and Steve worked the screen, also known as a sieve, at the river's edge. The sieve worked on the same principle as a sluice box, but it was a two-man operation. At the end of the week, the trio had $23 worth of gold dust between them.

August 23, 1864 *Oh, great tarnation, these tired, aching muscles and joints! Tonight, when I went into the tent, I flopped face first down on my cot out of pure exhaustion. My arms felt like lead as if someone had thrust a sledgehammer upon them a thousand times. Never have my muscles and joints endured such powerful bending and lifting. I rested for nigh on a hour, then when Ben announced beans and bacon, I arose and ate. After taking food, I wandered back inside the tent, fell once more onto the cot and was dead to the world.*

***

That night, once all the miners were gathered around the campfire, Scratchy, who always served as emcee, turned to Ben.

"Ben! You want to tell a story?"

The old miner hesitated for a moment, then began.

"When I was at Jackass Hill two years ago, I had a friend

170

named Jim who would bet on anything and everything from horse races to dogfights to the health of the local parson's wife. So one day, ole Jim catches a frog who he names Daniel Webster and spends three months teaching that critter to jump. So, when a stranger visits the camp, Jim shows off the frog and offers to bet $40 that it can outjump any frog in Calaveras County. The stranger, who was unimpressed, allowed that he would take the bet if he had a frog. So ole Jim goes out to catch another frog and leaves Daniel alone with the stranger. While Jim is gone, the stranger pours lead-shot down Daniel's throat. When Jim returns, they set the frogs down and the race is on. The stranger's frog jumps away while Daniel didn't budge. So Jim pays the $40 to the stranger, who went on his merry way. When Jim, disgusted at losing the bet, checked on Daniel, he noticed he seemed heavier than usual. Suddenly, the frog belches up a double handful of lead-shot. Then, realizing he had been cheated, ole Jim went running after the stranger but never caught him."

Several of the miners applauded and broke into laughter at Ben's story. Then Scratchy stood up again, then looked around the group.

"Texas Bob!" he said, pointing to one of the miners. "You got a yarn for us?"

Texas Bob, a stocky man in his early forties with a jowly, clean-shaven face and a paunch hanging over his jeans, stood up and withdrew a folded paper from his shirt pocket.

"I wanted to tell you boys…" he said, unfolding the paper, "this is the most truthful poem I ever set my eyes on."

He paused.

"Now all y'all got to stay quiet till I'm finished."

"They won't disturb you," Scratchy said. "Read the poem."

Texas Bob cleared his throat and began reading.

"The name of this poem is Ozymandias. It goes like this.

I met a traveller from an antique land,
Who said—"Two vast and trunkless legs of stone
Stand in the desert. . . . Near them, on the sand,
Half sunk a shattered visage lies, whose frown,
And wrinkled lip, and sneer of cold command,

Tell that its sculptor well those passions read
Which yet survive, stamped on these lifeless things,
The hand that mocked them, and the heart that fed;
And on the pedestal, these words appear:
My name is Ozymandias, King of Kings;
Look on my Works, ye Mighty, and despair!
Nothing beside remains. Round the decay
Of that colossal Wreck, boundless and bare
The lone and level sands stretch far away."

Once he was finished, quietness prevailed for a long moment.

"That ain't no poem," said Arky Wilkerson. "The lines don't rhyme."

"They weren't meant to rhyme," said Three-finger Brown. "Some poems don't rhyme."

"Shhh!" said Texas Bob.

The other miners grew quiet again.

"What the poet is saying," Texas Bob continued, "is that no matter how famous, how rich or how powerful you become in this world, finally all you'll be is dust to be blown away by the wind."

"Who wrote it?" asked one of the miners

"I don't know," Texas Bob said. I think it was an Englishman by the name of John Keats."

Suddenly, Bret Harte, who had been silent all night, spoke up.

"It was Shelley," he said. "Percy Bysshe Shelley."

"How come you know so much?" asked another miner.

"I'm a poet myself," he said.

Over the next hour, several other miners told stories. Three-finger Brown told the story of how he once won four jackasses in a card game with a pair of deuces. Claude Farlow related a story about his mother's death back in Kansas and how her ghost returned again and again to visit the family home. Finally, with the usual close, all the miners joined in to sing "My Old Kentucky Home" and, once finished, the session was at an end.

As the miners started back to their claims, Sam sidled up

to Bret Harte.

"You say you're a poet?" he said.

"That's right!"

"I'm a writer myself," Sam said. "I've never tried poetry."

"What have you written?"

Sam explained his newspaper days with the *Hannibal Journal* and the *Territorial Enterprise*.

"I'd like to hear more from you," Harte said. "Tomorrow night, after the work is done, why don't you come down to claim #43? We can drink some cheap whiskey and maybe learn something from each other."

"Agreed."

***

The following night, while Ben and Steve went to the campfire, Sam told them he was going to visit Bret Harte. Claim #43 was four claims south of Ben's along the river's edge. There he was introduced to Bret's partner, Bill Stark. Afterward, Sam and Harte took a pint of whiskey and three cigars and went to the river. There they took seats on an old log jutting out into the river.

"I grew up in Albany, New York," Harte said. "My parents were well off and I guess you could say I was raised with a silver spoon. I wrote my first poem when I was 11, a little satire titled 'Autumn Musings.' I remember how proud I was to show it to my family. When they saw it, they laughed and mocked me. I ran away from them and hid in my shame. Their ridicule was such a shock that I wonder I ever wrote another line of verse."

"Why did you come west?" Clemens asked.

"Oh, I read all of the western dime novels I could get my hands on. Stories about Indian massacres, gunfights, vigilante justice and such filled my imagination when I was young. In my heart, I knew I wanted to write poems and stories, and the West held forth some of the most interesting material I knew."

"Why did you get into mining?" Sam said.

"For the pure adventure of it," Harte said.

Sam laughed.

"I know the sentiment," he said. "Only too well."

***

Over the next four months, Sam, Ben and Steve toiled away at their claim. Day after day, they hauled one wheelbarrow load after another from the hill, then transported it to the river for processing. At the end of three back-breaking weeks of work, they had a total of $42. One morning, while Ben was gone into town, Sam and Steve took a break and seated themselves under a cottonwood tree to rest.

"I'm getting weary," Sam said, wiping the sweat off his face. "Working like a mule all day and getting nothing in return."

"Me too," Steve replied.

"I'd just like to get back the $150 I put into this venture. If I got that, then I'd hightail it out of here."

"Where would you go?" Steve asked.

"I'm not certain," Sam said, "but I wouldn't be here."

A long pause.

"I think I'll tell Ben tonight that I'm cutting loose," Sam said.

"No, let's stuck it out for a mite longer," Steve said.

Sam looked at him.

"Just for the old man's sake," Steve said.

"All right," he said. "I'll bear the misery a bit longer."

***

That night, as the Jackass Hill miners sat around the campfire, a new face joined them. The moment the strange man stepped into the firelight, the other miners went for their weapons.

"Hold it, boys!" the stranger said. "I don't mean you no harm. I'm a miner just like y'all. I'm just passing through."

Once satisfied he was harmless, the other miners replaced their pistols.

"Where you headed?" asked Scratchy.

"Angels Camp in Stanislaus County. They hit a rich vein

of gold at Dead Horse Ravine. They say the vein runs right under that mountain, and the further it goes, the bigger it gets. Some are getting $10,000 a day.”

“I’ve heard stories like that ever since I been prospecting,” Ben said. “I don’t believe any of them.”

“It’s true,” the man said. “A friend of mine pulled $15,000 out of a small claim, then hightailed it out for San Francisco.”

“I’m with Ben,” said Howard Willingham. “Stories about quick riches in the gold fields are as plentiful as grains of sand.”

“You boys can believe what you like,” said the stranger. “Me, I’m a believer.”

***

The following morning, Sam, Ben and Steve were toiling away. Sam was working the sluice boxes while Steve and Ben used the screen, swirling the fresh earth around, closely watching the sediment for yellow metal. Suddenly, Ben looked up from his work to the side of the hill behind them, then he stopped. There he saw Arky Wilkerson, who owned the adjacent claim, using a pick and shovel to fill a wheelbarrow.

“What the hell is he doing?” Ben said. “He’s on our claim.”

Ben turned to Steve.

“Let’s put this screen down,” he said. “I’m going to have a talk with Mr. Wilkerson.”

Once the screen was safely at the river’s edge, Ben checked his sidearm, then strode up the hill.

“Arky!” he called. “Why are you digging on my claim?”

“Your claim, hell! This is my property.”

“No such thang,” Ben said. “My claim extends all the way to that gully,” he said, pointing to a small ravine. “That gully is the line between the two claims.”

“No! No! My claim goes twenty feet on the other side of the gully.”

Ben turned and walked to the edge of the gully.

“Anything from here southward is my claim,” he said.

“You’re a liar!”

“Who you calling a liar?” said Ben.

175

"You! You old goat!"

The two men glared angrily at each other.

"I know what's mine!" Wilkerson said. "I'm going to mine this ground, whether you like it or not."

"Like hell you are!" Ben replied.

Suddenly, Wilkerson rushed at the old miner with the shovel, poised to strike. Quickly, Ben stepped aside, pulled his sidearm and slapped the other man across the face with the weapon as he lunged past. Instantly, Wilkerson went to the ground, holding his hand to his face. Blood was coming from his nose and mouth. He looked at the blood, then back at Ben.

"You son of a whore," he said. "I'll have you for this."

"Get off my property!" Ben said. "Now!"

Wilkerson, livid anger in his face, slowly raised himself to his feet, threw the shovel and pick into the wheelbarrow, then started pushing it down the side of the hill.

"And don't come back!" Ben shouted as the other man reached the bottom of the hill.

Wilkerson didn't look back.

***

That night at the campfire, Scratchy told the story of his Aunt Bessie who killed two of her three husbands and escaped justice. Texas Bob read another poem and Claude Farlow recalled how his brother, a one-eyed man, killed another man over a woman. Finally, at the end, the miners launched into "My Old Kentucky" Home while Scratchy strummed his guitar. As the group launched into the second verse, two loud cracks from a rifle suddenly pierced the night air. At the sound, Ben, who was standing in front of the fire, pitched forward into the dirt. Seeing this, Scratchy stopped playing.

"Ben Coon is shot!" said one of the miners.

Quickly, the other miners rushed to the prostrate form in front of the fire.

"He's dead," said Three-finger Brown. "Somebody ambushed him."

"The only person with a reason was Arky."

"Where is Arky?"

"He hasn't been here tonight."

"Let's go check his claim," said Howard Willingham.

Ten minutes later, using torches and lanterns, the other miners strode along the river's edge to Wilkerson's claim. Arky and all of his personal items were missing.

"It was Arky all right," said Texas Bob. "He's took everything and hightailed it out."

"We going to have to bury Ben," said Scratchy.

"We'll do it tomorrow when there is light," said Texas Bob.

***

The following morning, the miners dug a grave for Ben Coon on the hillside overlooking his claim. Once the grave was dug, the other miners gathered around, removed their hats and solemnly waited for Scratchy to deliver the eulogy.

"Old Ben has gone to a better place," Scratchy said. "A place way up there in them clouds where the digging is easy, the wheelbarrows are light, and the nuggets are big as your fist. Adding to that, I'm hoping somewhere up in them clouds, old Ben will meet up again with Elmira Rossiter, the woman he loved with his total heart. Next to gold, there wasn't anything old Ben loved more than Elmira. Rest in peace, Old Ben!"

"Cover him up, boys," Scratchy said. Then, as Scratchy read the Lord's Prayer, the other miners began throwing fresh earth into the grave until it was heaped high.

***

Ten minutes later, Sam and Steve were walking back to their claim.

"With Ben gone, I guess all this equipment belongs to us," Steve said.

"Yeah, but what are we going to do with it?"

"Let's go to Angels Camp in Stanislaus County," Steve said. "You heard what the stranger said the other night. There's got to be some truth to it."

"I'm ready to try about anything," Sam said. "I despise the very sight of this river and these hills. Let's ask Bret if he wants to go."

"You go talk to him," Steve said. "I'm going to start loading up the wagon."

Ten minutes later, Sam was at Harte's Claim. Clemens told him about his new plans. Harte, without hesitation, turned and strode to the side of the river to talk to his partner Bill Stark.

"Leaving?" Bill asked.

"I'm going to Angels Camp," Harte said.

"What about your interest in the equipment?"

"You keep it. Most of it is yours anyway. The boys I'm going with have plenty of equipment."

"Suit yourself," Stark said, offering his hand. "Good luck!"

***

Over the next two days, in a wagon loaded with mining equipment, Sam, Bret and Steve crossed the rugged, rolling foothills of the Sierra Nevada past giant forests of redwoods, eucalyptus and box elders. Their journey took them through the heart of Yosemite Valley, past the towering crags and raging rivers, then north through the mining towns of Groveland, Gouge Eye and Sonora, then straight north into Stanislaus County. On the afternoon of the second day, the wagon rolled into Angels Camp.

***

By the early winter of 1864, Angels Camp had become one of the oldest and most well-known gold rush communities in California. In 1851, after Henry Angel discovered a large vein of gold at the confluence of Angel's Creek and Dry Creek, he pulled more than $10,000 out of the claim in less than a year. As word spread, other miners, hungry for the yellow metal, converged on the area and, by the end of 1852, more than one hundred tents and cabins were scattered along the banks of the two creeks. Now, thirteen years later, Angels Camp had grown into a thriving settlement with two mercantile stores, a bank, three saloons, a harness shop, a hotel and a brothel, everything a miner needed to work his trade.

That afternoon, as their wagon trundled into town, the three adventurers scanned the row of business establishments on Main Street for the claims office. Finally, they spotted it between a funeral home and a harness shop.

Ten minutes later, the three were out of the wagon and inside the claims office.

The clerk was a medium-height, balding man in his mid-forties with a clean-shaven face and round glasses.

"All mineral rights belong to the state of California until someone stakes out a claim," the clerk said. "When a miner makes a claim, he don't own the property, only the right to mine it for minerals. If a claim is left unworked for a year, it returns to state ownership."

"Don't you have some old, unclaimed mines?"

"Several," the clerk said. "They're mostly properties that have been claimed multiple times without producing ore."

"Let's see what you got," Sam said.

The clerk hefted down a large map that listed all the mining claims and spread it out on the counter. Sam, Steve and Bret gathered round.

"Now right here," he said, indicating on the map, "is 'Crazy Bill' Watson's old place. He mined it a few years, took some ore, then killed a man in a gunfight over a woman. Last I heard, he left the States and was back in Winnipeg."

"How long since it's been mined?" Steve asked.

"Two, maybe three years."

"What else you got?" said Sam.

The clerk surveyed the map.

"Now here," he said, "claim number 63 is something you might be interested in. The last feller to mine it was a man named Duke Harralson. He worked it for over a year, then, after he didn't make enough to buy beans, he went back to Kansas."

"Any claims at Dead Horse Ravine?" Sam asked.

"Everything near Dead Horse Ravine has been claimed over a year now," the clerk said. "They made a big strike there in the fall of '64."

Still not satisfied, Sam studied the map.

"What about this one?" Sam said.

"Oh, that's Portuguese Joe's old place. It hasn't been mined in years. Three years ago, a feller from Chicago claimed it and worked for a year, then disappeared."

"Wasn't somebody telling a story about Portuguese Joe at the campfire in Jackass Hill?" Sam said.

"Yeah, something about an old miner filling sardine cans with gold dust, burying them, then forgetting where he buried them."

"That's the story they tell about Portuguese Joe," the clerk said. "Some say old Joe's ghosts still wanders around the claim at night."

"It's just an old miner's tale," Steve said. "What else you got?"

"No, wait!" said Sam. "Let's claim this one."

"Why?" Steve said. "Sounds like there is nothing to be gained."

"I got a hunch," Sam said. "This is the one I want to claim."

"No," Steve said. "I want something that offers some promise."

Sam turned to Bret.

"What do you say?"

"Looks like a roll of the dice," he replied. "From the looks of things, one is about as good as the other."

"Let's get this one," Sam said. "Why, we might even see old Portuguese Joe's ghost."

"This no time for funning," Steve said.

"I'm with you, Sam," Bret said.

Bret turned to Steve.

"The more I hear about this claim, the more I like it. Let's get this one," Bret said.

Steve slowly shook his head with indecision, then took a deep breath.

"Oh, what the hell?" he said. "We could go round and round and still not know what we got till we start digging.. Let's do it."

"How much to file a claim?" Bret said.

"Fifty dollars."

"We'll have a piece of paper giving us legal claim?" Sam said.

"Yep. Signed, sealed and legal."

Twenty minutes later, the three men paid their money, signed the necessary papers and left the claims office.

"Come on," Sam said. "Let's have a drink to celebrate."

Ten minutes later, the three walked into the saloon at the Angels Hotel. As they entered, Sam saw two billiard tables in the back.

"Ha!" Sam said, upon seeing the pool tables. "This is the place for me."

Ten minutes later, the three were seated at the bar drinking beer.

"Now, I want you boys to understand me," Steve said. "I'm putting just a few weeks into this little venture. If we haven't dug up anything worthwhile by Christmas, I'm hightailing it."

"Why until Christmas?"

"That's plenty of time to find out if our luck is going to change," Steve said. "Christmas day. That's the moment of truth."

***

The following day, Sam, Steve, Bret and their wagon slogged up the muddy banks of Angel's Creek to claim number 116. Once the wagon was unloaded, they set up tents, hauled out their equipment and started working the claim. As before, Sam worked the sluice boxes while Steve and Bret handled the sieve. Over the next two weeks, day after day, the three men dug shovelful after shovelful of earth from the hillside, then processed it in the sluice boxes and sieves in search of the elusive gold metal. At the end of the second week, they had $28 in gold.

***

The following afternoon, an old tomcat, a dark yellow color like quartz, wandered into their encampment. Seeing the creature was hungry, Sam fed it some left-over beans and rice and, after he had repeated that for several days, the cat became a regular at their camp. At night, as the miners sipped cheap whiskey and smoked, Sam and Bret would throw a rubber ball between them and watch the old tomcat chase it across the grass.

"What are we going to call him?" Bret said.

"We'll call him Tom Quartz," Sam said.

***

Over the next few days, the three adventurers continued to suffer the same setbacks they had endured at Jackass Hill. Day after day, they strained their backs, fought the insects and dealt with the heat, the dust and the callouses. At the end of the third week, on Christmas day, they had accumulated $18 in gold dust.

The next morning, when they woke up, Gillis announced he had had enough.

"This is the end of the line for me, boys," he said. "I'm packing up and heading to the big city."

"Give it one more day," Sam said.

"No, I'm finished," Steve said. "Too much work, too little pay. I'm finished with mining."

"We might hit a big vein today," Sam said.

"Good luck!" Gillis said. "I won't be here."

Over the next hour, Gillis gathered his personal belongings, said his good-byes, then, with a knapsack slung over his back, disappeared down the road toward Angels Camp.

***

The following morning, Sam woke up, made coffee and went to Bret's tent to rouse him out of bed. Moments later, Bret was out of his tent having coffee in front of the fire. As Sam returned to his own tent, he glanced into the nearby underbrush and saw a strange yellow-looking object. Curiously, he moved closer. It was the old tom cat.

"Tom Quartz is dead," Sam said.

"Where?"

"Over there!" Sam said, pointing to the underbrush.

Bret stood up and walked over to inspect the carcass.

"We better get him buried," Sam said. "He'll be smelling before long."

Ten minutes later, Sam had a shovel and was digging a grave for the dead cat. Bret was standing beside him holding the cat's corpse in another shovel.

After Sam had tossed aside several shovelfuls of earth, the blade of the shovel suddenly hit something hard and stopped. Sam peered into the hole and saw that his shovel had hit a shiny tin-looking object. Then he reached into the hole and withdrew the object. It was a sardine can with a rotting cloth and wire wrapped around it. For a moment, both men peered at it.

"Are you thinking what I'm thinking?" Sam said.

"Let's open it."

They pulled away the wire and the cloth and opened the can. It was filled with gold nuggets.

"Hallelujah!" Bret said. "This is one of Portuguese Joe's hideaways."

"Let's see if there are others," Sam said.

"We couldn't be that lucky," Bret said.

Sam began to dig around the edges of the hole. After a while, he turned up two more sardine cans wrapped in rotting cloths and bound with wire.

Sam threw down the shovels and raised his arms in victory.

"We've discovered Portuguese Joe's hidden stash."

Over the next hour, Sam and Bret opened the three sardine cans and removed their contents. All three were filled with gold nuggets.

"Who would ever have dreamed we could be so lucky?"

"How much you think all this gold is worth?" Sam said.

"Let's go into town and cash it in," Bret said. "Then we'll know."

***

That afternoon at the assayer's office in Angels Camp, they presented their find to the proprietor.

"What do you have there?" the assayer said.

"Three sardine cans filled with gold," Sam said.

"I don't believe you!"

They spread the contents of the three cans beside the assayer's scales. Finally, after more than an hour of grading and weighing and adding, the assayer turned to Sam and Bret.

"You have a total of $16,722.81 in gold," he said.

Sam turned to Bret and shook his hand, then together, they jumped up and down in jubilation. Once the celebrating was over, Sam turned serious.

"What are you going to do now?"

"I'm going to San Francisco to live the high life," Bret said.

"I'm going with you," Sam replied.

12
San Francisco

On the afternoon of January 3, 1865, the stagecoach carrying Sam Clemens and Bret Harte rolled into San Francisco. Upon arrival at the Hyde Street station, they took a cab carriage to the exclusive Queen Anne Hotel where they booked rooms. Known as "the finest accommodation in the city," the Queen Anne sat high atop Knob Hill and served as a shining example of the lavish lifestyle that awaited those miners fortunate enough to find great wealth in the gold fields. Each of its forty-two rooms featured a panoramic view of the bay, king-sized brass beds, hand-made quilts, the latest period furniture, an athletic club, a reading room and a gentlemen's parlor where male guests could drink, smoke and play billiards at their leisure.

The following morning, Sam dashed off a letter to his brother Orion informing him of his new situation. Then, after he and Bret had a breakfast of scrambled eggs, ham, grits and hot biscuits in the hotel restaurant, they went shopping. By noon, each had been outfitted with new tailor-made suits, silk shirts, matching cravats, patent leather shoes with wool stockings and stylish gentlemen's hats.

"We are now equipped to fulfill our roles as true gentlemen," Clemens said. "Now let us entertain ourselves with some billiards."

Upon arrival in the gentlemen's parlor, they discovered an ornately-decorated room with a full-service saloon, three billiard tables, a small sandwich bar and a tobacco shop. Upon arrival, Sam and Bret took a table, then commenced playing a game of eight ball.

When their game was finished, Sam was approached by a short, well-dressed man in his early thirties with a thin face and a well-trimmed mustache.

"Interested in playing ten games of rotation pool for $1 per game?" he said.

"Rack 'em up," Sam said.

Over the next two hours, Clemens won eight of the ten billiard games. As he prepared to shoot the fifteen ball for the final game, the other man, obviously displeased, hung up his cue and threw eight dollars on the table.

"Lucky!" he said, anger in his eyes. "You're not a truly talented billiards player. Simply lucky!"

"No need to be a sore loser," Sam replied.

"Sore loser?" the man said. "You were lucky."

"I beat you straight up," Sam said. "In three racks, you didn't pocket a single ball."

"Luck. Not talent!"

Then he turned and stalked out of the gentlemen's parlor.

"Some people have no sense of humor," said Bret, who had been watching the contest.

Sam pocketed his money and hung up his cue.

"Who was that man?" Sam asked.

"His name is Ambrose Bierce," Bret said. "He's an author."

Sam pondered for a moment, then shook his head.

"Never heard of him," he said. "What's on our agenda for tonight?"

"I want you to meet Ina."

"Ina who?"

"Ina Coolbrith. She's a poet, an essayist and the matriarch of the local literary crowd. She's having a social function at her home tonight."

"Sounds interesting," Sam said. "Introduce me as Mark Twain."

***

That night, when Sam and Bret left the hotel, they were dressed to the nines in their stylish new clothing. As they passed through the hotel lobby, they stopped in front of a wall mirror to admire themselves.

"If only Scratchy Mitchell and Texas Bob could see us now," Sam said with a big laugh.

Outside, they hailed a cab carriage, then Harte guided the driver across town to the exclusive Russian Hill area of the city. Finally, it stopped in front of a two-story Victorian mansion that reeked of elegance. Constructed of orangey-red Flemish bricks, the home featured high French windows, a black metal roof with three spires, and a lush, well-manicured garden.

At the door, a servant greeted them, took their coats and hats, and ushered them into a ballroom, where a throng of elegantly-dressed guests were having drinks, snacking, mingling and enjoying themselves. Moments later, after taking glasses of French champagne from a server's tray, they surveyed the crowd.

"Bret! Bret Harte!" a voice suddenly called.

The two turned to see a tall, well-dressed older gentleman coming toward them with his hand outstretched.

"Thomas! Thomas Whipple," Bret said, shaking his hand. "A pleasure to see you again, sir."

After pleasantries, Bret turned to Sam.

"I want you to meet my friend Mark Twain," he said. "He's a reporter and writer."

Whipple shook Sam's hand, then studied him for a moment.

"Are you the Mark Twain of *Territorial Enterprise* fame?"

"That would be me."

"I'm familiar with your work," Whipple said. "In fact, I published some of your articles in the *Gazette* several years ago. Are you based in San Francisco now?"

"For a while."

"Perhaps you could stop by my office tomorrow and we could discuss your possible employment at the *Gazette*."

"Absolutely!" Sam said. "What time tomorrow?"

"Say about one?"

"Perfect."

"I'll meet you tomorrow," Whipple said.

Whipple then shook hands with Sam and Bret again and melted back into the crowd.

Sam turned back to Bret. Harte's eyes were scanning the

guests. Suddenly, he stopped.

"See the woman over there?" Bret said, indicating with a nod of his head.

Sam's eyes searched through the crowd.

"Which one?"

"There!" Bret said. "The petite woman in the powder blue dress with all the men around her."

"Oh yes. I see her."

"That's Ina Coolbrith."

"My! My! She's a beauty! When you said matriarch, I was expecting an older woman."

"She's twenty-four," Bret said. "Beauty AND brains. Come, let me introduce you."

Bret, leading the way, guided Sam through the crowd. Once they were within earshot, Sam could see the woman up close. Short-statured and in her mid-twenties, Ina Coolbrith was just over five feet tall with dark hair, large, piercing eyes and a perfect cupid's bow mouth.

"Ina?" Bret called.

The woman turned to face them. Upon recognizing Bret, a bright smile flashed across her face; she stepped forward.

"Bret Harte! For Heaven's sake, I didn't expect to see you tonight," she said, offering her hand. "I heard you were in the gold fields trying to strike it rich."

"I thought I would return to civilization."

She laughed.

"I'm so happy to see you!" she said.

Bret turned to Sam.

"I want you to meet my friend Mark Twain," he said.

"Why hello!" she said, offering her hand. "Are you the Mark Twain of Nevada fame?"

"One and the same," Sam said.

"I know your work. I remember the petrified man piece. It was published in several local publications."

She turned to Bret.

"Can I take Mr. Twain around and introduce him to my literary friends?"

"Absolutely."

Moments later, Ina was escorting Sam around the ballroom.

First, there was Joaquin Miller, a tall man with an emaciated look who Ina introduced as a short story writer. Next was Charles Warren Stoddard, a thin man with sad eyes and a pale, sensitive face. After a short chat with each, Ina led Sam through the crowd to another guest who had his back to them. Ina tapped him on the shoulder.

"Ambrose!" she said.

The man turned. It was the same man Clemens had thrashed at billiards earlier in the day.

"This is Ambrose Bierce," Ina said. "His new book, *The Devil's Dictionary,* is a best seller."

Sam peered coldly at the man.

"We've already met," he said.

"Yes, we have," Bierce said.

Then, ignoring Sam, he turned to the hostess.

"Ina! Is there anything I can get you? Another glass of champagne?"

"No, thank you! Perhaps later."

Then, still holding Sam's arm, Ina guided him away.

"What's the problem between you and Ambrose?" Ina asked.

"I gave him a sound thrashing at billiards this afternoon."

"Sounds like two young bulls butting heads," she said with a laugh. "Come! I have more guests for you to meet."

Over the remainder of the evening, Sam and Bret made new friends, dined on raw oysters and smoked salmon, had several glasses of champagne and engaged in literary discussions with other guests. Ina introduced Sam and Bret as authors from the "Sagebrush School" and noted that he was the notorious "Mark Twain" of *Territorial Enterprise* fame.

Around midnight, as guests began to depart, Ina pulled Sam and Bret aside.

"I am requesting that the two of you return to my home next Saturday night so we can discuss your contributions to the *Overland Monthly*, the publication I edit," she said.

"Agreed!" Bret said.

"Same here," Sam said.

Twenty minutes later, in the cab carriage back to the hotel, Harte turned to Sam.

"Ina likes you," he said.

"How do you know?"

"I could detect it by her furtive glances."

Sam smiled.

"Bierce is going to be jealous," Bret continued. "He has been trying to win her favor for some time and achieving nothing."

"That's my good fortune," Sam replied.

***

The following morning, Sam arrived at the offices of the *San Francisco Gazette* at the appointed time. The secretary took him straight into Whipple's office where he was seated.

"Twain, let me come straight to the point," Whipple began. "If you're interested, I'd like to offer you a staff job. If not, I want you to become a contributor."

"Contributor is more to my liking," Sam said.

"Can you produce new stories similar to those in the *Territorial Enterprise*?"

"I can."

"Then can I expect two articles a week?"

"What's the pay rate?"

"One hundred dollars per article."

"Agreed."

"When can I expect the first one?"

"Day after tomorrow," Sam said.

"Splendid!" he said. "I shall await it."

***

Later that afternoon, back in the hotel room, Sam took pen in hand and worked until the wee hours composing "The Celebrated Jumping Frog of Calaveras County," the yarn he had heard Ben Coon tell around the campfire while he was at Jackass Hill. Once finished, he went out into the night to post one copy to Whipple at the *Gazette* and another to William Dean Howells at the *Atlantic Monthly*.

***

As promised, Clemens and Bret were back at Ina's mansion the following Saturday night. Upon arrival, Sam presented her with a copy of the jumping frog story.

"Wonderful!" she said. "Please understand I can't pay you a lot, but your work will be read by the brightest literary minds in California."

She turned to Bret.

"What can I expect from you?"

"I am composing a short story which I should have completed over the next few days."

"What's the title?"

"'The Luck of Roaring Camp'."

"Splendid! Let me say it would behoove each of you to join the Golden Gate Literary Society. We could do author salons, schedule promotions at bookstores and promote one another's work to the reading public."

"I'm agreeable to that," Sam said.

"So am I," said Bret.

Just after 9 p.m., Bret announced his departure.

"I must be leaving," he said. "I have an appointment tomorrow with the editor of the *Northern Californian*."

"Go ahead," Sam said. "I want to spend some more time with Ina."

Bret then said his good-byes and left.

"We're alone now," Ina said. "Come, I want to show you my personal study."

Moments later, she led Sam into an elegantly appointed study with a view of the bay, a large mahogany desk and ceiling-high shelves filled with stacks upon stacks of books. She stopped in front of the shelves and took down a large book bound in gold gilt.

"This is my signed copy of Rousseau's *The French Revolution*," she said. "I received it in Paris three years ago."

"Oh, my!" Clemens said, taking the volume and thumbing through it. "Rousseau is one of my favorites. Unlike most of the other philosophers of today, he believes in the goodness of mankind."

"And the beauty of nature," she added.

He handed the volume back to her.

"When I die, I hope I'm reading Rousseau," he said.

She smiled.

Moments later, they returned to the sitting parlor where a cold bottle of champagne and glasses were waiting. Sam poured each of them a glass, and they seated themselves side by side on the settee.

"My father was Don Carlos Smith, youngest brother of Joseph Smith, the Mormon prophet," Ina said. "When I was eight, my family left Utah and migrated to Los Angeles where my father made a fortune in the shipping trade. When I was twenty-one, my father gave me my inheritance, and I moved to San Francisco. Since then, I have been a poet and editor of the *Overland Monthly*."

"What, may I ask, is the origin of your surname Coolbrith?"

"I was in a failed marriage when I was 18," she said. "After the divorce, I retained my ex-husband's surname."

A pause.

"Tell me about your life," she said.

Sam recalled his early days in Missouri, his experiences as a riverboat pilot and newspaper reporter in Hannibal, and finally, his journey across the plains to Nevada.

"Now, I have given up mining and returned to authorship."

"Have you ever written poetry?"

"Poetry is too confining for me," he said. "It's like trying to dance inside a box. There is no room to flail your arms and kick up your heels. I relish the leisurely freedom of prose where you can raise your face to the open sky and run free and wild among the daisies."

She laughed.

"You bring out the laughter in me, Mark Twain," she said.

Over the next hour, they discussed the works of Plutarch and Tacitus. She explained that Plutarch, in his book *Plutarch's Lives*, didn't do justice to Julius Caesar.

"The author seems to have had a personal preference for

Alexander the Great and therefore dealt more extensively with his life than Caesar's."

After Sam poured the fourth glass of champagne, Ina took a sip, then moved closer on the settee. She was getting tipsy.

"You know, you're a very handsome man," she said.

"You're a beautiful woman."

For a long moment, they peered into one another's eyes, then she set aside the champagne glass, took his face in both hands, and kissed him on the lips. It was a long, passionate kiss. She held it for several seconds, then broke it.

"Come!" she said. "I wish to know you better. Would you remove my shoes?"

Sam knelt on the floor, lifted the hem of her calico dress and slipped off her shoes. She had dainty little white feet.

"Will you carry them?" she said.

Sam took her shoes in hand, then Ina stood up.

"Let's go upstairs," she said,

Moments later, carrying Ina's shoes in one hand and holding her arm with the other, they started up the spiral staircase. Once they were safely locked in her bedroom, there was more kissing and fondling, then each removed the other's clothing. Once naked, Sam pulled back the covers and crawled into bed. Seconds later, Ina was beside him.

That night, Sam described the experience in his journal.

January 6, 1865 *After joining our bodies together, we lay naked in the brass bed, stroking and preening one another's bodies. That night, I learned, for the first time, to feel comfortable with my nakedness in the presence of a woman. Never before had I felt that peculiar sort of freedom in my nakedness. That was my jealous down-home upbringing trying to tell me that I wasn't worthy of a woman who was beautiful, intelligent, literate and knowledgeable about the ways of the world. From the first kiss, she had me locked in like a hungry hawk after a rabbit. And I was a more than a willing victim. My intoxication with her was such that I threw all caution to the wind. I gave no margin to the thought that I might contract a disease or impregnate her. My singular interest was the temptation that lay in front of me. I was under the covers before she was.*

***

A month passed. On a cold afternoon in early February, Sam returned to the Queen Anne to discover he had received a return letter from Orion.

February 8, 1865
My Dear Sammy:
My life has undergone several drastic changes since we last spoke.
After the Nevada territory became the thirty-sixth state last October, my appointment ended and I entered the general election as a candidate for the state's Secretary of State position.
In the election, I took a strong position against alcohol and it cost me the election.
Shortly after losing the election, Mary and I returned briefly to Hannibal, then relocated to Keokuk, Iowa, where I have been operating a printing business for the past three months.
I am currently engaged in writing my memoirs and now have 300 pages completed and another 200 proposed by outline.
Do you know influential people in the publishing business who can assist me in finding publication for my work once it is finished?
Hoping all is well with you.
Awaiting your reply.
Your brother,
Orion

That afternoon, Sam penned a reply.

My Dear Brother:
Congratulations on your efforts.
Once finished with your grand opus, prepare a readable manuscript and remit to me in care of the Queen Anne Hotel

in San Francisco.

I shall peruse it for my own benefit, then present it to the publishers I know both in San Francisco and back East.
Wishing you and yours the best of health and wealth.
Your brother,
Sammy.

***

The following Saturday night, Sam was back at Ina's mansion for another social function. Throughout the night, Ina was constantly at his side and all of the other guests could see from their body language they were lovers. This included Ambrose Bierce. At one point, when Sam went to the serving table for more champagne, Bierce sidled up to him.

"How did a cornpone hack like you ever win the heart of such a beautiful woman?"

"Quite simple. I'm handsome, intelligent and much taller than you."

"You're nothing but a country bumpkin. You don't deserve her."

"Your loss is my gain."

Bierce glared at him angrily, then turned and left the festivities. As Ina watched him take his coat and hat and leave, she approached Clemens.

"What happened to Ambrose?"

"As always, he's miffed about nothing."

***

Ten months passed. During that time, Clemens' star was on the rise as a man of letters in the city by the bay. The jumping frog story had not only been published throughout the States and in the East, but in Europe as well. His pieces in the *San Francisco Gazette*, making fun of San Francisco's mayor, exposing officers of the Grass Silver Mining Valley Company for bilking investors and his calls for fairer treatment of the Chinese in the city's courtrooms had won him a huge following. He was a correspondent for six different newspapers and the *Atlantic Monthly* and, as a speaker, he was in demand for social events. By Christmas of 1865, he was the toast of the town.

***

Meanwhile, his fling with Ina continued.

January 3, 1866 *For seven of the last ten nights, I have been with Ina in her bed putting my body together with hers. I have since realized that my life has been quite sheltered in such matters. To lie beside her is like standing in the shadow of Aphrodite or Helen of Troy. The feminine pulchritude she brings to the love nest is intoxicating. Only the second woman I had ever been with, she needed only a few nights to bring forth the furthermost reaches of my manhood. In retrospect, my sojourn with Laura Hawkins amounted to hardly more than child's play. We were two young puppies experimenting with our reproductive powers. In all surety, I can report that Ina was the first woman to bring forth the fullness of my manhood. I never imagined said manhood had so many different sides, so many disparate dimensions. Most of all, she brings forth the essence of the Bohemian, the freedom-loving gypsy inside me. It is irresistible.*

***

On the morning of January 12, 1866, Clemens received a heavy package in the mail. When he opened it, there were more than three hundred pages of Orion's autobiography. That night, he read it and, the following morning, penned a reply.

January 13, 1866
My Dear Brother:
It is a model autobiography.
Continue to develop your own character in the same gradual, inconspicuous way.
The reader, up to this time, may have his doubts about you, perhaps, but he can't say decidedly, "This writer is not such a simpleton as he has been letting on to be."
Keep your reader in that state of mind.

196

Stop re-writing. I saw places where re-writing had done formidable injury. Do not try to find those places or else you will mar them further by trying to better them.

I have penciled the manuscript in some places but see no need to make any criticisms or knock out anything.

Your brother,

Sammy

***

That afternoon, Sam dashed off a latter to his friend William Dean Howells to try and interest him in publishing portions of the autobiography.

January 13, 1866

My Dear Howells:

Some time ago, I told Orion to sit down and write his autobiography in a plain, simple truthful way.

He started in and I think the result is killingly entertaining; in parts absolutely delicious.

I'm mailing you 100 pages or so of the manuscript. Read it; keep it a secret and then tell me, if, after surplusage has been weeded out, you'll buy the stuff for the Atlantic *at the ordinary rates from unknown writers.*

Yours Ever,

Mark

***

On the night of January 14, 1866, an author's salon was held in the lecture hall at Brookstone's Literary Emporium, San Francisco's largest bookseller. In attendance were Clemens, present for his controversial articles in the *Gazette*, Ina to hawk her new book of poems, and Ambrose Bierce to promote his book, *The Devil's Dictionary*. The authors were seated at a table in front of the crowd with Harte serving as moderator.

When Harte introduced Sam as Mark Twain, some members of the audience applauded while others booed.

"You're the one that mocked our mayor," said one woman.

"You've been taking up for the slant-eyes," said a man. "You should be shot for supporting heathens."

"Quiet, please!" Harte said.

Once he took the podium, Clemens spoke at length about his love of San Francisco and thanked audience members for supporting him and his columns at the *Gazette*.

Once he was finished, Bierce spoke up.

"His columns represent more fiction than facts," he said. "Personally, I take each with a grain of salt."

Sam turned angrily to him.

"Fools like you fail to discern the difference between the two," he said.

Harte tried to bring calm.

"Gentlemen!" he said. "Please!"

Both Sam and Bierce, after exchanging angry glances, quietened down.

Upon introduction, Ina won a ripple of applause. She read her poem "After a Winter Rain" from her new book and asked audience members to buy it.

When Bierce was introduced, several members of the audience applauded. Then he proceeded to tout his new book, *The Devil's Dictionary*, as "a parody of wit relating the darker side of human nature."

Once finished, he received mild applause as well as boos.

As he started to return to his seat, Clemens spoke up.

"His book is little more than fodder for imbeciles."

Furiously, Bierce turned to him.

"Imbeciles such as yourself," Bierce said. "And the slut you've been consorting with."

Clemens froze at the words.

"What were those words?" he shouted.

Bierce turned to him and repeated the words, louder this time.

"Imbeciles such as yourself. And the slut you've been consorting with."

Clemens jumped angrily out of his chair. Bierce, who turned to see Clemens coming, tried to escape, but Sam was too fast, striking him first in the face with a hard right, then following with two quick blows to the head which sent Bierce to the floor.

For a moment, he sat on the floor, then raised himself to one elbow and put his hand to his mouth. Upon seeing the blood, he quickly arose to his feet, and he and Sam danced around with fists raised.

"Gentlemen! Gentlemen!" Harte shouted.

Quickly, Harte left the podium, rushed to the two combatants and grabbed Bierce's coat sleeve to try and separate them. Suddenly, a member of the audience grabbed Bret's shoulder, spun him around and delivered a right hand to his jaw. Harte went to the floor, then stood back up and began exchanging blows with the audience member who attacked him.

Pandemonium ensued as audience members who had earlier taken sides between Clemens and Bierce began fighting among themselves. Patrons threw chairs and books and fought with other attendees.

"Police! Police! Call the police!" someone shouted.

Twenty minutes later, when police arrived, the lecture hall at the bookstore was in shambles. Books, chairs and papers were strewn about the floor, a window was broken, a bookshelf had been toppled and the place was in total disarray. Once calm was restored, police arrested Harte, Bierce and Clemens and charged them with "disturbing the peace."

Early the following morning, Ina was at the jail. She paid $100 for both Sam and Bret's fines and $85 in property damages. Both men repaid her as soon as they were released.

***

That afternoon, back at the Queen Anne hotel, Sam and Bret had a surprise visitor. It was their old mining partner Steve Gillis.

"Steve!" Sam said. "How did you find us?"

"You boys are celebrities," he said.

Then he produced a copy of the *San Francisco Standard*, the *Gazette*'s cross-town rival. There was an illustration of Sam, Bret and Bierce on the front page. The headline read: "Authors arrested when Salon event becomes Riot."

Sam took the newspaper in hand and began reading out

loud.

"Three of the brightest stars in San Francisco's literary community were arrested and incarcerated last night after they initiated at violent brawl at a local bookstore…"

He burst out laughing, then turned back to Gillis.

"You're right, Steve," he said. "We are celebrities."

"Come on!" Steve said. "It's been awhile. Let's go celebrate."

"Where do you want to go?" Sam said.

"I found a new bar on Van Ness Street called the Weary Gentleman."

***

Thirty minutes later, the trio were seated at the bar at the Weary Gentleman Saloon on Van Ness Street. The bartender was a big man, six foot five with broad shoulders, a serious face and a drooping mustache.

"What'll you have?" he asked. "Make it snappy. I'm busy."

"That's not a very friendly attitude," Sam said.

"What do you want?"

Sam and Bret ordered beers and Steve ordered two shots of whiskey.

"That'll be three dollars."

"Can we pay when we're finished?"

"No! Cash up front! Now!"

Sam paid the bartender, then he turned to fetch their order. As he waited, Sam turned to another patron.

"What's the bartender's name?"

"Jim! 'Big Jim' Casey!"

"He's the rudest bartender I've ever encountered."

"That's Big Jim's way," the man said.

***

The following morning, Sam received a new letter from William Dean Howells, editor of the *Atlantic Monthly*.

January 16, 1866

My Dear Samuel:

Today, it came to my attention that several prominent New Yorkers, including Rev. Henry Ward Beecher, are planning a three-month pleasure excursion to the Holy Land this next summer aboard the steamship the Quaker City.

Trip will begin on June 1 and return to New York in November.

The steamer fare is $1250 plus another $500 for tour guides during the land portions of the excursion.

If you will pay $500 for the guides, the Atlantic Monthly *will foot the bill for your passage if you promise to send regular dispatches back to New York for publication.*

Please remit your reply as soon as possible as space for the excursion is limited.

Yours,
William Dean Howells

Upon reading the letter, Clemens quickly penned a reply with three short words: "Count me in!"

***

That night, Sam and Steve were back at the Weary Gentleman Saloon. Big Jim Casey, the bartender who had been so rude during the last visit, was on duty. Only moments after they had their drinks, there was a clamor of shouts and loud cursing at the end of the bar. They turned to see Big Jim cursing and grasping the shirt of one of the patrons.

"Who do you think you're talking to?" Big Jim said.

"You! You son of a whore!" the smaller man said.

With that, Big Jim released his grip, stepped around the bar and attacked the smaller man. The two fell to the floor and ended up with Big Jim atop the smaller man, slamming him again and again in the face with his fists. For several moments, other bar patrons watched the one-sided fight. Finally, Steve, feeling the smaller man had had enough, jumped off the bar stool, grabbed Big Jim's shoulders and pulled him off the smaller man.

The bartender turned and glared at Steve.

"Now it's your turn," he said.

Then he started for Steve. Steve was smaller, but faster, and dodged as Big Jim charged. Then, when he charged a second time, Steve stepped aside, grabbed a beer pitcher from the bar and slammed it into the bartender's head. Shards of broken glass flew around the barroom as Big Jim fell to the floor. For a long moment, quietness reigned, then one of the patrons went to the bartender.

"He's not getting up," said the man.

"We better get him to the hospital," said another patron.

***

The following morning, Sam received an urgent letter from Orion's wife.

January 3, 1866
Dear Samuel:
Something truly tragic has befallen Orion. I fear to tell you the true nature of my suspicions.
Can you send money? We are in terrible financial straits.
Can you come and visit? I know the distance is far, but your brother's life may depend on it.
Perhaps your presence can bring about some improvements in him and his health. As you know, there is no one on this earth he has more respect for than you.
Please forgive me for this desperate plea, but I have no other alternative.
Sincerely,
Mary Clemens

That afternoon, Sam sent a bank draft for $100 to Orion's Keokuk, Iowa address with a note explaining he would make arrangements to visit as soon as possible.

***

On Monday, three days after the incident at the Weary Gentleman, Big Jim Casey died in the hospital. That afternoon,

Steve Gillis was arrested and charged with murder. Sam visited him at the jail.

"They've charged me with murder," Gillis said. "Can you post my bail?"

"How much is it?"

"Five thousand dollars."

"That's a lot of money," Sam said. "Will you pay me back?"

"You know I will."

"If you skip town and I have to pay, it will wipe me out financially."

"Sam, I would never do something like that."

Clemens paused and shook his head undecidedly.

"Sam! You know I have always stuck by my word."

"You have, Steve! I believe in you. I'll sign your bail bond."

"I'm much obliged, Sam!"

***

A month passed. On February 19, 1866, two days before Steve's murder trial was scheduled, Sam went to McCurdy's boarding house on Van Ness Street to visit him. When he went to Steve's room and knocked, there was no answer. Then he went downstairs to the landlord's office.

"Steve Gillis?" the landlord said. "He moved out day before yesterday."

"Did he say where he was going?"

"Back to Oklahoma."

Sam took a deep breath.

Now he knew he was in trouble. It was time for drastic action.

***

February 20, 1866 *I am leaving San Francisco without a farewell to Ina. The truth is I am incapable of saying farewell to such a remarkable woman. There were too many nights of carnal pleasure, such that I would not commit an act which casts shadow on the glory of those memories. Despite my shortcomings, I feel confident her heart will not remain broken for too long. Someday soon, another young, hungry author will step into her life to seek out her literary wisdom. She will take him into her study and show him her signed copy of Rousseau's* French Revolution, *tell him he brings out her mirth, then, noting her tiredness, she will ask him to remove her shoes. Finally, arm in arm, with him carrying the shoes, they will go up the stairs to her bedroom. And the circle shall be recreated once more, this time with a different man.*

The following morning, a full two days before Steve's murder trial was scheduled to begin, Clemens was on a stagecoach bound for Keokuk, Iowa.

13
Death of Orion

Sam's journey back east to Keokuk, Iowa required a total of eight days. The first leg was a four-day stagecoach ride from San Francisco to Ogden, Utah, the latest terminus of the new transcontinental railroad. There he had a three-day train ride to Council Bluffs, Iowa, then another short stagecoach journey to Keokuk. Upon arrival, Sam took a cab carriage to Orion's home on Magnolia Avenue in the heart of town. As he emerged from the carriage, he saw Mary, Orion's wife, and their daughter, five-year-old Jennie, waiting to greet him.

"Sammy!" Mary said, rushing off the porch, then running to hug him. "I'm so happy you're here."

"Uncle Sam!" little Jennie squealed, running to hug and kiss him.

Once inside, Mary made a fresh pot of coffee and, while Jennie went out to play, Sam and Mary chatted at the kitchen table.

"Something terrible has befallen Orion," she began. "He has become another person, someone woefully different from the man I married. I fear...." She hesitated before she said the words. "I fear his mind is fading away. Oftentimes, he doesn't recognize me and imagines he is still in Nevada performing his duties as secretary."

"Where is he now?"

"He's in our bedroom sound asleep," she said. "Let's not disturb him."

"Can I have some vittles?" Sam said. "I've had a long journey."

"All I can offer is some sow belly and green beans."

"That's all you have?"

She nodded sadly.

Sam studied her for a moment, then arose from his chair, went to the pantry and peered inside.

"The cupboard is bare," he said. "No cornmeal for cornbread, no flour for biscuits, not even fatback for cooking?"

She nodded sadly.

"Come along," Sam said. "We're going shopping. Bring little Jennie."

***

An hour later, Sam, Mary and Jennie returned to the Clemens home, their arms filled with grocery bags. Over the next hour, Mary whipped up a full meal of cured ham, green beans, boiled potatoes, a large pone of cornbread and lemon pie for dessert. Once the meal was prepared, Mary and Sam were seated at the table ready to eat.

"Can you get Orion now?" Sam said.

Mary got up from the table and went into the bedroom.

Moments later, Orion appeared.

Seeing Sam, he smiled and rushed forward.

"Sammy!" he said, shaking Sam's hand and hugging him. "So happy to see you."

He took a seat at the table.

"Did your editor friend hearken to my manuscript?"

"Oh yes!" Sam replied. "He felt it was a model autobiography and predicted it would soon find a publisher."

"Does the publisher want to buy it outright or pay royalties?"

"He has not yet addressed that question."

Sam watched as Mary dipped Orion a plate of baked ham, green beans, potatoes and cornbread, then set it before him.

"Many years of hard labor went into the manuscript," Orion continued. "I trust there is something to be gained."

"The instant I have his answer, I will notify you."

That seemed to satisfy Orion.

Moments later, after Sam had served his plate, the group began to eat. As Sam sliced off a huge bite of ham and put into his mouth, Orion took a drink of milk, then a bite of cornbread. For a moment, he peered at the half-eaten piece of cornbread, then crumbled it up in his hands and sprinkled the crumbs over his head. The majority of the pieces fell on the table and to the floor. A few small pieces lodged in his eyebrows.

Sam, trying not to appear shocked, looked at Mary.

She continued eating, pretending not to notice.

"Father!" Jennie said. "Why are you dropping your cornbread over your head?"

Orion did not hear.

Sam tried to change the subject.

"Have you received any word from Mother?" he said.

Again, seeming not to hear, Orion suddenly jumped up from the table and began speaking loudly and gesticulating wildly.

"I have told you ranchers no water rights shall be yours until you pay the tax levies on the land. The legislature, in bill number 1411, made it perfectly plain that water rights would be rescinded to all parties who evaded the previous year's taxes. No paid taxes, no water rights!"

Little Jennie looked to her mother.

"Mama, what is Father talking about?"

"Shhhhh!" the mother said.

For several minutes, Orion continued to rant, directing his comments at unseen personages while the others ate quietly.

Finally, Sam spoke up.

"Orion, sit down and eat your vittles," he said.

Suddenly, Orion stopped as if he remembered where he was.

"Father!" Jennie said. "Why are you carrying on so?"

"I must persuade these thieving ranchers they should pay their taxes if they expect to receive government services."

"Oh!" the five-year-old said, as if she understood.

"Orion, sit down and eat your vittles," Sam said again.

For a moment, Orion peered at his brother. Then, seemingly calmer, he reseated himself at the table and began to eat again.

"Did your editor friend like my manuscript?"

"Haven't we already discussed this?"

"Does he want to buy the manuscript outright or pay royalties?"

Sam, seeing it was some sort of game, played along.

"I shall inform you once I have his answer."

A long silence at the table.

Mary began to cry softly.

"Mommy, why are you crying?"

"Hush up and eat your green beans," the mother replied.

***

That afternoon, Sam and Orion were sitting in the swing in the family garden at the rear of the house.

"With great fondness, I remember our journey across the plains," Sam said. "The Indian attack. The robbery. The jackass rabbits and sagebrush."

Orion peered at his brother for a long moment.

"Indian attack?" he said. "You mean the massacre at Apache junction?"

"No, the one on the stagecoach when we were in Wyoming. Remember the sociable heifer that killed the Indians?"

Orion didn't hear; he was lost in his own world.

A long silence.

Suddenly, Orion, launched into another round of senseless babble.

"Papa took Henry to the woodshed this afternoon for turning over the pee pot. You could have heard him bawling three counties away. The louder he yelled, the more Papa poured it on."

He stopped. Once again, all was quiet.

Sam, at the end of his patience, arose from the swing, turned to his brother and grasped him by the shoulders. Then, staring angrily into his face, he began to shake his brother.

"Orion! Orion!" he shouted. "Listen to me! I am Sam! You are Orion! There are no Indians. No attacks. Our father is long dead. Wake up!"

Then, still holding his brother's shoulders, Sam peered into his eyes. He saw only the blank stare he had seen earlier at the table.

"Come with me," Sam said. "Let's go inside."

Moments later, Sam was escorting Orion into the house. Mary met them at the door, then led them into the bedroom where she put Orion into bed.

"Should we call the authorities?" she asked.

"Oh, no, their first answer would be the asylum for the mentally disturbed. Let's keep him calm and humor him."

That night, Mary made a bed for Sam in the spare bedroom. Before he went to sleep, he took several sips of whiskey from a bottle Mary found in the closet, then drifted off to sleep.

*****

The following morning, Sam received a letter from Howells. Before he opened it, he noticed it had first been sent to the Queen Anne Hotel in San Francisco, then to the Keokuk, Iowa address.

February 12, 1866
My Dear Clemens:
I have read your brother's autobiography with close and painful interest. It wrung my heart, and I felt haggard after I had finished it.

The best touches are those passages which make the reader acquainted with you; and they will be valuable material hereafter, but the writer has laid his soul far too bare.

The material is shocking and downright vulgar in its content and I cannot risk such material in the Atlantic.

If you print it anywhere, I hope you won't let your love of the naked truth prevent you from striking out some of the most intimate pages.

Don't let anyone else ever see those passages about your father's autopsy. The light he sheds on your father's character is most pathetic.

Yours ever,
W. D. Howells

*****

March 1,1866 *I fear I am my brother's keeper, whether it be through moral choice or familial imperative. Since earliest childhood, Orion has been the foundation of my existence, the guiding beacon of wisdom and affection which has sustained me; in truth, Orion is the nearest figure to a father I ever possessed. Forthwith, I have ascertained that his mental capacities have become severely diminished and he can neither maintain the lives of his family members or his own. I shall endeavor, within all means available, to assist my brother and his family in their time of desperate need. I have not the heart to inform him that his so-called "memoirs" represent a bucket of vulgar garbage.*

***

Early the following morning, Sam was awakened by a knock on the door. It was Mary.

"Sam!" she said. "Wake up! Wake up! Orion is gone."

Quickly, Sam was out of bed. Once he was dressed, he and Mary made a thorough search of the premises. Orion was nowhere to be seen.

Sam turned to Mary.

"Where could he have gone?"

"I have no earthly idea."

An hour later, Sam was at the local sheriff's office and reported Orion missing. Immediately, the sheriff organized a search party and the group began scouring the woods, the rivers and the streets of the town. Late that afternoon, the search party discovered Orion asleep on the banks of a small creek not more than a mile from the home. Weak, hungry and coughing, he staggered to his feet.

"I wish to go home," he said.

"We've got to get you to a doctor," Sam said.

Moments later, Sam and Mary were escorting Orion up the creek bank to a waiting carriage when the sheriff pulled them aside for some questions.

"Has he wandered off like this before?" the sheriff asked.

"No! Never!" Mary said.

"He is not of sound mind," the sheriff said. "He should be in the asylum in Des Moines."

"We're not ready to do that," Sam said. "We would like to take custody of him and return home."

"You could well be out chasing after him again tomorrow," the sheriff said.

"We shall take our chances," Sam said. "We need to get him home and get some medical attention for him."

He turned to Mary.

"Can you go and fetch the doctor?"

"Can you pay for the services?"

"I can."

***

Thirty minutes later, Mary arrived back at the Clemens home with Dr. Tom Henderson, a youngish man with a shock of black hair and glasses. Immediately, he went into Orion's bedroom alone. Moments later, he returned.

"He has a case of the croup since he was exposed to the elements last night," the doctor said. "He has a temperature and his lungs are congested. Keep him warm and feed him plenty of soup."

With that, Dr. Henderson withdrew a bottle of pills, handed them to Mary, then turned to leave.

"May I have a private conversation with you?" Sam said.

"Absolutely."

Moments later, Sam and the physician were outside the bedroom, out of Mary's earshot.

"Lately," Sam began, "my brother has been acting strangely. He has delusions and suddenly begins ranting about subjects which have no bearing on matters at hand. His memory fades in and out…"

The doctor interrupted.

"Does he have the pox?"

"The pox?"

"Syphilis."

Sam stopped at the word.

"Not that I am aware of," he said finally.

"There is obvious mental derangement," the doctor said. "With those particular symptoms, that's the first illness that comes to mind."

Again, Dr. Henderson turned to go.

"Is it your intention to contact the authorities?" Sam said.

"He is your brother, not mine," the doctor replied. "You are his keeper, not I. Be certain that he takes his medicine."

***

That night, Sam and Mary kept a vigil at Orion's bedside. All through the night, Orion thrashed about the bed, one minute ranting about the legislator who refused to change his vote on the Washoe basin redistricting, then swearing revenge on the Indians who massacred three families at Desert Springs. Finally, in the early morning, he grew quiet and appeared to be sleeping soundly.

***

The next morning, Sam was sound asleep when he heard loud rapping again on his bedroom door. It was Mary.

"Sam! Come quick! Orion won't wake up!

Sam, in his bedclothes, rushed into Orion's bedroom. His eyes were open, staring straight up at the ceiling. Sam put his fingers under his brother's nostrils, then shook his head.

"Shall I fetch the doctor?" Mary asked.

"The doctor can offer no relief," Sam said. "He passed away in his sleep."

Instantly, Mary broke into heart-rending sobs.

Sam embraced her and held her protectively for several minutes.

"I'm sorry," he said again and again.

Finally, after several moments, Mary was calm again.

"Will you close out his affairs?" she said. "That's the way he always said he wanted it."

"I shall. What will become of you and little Jennie?"

"We will take the train and return to Hannibal to live with my parents."

"Will you be able to finance your trip?" Sam asked.

"No!"

"I shall attend to it," Sam said.

***

Late that afternoon, the owner of the local funeral parlor arrived at the Clemens home. With Sam's help, they loaded Orion's body into a waiting wagon hearse.

The undertaker then took a seat and turned to Sam.

"Can you come to the mortuary and sign some official documents?"

"I shall be happy to," Sam said. "I wish to have an autopsy performed. Can you assist with that?"

"I can speak to the coroner on your behalf. His office is three doors down from the mortuary."

***

Five days later, Orion was buried at White Springs Church, the oldest and largest Baptist Church in Lee County, Iowa. In attendance were Orion's friends, business associates and the entire living Clemens family. This included mother Jane, sister Pamela, her husband William and their daughter Annie, who had all arrived from St. Louis. After eulogies by Orion's business partner and Mary's uncle, eight pallbearers removed the coffin from the church and delivered it to the nearby cemetery. As the entire Clemens family gathered themselves around to pay respects to Orion one final time, thirty-one-year-old Samuel Langhorne Clemens wept like a little child.

March 5, 1866 *Today, at Orion's funeral, the floodgates of my sorrow were lifted wide as I watched the workmen lowering his body into the cold, black earth. Orion's passing represents the loss of the only father figure I have ever known. My own father had no time for me. It was Orion who sought out the remedy for my childhood illness; it was he who saved the family with his small printing press when our father took a powder; Orion instigated my entry into the newspaper industry and launched my adventures into the wilds of sagebrush country. Now that mentor, instigator, and fellow adventurer is no longer walking the face of this earth.*

***

The following morning, at the train station, Sam saw off Mary and little Jennie for their trip to Hannibal.

"I'm grateful for all the things you have done," Mary said. "I truly thank God for your presence."

"I'm happy to assist," Sam said. "I shall contact the family solicitor to oversee the sale of the home and the business. Rest assured that all of the proceeds shall come to you."

"You have my total confidence," Mary said. "You have my parents' address."

With that, Sam hugged the mother and daughter, then watched as they boarded the cab carriage which would take them to the train station in downtown Keokuk.

***

That afternoon, alone in the family home, Sam went into Orion's study and began rummaging through his papers. There, on the top of the stack, he found portions of Orion's autobiography. Interested, he withdrew several pages and began reading. He wanted to prove to himself that his brother's writing was as dreadful as Howells had concluded.

"As she pulled away the wrappers enveloping those melon-like white lilies, my manly need grew with gigantic proportions. Quickly, I was unclothed and, as I slipped under the covers..."

Sam shook his head, then glanced at another page.

"Our copulation was so violent, so vicious, so unseemly that a casual observer would have been unable to discern whether we were engaged in carnal embracement or fighting to the death."

Disgusted, he turned to still another page.

"Upon fulfillment, she began to groan intermittently and call my name again and again. 'Oh, Orion! Orion! Orion!' she screamed. Once quiet, she rested her naked body on mine and we…"

With that, Sam had had enough. Quickly, he threw the pages aside, then went to the fireplace and built a fire. Then, he went around the room, gathering and throwing anything that looked like a part of the manuscript into the roaring fire.

***

The following morning, Sam went to the Lee County Coroner's office to learn the autopsy results, but was informed that the coroner was not available. Then, he went back across town to the office of Orion's family solicitor and made arrangements to sell Orion's family home and the printing business. When he returned to the home, there was a new letter from Howells.

February 27, 1866
My Dear Sam:
This letter is to inform you that all of the machinery for your excursion with the "pilgrims" to the Holy Land next summer has been set into motion.
Yesterday, on your behalf, I booked passage and delivered a deposit for said passage on the steamship the Quaker City *for your grand adventure.*
It would be of great assistance if you could arrive in New York a week before the excursion begins so that we may discuss our plans for articles in the Atlantic Monthly.
Yours, as always,
W.D. Howells

***

That afternoon, Sam returned to the coroner's office. This time, when Sam asked, the coroner appeared.

"Is the autopsy complete?" Sam asked.

"It is."

"What was the cause of death?"

The coroner studied Sam for a long moment.

"Are you certain you wish to know?" he said finally.

"I am certain."

"He died from an advanced case of syphilis."

Sam took a deep breath.

"I suspected as much," he said. "Does that account for the memory loss and illogical behavior of his final days?"

"It does."

"I'm obliged to you for your work."

"It is my official duty," the coroner said.

Satisfied, Sam turned and left the office.

***

March 7, 1866 *The coroner's conclusion did not shake my expectations. Therein lies an important lesson for me. Today, I vow to never again have carnal knowledge of a woman who is not my wedded wife. The risk is too great. I shall not allow the fate which befell my father and brother to perch upon my shoulder. Rousseau admitted to masturbation. I fear I shall be obliged to confess likewise. Perhaps the hour has arrived for this unwashed, ill-mannered, wise-cracking no-count from Hannibal, Missouri to look for a young filly as a potential mate.*

14
Innocents Abroad

A month later, in April of 1866, Sam found himself in the deep South cruising up and down the Mississippi River gathering material for his *Life on the Mississippi* book. Over the next ten months, he visited his old haunts—Hannibal, St. Louis, Baton Rouge and New Orleans—and searched out old friends and colleagues. He found Captain Horace Bixby, now an old man, in a retirement home in Memphis. Tom Dempsey, the first mate on the USS *Pennsylvania* when Henry died, had an insurance company in Starkville, Mississippi. There were revisits to the old vessels he had piloted, the *A.T. Lacey,* the *City of Memphis* and the *Mississippi Queen.* All the while, he was making notes, rehashing old memories and renewing friendships with former boatmen he had known during his piloting years. In late May of 1867, when he boarded the train to New York for his adventure with the "pilgrims," *Life on the Mississippi* was almost half-written.

***

On the afternoon of May 29, 1867, when Sam arrived in New York City for his grand excursion with the so-called "pilgrims," he was met at Grand Central Station by William Dean Howells. At age 31, Howells was a stocky, heavy-set man with a round face, kind eyes and a drooping mustache. Once Sam had retrieved his luggage, they hailed a cab carriage to take them to Sam's favorite New York hotel, the St. Nicholas on Broadway between Broome and Spring streets. As they rode, Howells detailed the upcoming journey.

"It's a religious excursion to Europe and the Holy Land," he began. "It includes France, Italy, Sicily, Turkey, the Holy Land, Egypt and Spain. All those aboard are devout Christians making the journey to confirm their faith."

"As you know, I don't put much stock in religion."

"You don't have to let the other passengers know that," Howells said. "Just behave yourself. Pretend to be a good Christian for once in your life. There's going to be a bevy of top-notch celebrities on board."

"Like who?"

"General Sherman, Henry Ward Beecher, the Drummer boy of the Rappahannock...."

"Henry Ward Beecher?" Sam interrupted. "That pious old windbag! Preaching fire and damnation to all who will listen."

"Sam, he's the most respected minister in New England and the organizer of the excursion. Now don't go ruffling feathers. This is a magnificent opportunity for you. There should be plenty of fodder for a travel book as well as some lifestyle pieces for the *Atlantic Monthly*."

"You are aware the *Atlantic* is not exclusive for my dispatches," Sam said. "I also have agreements with the *Alta* in San Francisco and the *Herald* and *Tribune* in New York."

"I'm aware of that," Howells said impatiently, "but I was hoping, once the excursion is over, you would allow me to put all the dispatches together and edit the material for a book."

"Agreed!" Clemens said.

Moments later, the cab carriage arrived under the portico at the St. Nicholas Hotel. As Sam stood up to exit the carriage, Howells had some parting words.

"We're meeting Captain Duncan onboard the *Quaker City* tomorrow. All passengers must be approved by him."

"Approved by the captain? My fare has already been paid. What else does he want?"

"The captain reserves the right to interview each and every one of his prospective passengers. That's his policy."

"All right! All right!"

"Two p.m. tomorrow. Pier 141."

***

The following afternoon, after a few drinks at the hotel bar, Clemens took a cab carriage across town and met Howells at New York Harbor. It was the first time either of them had seen the mighty steamboat the *Quaker City*. A vessel of eighteen hundred tons and a top speed of ten knots, she boasted a length of 256 feet with steam-driven sidewheels and auxiliary sails. Before becoming outfitted as a tourist vessel, the ship had been used by the Union Navy during the waning years of the Civil War to enforce Union blockades at Confederate ports.

Before boarding, Howells turned to Sam.

"Have you been drinking?"

"I had a few shots in the hotel saloon."

Howells shook his head with disapproval.

"Remember, he's a very religious man. Don't go stirring up mischief."

Moments later, after presenting identification, both men boarded the ship and, after scrambling up a flight of stairs to the upper deck, went into the captain's cabin. Charles Duncan was a graying, fiftyish man with a bearded, jowly face and a noticeable paunch.

After introductions, the captain asked that he and Clemens be left alone. Once Howells was gone, the captain wasted no time coming to the point.

"Mr. Clemens, are you a man of God?"

"What exactly do you mean by that?"

"Has your soul been saved from the fires of hell by the graces of God?"

"Not to my knowledge. Oftentimes, it's all I can do to save myself from a bad case of heartburn after a full meal."

Sam laughed.

The captain peered sternly at Sam.

"This is not a laughing matter," the captain said.

Moments later, he spoke again.

"Are you familiar with the famous Biblical passage John 3:16?"

"I heard it from my mother a total of 1,413 times. For breakfast each morning, I got fried eggs, hard tack biscuits, sow belly and three helpings of John 3:16."

The captain peered warily at Sam.

"Are you aware that all passengers on this excursion must be God-fearing men who are well-versed in the teachings of our Lord and Savior Jesus Christ?"

"Sir, I am a writer, a scribe, a journalist, a man of letters and a mealy-mouthed scoundrel. If other men seek to have their souls cleansed by some supernatural entity beyond this known world, then that is their affair, their aspirations… not mine."

The captain's face screwed up in irritation.

"Every day," the captain replied, "I put my faith in great God almighty and He guides me to good health, wealth and happiness."

"If your faith is so propitious, perhaps you should ask God to reduce that great wad of paunch at your beltline?"

The captain looked down at his belly, touched it and turned back to Sam.

"Well… never have I been so insulted in such a short period."

"You should ready yourself for all assaults," Sam said.

A long pause.

Finally, the captain, looking very unhappy, cleared his throat.

"This interview is at an end," he said. "Send your sponsor back in."

Sam chuckled, then got up and went back outside.

"He wants to talk to you," Sam said.

Howells went back inside. After he had been inside for several moments, he returned. His face was filled with livid anger.

"God dammit, Sam! You've ruined it! You're not approved!"

"What did he say?"

"He said you smelled of John Barleycorn. He said you were rude and obnoxious. He said he refused to take an infidel on a trip to the Holy Land."

"Did you tell him my fare was already paid?"

"He said the sum shall be refunded."

Suddenly, Sam stopped and peered seriously at Howells.

"Holy Christ! So, I'm not going on the excursion?"

"That's right."

"What are we going to do?"

A pause.

"I'm not sure," Howells said finally. "Let me contemplate the matter. I'll return tomorrow and try to arrange a second interview."

"That old bastard!"

***

The following morning, Howells arrived back at the St. Nicholas Hotel.

"I spoke with Captain Duncan again. He has relented somewhat and agreed to a second interview. Can you be at the docks at 3 p.m. this afternoon?"

Sam didn't answer at first.

"Do you want to go on this trip?" Howells said.

"Of course," Sam said, "but I didn't realize it would take an act of Congress to board the ship."

"You've got to play along with the rules."

Sam took a deep breath.

"Very well!" he said. "I'll give it another go."

"Will you humor him this time?"

"Yes! Yes!"

"And act like a devoted child of God?"

"Yeah! Yeah!" Sam said impatiently. "I'll give him the full treatment."

***

Later that afternoon, Howells and Sam were back at Captain Duncan's cabin aboard the *Quaker City*. As before, Howells went in first, then returned and ordered Sam to enter.

"I seldom grant second interviews for prospective passengers," the captain began, "but I've made an exception this time."

"Praise the Lord!" Sam said. "What questions do you have, sir?"

"Are you familiar with the Biblical quotation John 3:16?"

"Yes, sir! For God so loved the world that he gave his only begotten son, that whomever loved him shall not perish, but have everlasting life."

"Very good!"

"Praise the Lord!" Clemens said.

"Have you been baptized?"

"When I was a mere lad of only nine," Sam said wistfully, "the right Reverend Jeremiah Blevins cleansed my soul of all sins and transgressions in the shallows of Bear Creek in Hannibal, Missouri. It was the happiest day of my life."

Another pause.

"These are wholly different answers than I received yesterday."

"It was the John Barleycorn, sir. The ruin and damnation of all God-fearing men. Praise the Lord!"

The captain nodded his approval.

"Woe unto those who take strong drink," he replied, "for they shall not enter the kingdom of heaven. Isaiah 1:22."

"Amen!" Sam said.

"Do you enjoy singing the great gospel hymns? Rock of Ages? I'll Fly away? Amazing Grace?"

Sam started to sing.

"Rock of ages, cleft for me… Let me hide myself in thee… Let thy water and thy blood…"

The captain motioned for Sam to stop.

"Very good," the captain said. "I think that shall be sufficient. Thank you for your interview. You may send in your sponsor again."

Moments later, Sam was back outside.

"How'd it go?" Howells said.

"He has never witnessed a more devout Christian in his entire life."

Howells peered at him for a moment, then went back into the captain's office. Moments later, he returned. There was a smile on his face.

"Am I in?"

"Not quite," Howells said. "He was impressed with the second interview, but he wants you to demonstrate your Christian charity."

"Christian charity?"

"He wants us to make a small donation to have the ship's organ fixed and he insists you join the ship's gospel choir."

"How much is the small donation?"

"One hundred dollars."

Sam laughed.

"Sounds like a bribe to me."

"Perhaps it is, but it will get you on the excursion."

Sam reached for his wallet.

"Never mind," Howells said. "I'll shall attend to it."

***

So, Sam became an official protege of the so-called "New Pilgrims," a brave troupe of Christian devotees, mostly middle-class Midwesterners and well-heeled eastern aristocrats, determined to refortify their faith. Little did they know they would be immortalized beyond their wildest dreams when "The wild humorist from the Pacific Slope" was added to their passenger list.

***

June 6, 1867 *We leave tomorrow at 3 p.m. We have a fine side-wheeler at our disposal which should skim across the waves with the greatest of facility. We've got a crowd of tip-top people and shall have a jolly, sociable, homelike trip of it for the next six months. And then, if we all go to the bottom, I think we shall be fortunate. There is no unhappiness like the misery of sighting land again after a cheerful, careless voyage.*

***

On the night before the excursion was to begin, Sam went out on the town and threw a Washoe-style drinking binge with his editor friends at the *New York Tribune*. Finally, he flopped into bed at 2 a.m. The following afternoon, he made his way woozily, unsteadily, up the gangplank to the decks of the *Quaker City* while a ship's steward pulled his personal baggage behind them.

Some ten minutes later, Sam and the trailing steward arrived at his upper deck cabin and went inside. There, sitting by a window and reading, Clemens saw the person who was to be his cabin mate.

"I'm Sam Clemens," he said, offering his hand.

"Charles Langdon," the man said. "I hail from Elmira, New York."

Sam looked him up and down. Medium height with wheat-colored hair, he was twentyish, slim and had an overall well-kept appearance.

"What sort of work does your father do?" Sam asked.

"My father is Jervis Langdon," Charles said. "He is a coal magnate and one of the wealthiest men in the state of New York."

"I'm from Missouri myself," Sam said. "A small hamlet on the banks of the Mississippi called Hannibal."

Over the next twenty minutes, Sam and Charles made small talk about their past and hopes for the future. Finally, Charles got up to go.

"Shall we go to dinner tonight?" Charles said.

"Splendid idea."

***

That first night at dinner, Sam and Charles were seated among other journalists who would be dispatching articles back to state-side publications.

Across from Sam sat Mrs. Julia Newell, a thirtyish, dark-haired woman who hailed from Wisconsin. During the excursion, she would be sending dispatches back to her hometown newspaper, the *Janesville Gazette*.

"With great interest did I read your jumping frog story in the *Tribune*," Mrs. Newell said. "A delightful yarn which I passed on to my husband."

"It has been one of my most popular pieces."

"Since both of us shall be dispatching copy back to the States," Mrs. Newell continued, "Would you be interested in critiquing one another's articles? An objective eye can improve one's work."

Sam studied her for a moment.

"Splendid idea," Sam said finally. "I look forward to perusing your work."

Just after 10 p.m., the dinner came to an end and Sam and Charles returned to their cabin. The minute they walked in, Charles angrily threw off his tie and turned to Sam.

"My God, Sam!" he said. "Don't you know when to use a salad fork? Have you had no training in social graces? And those nose hairs, you've got to trim them. There is nothing worse than talking to someone while looking at their protruding nostril hair."

Clemens was taken aback at the sudden attack.

"I had never really noticed them," he said.

Then he strode across the room to a mirror and examined them.

"Yes," he said. "They could use a trim. I shall attend to that before we go out again."

"Further, you should learn to use a salad fork and a napkin. It's just good manners."

***

June 7, 1867 *This roommate of mine is a well-kept, prim and proper silver spooner; his face is pleasant enough; he has darting eyes like a cat, a well-trimmed mustache and is given to considerable pomp and circumstance. Rest assured this sort of lad has never squished his toes in river mud, went hungry or was whipped for turning over a pee pot. I also discern a certain uppity air he affects from time to time which lends itself to outright snobbery, but I shall hold my tongue.*

***

On June 8, 1867, after a one-day delay for high seas, the *Quaker City* fired up its boilers and pointed itself toward its first port of call, the Azores, off the coast of Spain. Once the excursion was underway, the final passenger list was a far cry from the original. Rev. Henry Ward Beecher, initial organizer of the trip, withdrew, noting that urgent religious duties required his attention. General William Tecumseh Sherman, he of "March to the Sea" fame, also dropped out, claiming the Indian wars compelled his presence on the western plains. The "Drummer Boy of the Rappahannock," a Union Civil war hero, also deserted after contacting a case of measles.

Over the next five days, passengers mixed, mingled and entertained themselves as best they could with the ship's recreational facilities as they steamed toward Europe. Charades proved to be popular as well as horse billiards, dominoes and ballroom dancing. Regarding the latter, Sam noted:

June 13, 1867 *The music was bad, but the dancing was infinitely worse. When the ship rolled to starboard, the whole platoon of dancers came charging down to starboard with it, and brought up en masse at the rail; when the ship rolled to port, dancers went floundering down to port with the same unanimity. Waltzers spun around precariously for a matter of fifteen seconds, then went scurrying down to the rail as if they meant to go overboard. The Virginia reel, as performed on board the* Quaker City, *had more genuine reel about it than any reel I ever saw before. We gave up dancing, finally.*

Another favorite recreation was mock trials.

June 14, 1867 *The defendant was accused of stealing an overcoat from stateroom No. 10. A judge was appointed; also clerks, a crier of the court, constables, sheriffs; counsel for the State and for the defendant; witnesses were subpoenaed, and a jury empaneled after much challenging. The witnesses were stupid and unreliable and contradictory, as witnesses always are. The counsel was eloquent, argumentative, and vindictively abusive of each other, as was characteristic and proper. The case was at last submitted and duly finished by the judge with an absurd decision and a ridiculous sentence.*

***

Over the first few days of the voyage, Sam and several other rowdy young male passengers formed a close-knit group which fellow travelers dubbed "the *Quaker City* nighthawks." Members included Sam, Charles and Dan Slote, a short, fat, fortyish owner of a New York millinery firm. Many nights, Sam would invite the other members to his and Charles's cabin where they would drink, play cards, smoke and swear until the wee hours of the morning. They quickly became known as the excursion's mischief makers and practical jokers.

On June 24, 1867, the *Quaker City* made a stop at Gibraltar just long enough for the "night hawks" to take a side trip to Tangiers, then move on to Marseilles, France where they boarded a train for Paris to see the Grand International Exhibition. America's contribution at the show was the new Cyrus McCormick reaper and the Elias Howe's sewing machine. After witnessing the risqué can-can at a Paris night club, Sam noted:

"I placed my hands before my eyes out of pure shame, but I peeked through my fingers."

***

A week later, Sam and his pious companions arrived in Milan, Italy, where he and the other "night hawks" decided to have a public bath. Sam lost no time making fun of Italians' lack of cleanliness.

July 3, 1867 *We had a bath in Milan in a public bath-house. Initially, they were going to put all three of us, me, Charles and Dan, in one bath-tub, but we objected. Each of us had an Italian farm on his back. We could have felt affluent if we had been officially surveyed and fenced in. We chose to have three bathtubs, and large ones—tubs suited to the dignity of aristocrats who had real estate. After we were stripped and had taken the first chilly dash, we discovered that haunting atrocity that has embittered our lives in so many cities and villages of Italy and France—there was no soap. I called. A woman answered, and I barely had time to throw myself against the door—she would have been in, in another second. I said: "Beware, woman! Go away from here—go away, now, or it will be the worse for you. I am an unprotected male, but I will preserve my honor at the peril of my life!"*

***

That night, back in their cabin, Sam waited while Charles groomed himself for dinner. As he waited, his eyes fell on an ivory miniature portrait of a young woman on Charles' bedside table.

"Who is that?

"That's my sister Olivia."

Sam picked up the portrait and examined it.

"She's a beautiful young woman."

"She's in a wheelchair."

"For what reason?"

"She was in an ice-skating accident when she was sixteen. Been partially paralyzed since."

"How old is she?"

"Turned twenty-two last month," Charles said, making one final stroke on his well-coiffed blonde hair.

Then he turned to Sam.

"Let's go to dinner."

Sam took one final glance at the portrait, then returned it to the bedside table.

***

After Milan, there were brief stops in Pisa, Perusia and Tuscany. In Florence, Sam poked fun at the Arno River, which had been described in the excursion prospectus as "the mighty Arno."

August 13, 1867 *After visiting the Ufizzi Gallery, we stopped and stood briefly on the bridge to admire the trickle of water they call the Arno. It is a popular pastime to admire the Arno, a great historical creek with four feet of water in the channel and some scows floating around. It would be a very plausible river if they would pump some water into it. They all call it a river, and they honestly think it is a river, do these dark and bloody Florentines. They even help out the delusion by building bridges over it. I do not see why they are too good to wade.*

***

In Venice, at the Doge's Palace, Sam's guide was a young black man, born to slave parents in South Carolina.

August 21, 1867 *The guide we had today is the only one we have had thus far who knows anything. He was born in South Carolina of slave parents. They came to Venice while he was an infant. He has grown up here. He is well-educated. He reads, writes, and speaks English, Italian, Spanish, and French, with perfect facility; is a worshipper of art and thoroughly conversant with it; knows the history of Venice by heart and never tires of talking of her illustrious career. He dresses better than any of us, I think, and is daintily polite. In Venice, Negroes are deemed as good as white people and so this man feels no desire to go back to his native land. His judgement is correct.*

***

That night at dinner, Mrs. Newell had some pointed criticism of his dispatch about the cleanliness of Italians.

"It is insulting," she said. "Travel pieces are meant to glorify and inform about a culture, not to demean and make comedic light."

"The dispatch was no more insulting than your diatribe about the snobbery of the French in Marseilles," Sam said. "You portrayed the entire nation as a bunch of pious, self-absorbed aristocrats."

"Totally untrue!" she shot back. "I hinted at the notion, but I never said the words outright."

"Read your dispatch again," Sam said. "Only then will you

get my meaning."

"Come along," she said. "We shall go to by cabin and read it together."

***

Ten minutes later, Clemens and Mrs. Newell were in her cabin reading her dispatch about the French in Marseilles. After rereading the piece, she turned to him thoughtfully.

"Your point is well-taken," she said. "Perhaps I was a bit harsher than I intended."

Satisfied, she returned the dispatch to a nearby sheaf of papers, then she turned back to Sam.

A long pause.

"You're a very handsome man, Mr. Clemens," she said, moving closer and placing her hand on his arm. "I would like to inform you that I have talents other than composing dispatches."

"What about your husband?" he said.

"He doesn't give a flip for me," she said, as her hand reached his thigh. "All he cares about is his damned newspaper."

Sam peered at her.

"Further," she continued, "what he doesn't know won't hurt him."

Sam smiled.

Mrs. Newell then stood up, took Sam's hand and started to the bed.

"Come!" she said. "I wish to show you my secondary talents."

Sam pulled his hand away.

"The hour is late," he said. "I must be going."

"Were my words offensive?"

"I must be going!" Sam said.

Then he turned and started for the door.

"Mr. Clemens!" she called after him. "Please don't go! Did I say something wrong?"

Sam didn't hear. He was already out the door.

***

In Rome, Clemens described the treatment of Jews. As always, he pulled no punches.

September 4, 1867 *Jews here are treated just like human beings, instead of dogs. They can work at any business they please; they can sell brand new goods if they want to; they can keep drug-stores; they can practice medicine among Christians; they can even shake hands with Christians if they choose; they can associate with them, just the same as one human being does with another human being; they don't have to stay shut up in one corner of the towns; they can live in any part of a town they like best; it is said they even have the privilege of buying land and houses, and owning them themselves, though I doubt that, myself; they never have had to run races naked through the public streets, against jackasses, to please the people in carnival time; a Jew is allowed to vote, hold office, yea, get up on a rostrum in the public street and express his opinion of the government if the government don't suit him!*

***

That night, after a day of sight-seeing in Rome, Sam and Charles were back in their cabin preparing for bed. As Sam pulled on his night shirt, he again noticed the portrait of Charles' sister on the bedside table. He picked it up and examined it.

"Does your sister have any suitors?" Sam asked.

"Not that I'm aware of," Charles said. "She's in a wheelchair."

"That doesn't mean she can't fall in love."

Charles shrugged.

Sam turned back to the portrait.

"Can I have this portrait," he said.

"Of course not! That's the only one I have."

"Once the trip is finished, may I come visit you and meet her?"

"If you like," Charles said, "but you must trim your nose hairs and learn to use a salad fork. She very meticulous about propriety."

Sam laughed.

"I would be pleased to meet her," he said, returning the portrait to the bedside table.

***

In mid-September, the *Quaker City* landed at Beirut, where Sam and other members of the Night Hawks decided their journey to the Holy Land would not be complete without a trip by pack train.

September 15, 1867. *In Syria, at the headwaters of the Jordan, a camel took charge of my overcoat and, while the tents were being pitched, he examined it with a critical eye; all over, with as much interest as if he had the idea of having one made like it; then, after he had done figuring on it as an article of apparel, he began to contemplate it as an article of diet.*

He put his foot on it and lifted one of the sleeves out with his teeth, and chewed and chewed at it, gradually taking it all in, and all the while, opening and closing his eyes in a kind of religious ecstasy as if he had never tasted anything as good as an overcoat before, in his life. Then he smacked his lips once or twice, and reached after the other sleeve. Next he tried the velvet collar, and smiled a smile of such contentment that it was plain to see he regarded that as the tastiest part of the garment. The tails went next, along with some percussion caps and cough candy and some fig-paste from Constantinople. Then, when the creature discovered paper manuscripts of my dispatches which had fallen out of the overcoat pocket, the camel began to consume them. Suddenly, the creature began to gag and gasp, and his eyes to stand out and his forelegs to spread, and, in the twinkling of an eye, he fell over as stiff as a carpenter's workbench and died a death of indescribable agony.

***

In early October, Sam and his pious companions landed in what is today modern Israel.

October 18, 1867 *Today, on the banks of the Sea of Galilee, while imagining Jesus preaching to the local fishermen, my fellow adventurers and I tried to barter for a ride on one of the local fishing boats. After an unreasonable price of two Napoleons was put forth, the "innocents" countered with an offer of only one. They were then shocked to see the fisherman turn around and sail off, leaving them stranded on the shore. Instantly, there was wailing and gnashing of teeth in the camp. We, who had dreamed all our lives of someday skimming over the sacred waters of Galilee and listening to the hallowed story in the whisperings of its waves, and had journeyed countless leagues to do so, had been left stranded because the fare was too high. Impertinent Mohammedan Arabs, to think such things of gentlemen of another faith!*

***

October 27, 1867 *Between the tender ages of fifteen and eighteen, I experienced my time of self-education by touring the country setting type and spending nights in libraries reading books. At the time, I had no knowledge as to how this vast plethora of information would benefit me. Today, when the tour guide mentioned Hammurabi and his famous legal code, I knew precisely who the famous Babylonian king was and his place in history. In Greece, when tour guides mentioned Diogenes, Plato or Alexander the Great, I knew precisely who these historical figures were. In Italy, as a result of my self-education, I was quite capable of framing Caesar, Leonardo, Cicero and Tacitus into the conversation. The days of my self-education prepared me for the dispatches I would compose over the course of this excursion. Somehow, destiny prepares you for your future without your realizing it at the moment the preparation is occurring.*

***

Over the next ten days, Sam and his pious companions completed the final leg of their excursion when they made stops at Malta and in Spain, stopping for visits in Valencia, Cartagena and Malaga. On the afternoon of November 5, the *Quaker City* steamed westward back through the straits of Gibraltar to begin the return trip across the Atlantic to New York.

***

Finally, on the cold wintry afternoon of November 12, 1867, the *Quaker City* steamed back into New York Harbor to a scene of total pandemonium. Despite the chilly weather, thousands of people—curiosity seekers, friends and families of passengers, newspaper reporters and well-wishers—had crowded on the pier to await its arrival. The dispatches from the journalists onboard and the subsequent newspaper articles had made the *Quaker City*—and the voyage—famous throughout the nation.

As the ship dropped anchor, Sam and Charles were at the railing on the promenade deck saying their final goodbyes.

"I have very much enjoyed my time with you on the excursion," Charles said. "You must come up to Elmira and visit me this next spring."

"I would be pleased," Sam said. "Hopefully, I can meet your sister."

"Do you have my address in Elmira?"

"I do. If you wish to contact me, I'll be at the St. Nicholas Hotel in New York."

"Very well," Charles said.

"One last thing," Sam said.

"What's that?"

Sam held up a letter.

"Will you give this to your sister?"

"What is it?"

"A note of introduction from yours truly."

"It shall be delivered," Charles said, taking the letter.

"Much obliged!" Sam said.

The two friends shook hands one final time. Then Sam watched as Charles, his bags in tow, turned and melted into the stream of passengers striding down the promenade deck to the gangplank.

Moments later, when Sam and his luggage appeared at the end on the gangplank, William Dean Howells, smiling ear to ear, was there to greet him.

"You're a hero!" he said, shaking Sam's hand and hugging him. "The whole world is saying your name. Your dispatches are the talk of the publishing community. You're going to be rich!"

Once Sam's luggage was loaded on the cab carriage, Howells rode with him to the St. Nicholas Hotel. Before he got out of the carriage, Howells turned to Sam.

"I had lunch with Elisha Bliss, owner of American Publishing last week. I told him about your *Quaker City* excursion. He is very interested in publishing a book about your adventures."

"I shall attend to it next week," Sam said.

15
Olivia

That first night back in New York, Sam settled into his fifth-floor room at the St. Nicholas Hotel and began making plans to sell the dispatches from the *Quaker City* excursion as a book. When he checked in that afternoon, he picked up a bundle of waiting mail at the desk, but promised himself he would wait until the morning to go through it. That night, free of the constant noise and swaying motion of the steamship, he got the first good night of restful sleep he had had in six months.

The following morning, after a hearty breakfast of fried eggs, grits, ham and biscuits in the hotel restaurant, he returned to his room and began sorting through his mail. One of the first letters he opened was from Elisha Bliss Jr., owner of American Publishing Company.

November 10, 1867
Dear Sam Clemens:
On November 5 past, William Deans Howells informed me of your plans to consolidate the letters from your Quaker City *excursion into a book.*

I feel such a project is worthwhile and American Publishing Company would like to have you get up a book for us. We think we see clearly that the book will sell; a humorous work—that is to say a work humorously inclined. The first thing then is.... will you make a book?

We can either buy the finished manuscript outright for $10,000 or pay you four percent royalty on each sale, whichever is your choosing.

Can you arrive at my office on the morning of Nov. 16 to discuss details?
Sincerely,
    Elisha Bliss Jr., publisher

***

Four days later, Sam was in Bliss's New York office negotiating a deal.

"I'm expecting a five percent royalty with a $2,500 advance," Clemens said.

"Sam, the most we have ever paid any author is four percent. We can't afford more than that. Printing costs are going up, delivery is becoming more expensive and staff wages are becoming higher and higher."

"That's my offer," Sam said. "Accept it or I shall take it elsewhere."

Bliss, a short-statured, fiftyish man with a balding head and glasses, hesitated before he answered.

"All right, Sam," he said finally. "I'm well aware of how popular your work is among readers. Let's draw up an agreement and I'll meet your offer."

Two hours later, when he left the office, Sam had signed a contract and had a bank draft for $2,500 in his pocket. The agreed upon deadline for delivery of the manuscript was July 1, 1868.

***

That afternoon, when he returned to the St. Nicholas Hotel, there was a new letter awaiting him. When he saw the Elmira, New York postmark, Charles' sister popped into his mind. Back in his room, he feverishly opened it.

November 14, 1867
Dear Mr. Samuel Clemens:
Initially, I wish to express my gratitude at your interest in becoming acquainted with me as a possible suitor.
I must tell you, at this juncture, I feel it would be unwise to

237

pursue such a course of action.

I have discussed your moral character with my brother Charles and he has reported to me that you are a most unchristian man; a man who smokes, swears, curses, imbibes intoxicating liquors and sees religion as a subject of contemptuous drollery.

In all honesty, I fear I never could or would love a man with such unwholesome qualities.

With this in mind, again permit me to express my gratitude for your interest, but I can see no future in a relationship between two personages as starkly different as you and I.

Sincerely,
Olivia Louise Langdon, a soldier for Christ.

Sam looked up from the letter, then threw it aside.

"Oh, the trials and travails of true love," he said to himself. "I shall not surrender so easily."

***

A week passed. On Thursday of the following week, Sam went to the offices of the *New York Tribune* to check his mail. When in New York, Clemens used the *Tribune* offices as a base of operations. As an ongoing correspondent, he had a desk in the office and would often drop by to say hello to George Ripley, his long-time friend and editor who handled his *Quaker City* dispatches.

"Sam!" Ripley called out when Clemens entered the office.

Ripley, a tall, late-thirtyish man with dark hair and a well-trimmed beard, arose from his desk and walked across the newsroom to shake Sam's hand.

"Our readers devoured the *Quaker City* letters," he began. "Circulation shot up twenty percent when the series began and has remained steady since. I understand you plan to compile the letters into a book."

"I have already struck a deal with American Publishing."

"Elisha Bliss! That old skinflint. How much is he offering?"

Sam explained the terms of the deal.

"Five percent!" Ripley said. "You must have twisted his arm."

"I did!" Sam said with a laugh, then he turned to the three letters on his desk. Two of the letters were advertisements from a harness shop and a dentist. The third was an odd-looking letter with a San Francisco postmark. Curious, he opened it.

November 19, 1867
Mr. Samuel Clemens:
Our company have been made aware that you intend to publish a book from the letters you dispatched to the California Alta during your Holy Land excursion.
We wish to remind you that the copyright to the letters which were published do not belong to you, but are the exclusive rights of the Alta publishing company.
Rest assured that any attempts to publish the letters without the express written approval of Alta Publishing Company will result in vigorous legal action against you.
Be forewarned in this matter!
Sincerely,
Albert S. Evans, editor-in-chief

Clemens looked up from the letter to Ripley.

"Great Caesar's ghost!" he said. "Those consarned thieves. They're trying to steal my work."

"Did you sign over the copyright to the Alta when you struck the deal?"

"Of course not."

"You must confer with the *Tribune* copyright attorney," Ripley said. "He'll know the most effective course of action."

"Will you introduce me?"

***

Two hours later, Sam was conferring with the *Tribune*'s in-house attorney about the Alta dilemma. The lawyer, one Harley Crutchfield, was a heavy-set man, early forties with a round, clean-shaven face and glasses.

"If the Alta publishes the letters," he said. "It's going

to take the bloom off any book you might publish on your own."

"So, what should I do?"

"You must take action in the local jurisdiction," Crutchfield said. "As long as there is 1,500 miles between you and them, they will try to take advantage at every turn."

"What do you suggest?"

"I'm going to contact my friend Louis Hendershot, a San Francisco copyright attorney. He will send a cease-and-desist order to California Alta. If they persist, he'll file an action against them."

"When will you contact your friend?"

"The letter will go out this afternoon."

***

Over the next few months, Sam and Howells worked day and night to compile a book from the *Quaker City* dispatches. Several times, while editing, Howells was harshly critical of Sam's words.

"Your prose tends to be too ribald," Howells said. "The range of your mind is such that you use certain words and venture into areas which some readers would consider ill-placed or outright ugly. It's bad taste to say Syrian women cover their faces with hajibs because they're ugly. Further, you should be more forgiving of the other pilgrims. Wit without vulgarity! That's what you want."

At first, Sam started by rewriting portions of the letters into original copy, but discovered it was far too time-consuming. Then he shifted from original composition to preparing line-edited versions of the Alta, *Tribune* and *Herald* dispatches. Again, this was too laborious. Finally, many pages of the manuscript were pasteups of the columns with revisions scrawled in the margins. It was a rag-tag approach to authorship, but Sam hoped it would suffice.

***

In early August of 1868, Sam received a letter from Charles

Langdon.

August 10, 1868
Dear Sammy:
*It would warm my heart to see you, to slap you on the back
and hear your laughter.*
*Will you pack your bags and pay me a visit in Elmira? You
can meet my family; we can entertain ourselves fishing,
hunting, doing some serious drinking and recalling our
exploits aboard the* Quaker City.
*Also, you can meet my sister. From a recent conversation,
I understand she is not happy with you. Be that as it may, the
two of us can knock back a few, check out the local ladies and
play some pool.*
If my sister wants to sulk, then we shall permit her to do so.
Awaiting your reply.
Sincerely,
Charley

That afternoon, Sam dashed off a letter notifying Charles
he would arrive in Elmira on the afternoon of August 21.

***

In the early morning hours of August 21, 1868, thirty-two-
year-old Sam Clemens boarded the Express Mail train from
mid-town Manhattan to Elmira in western New York state. It
was an uncomfortable seven-hour trip. A crowd of unruly
soldiers were on board and the middle-aged woman and her
daughter in his passenger compartment chattered endlessly
about their dogs. Late that afternoon, when he arrived in
Elmira, Charles was waiting at the platform.

"Sammy!" he said, offering his hand and hugging his old
friend. "Great to see you. Now perhaps I can have some
excitement in my life."

Fifteen minutes later, they were in a cab carriage en route
to the Langdon home. As they rode, Charles peered at the
yellow duster and the old battered straw hat Sam was wearing.

"Don't you have better clothes than that?"

"Oh yes. I have a fine, brand-new suit and hat in my bag. Nobody will recognize me when I present myself for dinner tonight."

"Will you kindly trim your nose hairs before we go to dinner?"

Sam smiled.

"As I said, you won't recognize me tonight," Sam said. "How is your sister faring?"

"As pious and headstrong as ever."

They rode quietly for a moment.

"As you know, she's in a wheelchair," Charles said. "For God's sake, don't try to assist her. She loves her independence. Can you remember?"

"I can."

Thirty minutes later, when the cab carriage pulled up in front of the Langdon home on Elmira's exclusive north side, Clemens entered a world like he had never seen before. The Langdon family home, an imposing, three-story structure surrounded by giant white oaks, occupied an entire block. Constructed of orange-red Flemish bricks, it featured French windows, matching white lions guarding the entrance and a shiny black metal roof complete with spires. Visitors had to pass through three separate automatic gates to get to the front door. It was the epitome of nineteenth-century architectural and technological elegance.

The family patriarch, Jervis Langdon, was a one-time country storekeeper who became a millionaire after cornering the coal market. At age 16, he was apprenticed to a wealthy merchant in Ithaca, where he learned the mercantile business. At age 23, he was running several stores and, after a few years, amassed sufficient capital to buy several hundred acres of Allegheny County pine-tree land, which turned out to be rich in coal deposits. This single happenstance fed the factory-fueled demand for weaponry and supplies throughout the Civil War and, ultimately, Langdon owned coal mines from Pennsylvania to Nova Scotia and a rail transport system to move the yield. Now, at age 61, he was a staunch abolitionist and a "conductor" on the Underground Railroad.

***

At dinner that night, Jervis was seated at the head of the table with Sam to his left. Henry, the Negro manservant charged with caring for Olivia, brought her into the dining room in a wheelchair; then, with the help of a cane, she made her way to the table and seated herself beside Sam. Mrs. Langdon and Charles were seated on the opposite side. Once the food was served, Jervis, who had a jowly face, long sideburns and a noticeable paunch, said a short blessing, and the group dug into a sumptuous meal of roast beef with green beans, mashed potatoes and all the trimmings.

After several moments, Jervis opened the table conversation.

"The New York state constitutional convention passed a new law last week that gives all citizens over the age of 18, both men and women, the right to vote," he said. "This could very well mean some sweeping changes in the upcoming election."

"It's not a moment too soon," said Mrs. Langdon, a late-fortyish woman with sad eyes and curly dark hair. "Women have been neglected in the state's electoral process for far too long.

"Amen!" Olivia said. "Women have just as much right to vote as men. Don't you agree, Mr. Clemens?"

"That's the new thinking," Sam said, "that women are equal to men. When I was growing up, I was taught that men should tend to affairs of business and politics while women were bound to home and family."

"Nonsense!" said Olivia. "Women are just as well-qualified for business and politics as any man. In fact, the world would be much better off if their leaders were all women."

"What gives you that notion?" Charles said.

"Women understand the ways of the human heart," Olivia said. "Men, in their infinite pursuit of manly prowess, are given to violence and physical force in decision-making."

"I prefer Rousseau's stance on the subject," Sam said. "In

his work, *Women, Family and Freedom*, he says woman was specifically made to please man. This is the law of nature, which is older than love itself."

"Mr. Clemens! I beg your pardon!" Olivia said. "There is no such quote in all of Rousseau. At no time does he say woman is made to please man."

"Do you have a copy of the work?"

"In the library."

"May we examine the validity of my statement?"

"We shall do that tomorrow," Olivia said.

The group ate quietly for a long moment.

"You seem quite well-read, Mr. Clemens," Olivia said finally. "Which other French philosophers are you familiar with?"

"Rousseau is my favorite, but I'm also familiar with the works of Descartes and Voltaire."

"Where were you educated?" Olivia said.

"At the university of Samuel Langhorne Clemens."

Charles chuckled.

"Excuse me?" Olivia said.

"I'm only making mirth," Sam said. "I'm self-taught. As a young man, I spent over four years as a travelling typesetter and most of my nights were in libraries reading books. I read the Greeks in Philadelphia, the Romans in Washington and the Philistines in New York."

Suddenly, Charles erupted in raucous laughter.

Olivia sensed she was the object of their fun.

"Mr. Clemens!" she said. "Why must you take the conversation from the sublime to the ridiculous?"

"I was only having fun," Sam said. "You don't enjoy mirth?"

Olivia, caught off guard at the question, hesitated before answering.

"Well..." she said finally. "I suppose I do enjoy a bit of frivolity in my life. I have never truly put any serious cogitation into the matter."

***

Once dinner was finished, Charles announced that he and Sam were going into town.

"Where are you going?" Olivia asked.

"To the library."

"The library is closed. You are going to imbibe intoxicating liquors."

"If you knew, why did you ask?"

"You're hopeless!" she said, waving him away. "Go ahead! Ruin your life!"

An hour later, Sam and Charles were at McSorley's Ale House in downtown Elmira having drinks and playing billiards. Between whiskey shots, they recalled the days when they saw the saucy can-can in Paris, tried the public baths in Milan and watched a hungry camel eat Sam's coat in Syria. Later that night, Sam struck up a game of eight ball with another saloon patron and won eight dollars. Finally, when the establishment closed at midnight, Sam and Charles caught a cab carriage back to the Langdon home. Charles was so drunk, Sam had to help him into bed.

***

August 23, 1868 *Upon meeting Olivia for the first time, I must aver she is undeniably delightful. At 22 years old, she is lovely, highly-religious, headstrong and much better educated than I. She reads voraciously and attended Miss Clarissa Thurston's Female Seminary and the Elmira Female College. She continues to show some incapacitation from the ice-skating injury, but it only manifests itself when she walks. She hobbles uncertainly about, but, to my eyes, this incapacitation does not diminish her beauty in the least. Although she prefers to be shifted about in her wheelchair, she can walk reasonably well with the assistance of a cane. She is small of body, but her fragility and the incapacitation only seem to add to her beauty.*

***

The following afternoon, Sam and Olivia retired to the lush

family garden at the rear of the mansion. Maintained by two full-time horticulturists, "Olivia's Garden," as Jervis called it, was the centerpiece of the mansion grounds. Around a sitting area of oaken benches and chairs, row upon row of roses, dahlias, hyacinths and lilies had been planted in successive tiers to form a virtual bowl of color and fragrance. Now, in mid-August, the garden was ablaze with brilliant reds, blues and yellows and the fragrant scent of roses. Olivia, seated comfortably in her wheelchair, was reading the final lines of William Cullen Bryant's poem *Thanatopsis*.

"So live that when thy summons come to join that innumerable caravan which moves constantly into the silent halls of death, go not, not as quarry slave by night scourged to his dungeon, but soothed and relaxed as the sleeper who draws his drapes about him and reclines to peaceful dreams."

She stopped reading and turned pensive for a moment.

"The poet is telling us how to die," she said thoughtfully. "He is saying that we should not dread the approach of death, but accept it gladly as if we were about to begin a long slumber."

"That's the obvious interpretation," Sam said. "The distinctive characteristic of the poem I admire is that it has no religious overtones. No mention of sin, salvation, heaven and hell, milk and honey…. none of that. The poem leaves the listener his freedom to decide those matters on his own."

Olivia's face slowly screwed up in disapproval.

"Mr. Clemens, you are such an unchristian man! One cannot separate death and the existence of God. The two are inextricably entwined."

"We have a difference of opinion."

"The existence of God is not an opinion. It is an undeniable fact of life. It is as constant and as forthcoming as the sky, the stars, the earth, the seas…even the very air we breathe comes from God. Are you not aware that God is providing you with every breath you take?"

"Well, he must be giving it to me free of charge. I have never had to ask him for it and I've certainly never received a bill."

"Once again, you have taken the conversation from the

sublime to the absurd."

"I like to have fun," Sam said.

Olivia set aside the book of Bryant's poems.

Sam peered at the volume.

"Your book of Bryant poems has seen better days."

Olivia examined the well-worn volume. The book was in two separate pieces held together by a band of white cloth.

"I've sought to purchase a new volume, but I'm unable to secure one."

Then she reached into the side pocket of the wheelchair and withdrew another book, Rousseau's *Women, Family and Freedom.*

"Remember our discussion of last night?"

"I do."

"Where in this volume does Rousseau say women were made to please men."

"Page 168, halfway down the page."

Olivia, startled at his quick answer, opened the book, turned to the page and began reading.

"'With the establishment of this principle, woman was specifically made to please man. If man ought to please her in turn, it is less direct. I grant you this is not the law of love. This is the law of nature.'"

She stopped reading, then turned to Sam.

"You were correct, Mr. Clemens. You have my apologies."

"I have one burning question I wish to ask."

"What might that be?"

"Will you marry me?"

Suddenly at a loss for words. her face screwed up in disapproval. Finally, she spoke.

"Mr. Clemens, this is not the time or place for such a conversation."

"Will you marry me?" Sam said again.

Suddenly, Henry, the black manservant, appeared.

"Miss Olivia! Dinner is being served."

For Olivia, it was a welcome relief.

"Mr. Clemens! Let us go inside to sup."

***

A week passed. During that time, Sam and Olivia continued their conversations in the garden about politics, world affairs and famous authors. At night, Sam, Jervis and Charles played whist, smoked cigars and drank brandy while Sam regaled them with tales of his days on the western frontier. Some nights, Sam would join in with the family to play charades and sing gospel hymns while Mrs. Langdon played the piano. When not participating in family parlor games, Sam and Charles were drinking and playing billiards at McSorley's tavern.

***

After dinner on Thursday night of the following week, while having brandy and cigars, Jervis made an invitation to Sam and Charles.

"I've been invited to spend the upcoming weekend with my friend David Gray at his lodge," he said. "Would the two of you like to accompany me?"

"Splendid idea!" Charles said.

"What would we do?" Sam said.

"It would be great fun," Charles said. "We could go hunting, fishing, skeet-shooting. Most of all, we could be away from the women for a while and do some serious drinking."

"Sam, I want you to meet my friend David Gray," Jervis said. "He is publisher of the *Buffalo Express.*"

"He's a newspaper man?" Sam said.

"Oh, yes," Jervis replied. "And a fine one."

"Count me in," Sam said.

"We'll leave Saturday morning."

***

Two days later, on a warm Saturday morning, the Langdon family coachman brought around a two-horse buckboard to the front of the mansion, which would take Sam, Jervis and Charles to the Chemung River where Jervis's friend owned a sporting lodge. After an hour's journey, the buckboard pulled up in front of a massive log structure nestled in the dense forests along the river's banks. The 100-acre backwoods getaway was essentially an upscale gentlemen's club where men could get away from their womenfolk and be men. Upon arrival, the trio went inside, registered with the front desk, then were escorted to their rooms.

At dinner that night in the lodge dining hall, Sam met David Gray, a tall, neatly-dressed man in his late forties who was publisher of the *Buffalo Express*.

"You're Mark Twain!" Gray said, upon shaking Sam's hand. "With great pleasure, I have read your work in both the *Atlantic Monthly* and the *Tribune*. I had some robust belly laughs from your Holy Land excursion."

"I'm obliged for your kind words," Sam said.

"Ever think about working exclusively for one newspaper?"

"Why would you be asking?"

"I'd love to have a well-known name like yours gracing the columns of the *Buffalo Express*."

"Buffalo?" Sam said. "I hear it gets mighty cold up there."

"It's does, but you learn to acclimate."

Sam peered at him.

"What did you have in mind?"

"Your humorous pieces would be a perfect fit for the *Express*. Our readers would love to read more sketches about your days in the Wild West. Further, your political satires are quite entertaining."

"How much is the pay?"

"If you're interested, we can discuss the details."

"Fair enough," Sam said.

Charles turned to Sam.

"Let's go to the bar and have a few."

"Come on!" Sam said.

Once Sam and Charles were gone, Gray turned to Jervis.

"You say that young Clemens is courting your daughter?"

"Yes, although he's not making much progress."

"He would be a fine catch for any woman."

***

On Sunday morning, before saying good-bye to his lodge guests, Gray sweetened his offer.

"It would please me highly to have a journalist of your caliber on the *Express*," Gray said. "If you were serious about coming onboard, I would even consider offering you part interest in the publication."

"At what price?"

"I would sell one-third interest for $15,000."

"What is your circulation?"

"Around 8,000 daily."

Sam inhaled, then studied Gray for a long moment.

"That's a fair price, but a mite strong for my blood. I appreciate your offer, but my financial resources will not allow it at this time."

"If you change your mind, please inform me," Gray said.

"I shall," Sam said.

***

On Saturday morning of the following weekend, Sam's bags were packed and he was completing his three-week visit to the Langdon family home. Clemens and Olivia were alone in the garden.

"I shall be leaving tomorrow," Sam said. "I wish to remind you that my offer of marriage still stands."

"I must refuse your offer once more," she said, "but I shall grant you the privilege of corresponding with me."

"I'm obliged for your graciousness."

"But only as a brother," she said. "A Christian brother."

Sam peered thoughtfully at her for a long moment, then, crest-fallen, he shook his head sadly.

"I reckon that's better than nothing," he said. "I shall honor your wishes."

With that, Sam said his good-byes to Mr. and Mrs. Langdon and Charles, then boarded the cab carriage to the train station. In town, while waiting for his train, Sam penned a new letter to Olivia.

September 14, 1868
My honored "Sister,"

I do not regret that I have loved you, still love and shall always love you. I accept the situation, uncomplaining, as hard as it is. Of old, I am acquainted with grief, disaster, disillusionment and disappointment and have borne these troubles as becoming a man.

So also shall I bear this last and bitterest. Even though it breaks my heart, my honored sister—give me a little room in that great heart of yours—only the little you have promised me—and if I fail to deserve it, may I forever remain the homeless vagabond I am.
Sincerely,
Samuel

***

That night, after Sam was gone, Jervis and Mrs. Langdon discussed Olivia's suitor while sitting alone in the family garden.

"He is too crude and rough-hewn for my taste," Mrs. Langdon said. "His clothes are poorly kept and his hair is unruly. He has a lazy way of talking like Southerners and there is the constant smell of tobacco about him."

"Dear, you tolerate my pipe."

"I do, but your pipe doesn't emit the harsh smell of his cigars. Further, one never knows what new coarseness or vulgarity will arise from his lips. He is far too unpredictable for my tastes."

"He has a certain down-home charm about him," Jervis said. "He has experience, wit, wisdom and conversational skills. Did you notice that Olivia seems to be livelier and more enthusiastic since he has been here?"

"How do you mean?"

"She has spent less and less time in her wheelchair."

Mrs. Langdon turned to her husband.

"I see the truth of that."

***

Back in New York that night, Sam had a letter from Crutchfield's San Francisco friend about the Daily Alta California dilemma.

September 8, 1868
Dear Mr. Clemens:
We have prevailed in our legal action against Alta Publishing Company.
Not only did I secure the original copyright to the letters, but I have won two other points of contention.
The Alta has agreed to pay you royalties on any further publication of the letters; also, I refused to include a preface which thanks the Alta for waiving its rights; further, sister papers of the Alta are prohibited from publishing the letters.
Earlier today, I remitted a letter to Elisha Bliss, your New York publisher, notifying him of the good news.
Sincerely,
Louis Hendershot Esq.

***

Six weeks later, *Innocents Abroad,* the book version of the *Quaker City* dispatches, was printed and began appearing on bookstore shelves and in homes as subscriptions across the nation. It would sell more than 100,000 copies in the first two years; only Tom Paine's *Common Sense* and *Uncle Tom's Cabin* had sold more in the same time frame. Two months after the initial printing, Sam boasted to a friend that the book was "waltzing me out of debt so fast that I shall not owe any man a penny this time next year. We keep six steam presses running day and night and still we can't catch up with orders. Hallelujah!"

***

Two years passed. During the spring and summer of 1869, Sam promoted *Innocents Abroad* with lectures, personal appearances and book salons in bookstores and retail outlets.

During the spring of the following year, he spent two months researching and outlining a novel about a young white boy who was captured and raised by plains Indians. In the fall, he was occupied with editing a novel for Howells titled *Their Wedding Journey.*

All the while, Sam continued to bombard Olivia with letters professing his love. When Howells came to New York to visit him in the fall of 1870, Sam was writing a new letter to Olivia almost every day. One night, Howells called him out about it.

"Every time I turn around, you're writing a new love letter," Howells said. "How many is that now?"

"More than two hundred over the past two years."

Howells laughed.

"You must truly love her," he said.

"That I do," Sam replied.

***

That same night, more than 240 miles away in Elmira, Jervis Langdon was in Olivia's bedroom having a daughter-father conversation.

"I'm concerned about you," he said. "You seem to have undergone some profound changes since you brushed off that young Clemens fellow."

"What are you saying?"

"You've been quite morose since he has been gone. When he was here, there was a liveliness about you. You were forever laughing, smiling, talking. Most importantly, you were spending more and more time out of that damned wheelchair."

"It is true that there are times Mr. Clemens evokes happiness in me. Despite his rough-hewn manners and his lack of Christian virtues, I realize he is intelligent, knowledgeable of the world and quite humorous at times."

"Have you forgotten him?"

"Father, how could I forget him? He has sent me more than 200 love letters over the past two years, each and every one professing his love. Most have gone unanswered."

"Again, I say you were happier and your life was much

fuller when he was present in this house."

"Are you implying I should reconsider his proposal?"

"Perhaps. Ultimately, you are the one to make the decision, not I."

***

In early November of 1870, Sam received a letter from Jervis asking him to come visit a second time. A week later, when Sam arrived at the Langdon home for the second visit, he had a bouquet of roses and a new hardback copy of William Cullen Bryant's *Collected Poems*.

"Oh, my!" Olivia said, upon seeing the book. "This makes me very happy."

"Where is Charles?" Sam asked.

"He's in Buffalo on company business," Jervis said. "He won't be back for a week, maybe longer."

***

When the family sat down for dinner that night, Jervis announced he and Sam would be returning to the sportsman's lodge the following morning to do some fishing. Before Jervis blessed the food, Olivia turned to Sam.

"Mr. Clemens! May I make some requests of you?"

"Anything."

"Will you limit yourself to one glass of wine?"

"Done."

"Will you have only one cigar after your meal?"

"As you wish."

"Will you promise not to swear at the dinner table?"

"Done."

"Will you attend worship services with us this Wednesday?"

"I shall."

"The fulfillment of each of those matters would make me happy," she said. "Very happy!"

"That is my goal," Sam said.

***

The following morning, the family coachman brought around the buckboard which would take Sam and Jervis once again to David Gray's fishing lodge. Mrs. Langdon and Olivia were there to see them off. Sam, dressed in outdoorsmen clothes, a plaid shirt and boots, entered the buckboard first. As Jervis started to board, he noticed one of the back wheels was wobbling on its axle.

He turned to the driver.

"Horace! Can you take a look at that back wheel?"

Instantly, the coachman was out of the driver's seat and on the ground to inspect the wheel. As he stepped down out of the buckboard, the horse suddenly bolted, then started running aimlessly across the front yard with Sam inside holding on for dear life. As the buckboard slashed across the yard, one corner hit the base of a cherubic fountain and threw Sam out of the carriage. He flew some five feet through the air and his head landed on the concrete base of the fountain. For a moment, he stood up, then collapsed to the ground.

Suddenly, Olivia let out a shriek of horror, then, with the use of her cane, hobbled to the point where Sam was lying and knelt beside him. His eyes were closed and blood was trickling down the side of his head.

"Samuel! Samuel!" she shouted. "Are you hurt? Are you in pain? Samuel! Samuel! Speak to me!"

Jervis stepped over and knelt beside Sam.

"He's unconscious. Call Henry to help us get him inside. I'll fetch the doctor."

***

Three hours later, Sam was awake and propped up in bed in the guest room; his head was bandaged, the bleeding had stopped. Dr. Ezekiel Wilson, the Langdon family physician, was in attendance.

"You're going to have a lump on the top of your head for the next few days," the doctor said. "You're young and healthy and should be fit as a fiddle again in a couple days."

He handed Sam a bottle of pills.

"Take two of these before bed. They'll help you sleep."

***

All that night, Sam slept peacefully. He awoke shortly after sunrise and began reading from Rousseau's *Social Contract*. After he had been reading almost an hour, there was a knock on the door. It was Olivia. He was sitting up in bed.

"Good morning! Did you rest well last night?"

"Will you marry me?" Sam said.

Startled by the suddenness of the words, she needed a moment to regain herself. First, she started laughing. Then, she began crying. Finally, she wiped her eyes, knelt beside the bed and took Sam's hands in hers.

"Oh yes, Samuel darling. Yes, I'll marry you. I love you and I want to be your wife."

***

January 12, 1870 *When I awoke this morning and heard Olivia's pitying remarks drizzling over me, I realized the carriage accident was one of the happiest moments of my life. That single happenstance did more to gain me her heart-felt affections than all of the courting, the happy flowers, the gushy letters, marriage proposals and denials, witty comments and improvised gentility I have doled out upon her over the past year and a half.*

***

Two weeks later, on February 2, 1870, Sam and Olivia were married in "Olivia's Garden" among the lush, fragrant beauty of the roses, dahlias and lilacs. Olivia, standing unsteadily beside Sam without her cane, was radiant in a white taffeta wedding gown. Officiating was Rev. Joseph Twichell, a tall, thirtyish congregational minister Sam had befriended on the *Quaker City* trip. For the ceremony, Sam recycled the engagement ring he had given Olivia when she accepted his proposal, one he described as "plain, and of heavy gold." In later years, Sam would have their wedding date engraved inside the ring, although this proved superfluous since "it was never again removed from her finger for even a moment" and, at Sam's insistence, it was buried with her.

***

Late that afternoon, once wedding festivities were finished and guests had departed, Jervis pulled Sam aside.

"I want you and Olivia to make a trip with me to Buffalo tomorrow."

"Buffalo?" Sam said. "What's in Buffalo?"

"I have something I want to show you."

"What might that be?"

"I want to show you the boarding house where you and Olivia will be living."

Sam's face took on a puzzled look.

"Boarding house?"

Jervis smiled, a twinkle in his eye.

"Just come along," he said. "You'll discover our purpose soon enough."

16
Buffalo

At noon on the following day, Mr. and Mrs. Langdon, along with Sam Clemens and his new bride, were on a passenger train streaking through the rolling, snow-covered hills of western New York state to the city of Buffalo. Once the train pulled into the station that afternoon and the travelers retrieved their luggage, Jervis hired a snow sleigh to deliver them to the so-called "boarding house" where Sam and Olivia were to begin their married life. After riding around the city's wintry streets for more than hour, Sam grew impatient.

"Whereabouts is this boarding house?" he said. "I'm getting cold."

As he said those words, the sleigh pulled to a stop in front of a magnificent brick home along Buffalo's fashionable Delaware Avenue.

"Why are we stopping?" Sam said.

"We have arrived," Jervis said. "Come see your new boarding house."

Sam peered at the dwelling before him.

"That's the finest looking boarding house I've ever seen."

"Come along," Olivia said, taking his hand and leading him out of the sleigh. "This is our new home. It is my father's wedding gift."

Unbeknownst to Sam, during the four months between the accepted proposal and the wedding, Jervis and Olivia had conspired to buy, furnish and staff the home as a surprise. Once they were inside, Olivia gave Sam a cook's tour of the premises. Constructed of Belgian red bricks with French windows, Gothic spires and a black metal roof, the home featured eight rooms on each of the first two floors, which included a gallery, a foyer, a sitting room, a formal dining room, a ballroom, a large library and stables with two fine Arabian horses. Furnished to Olivia's personal tastes, the household staff included five kitchen servants, a coachman, three maids and a gardener. The total package had cost Jervis $42,000, a small fortune in 1870.

Once the tour was finished, Sam announced that his favorite room in the new home was a writing parlor on the third floor which looked out on the family garden.

"I promise to make proficient use of this room," he said.

Then he turned to Jervis.

"I thank you from the bottom of my heart."

"You're quite welcome," Jervis said. "There is more."

Sam watched as Jervis pulled a sheaf of papers out of his pocket.

"What might that be?"

"These documents make you half owner of the *Buffalo Express*," Jervis said. "You're now set for life! My congratulations!"

Two days later, Clemens put a sign in the front yard of the new home which read: "I live here, but my father-in-law pays the rent."

The following day, the sign disappeared.

In the marital bed that night, Sam asked Olivia about the fate of the sign.

"I had it removed," she said. "I will not allow you to make fun of my father's generosity."

***

February 4, 1870 *Flush times and the cornucopia of plenty have arrived once again! With $80,0000 in* Innocents Abroad *profits, a magnificent, fully-staffed new home and a partner's interest in the local newspaper, I reckon I can call myself a wealthy man. This reminds me of the time me and Bret Harte found those gold nuggets Portuguese Joe had buried in the sardine cans in Calaveras County. Suddenly, money is as* *plentiful as water.*

***

Over the next few weeks, Sam and Olivia settled into their new lives in Buffalo. In his role as co-owner and associate editor at the *Express*, Sam began writing editorials about local politics and providing Wild West sketches for the paper's entertainment section. As co-publisher, he also found himself poring over financial records, adjusting printing schedules and making decisions about hiring and firing. Co-owner David Gray, a perfectionist and a stickler for details, often kept Sam in the office late at night for discussions about the business and its future. After only a few weeks, however, Sam began to balk at the daily routine of being in the office at nine, having meetings and performing administrative chores until lunch; then attending even more meetings and performing more administrative chores until he could leave the office, sometimes as late as 8 p.m.

March 21, 1870 *First and foremost, I am a writer, a scribe, a man of letters, one who imparts words to paper with ink. My very essence has been embodied within that exercise for as long as I can remember. I am not befitted for sitting in smoke-filled rooms listening to voices arguing over interest payments, delivery schedules, poor proofreading, libel suits, delivery wagon break-downs and decisions about which supplier to buy printing paper from. The act of putting words to paper is my destiny. Making day-to-day business decisions does not befit my soul.*

***

During those first few months, Sam and Olivia made a new set of friends who were frequent dinner guests at their home. One of these was Charles Dudley Warner, a former business editor at the *Express* who was now employed by the *Hartford Courant*. One Saturday night in late April, Sam, Olivia, Warner and his wife Susan were having dinner when Warner's wife mentioned that she had recently finished a new book about James J. Hill, the Canadian-American railroad magnate who owned the Great Northern Railway and had amassed a personal fortune of $15 million.

"That one man has more money that the US Government," Warner said, a tall, early thirties man with stooped shoulders and a full beard.

"Just another robber baron that used a monopoly to make himself rich while riding the backs of the poverty-stricken," Olivia said.

"He's not the only one," Susan said. "There are others… Carnegie, Morgan, Vanderbilt, Gould…"

"It's shameful," Olivia said.

Warner turned to Sam.

"Why don't we write a book about it, Sam?"

"Capital idea!" Clemens said. "We could expose the greed and political corruption which grew out of the Civil War."

"How should we handle it?"

"Let's sit down and put together a synopsis," Sam said. "Next week, I'll come down to Hartford and we'll pitch it to Elisha Bliss."

"Splendid!" Warner replied.

***

That night, Olivia offered some advice on the new project.

"You've never written a novel before, so you'll need to get organized. First, you must determine the outline for the story, then divide up the chapters between the two of you."

"How will I get my chapters to Warner and Bliss?"

"You could post them," Olivia said.

"That's a risky business," Sam said. "I would be fit to be tied if my chapters were lost in the mails."

"Then you will have to travel periodically to Hartford," she said. "You can deliver your chapters to him and you can read his."

"That's a lot of travelling."

"If you refuse to use the post, you have no choice."

***

Over the following day, a Sunday, Clemens and Warner put together a summary of the novel they planned to write. The major story line focused on a poor, rural family in Tennessee and their efforts to become affluent by selling 75,000 acres of unimproved land which had been acquired by their long-dead patriarch. Most of the story took place in Washington, D.C. where the patriarch's granddaughter, the beautiful Laura Hawkins, lobbies members of Congress to buy the land from her family. Subplots focused on the greed and lavish lifestyles of corrupt political leaders and the so-called "robber-barons." Once finished, the rough outline called for a total of thirty-three chapters with Sam writing the first two, Warner the next two and so on.

"What will we call it?" Warner said.

"*The Gilded Age*," Sam said. "From the line in Shakespeare's King John which reads: 'Gilding gold, which would be to put gold on top of gold, is excessive and wasteful.'"

"Perfect!" Warner replied.

***

During the following week, Sam wrote the first two chapters of *The Gilded Age*, then, on Sunday, announced to Olivia he was going to Hartford to show them to Warner.

"Next time you go, I wish to go with you," she said. "I want to visit my parents while you're in Hartford. It's been four months since I've seen them."

Late that afternoon, when Clemens arrived in Hartford, Warner was waiting in a cab carriage at the train station to take him to his home. Twenty minutes later, they arrived at Nook Farm, a sprawling 144-acre enclave of shady, fashionable homes located on Hartford's west side. Upon seeing the setting, Sam sat up in the carriage and took an immediate interest.

"What sort of place is this?"

"It's a literary community," Warner said. "My neighbors are some of the most famous authors in New England. Over there," he said, pointing to a magnificent home, "Is the home of Harriet Beecher Stowe. Here, in the gray stone house, is the residence of Sen. Francis Gillette, father of playwright William Gillette. Isabella Beecher Hooker, Harriet's sister, lives in the brownstone home on the corner."

"Very interesting," Sam said.

May 8, 1870 *Today in Hartford, I conferred again with Warner; he read my chapters; I read his, then we went into New York and showed them to Bliss. The old curmudgeon showed a modicum of interest, then rattled on and on that, in order to make the book saleable, we needed a plenitude of material which demonstrates "the greed and lavish lifestyles of the ravenous captains of industry." We assured him our work would contain an abundance of such material. Finally, he said, once we had presented him with a total of eight chapters, he would make a decision on publishing it.*

***

Two days later, a Sunday, Clemens was back in Buffalo, and he and Olivia were preparing for church. Olivia was unable to find a pair of black shoes she wanted to wear and she had Sam digging through her closet to find them. As he searched, he pulled out her old walking cane.

"Remember this!"

"How could I forget? It was my instrument of mobility for over six years. Your love bore me away from that tragedy."

He smiled and turned to her.

For a long moment, she peered lovingly into his eyes.

"What's going on inside that pretty little head?" he said.

"I have something to tell you."

"What night that be?"

"I visited the doctor yesterday," she said. "He said I'm with child."

Sam smiled and turned to her.

"I love you, darling Livy."

"I love you, Samuel," she said.

***

In the years following the marriage, Olivia's handicap which resulted from her childhood ice-skating accident never totally disappeared. Over the first few years, she gradually ceased to use the cane; on some days, especially if the weather was cold or rainy, she would take it down occasionally and use it. Over the succeeding years, Olivia taught herself to walk comfortably without the use of the cane, but there was always a slight limp.

***

That night, in the marital bed, Sam asked Olivia for her thoughts on the front-page editorial he had written for the *Express* about the city of Buffalo's new fire wagons.

"You couched your points so heavily in comedy that you didn't make a valid point," she said. "All you did was make fun of the firemen and their new wagons. You are so inclined toward comedy that you ignore your serious side."

"Humor and making fun of the world has always been my long suit," Sam said. "What are you suggesting?"

Olivia peered at her husband for a long moment.

Finally, she spoke.

"Over the past year, you've related to me many stories about your childhood days with Tom Blankenship."

"Oh yes!" Sam said. "Tom and I had some great adventures. Some of the happiest days of my life."

"You should write a serious novel about your relationship with Tom and overlay it with political themes. You should be more didactic."

"More what?"

"Didactic! When one attempts to teach moral lessons in one's craft."

Sam peered thoughtfully at her.

"Since you enjoy talking about your days with Tom so much," Olivia continued, "it should be quite easy to write a book about it."

"Well, I never put too much thought into it," he said. "I reckon it would be fun. What would I call it?"

"*The Adventures of Tom Blankenship*," Olivia said. "You could alter it later, but that could be your working title."

"Splendid idea. I'll start making notes tonight."

***

On the morning of May 18, Clemens had finished two more chapters of *The Gilded Age* and he and Olivia were preparing to travel, Olivia to visit her parents in Elmira and Sam his writing partner in Hartford. When they arrived in Elmira that night, Sam got off the train just long enough to say hello to Mr. and Mrs. Langdon, then, after promising to visit on the return leg, he reboarded. The following day, after Clemens conferred with Warner and Bliss about their project, he caught a train back to Elmira.

Over dinner that night, Sam and Olivia discussed their new lives in Buffalo with their in-laws and the prospects of a new addition to the family. Once the meal was finished, Jervis and Sam retired to the family garden.

"I have some bad news," Jervis said. "The doctors have diagnosed me with stomach cancer. I don't have long for this earth."

"I'm so sorry to hear that," Sam said. "It's going to break Livy's heart."

"I know," Jervis said. Let's keep it a secret from her until the end is near. I don't want to worry her, her being with child."

"Will your wife follow suit?"

"She will."

"How long do you have?"

"The doctor says one, maybe two months."

***

By early June, Sam had finished another two chapters of *The Gilded Age* and, the morning after, he was on the train

265

again for Hartford. When he returned to Buffalo two days later, he was at his wit's end.

"This madness must come to a halt," he said. "Here we are in Buffalo and my writing partner is in Hartford, Connecticut. The train trips for editorial conferences are requiring more time than the time needed to write the chapters."

"Your point is well-taken, dear," she said. "What should we do?"

"We're going to have to shift our home to Hartford."

"That might be more easily said than done," she said. "You can't endure the travel until *The Gilded Age* is finished?"

"It's less than one-third written," Sam said. "That means another ten to fifteen trips to Hartford."

"You know I'm due to deliver around Christmas."

"I know, but this incessant traveling has to end."

"Then you should begin seeking out a new home in Hartford. Don't tell my father until we're ready to move. It will break his heart."

***

Three weeks later, when Sam returned home one night from the office, Olivia met him at the door. She was holding an opened letter in her hand.

"Why didn't you tell me my father was ill?"

Sam shrugged and peered sheepishly at her.

"Your father wanted to keep it a secret, you being with child and all."

"Well, the cat's out of the bag now," she said. "I opened his letter to you. He says he has only a few days to live. I want to be on the train for Elmira tomorrow morning."

***

Late afternoon of the following day, Sam and Olivia arrived in Elmira, then took a cab carriage to the Langdon mansion. Once they arrived, they could see that a death vigil was already underway. The mansion's foyer and family room were littered with bouquets of flowers and cards of condolence.

Jervis's old friends, relatives and business associates milled solemnly about the premises, eating, drinking and whispering among themselves. One of the first people they saw was Charles.

"Hello, old man!" Charles said, shaking Sam's hand.

"How does it look?" Sam asked.

"Bad. Very bad," Charles said, shaking his head sadly. "Let's go up."

Moments later, the three were upstairs in Jervis's bedroom. When they entered, they saw a nurse on one side of the bed and Mrs. Langdon on the other. Jervis was sitting up in bed, his eyes were closed and his head resting on his chest. Instantly, Olivia started toward the bed.

The nurse stepped forward.

"He shouldn't be disturbed," the nurse said.

"Remove yourself!" Olivia said. "This is my father and he's dying."

Olivia roughly pushed the nurse aside and turned to her father.

"Father!" she said.

No response.

"Father!" she said again, louder this time.

Jervis slowly raised his head and opened his eyes.

"My darling Olivia," he said. "My time is not long. Sit beside me so I may say good-bye."

Olivia limped over, seated herself beside the bed and took her father's hand in hers. For a long moment, she peered into his feeble eyes, then broke down in uncontrollable sobs.

"My darling! Weep not for me," he said. "I'll be waiting in heaven."

Olivia regained herself, then wiped her eyes.

"Oh yes, my dear father," she said. "This is not the end. We shall meet again someday. Oh, my father! I love you so."

"And I love you with all the fullness of my heart."

Jervis looked up and saw Clemens.

"Sam! Come forward and shake my hand one last time."

Sam stepped to the bedside and clasped Jervis's hand in his.

"Good-bye!" Jervis said. "Do you promise to take care of

my daughter?"

"I shall do so," Sam said. "From the bottom of my heart, I wanted to say I was much obliged for your generosity."

"You were more than deserving," Jervis said. "You have made me very proud. Now I want everyone to leave so I can rest. I'm very tired."

***

Just after midnight that night, with his family gathered around him, the rattles of death came calling and Jervis's breathing became progressively louder and more strained until it could be heard throughout the house. With each successive breath, his body labored with more and more difficulty to draw in the breath of life. At thirty minutes after midnight, the labored breathing stopped. Jervis Langdon was dead.

***

Three days later, more than 1,000 people attended Jervis's funeral at St. Peter's Episcopal Church in southwest Elmira. There was not enough room inside for all of the mourners, so those who were unable to get inside milled around or peeked in windows. They were friends, relatives, current and former employees, politicians, and business associates as well as curiosity seekers who wanted to see how extreme wealth appeared in death. Once services were over, a funeral procession of more than three hundred carriages accompanied the body to nearby Woodlawn cemetery.

There, Sam, holding a weeping Olivia close, watched as eight pallbearers trudged up the muddy hillside to deliver Jervis's remains to its final resting place. Once workmen began to lower the coffin into the cool, black earth, mourners stepped forward to drop mementos into the grave. There were bouquets of flowers, chunks of coal, a Bible, a miner's lamp, the lyrics to "Amazing Grace," a piece of white cloth with Jervis's stitched image, and the worn copy of William Cullen Bryant's poems. Olivia dabbed her eyes as she witnessed the spectacle, and Charles, always the happy-go-lucky rake, broke down and wept like a little child.

***

Four days later, Mrs. Langdon, Charles, Sam and Olivia were in the family solicitor's office for the reading of Jervis's final will and testament. The total estate had been divided up three ways between Mrs. Langdon, Charles and Olivia. When the reading was finished, Olivia had received $1.1 million in cash from her father's estate.

***

Sept. 12, 1870 *Over these past few weeks, my darling Livy has wrapped herself in a cocoon of misery. She is happy neither day nor night. She eats little, sleeps little and is constantly on the brink of an emotional outburst. Last night, while we were having dinner, she suddenly burst into tears and left the table. I followed her to our bedroom where I found her sprawled across the bed, sobbing uncontrollably. I lay down beside her, took her into my arms and wept with her. I knew of nothing more to do. I trust this avalanche of unhappiness does not affect the growth of our child.*

***

November 7, 1870 *This morning, at 8:36 a.m., my beloved Livy delivered my first child, a son whom we have named Langdon. What a poor, weary-looking little fellow he is! Born two months premature, he was thirteen inches long and weighed four pounds. Dr. Morgan proclaimed the infant would have poor resources for fighting off disease and would be plagued with frequent coughs and colds. Further, the doctor continued, his development would be severely retarded, slow to talk, to walk and to teethe. Ideally, the doctor said, the infant should be in a hospital for the first few months. If that was not possible, he said, an at-home nurse would be required. Upon hearing these words, Olivia told the doctor a nurse would be hired and explained: "We shall nurture and love that which*

God has given us."

***

With the birth of Langdon, Olivia's deep depression at the death of her father quickly faded away. Overnight, she threw herself into the care of the newborn, reading books about premature babies, discussing his condition with the nurse, ensuring the child had his medications and constantly monitoring his overall well-being. His crib was placed in his parents' bedroom, and some nights, he would sleep soundly all night. Other nights, his seemingly endless crying would keep Sam and Olivia awake all night.

***

In Buffalo, the winter of 1870 proved to be one of the most brutal in its history. While October and November had been relatively mild, two savage nor'easters had blown through in late December and dumped more than nine feet of snow on hapless residents in less than a week. Daily temperatures hovered in the mid-teens; vast stretches of Buffalo harbor were frozen solid and giant sailing ships and steamers were trapped firmly in their moorings. In suburban areas, city crews worked day and night to keep streets and sidewalks clear of snow so businesses could open and citizens could go about their daily activities. Workers with huge shovels would load wagon after wagon to the brim with fresh powder, then follow them to the harbor where it would be dumped. At the Lackawanna Public Park on Louisiana Street, where snow went untouched during such times, the massive drifts lay ten to twelve feet deep. This foul weather only aggravated little Langdon's health and he was constantly ill with the croup.

***

Meanwhile, Sam continued to write the chapters of *The Gilded Age* and travel between Buffalo and Hartford for conferences with Warner and Bliss. In February of the new year, he made his fifth trip to Hartford with the eleventh and twelfth chapters. After Warner had reviewed them, both he and Clemens went into New York to show them to Bliss.

"I love it!" Bliss said. "I can see this book taking form now. It's going to be a bestseller. How soon can you have it finished?"

Sam turned to Warner.

"Let's shoot for next January," he said. "It's almost half written. That should give us plenty of time."

"Done!" Bliss said.

Once the conference was finished, Warner and Sam were in a cab carriage returning to Warner's home so Clemens could collect his bags and catch the train back to Buffalo.

After they reentered Nook Farm, Sam's eyes fell on a quaint little cottage four doors down from the Warners' home.

"Such a delightful dwelling," Sam said.

"It's for rent," Warner said. "It's owned by Isabella Beecher Hooker. She moved out six months ago."

"You are referring to the famous suffragette?"

"The one and the same."

"Can we stop for a moment?"

Warner ordered the driver to stop.

Moments later, Sam and Warner were inspecting the grounds and the home. Built on two acres, the pale-blue dwelling had a dainty Scandinavian cottage look with a steep roof, two garrets, a huge bay window in front and a lush garden with several maple trees in front.

"How much is she asking in rent?"

"Not sure," Warner said. "I can speak to her sister Harriet if you like."

"I would be obliged," Sam said.

***

April 4, 1871 *Our little Langdon, now six months old, is constantly ill. The slightest draft or exposure would cause him to start coughing. Twice, doctors visited him this week and*

271

announced that he should be kept warm and quiet and fed his medicines at the designated times. Despite the best efforts of both Olivia and his nurse, the poor little thing has shown little or no progress in regaining his health. It seems that he never ceases crying. Over the past four months, I have not had a single night of natural, restful sleep. I had thought the vials of hellfire bottled up for my benefit had been emptied. If this baby goes on crying like this, I shall burst my frantic brains out to try to get some peace.

***

Throughout the month of May, Sam completed six more chapters of *The Gilded Age* and made four more trips to Hartford to show them to Warner. During one trip, he learned from Warner that Isabella Beecher Hooker was asking $100 a month to rent the cottage he had seen at Nook Farm. Warner explained she had been living in Boston for the past year working with the New England Women's Suffrage Association for women's rights. If Sam wanted to rent the cottage, Warner said, the negotiations would have to be conducted by mail.

"Do you have an address for her?" Sam said.

"I do."

***

On the morning of June 5, 1871, little Langdon, after suffering a severe case of croup for almost two weeks, was diagnosed with diphtheria and taken to the Buffalo hospital. That afternoon, Sam, with two more chapters of *The Gilded Age* in hand, prepared to make still another trip to Hartford.

"Dear, are you going to Hartford with Langdon in the hospital?" Olivia asked.

"My darling Livy! There is nothing I can do for him. His life is in God's hands now. We must press on with our lives."

She took a deep breath before replying.

"I know you are correct, Samuel," she said. "Will you be seeking a new home for us in Hartford?"

272

"Do you wish for me to secure one without you having seen it?"

"I want to escape this horrible Buffalo weather as soon as possible."

"I have sent Isabella Beecher Hooker a letter informing her that we wish to rent the cottage at Nook Farm."

"Inform me the minute you have an answer," she said. "I want away from this wretched city."

***

On the afternoon of June 9, 1871, Sam arrived back in Buffalo. The moment he walked into the family home and saw the face of little Langdon's nurse, his worst fears were confirmed. Langdon was dead. Upstairs, he found Olivia in our bedroom weeping.

"Oh, Samuel," she said. "Is there no end to the suffering we must endure in this world? What sin, what transgression did we commit to deserve such great sorrow?"

"We can't succumb to our sorrows," he said. "We must gather ourselves together and press on."

She sat up and dried her eyes.

"I firmly believe God was showing his mercy when he took Langdon," she said. "Now he is free of the pain, the misery and suffering of this world. He has gone to a better place."

She looked Sam in the eyes, then burst into tears.

For several moments, Sam took her into his arms and held her until she stopped crying.

"Did you secure our new home in Hartford?" she asked.

"I did. It is the most delightful little home in all creation. It sings. It dances. It is the most exquisite and enchanting home that can be found in America. I'm sure you will love it."

"When are we shifting our house?"

"You've never even seen it."

"No matter. I want to flee the miserable city of Buffalo at once. The winters are enough to drive you insane."

***

June 10, 1871 *Poor Langdon never really had a chance in this world. From the day he was born, the little fellow caught every ailment, every disease, every infection that came his way. Perhaps if I hadn't taken him for a walk on Friday of the last week, he would not have caught diphtheria and might still be with us. Of course, all those around me think what a mercy it is that he is at rest, but his poor mother is heartbroken. I can only hold her in my arms and weep with her.*

Two days later, Langdon was buried beside his late grandfather in the Langdon family plot at Woodlawn Cemetery in Elmira. Somehow, Olivia was noticeably silent during the services, not weeping but staring stoically ahead. Once the ceremony was finished, Sam and Olivia were making their way back across the cemetery grounds to the family carriage.

"My darling Livy?" Sam said.

She turned to him.

"Will you ever arrive at peace over this?"

"What must be, must be," she said. "I can only follow God's will."

***

On July 12, 1871, Sam and Olivia, along with four steamer trucks containing their personal possessions, were on a train traveling southeast across western New York State to their new home in Hartford. The Buffalo house was sold fully furnished and the only items they took were mostly personal items and memorabilia. Sam sold his interest in the *Buffalo Express* at a $12,000 loss. Only six more chapters remained to be written on *The Gilded Age*.

As the train rattled across the rails en route to Hartford, Olivia turned to Sam.

"What progress have you made on the Tom Blankenship book?"

"I have a compendium of incidents and I have established my main characters, but the writing is excruciatingly slow."

"Why?"

"It is torture to relive one's childhood days. It is an

absolute, sheer embarrassment, like standing naked in a public place."

"You cannot allow that to thwart your efforts."

"I'm not about to, but I have determined that writing this book is like picking hen's teeth. It's going to be slow, tortuously slow."

Satisfied with his answer, Olivia returned to her reading. They rode quietly for several moments, the only sound being the loud clickety-clacking of the steel wheels on the rails beneath them.

"It was a mistake to move to Buffalo," Sam said finally. "I'm not fully certain as to why we went there."

"You know full well why we went there," she said. "To take possession of the house and please my father."

"And we happily agreed. It was a mistake, but no one is to blame. Now let's go to Hartford and start again."

***

July 13, 1871 Jervis Langdon was the most generous man I have ever known in my entire life. I reckon when a man has more money than God, he can afford to display that level of generosity. Though I could forever see a certain sadness in his eyes, his heart was made of gold. Especially toward his family. Perhaps his sudden death is a secret mercy, for I would not have wanted him to know that Olivia and I had abandoned the lives he set up for us in Buffalo.

17
"Our Forever Home"

It was August of 1871 and Sam and Olivia had been living in Hartford for just over a month. Overnight, they had fallen in love with the quaint country cottage Sam had rented from Isabella Beecher Hooker at Nook Farm, the sprawling 140-acre literary community on Hartford's West Side.

The history of Nook Farm began in the late fall of 1853 when Isabella's husband John, the famous abolitionist, lawyer and political activist, joined up with his brother-in-law Francis Gillette, well-known actor and playwright, and they purchased the farmland to develop the real estate. First, they built their own homes, then sold parcels of land to relatives and friends to do likewise.

As a result, a colony of writers and intellectuals quickly took hold that included Hooker and his wife, the Gillette acting family, Charles Dudley Warner, former governor Charles Roswell Hawley, and Author Harriet Beecher Stowe as well as several other prominent journalists, feminists, spiritualists, writers, and reformers of the day. Almost overnight, the settlement became known as Nook Farm, taking its name from the bend, or "nook," in the Park River, which bordered the property on the west and south.

***

Once they were settled in, Sam and Olivia fell quickly into the intellectual life of Nook Farm. After only a week, Sam was invited to join the Monday Evening Club, a small band of community members who met at one another's homes on

Monday nights to have dinner and listen to lectures by one of its members.

Over the first two months, Sam delivered a total of seven Monday Evening club lectures, some of which may have seemed out of place for the venue. These included "The decay of the art of lying" and "A protest against taking the pledge." His first presentation, "License of the press" was delivered in front of an audience that included publishers of the *Hartford Courant*, the district's congressman and several local politicians.

As always, Sam's speech managed to ruffle feathers.

"The press has scoffed at religion until it has made scoffing popular. It has defended official criminals, on party pretext, until it has created a United States Senate whose members are incapable of determining what crime against law and dignity is; they are so morally blind, it has made light of dishonesty until we have, as a result, a Congress which contracts to work for a certain sum, then deliberately steals additional wages out of the public pocket and is pained and surprised that anyone should worry about such a little thing."

Over those first two months, Olivia eagerly attended the Monday Evening sessions with Sam and engaged in the lively debates, but, in September, she announced she was pregnant again and this caused both her and Sam's attendance to wane.

***

Meanwhile, Sam and Warner pushed on with the writing of *The Gilded Age*. By November, the originally proposed 33 chapters had been written, but the authors were undecided about the ending. Warner called for the novel to have a tragic ending and leave the reader with a sense of remorse and hopelessness about post-Civil War America.

"The novel should end on a positive note," Olivia counselled. "The main story can end in tragedy, but the last few pages should engender a feeling of hopefulness and optimism in the reader."

"What do you propose?" Sam said.

"At the end, Laura fails to convince the U.S. Congress to purchase the Hawkins family's land. Thinking the land is worthless, she kills her married lover in a fit of desperation, then takes her own life."

"There is nothing hopeful in that," Warner said.

"Permit me to finish," Olivia said. "After Laura dies, Washington, the youngest member of the Hawkins family, uses his engineering skills to discover a massive vein of coal on the land, develops it and becomes fabulously wealthy. This allows his late father's prediction that he would become 'one of the wealthiest men in the world' to come true."

"Splendid!" Sam said.

"Beautiful!" Warner said. "That will be our ending."

***

Two weeks later, Sam and Warner presented the manuscript to Bliss.

"I like it," he said, "but it's going to be a while before I can publish it. I've got several other books in the works."

"When will that be?"

"I'm not certain. Could be six months, maybe longer."

"Can you provide an advance?"

"Not until the book in published," Bliss replied. "There is a recession on and the last two books I published failed to pay for the printing."

"I reckon we'll just have to wait," Sam said.

***

That night, in the marital bed, Olivia goaded Sam about the Tom Blankenship book.

"Now that *The Gilded Age* is completed, you should be making haste on the Tom Blankenship book. This makes almost three years since you have been working on it."

"I know full well how long it's been."

"What progress have you made?"

"It continues to be slow; it almost frightens me."

"You are exploring your serious rather than your comedic side, Samuel," she said. "That's what frightens you. You must remember you have never attempted this before."

Sam peered at her for a long moment.

"Perhaps you're right," he said finally.

"You must work within yourself to overcome such counter-productive emotions."

"I'm making every effort, but it is proving difficult."

***

Five months passed. In mid-March of 1872, Olivia delivered the couple's second child, Olivia Susan Clemens. The morning after the birth, Sam held the newborn in his arms for the first time.

March 13, 1872 Olivia Susan Clemens is the most beautiful child God ever made. A shock of curly dark hair, large shining eyes and the face of a cherub, she is chomping at the bit to become a part of this world. When I first took her in my arms, she smiled at me and her little hand slipped to my finger and she grasped it as if she were pulling me to her. She cries little, is in perfect health and her large brown eyes search every nook and cranny of your face. Providence was watching over me when He gave me this child. This is the offspring I'm been waiting for.

***

The following November, *The Gilded Age* was published to mixed reviews. Critics complained that the narrative was uneven and readers could detect distinct differences between each author's writing style.

"It's a poorly mixed salad dressing," said one critic, "in which the ingredients are capital, but the use of them quite faulty."

Another reviewer called the book "a praiseworthy, though flawed representation of post-Civil War America."

Despite the reviews, Sam already had a solid following of

readers and, after only six weeks, the book had sold more than 50,000 copies. Subscription houses were overwhelmed with orders. Bliss suggested Sam do a lecture tour to promote it, which Sam declined. Letters praising the book as well as its author came pouring in to the publishing house while huge royalty checks followed. Sam was delighted. Even Bliss was surprised.

Only months after the book was published, a stage production opened at the Park Theater in New York. Although the stage play, like the book, received tepid reviews, the production would run for over two years.

Eight months later, when Sam received a royalty check for $1680 from the play's proceeds, he said: "It's free money. It wasn't written to make money as a stage play, but I'll take it."

***

During the spring and summer of 1873, Sam pulled out all of the stops on the Tom Blankenship book. One morning in late August when Sam came to the breakfast table, he seemed especially full of himself.

"I am happy to report I am now slaying the Tom Blankenship book. I wrote 5,000 words yesterday. Today I wrote 7,000."

"What was your breakthrough?"

"I told myself that writing this book was not a choice, but a duty."

"So, the waters of creativity are flowing freely?"

"They are rushing forth in great torrents. It's amazing what a kick in the rear will do. Especially from someone you love."

Olivia smiled.

"I was at the doctor's office yesterday afternoon."

"Any news?"

"I'm pregnant again," she said.

***

Eight months passed. In early June of 1874, Olivia

delivered the fourth member of the Clemens clan when Clara Langhorne Clemens, a whopping eight and a half pounds at birth, made her appearance. Instantly, Sam anointed the newborn "the Great American Giantess."

June 13, 1874 *Our newest arrival Clara has the facial features of her grandmother, Mrs. Langdon. She seems frightened, her little eyes dart about furtively as if she fears some impending danger. She smiles little, cries a lot and seems to be forever on the brink of sorrow. She fails to exude the warmth, the rock-steady calmness of Susy. While Clara strongly resembles Olivia's mother, I hope she doesn't turn out to be as ornery, stubborn, pig-headed and self-righteous as her grandmother.*

***

Two weeks after the birth of Clara, Sam made a proposal to Olivia at the breakfast table.

"It's time we had larger, more commodious quarters," he said. "Our family is growing; our lives are expanding, and this cottage is too small to accommodate our needs. I need a larger study, Susy needs her own room and, in a few years, little Clara will require the same."

"What do you propose?"

"I want to build a grand home on top of the hill on Farmington Avenue," Sam said. "A magnificent home that looks down into the valley and across the treetops to the Park River below. It will be a home where we can raise our family and live out the remainder of our lives."

"A splendid idea!"

***

Two months later, in August of 1874, Sam and Olivia bought a five-acre plot on Farmington Avenue and hired famous New York architect Edward Tuckerman Potter to design the new home. From the first, Sam knew exactly what he wanted.

"I want the most glorious house in town," he told Potter. "No expenses will be spared. Three floors, nineteen rooms, five bathrooms, turrets, balconies, a billiards room, a ballroom… anything that will set my house apart from all the others. A house like no other in town."

***

Potter's drawings for the design were finished in September and work began on the new home in October. As work progressed, Sam took off time from writing the Blankenship book to make daily inspections of the construction. Two to three days a week, Sam was on the site comparing the work being done to the drawings Potter had provided him. From foundation to roof, Sam meticulously oversaw every part of the construction.

When Olivia asked him why he was going to the site so often, he said, "I want to be sure the job meets each and every one of my specifications. We're going to reside there for many years."

***

Another year passed. In late September of 1875, although the new house was not completely finished, workmen began moving the family's belongings from the Hooker cottage into their new quarters on Farmington Avenue. The shifting of furniture, the packing and unpacking of personal items plus having to deal with a bevy of pestering contractors left Sam in a foul mood.

"I've been bull-ragged all day, by the builder who wants instant decisions on God knows what. Then, by his foreman, by the architect, by the tapestry devil who is upholstering the furniture, by the idiot putting down the carpets, by the scoundrel setting up the billiards table (and has left the balls in New York), by the wildcat sodding the ground and by some book agent whose body is in the backyard with the coroner notified. Just imagine all of this going on the whole day long, and I am a man who loathes details with all my heart. But I haven't lost my temper and I've made Livy lie down and calm herself most of the time. Could anybody on this earth make her lie down all the time?"

Although Sam groused about being pestered by the workmen, the dwelling turned out to be everything he had hoped, a masterpiece of Victorian Gothic architecture. The imposing three-story, terra cotta-colored structure featured lofty stone facades, steep roof pitches, arched windows and spiraling turrets, all a stark reminder of the midland castles built in England and Europe during the Middle Ages. There were balconies with splendid views of the surrounding countryside, an elongated porch for lazy summer afternoons and "a gentlemen's parlor" to which male guests could retire to smoke cigars, sip brandy and play billiards.

Susy, the oldest child, had her own room on the second floor adjacent to the schooling room while Clara, at only four months, was housed in her own second floor nursery complete with all of the accessories needed to care for a young infant. Sam's favorite part of the house was the shady octagonal balcony off the third floor which was connected to the billiards room. It was there he strung a hammock, from which he loved to relax and peer down over the green tree tops or admire the clouds which were mirrored in the Park River below. Sam called the balcony his "Texas deck."

A total of nine servants were required to maintain the home. In charge of the household staff was Katy Leary, Olivia's long-time maid, who met promptly at 8 a.m. each morning with Livy to receive the day's instructions. When the Clemenses initially moved in, an African-American man named George Griffin showed up to wash the windows, but stayed on to become butler at the residence for the next twenty-two years.

"George has a talent for turning away unannounced visitors with polite tactfulness," Sam told a friend. "He's a keeper."

Patrick McAleer, a quiet, unassuming man and a blacksmith by trade, served as the family coachman for the Clemenses from the day of their marriage until they left the Hartford home.

At a time when the average household income in America

was $500 a year, Sam was spending $30,000 a month to maintain his home.

*****

In mid-October, William Dean Howells and his son John came to visit. The eight-year-old was awestruck at the grandiosity of the mansion.

"They even have their soap painted," the child explained to his father when he saw a bar of pink soap at the bathroom sink.

The following morning, when the child saw a servant serving breakfast, he rushed to awaken his father.

"Better get up, Papa," the child said. "The *slave* is setting the table."

Even Howells was impressed.

"The Clemenses are whole-souled hosts," he later wrote his wife. "With an unextinguishable supply of money and a palace for a home."

During Howells' visit, Sam showed him the nearly-finished manuscript for the Tom Blankenship book.

"The structure of the book is masterful," Howells said, "but you should tone down the cursing. Throughout the work, you should change 'hell' to 'thunder.' Further, change 'damnation' to 'tarnation.'"

Sam peered at his old friend for a long moment.

"Your point is well-taken."

"I'm assuming your friend Tom Blankenship is the model for the main character?"

"That is correct."

"Who was your model for Aunt Polly?"

"My mother."

"And Becky Thatcher?"

"Laura Hawkins."

"And Huck Finn is based on you?"

"Correct on all counts!"

Howells smiled, then continued.

"This book will become one of the most enduring works in all of American literature. It will live in the hearts and minds of Americans for generations to come. It will define the pre-Civil War era in America."

"You're being too kind," Sam said.

"I know that of which I speak," Howells said. "It will become more famous than *Innocents Abroad*. And make more money."

Sam laughed.

"I hope you're correct," he said. "Let's see what the old curmudgeon has to say."

"Go to the Blueprint Shop on Third Avenue and get two additional copies made of the manuscript," Howells said. "That way, you'll have extra copies to shop around overseas."

"Splendid idea."

***

That night, in the marital bed, Sam told Olivia what Howells had to say about the Tom Blankenship book.

"He loved it and predicted it would be a classic."

Olivia didn't answer at first.

"How much more work is needed on the book?" Olivia said.

"It's as finished as it will ever be," Sam said. "I don't know what further work I can put into it to improve it."

"Have you decided on a title?"

"I'm going to call it *The Adventures with Tom Blankenship*."

Olivia quickly shook her head.

"That name is far too sophisticated for your main character," she said. "You need a last name that has a more rural, rustic connotation. Something with a down-home folksy sound."

"I'll have to put some thought into it," Sam said.

***

Over the next few months, Sam and Olivia fell into their lives in the new home. Only a week after they took residence, Sam moved his writing desk from his study on the second floor to the billiards room on the third floor so the girls would not disturb him. When Sam was at home, he expected to be the center of attention and his moods were volatile. One Sunday morning, neighbors watched as Sam threw all of his shirts out the second-story window because one was missing a button.

Despite his mercurial temper, Sam always found quality time to spend with his girls. One favorite pastime was playing big-game hunting in the library. There, with a fountain gently splashing in the adjacent conservatory, Sam would play the elephant, scrambling about on all fours across the Turkish carpets while Susy and Clara, who were the hunters, hung on to his back and neck. Many evenings, Olivia would read the two girls bedtime stories from *Grimm's Fairy Tales* and *Robinson Crusoe*.

Sam and Olivia's bed in the master bedroom was, in his own words "the most comfortable bed there ever was, with space for the entire family and carved angels on the bedposts to bring peace and pleasant dreams to the sleepers." Sam and Olivia loved the wooden angels so much, they slept with their heads at the foot of the bed so they could admire the charming cherubs. In later years, Susy and Clara recalled how they loved the cherubs as much as their parents and would spend many hours dressing up the wood carvings in dolls' clothing.

Sam's foremost complaint about the new home was his worrisome neighbor Harriet Beecher Stowe, famous as the author of *Uncle Tom's Cabin*. Sometimes, in the wee hours of the morning, Sam would be awakened by a piano playing loudly and an almost disembodied voice from next door singing "Rock of Ages" or "Battle Hymn of the Republic."

"Now what kind of human being goes singing religious songs at 3 a.m. in the morning?" he groused. "Can't she see fit to wait until sunrise for her overly-zealous yawling?"

Some mornings, Mrs. Stowe would tear out hyacinths and zinnias by the roots from the Clemenses' greenhouse, then appear as the front door and present them to Olivia as if they were her own. Rather than confront her neighbor about her strange behavior, Olivia put a pair of scissors at the greenhouse door, hoping the famous author would use them to harvest the flowers rather than tearing them out by the roots. But she never did.

***

In early November, the family's head gardener came to Sam and announced he had taken another position. Two days later, Clemens hired a new gardener. That night, in the marital bed, Olivia asked Sam about the new employee.

"He seemed like a capable fellow," Sam said, "so I hired him."

"What sort of work did he do in the past?"

"He worked at a sawmill."

"Doing what?"

"He was a sawyer."

Olivia quickly turned to her husband.

"A sawyer?" Olivia said.

"Yes. At the lumber mill, he makes useable lumber out of logs."

"That's the last name for your character," Olivia said.

"What character?"

"The main character in the Tom Blankenship book. The title should be *The Adventures of Tom Sawyer*."

Sam studied her for a moment, then he smiled.

"Brilliant!" he said with a big smile. "My darling, I would be lost without you."

***

A month passed. In early December, over breakfast, Sam suggested they stage a huge Christmas gathering to celebrate their new home and their successes over the past year.

"A wonderful idea, Samuel," Olivia said. "God has so blessed us this past year. We have a bounty of blessings to be thankful for. We'll put up an enormous tree, invite our friends and neighbors and have a bountiful Yuletide feast. We will hire a twelve-piece band and initiate the new ballroom with music and dancing."

"Oh, yes!" Sam said. "It will be a Christmas celebration

like Nook Farm has never seen before."

***

Three weeks later, the Christmas celebration for their new home turned out to be everything Sam and Olivia had hoped. Friends, members of the Monday Evening Club, business associates, including Elisha Bliss, were all in attendance. The revelers sipped champagne, mixed and mingled, and danced away the evening. Just after midnight, the revelers began to break up and the servants were left to clean up. Once the house was quiet, Sam and Olivia were snuggled up on the settee in the drawing room with a warm fire burning in the fireplace. Somewhere nearby, carolers were singing *Silent Night*.

"God has blessed us in innumerable ways," Olivia said. "He has graced us with two beautiful children, an unimaginable bounty of worldly goods and a magnificent home. We shall rear our children and live out the remainder of our lives in this house. It will be our forever home."

18
The Tom Blankenship Book

On the morning of January 3, 1876, Sam made the two-hour train ride from Hartford to New York and presented his manuscript for *The Adventures of Tom Sawyer* to his publisher Elisha Bliss. With his usual air of ornery grumpiness, Bliss groused when Sam handed him the sheaf of papers.

"What's it about?" Bliss said, thumbing through the pages.

"It's a hymn to my childhood," Clemens replied. "A story about a young boy growing up on the Mississippi River that recounts his adventures, his misadventures and mischief-making with his friend Huckleberry Finn."

Bliss's face screwed up in a frown.

"Is it a book for children?"

"Not necessarily. It can be read and enjoyed by both children and adults."

Bliss studied Sam for a long moment, then shook his head and put the manuscript aside.

"I've got two books ahead of it," he said. "I can't publish it until this spring."

"It can't wait that long."

"That's the best I can do."

Sam shrugged.

"I'll read it in the next few days," Bliss said. "Come back to my office in a week and I'll have an answer."

***

The following day, over lunch, Sam told Howells Bliss was dragging his feet with the Tom Sawyer book.

"I wouldn't waste time with him," Howells said. "The older he gets, the harder he is to deal with. You should speak with Moncure Conway."

"Who is Moncure Conway?"

"He's an author, a publisher and the American agent for Robert Browning."

"The poet?"

"One and the same. He has an office on 53rd Street and represents some of the biggest publishing houses in London. Take a copy of the manuscript to him."

"Splendid idea!"

***

Two days later, Sam and Howells were having lunch with Moncure Conway at the Knickerbocker Restaurant in lower Manhattan. In his late forties, Conway was a slim, balding man with a serious look, intelligent, twinkling eyes and clean-shaven face. Although he was born in Virginia, he had spent most of the past twenty years in England, where he published biographies of Nathaniel Hawthorne and Thomas Paine.

"Howells recommends your book highly," Conway began. "He says it is destined to become a classic."

Sam looked at Howells and smiled.

"Howells tends to be overly-enthusiastic," he said. "But in this case, I trust he is correct."

Sam opened a shoulder bag and handed Conway a copy of the *Tom Sawyer* manuscript.

Conway took the sheaf of papers and thumbed through them.

"Quite interesting," he said. "We'll need to sign an agent's contract."

Moments later, after both men had signed a contract, Sam explained he wanted Conway to sell it in England.

"I'll need a few days to go through the manuscript and decide where and how to pitch it," he said.

"Take your time," Sam said.

"Oh, I'm not accustomed to waiting," Conway said. "You'll have my reply within two weeks."

***

The following week, Clemens was back in Bliss's office.

"I read it and I must tell you I was not particularly impressed," Bliss began. "I have never witnessed another book quite like it, and when a book doesn't fit a proven pattern, you may rest assured it's certain to lose money."

"The fact that it's different from all the other books you've published is the characteristic what makes it singular and therefore attractive to the reader. All you know how to appreciate is what has already been tried."

"What can the reader learn from it?" Bliss said. "If all of today's boys were out trying to free slaves, dodge school and church, and consorting with the town's most lowdown, sorrowful riff-raff, where would our nation be? Children today should be taught morals, not encouraged to be even more lawless. I don't think it will sell. It's not a book for young boys."

Sam studied Bliss for a long moment.

"So, you don't want to publish it?"

"Not at the moment."

"Then I'll take it elsewhere."

"That's your right," Bliss said. "Just remember that, in the United States, your contract is exclusive with me."

"I know! I know!" Clemens said.

***

As promised, two weeks after their initial meeting, Clemens received a letter from Conway asking him to come to his office.

"We have a deal," Conway said. "The publisher Chatto and Windus of London wants to publish your book."

"When?"

"Next month," Conway said. "They love the book and want to rush it right through."

"What's the royalty percentage?"

"Six percent. Subscription teams are already out

canvassing readers."

"Splendid!" Sam said. "When will it go into bookstores?"

"Early March," Conway said. "The publishers see it as a best seller."

***

When Susy turned two, Clemens purchased a set of wooden letter blocks and began teaching her how to arrange them to make simple words like *cat*, *rat* and *dog*. After only a few months, Susy could recite her ABCs and, when Sam bought a small slate and chalk for her third birthday, she began spelling words. Now, in early February of her fourth year, Clemens had purchased a copy of *McGuffey's First Eclectic Reader* and wasted no time teaching her to read.

One afternoon, Sam and Susy were sitting in the conservatory practicing her reading as Olivia and Clara sat nearby and listened. While Susy sat in his lap, Sam held the book in front of them and pointed to a picture of a cat sleeping on a mat.

"Do you see the cat on the mat?"

"Yes, Papa!"

"Now let's read," Sam said, using his finger to guide her eyes along the lines.

"The cat," Susy read. "The mat. Is the cat on the mat? The cat is on the mat."

"Very good," Sam said, turning the page and running his finger along the new lines again.

"Do you see the man with a pen in his hand?" Sam said.

"Yes, Papa!"

"Now read…"

"The man. A pen. The man has a pen. Is the pen in his hand? The pen is in his hand."

Sam smiled from ear-to-ear.

"You're so intelligent," he said, pulling Susy to him and kissing her on the side of the head.

A pause as Sam turned the page.

"Papa, can you read with me?" Clara said.

"Darling, you're not old enough," he replied.

"Please…"

"First, you should play with Susy's letter blocks and learn your ABCs. Then I will read with you."

"When will that be?"

"When you get to be Susy's age, we'll read together."

"I want you to read with me now."

"I'm afraid we'll have to wait until you're older."

Clara looked at her mother, then put her face into her mother's bosom and began to cry softly.

"It's all right, darling," Olivia said. "Let's go to the greenhouse and pick some lovely flowers."

***

In mid-March, the *Tom Sawyer* book was published in England to rave reviews.

"The most notable work which Mark Twain has yet written," Conway wrote in a London *Telegraph* review. "It will certainly add to his reputation for a broad variety of literary powers."

In an *Atlantic Monthly* review, Howells wrote:

"The story is a wonderful study of the boy-mind which inhabits a world quite distinct from that in which he is bodily present with his elders. In this lies the manuscript's great charm and its universality, for boy nature is the same everywhere."

***

By late April, after only six weeks, the book had sold more than 13,000 copies in England and Howells was quick to congratulate Sam.

"Does Bliss know about your success in England?" Howells asked, during one of his visits to New York.

"I'm uncertain," Sam said. "I haven't heard from him."

"I'm having lunch with the old curmudgeon tomorrow," Howells said. "I'll inform him of your good fortune."

"Why do you think it's selling so well in England?"

"First, it's a good story with universal appeal," Howells said. "Further, it gives the English an outlet for their sense of superiority."

"What is your meaning?" Sam said.

"The British have always considered Americans a bunch of shiftless, uncouth, lawless, unwashed savages," Howells said. "The *Tom Sawyer* book proves it."

Sam burst out in raucous laughter.

***

Three days later, Clemens received a letter from Bliss asking him to come to his office. Clemens wasted no time hearing what his publisher had to say.

"I've changed my mind," Bliss began. "I've made the decision to publish the *Tom Sawyer* book."

"You noticed it's selling well in England."

Bliss's face screwed up in disapproval.

"That possibly had something to do with it."

"It has everything to do with it," Sam said. "And you are well aware."

"I'll pay five percent royalty."

"I want six percent," Sam said. "That's what England is paying."

"Absolutely not! The most I have ever paid any author is five percent."

Sam stood up to leave.

"Very well, if you change your mind…" he said, "you may let me know. Good day!"

Then he turned to go.

"Wait! Wait!" Bliss aid. "Perhaps I was a bit hasty."

"Six percent or I'm out the door."

"All right, dammit, I'll do it!"

"I'm happy to see you finally came to your senses," Sam said. "When will it go to press?"

"In a few weeks," Bliss said. "I still have books ahead of yours."

"When will you notify the subscription houses to start selling it? They need to have commitments before the book is published."

"Next week," Bliss said.

"Very well, Sam said. "Let's draw up the contract. I'm happy to see you arrived back at your senses."

***

After leaving Bliss's New York office, Sam stopped at a toy store on 53rd Street and Broadway to buy gifts for the girls. After searching more than an hour, he finally decided on a rolling hoop for Susy and paper dolls for Clara. When he arrived back at home, he presented them to the girls.

Once Olivia saw the paper dolls, she took the package and seated her and Clara on the floor in the drawing room.

"My! My!" Olivia said as she spread out the outfits. "Look at this! You can dress up the little girl with all these dresses and hats and shoes."

The two-year-old peered curiously.

"What is it?"

"Paper dolls," Olivia said. "Let me show you how to use them."

Moments later, mother and daughter were on the floor dressing up the cardboard model with various costumes.

The moment Susy opened her gift, a small metal hoop with a baton, she seemed confused.

"What shall I do with it, Papa?" she said.

"Come outside and I'll show you," Sam said.

Moments later, they were in the front yard where Sam demonstrated by starting the hoop rolling with his hand, then keeping the hoop rolling upright by striking it intermittently with the baton. After only two attempts, Susy was rolling the metal hoop all around the yard.

"Look at me, Papa!" Susy squealed.

Sam was delighted.

Moments later, when Sam returned to the drawing room, he saw the paper dolls scattered aimlessly about the floor with Clara nowhere in sight.

"What happened?" he asked.

"She didn't like her toy," Olivia said. "When you and Susy went to the front yard, she started to destroy it."

"Why?"

"I have no earthly idea," Olivia said. "I sent her to her room."

"I've never seen a young girl that didn't like paper dolls."

"She may be a bit too young," Olivia said.

***

A month passed. In late May, Clemens was back in Bliss's office checking on publication of the *Tom Sawyer* book.

"Why hasn't the book been published?" Sam said.

"I informed you that there were two other books ahead of it," Bliss said. "I can't go pushing a book into publication when I have others I feel will be more profitable."

"You're dragging your feet," Sam said. "If you don't want to publish it, I want it back."

"You signed a contract," Bliss said. "You can only have it back when you're released from the contract."

"Suppose I filed a legal action?"

"That would be your death warrant with my company."

Sam got up to go.

"Where are you going?"

"I'm giving you one month more," Sam said.

"Then what?" Bliss shot back.

Sam didn't reply. Then he turned and left the office, slamming the door behind him.

***

During the summer of 1876, the Clemens family, as they often did, spent the months of June and July with the family of Olivia's adopted sister Susan in Elmira. When Olivia's father and mother were first married, Mrs. Langdon was unable to conceive a child for the first three years, so they adopted Susan Crane in 1840 at the age of four and reared her to adulthood. In 1858, Susan married Theodore Crane, one of Jervis's business associates, and in 1870, when Jervis died, the Cranes inherited the family vacation home known as Quarry Farm. Although Susan was almost ten years older than Olivia, they remained close throughout their lives.

While the Clemens family visited the Cranes that summer, Sam spent his mornings writing, but, during the afternoons, the family and household staff would gather on the front porch to listen to what he had written that day. One such listener was Mary Ann Cord, a sixty-year-old, mannish-looking former slave who served as cook at Quarry Farm. One afternoon, after reading the day's offering, Sam asked Cord for her opinion about his writing.

"Sounds like them people had lots of troubles," Cord said.

"Have you ever had troubles?" Sam asked. "How did you come to live sixty years and never have any trouble?"

"Oh, Mr. Clemens, I've had my troubles," she said.

"Would you like to tell us about it?"

Cord began by explaining she was born a slave in Virginia on a tobacco plantation where she married and gave birth to seven children. Then, in 1852, her entire family was torn apart.

"The master sold my old man and they took him away. Then they began to sell my children and take them away too. I started to cry and the master said: 'Stop yo' blubbering!' and he hit me on the mouth with his hand.

"Finally, all of my children was gone but my little Henry. When they came for Henry, I grabbed him and pulled him close to my breast. 'I'll kill the man that touches this child,' I told them.

"But my little Henry whispered in my ear, 'I'm going to run away, then I'll work and buy your freedom.' Oh Lord bless this child; he was always so good. But they got him, they took him, the men did, but I hit at them and struck one with my chain and then they give it to me in my face and head, but I didn't mind that."

Over the next ten years, Cord said she lost contact with her husband and all of her children. Years later, during the Civil War, Cord was living in North Carolina when black Troops fighting for the Union came through and took over her master's plantation as their headquarters and designated Cord as their cook.

"One morning while I was stooping by the stove, I had a pan of hot biscuits in my hand and I was about to raise up, when I saw a black face coming around under mine and these eyes gazing into mine. I just stopped right there and never budged. Just gazed and gazed into that black face. Then the pan began to tremble, and all of a sudden, I knew. The pan dropped to the floor and I grabbed his arm and shoved back the sleeve… then I goes for his forehead and pushed the hair back so I could see his face in full.

"Boy!" I said. "If you ain't my Henry, what you doing with that welt on your arm and that scar on your forehead? Dear Lord of heaven be praised. I got my own again."

The old black woman stopped and turned to Sam.

"Oh, Mr. Clemens, I ain't had no trouble. And no joy."

Sam was so moved by her story that he wrote it down exactly as he had heard it and filed it away in his desk drawer. In the story, he gave Cord the fictitious name "Aunt Rachel."

***

By the fall of 1876, at age four, little Susy was reading everything in sight. Together she and Sam had read the classic *The Princess and the Goblin* together at least twenty times. Then there was Aunt Louisa's *Oft Told Tales*, *Through the Looking Glass*, *A Flatiron for a Farthing* and *Black Beauty*. Every time they would read *Black Beauty*, Susy would always ask Sam to read the last page twice.

At Thanksgiving, Sam bought her a large blackboard and he would spend endless hours with her practicing writing simple sentences. One morning in the drawing room, Sam and Susy were practicing writing while Clara sat nearby in Olivia's lap and watched.

Susy had written the sentence "My father is Samuel Clemens."

"Now read it to me," Sam said.

"My father is Samuel Clemens," she said.

"Well done!" Sam said.

Then Susy started to write something of her own choosing.

"My mother is Olivia Clemens," she wrote.

Sam and Olivia broke out in laughter.

Susy wrote something else.

"I love my father and mother very much."

Again, the parents laughed proudly.

"And we love you very much, darling," Olivia said.

Then Susy went to her father and hugged him. Moments later, she turned to her mother and did the same.

When Susy returned to the slate, Clara turned to her mother.

"Don't you and Papa love me?" she said.

"Of course, we love you!" Olivia said. "We love each of you equally."

***

That night in the marital bed, Sam and Olivia discussed the incident.

"You're going to have to start paying more attention to Clara," Olivia said. "She feels you ignore her. That you don't love her."

"She is just so inexorably contrary," Sam said. "Nothing I say or do pleases her."

"I'm aware," Olivia said. "She takes after my mother."

Sam laughed.

"At least you understand the origins."

Olivia turned pensive.

"Let's give her some time. I believe she will grow out of it."

***

It was Christmas morning of 1876 at the Clemens household. The four family members, in their pajamas and bedclothes, were gathered around the Christmas tree in the drawing room opening their presents. Wrapping paper, both opened and unopened boxes and packing material were scattered about the drawing room floor. Olivia had bought Sam a new bathrobe, bedroom slippers, a new briarwood pipe and a copy of Rousseau's *Discourse on Inequality*. For his wife, Sam had purchased a copy of Tolstoy's *Anna Karenina*. Susy had received the popular board game, the Snake Game, several new dresses and a copy of Charles Kingsley's *The Water-Babies*.

Clara had received a set of wooden letter blocks, a cup and ball toy, several dresses and a huge toy doll which was almost as big as Clara. For the entire family, Sam had bought a Zoetrope, a contraption which featured a lion jumping off and on the back of a horse as it spun around a circus arena to create the illusion of moving images.

Finally, all of the gifts had been opened. Susy was sitting quietly reading her new copy of *The Water-Babies*; Sam, peeping through the aperture of the Zoetrope, was watching the lion jump off and on the horse's back, while Olivia was reading excerpts from her new book. For a moment, she looked up from the book to Clara, who was sitting on the floor dressing her oversized doll.

"Do you like your new doll?" Olivia said.

"No!" Clara said, throwing the doll aside. "I wanted a rocking horse. I told Santa Claus to bring me a rocking horse."

"Darling!" Olivia said. "Susy already has a rocky horse. You can ride hers."

"No! I want my own!" Clara said. "Santa Claus doesn't love me. Mommy, why doesn't Santa Claus love me?"

"Clara, baby! Of course, Santa Claus loves you. He brought you all these beautiful toys."

"It wasn't what I wanted."

Sam turned to Clara.

"Now you mind your manners, young lady," he said. "Or I'll give you a spanking."

Clara, who didn't seem to hear, suddenly began kicking the partially dressed doll.

"Clara! Clara! What are you doing?" Olivia said. "Why are you hurting your doll?"

"Because I hate it! I wanted a rocking horse."

Quickly, Sam stepped forward.

"You will not behave like that," he said.

Then he turned Clara over his knee and began spanking her. Clara began to wail. Susy looked on solemnly.

Moments later, the punishment over, Clara broke away from Sam and rushed to her mother's arms crying and screaming. Finally, Olivia managed to calm her down.

"Oh, Mama!" Clara screamed. "Santa Claus doesn't love

me! He loves Susy, but he doesn't love me."

***

By Christmas of 1876, six months after publication, *The Adventures of Tom Sawyer* had sold only 3,000 copies in the States, a tenth of what *The Gilded Age* had sold over the same period. Sam was livid and, only a few days after Christmas, he was in Bliss's office for a showdown.

"I told you it wouldn't sell," Bliss said.

"The book, it was not," Sam said. "It sold more than 50,000 copies in England in six months," Sam said. "It failed to sell in the States because you mangled the sales plan. That wouldn't have happened if you hadn't dragged your feet with the subscription houses."

"I had other books to promote first."

"You lying old coot!"

"Don't you call me a liar!" Bliss said. "It failed to sell in the States because the Canadians and the Germans pirated it. That would not have happened if you hadn't published it in England."

"What choice did I have? You turned me down!" Sam shouted.

"I refuse to publish a book which I believe will lose money."

"You lying scoundrel," Sam shot back. "The book failed to sell because you destroyed the selling of it. It took me six years to write the book and you only needed four months to make it a failure. You were tardy with the subscription houses. The book should have been sold by subscription houses before it was published. Not after…"

Bliss's face screwed up in anger.

"Get out of my office!" he shouted.

Livid anger flashed across Sam's face. Instantly, he arose from the chair, strode across the room, reached across the desk and grabbed a fistful of Bliss's shirt.

"If you were twenty years younger, I'd show you what being a man was."

"Get your hands off me!" Bliss shouted.

For a moment, Sam held the older man in his grasp, then roughly pushed him back down into the chair.

Instantly, Bliss recovered himself, reached into his desk drawer and withdrew a pistol.

Sam stared at him for a moment.

"You put your hands on me again and I'll blow a hole in you that you can throw a dog through."

Sam glared at him for a moment.

"Get out of my office!" Bliss said. "Now!"

Sam, calmer now, threw his hands in the air.

"To hell with you and your publishing company," he said. "You've defrauded, cheated and hornswoggled me for the last time. I'm finished with you."

"Get out!" Bliss said, pointing the gun at Sam. "Now!"

"You low-life son of a whore," Sam said, shaking his fist at Bliss. "You take your publishing house and stick it where the sun don't shine."

"Get out! And don't come back!"

"Don't you worry!"

For a moment, Sam stood glaring at Bliss, livid anger in his eyes.

Then, he turned and stalked out, slamming the door behind him.

***

Sam needed only two months to find a new publisher.

The following February, he sent the story he had heard from the former slave at Quarry Farm to Howells and asked him to publish it in the *Atlantic Monthly* under the title "A True Story." Howells was delighted.

After the story was published, Howells sent a letter to Clemens explaining that James Osgood, a local publisher friend, had read the story and wanted to publish it as a small book with illustrations.

"You should come up to Boston and meet James," Howells said in the letter. "He's a publisher that loves his authors. You and he will get along famously."

"Can I take quarters at your place?"

"Absolutely!" Howells replied. "My accommodations are not as grandiose as yours, but I promise you'll be quite comfortable."

***

Four days later, Clemens was on a train for Boston. Upon arrival, Howells met him at the train station and, once Sam was settled into his quarters, Howells introduced him to Osgood over dinner.

James R. Osgood was a balding, dour-faced man in his mid-forties with a well-trimmed mustache, piercing eyes and glasses. A child prodigy, Osgood could read and write Latin at age three and entered college at age twelve. As president of Osgood and Company Publishing, he had already had great success with Howells' *The Lady of the Aroostook* and Walt Whitman's *Leaves of Grass*. From the first moment Osgood met Sam, he was mesmerized.

"Oh, Mr. Clemens!" he said. "It is truly an honor to meet you. Of all American authors, you're my favorite. I read the jumping frog story many years ago and now, after all these years, it remains my favorite."

Over dinner that night, Osgood explained that he wanted to begin publishing Sam's books, beginning with *A True Story*. He promised to pay six percent royalties and give Sam final editorial approval of all future manuscripts before publication. Sam eagerly jumped at the opportunity.

***

When *A True Story* was published two months later, sales far exceeded Sam's expectations. Although it was a small book of only forty-six pages, it included vivid illustrations of slaves and plantation life, which brought the tragic story to life. When Howells published the story in two parts in the *Atlantic Monthly*, it received glowing reviews since it served as a stark reminder of the evils of slavery. After only three months, *A True Story* had sold 28,000 copies, more than four times the number the *Tom Sawyer* book had sold in the same period.

The Adventures of Tom Sawyer would not sell briskly until 1885, nine years after its initial publication, when it became linked in the public's mind with the *Adventures of Huckleberry Finn,* which was published that year. The saturation of the pirated Canadian editions which were sold in the States was the primary reason for the poor sales. Bliss allowed Bret Harte's book *Gabriel Conroy* to stall American Publishing's marketing efforts on behalf of Sam's book. Despite this, over the course of his lifetime, *The Adventures of Tom Sawyer* would sell more copies than any book he had ever written.

19
Paige the Perfectionist

The year was 1880. Rutherford B. Hayes was president; Sioux Chief Sitting Bull had surrendered at Ft. Buford, North Dakota; Thomas Edison invented the electric light bulb; Kansas became the first state to prohibit alcohol; P.T. Barnum unveiled General Tom Thumb to the world; and Samuel Langhorne Clemens, his wife Olivia and their brood, Susy, aged eight, and Clara, aged six, were still living in their "forever home" in Hartford. On February 2 of that year, Clemens and his beloved Livy were due to celebrate their tenth wedding anniversary and, for the occasion, Sam wanted a very special gift to commemorate it.

One day in mid-January, after a dentist's visit in downtown Hartford, Sam stopped in to see his old friend Dwight Buell at his jewelry shop. Buell, who had become fast friends with Clemens after delivering a lecture to the Monday Evening Society at Nook Farm, was a smallish man in his early forties with a balding head, a sallow face and glasses.

"I want a gold ring with an inset of ten small diamonds in a circle," Sam said. "Inside the band, engrave the words 'I shall always love you.'"

Buell studied Sam for a moment, then proceeded to make a drawing of the proposed piece. Once complete, Clemens examined the drawing.

"That's the piece I want," he said.

"I'll deliver it to your home on the night on February 1," Buell said.

"Splendid!" Sam said. "We'll have cigars and brandy and play some eight ball."

"May I bring a friend?" Buell said.

"Absolutely," Clemens said. "I wish the gift to be a surprise, so please be discreet with your delivery."

***

Two weeks later, on the night of February 1, Buell and another man appeared at the Clemenses' home. Earlier that evening, Sam had suggested to Olivia, who was three months pregnant, that she spend a quiet evening with the girls and the household staff downstairs while he entertained his friends upstairs in the billiards room. When Buell appeared, the man with him was a smallish, clean-shaven, smartly-dressed man in his late thirties who introduced himself as Thomas W. Paige. Once introductions were over, Sam provided cigars and brandy, then the trio proceeded to play a game of rotation billiards.

"What sort of work do you do?" Sam asked as he chalked his cue.

"I'm an inventor," Paige said. "At the moment, I'm perfecting a typesetting machine."

Sam stopped and studied the man.

"A typesetting machine?" he said finally. "I know a thing or two about typesetting."

"My machine, once perfected, will do the work of ten typesetters using the manual galley method."

"That's an impossibility," Sam said. "Can your machine think?"

"In a manner of speaking," Paige said. "When perfected, it will be able to set 3,000 Ems of type per hour."

"You should see it," Buell interrupted. "It's a truly marvelous machine. I have already invested $10,000 in it."

"Why don't you come by and see the prototype," Paige said. "The machine is being built as the Colt Arms Manufacturing company here in Hartford."

"May I pay you a visit on Monday?" Sam said.

"Absolutely!"

***

February 2, 1880 *Today, my beloved Livy and I celebrated our tenth wedding anniversary. Over the course of those years, Livy has managed to "civilize" me despite my ornery, shiftless, God-forsaken ways. Under her esteemed guidance, I am duty-bound to shave every day, don clean undergarments, clean my teeth and clip the hairs in my nose. At her behest, I attend church and sing obediently along with the choir; I have been taught when to use a soup spoon, stand when ladies enter a room, never spit in public and when to use a salad fork. I am allowed two cigars a day, one glass of wine with the evening meal and forbidden to utter any blasphemous oaths. Lordy! Lordy! Whatever happened to that foot-loose and fancy-free devil by the name of Samuel Langhorne Clemens? If Scratchy Mitchell and Ben Coon could see me now, they would bust their britches with laughter. Such is the price of love.*

***

The following Monday morning, Sam was at the Colt Arms Manufacturing plant where Paige's typesetting machine was being built. When he first saw the contraption, Sam stopped, then walked around it to try to understand its various components. To Sam, it looked more like a miniature printing press than a typesetting machine. Standing more than seven feet high, four feet wide and weighing more than three tons, it was a complex composite of trays, channels, typefaces, levers and 18,000 moving parts.

Finally, after an initial examination, Sam turned to Paige.

"Let me see this thing operate," he said.

Then Sam watched as Paige took a seat at the operator's console and put the machine into action. Reading from a page of test copy, Paige pressed keys on a keyboard and the machine began making a rhythmic clicking sound that reminded Sam of a sewing machine. He watched as the different levers, trays and channels began moving back and forth. Moments later, the sound stopped and Paige reached down and withdrew a small block of lead type from a tray, then handed it to Sam.

Sam inspected the type.

"Let me see your copy," he said.

Paige handed him the sheet of copy.

Sam was astounded.

"Absolutely amazing!" he said. "But it's not justifying the lines."

"It will once I have it perfected."

"When do you determine that will be?"

"Not certain. Maybe another few months."

"I want to set down my name to invest $10,000," Sam said.

"Come into my office and we'll draw up the papers."

***

Five months passed. In the spring of 1878, while browsing in the family library, Sam had happened upon a copy of *The Prince and the Page,* by Charlotte M. Yonge, a story about a prince disguised as a blind beggar. Once he had read it, an idea came to him for an altogether different story of his own making. He would have a prince and a pauper exchange places, and through a series of adventures, each would learn the trials and tribulations of the other's life.

Several days later, Sam set about writing the story and spent most of the remainder of the year working on it. By the spring of 1879, the novel was almost eighty percent finished, then Clemens became disinterested and laid it aside. Over the next year, the manuscript went untouched, then, in March of 1880, Sam pulled out all of the stops to finish it. Now, in early July, the manuscript for *The Prince and the Pauper* was finally ready to present to James Osgood, his new publisher in Boston.

***

Sam's train trip to Boston the following morning was uncomfortable. The two brothers in his compartment chatted endlessly about the proceeds of their father's last will and testament. For lunch, Sam was served corned beef and cabbage, and afterward, he had to buy a digestive aid from the conductor. After five hours into the trip, the brothers left the train and a new passenger, a tall, thirtyish man wearing a priest's collar, entered Sam's compartment. Upon entering, he smiled politely and took a seat across from Sam. Once comfortably settled, he opened a traveler's bag, withdrew a sheaf of papers and began reading some handwritten pages.

For several minutes, Sam sat quietly, then, bored from peering out the window at the endless stream of passing farms, mountains, small towns and manufacturing plants, he turned to his fellow traveler.

"May I ask what you're reading?"

"Poetry," the man said. "Poems written by a recently-passed Jesuit priest."

"What was his name?"

"Gerard Manley Hopkins."

"Never heard of him."

"His poems have not been published. He died several years ago with his work unpublished. Before he died, he gave them to me and instructed me to destroy them."

"Interesting!" Sam said

"Would you be interested in reading one?"

"Absolutely!" Sam said. "I'm an author myself."

"An author?"

"My name is Sam Clemens, better known as Mark Twain."

"Oh, yes, Mr. Clemens," the man said, shaking Sam's hand. "I read your book *Innocents Abroad* some years ago. My name is Robert Bridges. I am the abbot of a Jesuit Abbey in Dublin."

The man then began rifling through the pages. Finally, he stopped.

"This is one of my favorites," he said, withdrawing one of the pages. "The title is *The Windhover*."

Sam took the page and began to read.

After he finished the poem, he was quiet for a moment

"Isn't a windhover a shore bird that lives along the coasts of the North Sea?"

"That is correct," the man replied. "The bird is commonly called a kestrel."

A long pause.

"What are your thoughts?"

Sam looked at him.

"Hold on!" Sam said. "Let me read it a second time."

Sam read the poem a second time.

Again, the priest peered at Sam for a response.

"I'm not much of a religious person," Sam said finally, "but I must say that is a beautiful poem. Will you permit me to keep this copy? I want to show it to my wife."

"Please do," the man said. "I have another."

"Much obliged!" Sam said. "My wife will take great joy in this poem. She is a religious person. When do you plan on having the poems published?"

Bridges flashed a quick smile.

"Some day!"

***

When Sam arrived in Boston that night, Howells met him at the station. Once Clemens had retrieved his baggage, they traveled across town to Howells' home in the trendy Beacon Hill section of the city and Sam was settled in for the night. After dinner, Sam showed Howells the manuscript for *The Prince and The Pauper*. Howells read the manuscript that night.

"This is a considerable departure from the *Tom Sawyer* book," Howells said the next morning over breakfast. "It is a well-defined children's book."

"At first glance, it appeals to younger readers, but there are overtones which render it attractive to adults as well."

"Oh, yes," Howells replied. "Further, the story has some far-reaching philosophical implications."

***

The following morning, Sam was in the offices of James R. Osgood Publishing in downtown Boston to show him *The Prince and The Pauper* manuscript. As always, Osgood was taken with Clemens.

"It's a pleasure to see you again, Mr. Clemens," he said. "I'm anxious to peruse your latest offering."

"I'll be expecting a six percent royalty," Sam said.

"Done."

"Also, I want final approval of the manuscript before it is published," Sam added.

"Agreed," Osgood said. "What new projects do you have in mind?"

"Sometime over the next year, I plan to write a narrative about my days on the Mississippi River as a steamboat pilot," Sam said. "The research was done several years ago. The working title will be *Life on the Mississippi*."

"I trust you will give me an opportunity to publish the book once the manuscript is ready."

"Let's determine the sales of *The Prince and the Pauper* first," Sam said. "If you can prove you can successfully sell that book, then I'll give you an answer."

"As you wish," Osgood said. "I shall provide a response to your latest book within a week."

***

Late the following afternoon, Clemens arrived back in Hartford and, when he showed up at home, Olivia and the two girls greeted him at the door with open arms. That night, in the marital bed, Olivia asked for his thoughts about Osgood.

"He doesn't have a fire in his gut," Sam said. "I agreed for his company to publish *The Prince and the Pauper,* but it is only a trial. If sales fail to meet my expectations, he won't get another."

"Were you not satisfied with sales of *A True Story?*"

"I was," Sam said, "but I'm hoping the day will come when I can publish my own books. I'm been bamboozled by publishers long enough."

A pause.

"Oh!" Sam said, remembering the poem. "I brought something for you."

Instantly, he turned to the bedside table and took a folded sheet of paper.

"I believe you'll enjoy this poem," he said, handing Olivia the single page.

311

"What sort of poem is it?"

"A religious poem. A deeply religious poem."

Olivia began reading silently.

"Read it aloud," Sam said.

Olivia cleared her throat then began reading.

"I caught this morning morning's minion,
Kingdom of daylight's dauphin, dapple-dawn-drawn
Falcon, in his riding
Of the rolling level underneath him steady air, and
striding
High there, how he rung upon the rein of a wimpling wing
In his ecstasy! then off, off forth on swing,
As a skate's heel sweeps smooth on a bow-bend: the hurl
and gliding
Rebuffed the big wind. My heart in hiding
Stirred for a bird, – the achieve of, the mastery of the thing!

Brute beauty and valor and act, oh, air, pride, plume, here
Buckle! and the fire that breaks from thee then, a billion
Times told lovelier, more dangerous, O my chevalier!

No wonder of it: sheer plod makes plough down sillion
Shine, and blue-bleak embers, ah my dear,
Fall, gall themselves, and gash gold-vermilion.

Olivia stopped reading. For a long moment, she waited so she could savor and digest the words.

"A truly magnificent poem," she said, looking up from the page. "It is a glorification of Christ our Lord like nothing else I have ever read. Only a man whose soul was close to God could have written such a poem."

"The poet was a Jesuit priest."

"I thought as much," she said. "When I die, I am requesting that you read this poem at my graveside."

"It shall be done."

"I love you, Samuel."

"And I love you, Livy."

***

July 27, 1880 *Last night, my darling Livy delivered a fifth member to the Clemens family in the form of Jane Lampton Clemens, a seven-pound, four-ounce bundle of bawling human flesh. Like Susy and Clara, she has soft brown eyes, a shock of silken dark hair and a scream that will wake up the dead. I remained with Livy throughout her labor and, although she has remained thin during her pregnancy, the birth passed without crisis. The new baby is thoroughly satisfactory, as far as it goes, but we had hoped it was going to be twins. Several months before the birth, we agreed that the child would be officially named after my mother, Jane Lampton Clemens, but Livy said she wanted to call her "Jean."*

***

Over the first few weeks, the new arrival was the center of attention in the household. Olivia was forever mindful to feed the infant regularly and keep her safe from drafts while Susy, at age eight, and Clara, at age six, were always anxious to help with the infant's care. After a few days, Olivia allowed Susy and Clara to take turns feeding the newborn with a bottle.

One morning, while the infant was sleeping and Olivia was downstairs supervising the household staff, Sam suddenly heard the baby crying, then loud voices from the marital bedroom. Quickly, he made his way to the floor below. When he arrived, the infant was wailing in its crib and Susy and Clara were fighting over the baby bottle.

"I want to feed her!" Susy said.

"No. It's my turn! You fed her last time!" Clara screamed, wrenching the bottle out of Susy's hands.

"Children! Children!" Sam said. "What's the problem?"

"I want to feed the baby," Susy said.

"No! I want to feed her."

"Whoa! Whoa!" Sam said. "This baby needs both of you! One to hold the bottle and one to rock the cradle. Give me the bottle."

Calmer now, Clara reluctantly handed over the bottle.

"Now let's go to the crib," Sam said.

The two girls obediently followed him.

At the crib, Sam handed the bottle to Susy.

"Now, you feed the baby," he said.

Then he turned to Clara.

"And you rock the cradle," he said.

"No! I want to feed the baby," Clara said.

"You're needed to rock the cradle."

Clara clenched her fists and slammed her foot on the floor.

"You give Susy everything she wants," Clara said. "You love her more than me."

"That's not true," Sam said. "I love both of you."

"You give Susy whatever she requests and you give me nothing."

Anger flashed across Sam's face.

"Young lady, you will not talk to me like that. I'm your father."

Instantly, Sam grabbed Clara's arm, seated himself in a nearby chair, tuned her over his knee and began to spank her.

Instantly, Clara began to wail. After Sam had delivered five or six blows to the child's behind, Olivia rushed into the room.

"Samuel! Stop that! Stop that now!"

Upon seeing Olivia, Clemens held his spanking hand, then released the child. Instantly, Clara ran into her mother's arms screaming and crying.

***

August 20, 1880 *For some consarned reason, I am unable to relinquish this Paige fellow and his typesetting machine from my mind. Six months ago, when I witnessed him putting the contraption through its paces, I was thoroughly amazed at its accomplishments. Somewhere, long, long ago, I dreamed such a machine existed in this world. A machine that would eliminate the drudgery of a typesetter building print lines one letter at a time. At that moment, however, I determined the idea was just that... a meaningless dream, an idle figment of my imagination. Now, as I remember that fateful day, I am of the settled opinion that Paige's machine could well be its realization. Over the next few days, I shall return to see the latest incarnation and confirm in my mind that Paige's contraption is the real McCoy.*

***

Two days later, Clemens was back at the Colt Arms Manufacturing company. When he arrived at Paige's office, he saw a secretary and, beyond the office through a glass window, he could see Paige hunkered down under the machine tinkering with the undercarriage.

"May I see Mr. Paige?"

"He's busy at the moment," the secretary said. "He can't be disturbed."

"I'm one of his investors."

"I'm sorry, but I have strict orders to not disturb him."

Sam, not to be denied, stepped behind the secretary's desk and rapped on the window.

"Wait!" the secretary said. "You can't do that!"

Paige, looking very haggard, looked up and saw Clemens.

Looking very irritated, Paige crawled out from under the machine and came to the window.

"I want to see the newest improvements in your machine," Sam said.

"I'm too busy at the moment," he said.

"Damnation, man!" Sam said. "I'm one of your investors."

"You're one of many," Paige said. "If you'll return next Thursday at noon, I'll make plans to meet with you."

Then, Paige pulled a curtain inside the room and blocked out all viewing into the room.

Sam turned angrily to the secretary.

"Who in tarnation does he think he is?"

"He's very busy making improvements on his machine."

***

During the hot, lazy days of late August, one of the favorite pastimes in the Clemens household was to invite friends and neighbors over for play-acting. For the performances, Sam would create a makeshift stage in the drawing room by stringing a curtain behind a settee. Sam's favorite skit, which he performed with Susy, was the children's poem "There was a Pretty Princess…," a story about a young princess who was put to sleep by an evil fairy then awakened by a handsome prince's kiss. In the roles, Sam would play the prince, eight-year-old Susy would play the princess, while other family members and neighbors would narrate the story from the poem as the scenes were acted out. Olivia always served as director.

One Saturday morning, the stage had been set, the actors were in their places and the performance was ready to begin.

"Are all the players ready?" Olivia said.

"We are!" said Sam and Susy in unison.

"Is the chorus ready?" Olivia said, referring to the group of Clara, Mrs. Charles Warner and her daughter Cathy.

"We're ready," the group announced.

The players took their places behind the curtain and the narrators began reading the first line of the poem to an empty stage.

"There was a pretty princess, a princess, a princess, there was a pretty princess long, long ago."

With that, Susy, decked out in a tiara and an elegant-looking satin dress worthy of a princess, appeared from behind the curtain and took a seat on the settee.

"An evil fairy cast a spell upon her, upon her, upon her; an evil fairy cast a spell upon her, long, long ago."

The evil fairy, played by Mrs. Warner's oldest, Emily, entered, all dressed in black. Then she slipped up behind the princess, touched her shoulder with a black wand, then darted behind the curtain again.

"The princess she went sleeping, went sleeping, went sleeping,
The princess she went sleeping, long, long ago."

Susy pretended to be drowsy, rested her head on her hands,

then reclined slowly on the couch as if sleeping.

"A handsome prince came riding, came riding, came riding,
A handsome prince came riding long, long ago."

Sam, with a silly-looking crown on his head and a white papier-mâché sword dangling at his side, came clippity-clopping in and stopped his horse in front of the sleeping Susy. He dismounted his horse, inspected her, then his face took on a quizzical look. Suddenly, he had an idea.

"It was then he kissed her, he kissed her, he kissed her,
It was then he kissed her long, long ago."

Sam bent over and kissed Susy on the forehead. Suddenly, she awakened, arose from the settee, rubbed her eyes, stood up and took Sam's hand.

"Suddenly she awakened, awakened, awakened,
Suddenly she awakened long, long ago."

Then, hand in hand, Sam and Susy danced off the stage and disappeared behind the curtain.

"Now everybody's happy, so happy, so happy,
Now everybody's happy, so happy now!"

Clara, Olivia and the others applauded. Moments later, both Sam and Susy reappeared from behind the curtain, took bows to further applause, then disappeared behind the curtain again.

Ten minutes later, the curtain had been removed, the settee had been replaced to its original position and the Clemens family, along with the neighbors, were enjoying cold lemonade in the conservatory.

"How was my performance, Papa?" Susy asked.

"Oh, sweetheart, you were wonderful," he said. "Someday you'll be a famous actress."

"No!" Susy said. "I want to be an author like you."

***

Three days later, Sam, Olivia and six-year-old Clara were in the greenhouse. Olivia, using scissors, was clipping the stems of yellow dahlias, then handing them to Clara, who had an armful. Sam, puffing on his pipe, stood nearby and watched.

Suddenly, Susy, holding a book in her hand, appeared.

"Papa," Susy said. "Can we go into the conservatory and read?"

"What book do you have?"

"The poems of Edward Lear."

"Of course! Come along, sweetheart."

Sam turned, Susy took his arm, and together they left the greenhouse.

Once they were gone, Clara turned to her mother.

"Mama, why does Papa call Susy 'sweetheart'?

"Because he loves her."

A long pause.

"Papa doesn't call me 'sweetheart.' Does he love me?"

"Of course, Papa loves you."

"Why doesn't he call me sweetheart?"

"Why don't you ask him?" Olivia said.

***

Ten minutes later, Olivia and Clara found Sam reading in his study.

"Samuel," Olivia said. "Clara has something to ask you."

Sam turned from his reading to face them.

"Then come sit on my knee and ask whatever you desire."

The six-year-old strode across the room and took a seat on Sam's knee.

"Now what is your question?"

"Do you love me?"

Sam looked at Olivia then turned back to Clara.

"Of course, I love you. You're my flesh and blood."

"Do you love Susy more or me more?"

"I love both of you equally."

"Do you love me enough to buy me anything I want?"

Sam stopped.

"Whoa!" he said. "I would not venture that far. Exactly what do you want?"

"Will you buy me a piano?"

Sam looked at Olivia.

She nodded.

"I'll see what I can do."

"Papa, is that a yes or a no?"

"It's a maybe. Give me a few days and I'll let you know."

***

On Thursday of the following week, Susy was busy with her math tutor most of the morning while Clara was up the street visiting with Emily Warner. When Mrs. Warner returned Clara to the Clemenses' home that afternoon, Sam and Olivia met their daughter at the door.

"How was your visit?" Sam asked

"Oh, it was such fun, Papa" Clara said. "We spent most of the morning listening to Emily's father tell stories about the Civil War. After that, Emily, her mother and I played charades."

"Sound like you had a grand time," Sam said. "Come with me to the ballroom. I have something to show you."

"What is it, Papa?"

"Come with me!" Sam said, taking her hand.

Moments later, they stepped into the ballroom, then Sam, with a wave of his hand, presented a new upright piano sitting in the corner.

"Voila!" he said.

"Oh, Papa!" she squealed with delight.

Then she ran to the piano, took a seat on the stool and began banging the keys.

"I want you to learn to play," Sam said. "We shall hire a teacher for you, but no practicing before noon each day because it will disturb my work. Is that understood?"

"I promise, Papa," Clara said.

Then Clara rose from the piano stool and ran to her father.

"Oh, Papa, I'm so grateful to you!"

"You're quite welcome, darling."

Then she hugged him.

"I love you Papa," Clara said.

"I love you too, baby."

Olivia glowed with pure joy at the sight.

***

The following week, at the appointed hour and date, Sam was back at the Colt Arms factory to see what updates Paige had made to his machine. When Sam arrived at Paige's office, he saw the secretary and, beyond the office through the glass window, he could see Paige sitting at the machine's console setting type.

"May I see Mr. Paige?"

"Oh, yes," the secretary said. "He is expecting you."

The secretary rose from her desk, then went to the window and tapped sharply.

Paige turned from the console and saw Clemens. Then he motioned him to come inside, so Sam entered. Paige, appearing very haggard, looked like he hadn't shaved or slept in days. The floor around the machine was scattered with intricate drawings, lever schematics and various parts for the machine.

"What's the latest development on the machine?" Sam asked.

"I've solved the justification problem," Paige said. "But it needs improvements in the way the letters fall into the casement channels."

"May I see the improvements?"

Moments later, Sam and Paige were at the machine and Paige was setting type. After a series of keystrokes, Paige removed a block of lead type from the tray and handed it to Sam.

"See for yourself," Paige said, handing the lead block to Sam.

Sam took the lead block and inspected it.

"It is justifying the lines, but this is only one column wide," he said. "I want to see it justify two columns of type."

Paige punched some keys again, the machine made a rhythmic clacking noise and, after several seconds, Paige pulled another block of type from the delivery tray.

"Marvelous!" Sam said. "I want to invest another $5,000. When do you feel it will be ready to manufacture?"

"Not anytime soon. It still requires many improvements. I want it to be perfect before we begin production."

***

September 14, 1880 *This Paige fellow has a crystal-clear mind and an inexhaustible will to work. He is a poet; a most great and genuine poet, whose sublime creations are written in steel. He is the Shakespeare of mechanical invention. He is an extraordinary compound of business thrift and commercial insanity. The performance I witnessed today did thoroughly amaze me. Here was a machine that was actually setting type, and doing it with swiftness and accuracy. Moreover, it was distributing the correct case each and every time. The machine fed itself from a galley of dead matter and, without human help or suggestion, began its work of its own accord when the type channels needed filling, and stopped of its own accord when they were full enough. Now that it can enable the justification feature, the machine is almost a complete compositor. I saw Paige set at a rate of 3,000 Ems an hour, which, counting distribution, was but a little short of six compositor's work. If perfected, it is my solidified opinion that it would presage a revolution not only in newspaper publishing, but in books and magazines as well.*

20
Publisher

Four years passed. It was early March of 1884. Chester A. Arthur was president, the cornerstone for the Statue of Liberty was being laid at New York harbor, Buffalo Bill Cody took his Wild West show to Europe, Harry Truman was born, Alaska became a US territory, and, in Hartford, Samuel Langhorne Clemens had finally realized his long-time dream of owning his own publishing company.

Three years earlier, *The Prince and the Pauper* was published to what Sam considered only mediocre success. With only 7,000 copies sold in the states and 3,000 in the UK over the first six months, publisher Osgood tried to paint the sales numbers as a great success, but Sam, after *Innocents Abroad,* knew otherwise. Two years later, when Osgood's company published his next book, *Life on the Mississippi*, sales were equally dismal, and Clemens, without a moment's hesitation, sent a letter to Osgood announcing he was ending their business relationship.

As a result, in the late fall of 1883, Clemens established his own publishing firm in Hartford and named it the Charles L. Webster Company, after his nephew-by-marriage. Webster, who was already in Sam's employ, was the husband of Annie Moffett Webster, daughter of Sam's older sister Pamela Moffett. Originally, Sam had hired Webster as his "business manager" with duties which included overseeing his investments, protecting his copyrights from piracy and finding a good plumber for the Hartford house. Now, as president of Sam's publishing house, Webster was responsible for not only overseeing the printing operation, but choosing profitable projects, although he had no publishing experience.

***

Now that he owned his own publishing company, Clemens set about finding manuscripts. In September of 1869, when Gen. Ulysses S. Grant came to Hartford to stump for that year's presidential campaign, Sam, at the behest of the city's mayor, introduced the famous general to the crowd. During that occasion, Grant and Clemens became fast friends and the famous general invited Sam to visit him at his home in Galena, Illinois. Over the following years, Clemens happily obliged.

***

Now, in early March of 1884, Clemens received word that a terrible tragedy had befallen the ex-president. Grant discovered that his business partner, one Ferdinand Ward, had swindled their banking company out of its assets. Although Ward was sent to prison for his crimes, Grant was financially ruined.

Humiliated and desperate to support his family, Grant decided to write his memoirs and took a tentative offer from a New York publishing house. When Sam heard about the offer, he paid a visit to his old friend and made his own proposal.

"My company will double the royalties," Sam said.

"I've already signed a contract with Century publishing," Grant said.

"I assure you, you will not receive the sales prowess from Century that my company offers."

"I'm surely interested," Grant said. "Let me talk to my solicitor."

***

Four months passed. On July 26, 1884, Sam's youngest daughter Jean was due to celebrate her fourth birthday and Olivia staged a spectacular birthday party. Servants baked a huge chocolate cake, a pile of birthday gifts were purchased and friends and neighbors were invited. Once all of the guests were assembled, Olivia lit the four candles on the cake, then she turned to Jean.

"Now, darling," she said. "Blow out the candles."

Jean, giddy with delight at her first birthday party, took a deep breath and prepared to extinguish the candles. Then, suddenly, she stopped and stared off into space.

"Darling, you must blow out the candles," Olivia said, but Jean didn't seem to hear. Suddenly, her body began to jerk in slight nervous twitches.

"Jean! Jean!" Sam said.

"Oh, dear God!" Olivia said.

Instantly, she sprang from her chair, went to Jean and took her in her arms.

"Baby! Baby! What's wrong?"

The four-year-old's eyes rolled back into her head and, for several seconds, the spasms became more violent as her body jerked uncontrollably one way, then another. Then, just as suddenly as the spasms had begun, they stopped.

Jean, pure horror in her eyes, turned to her mother and began sobbing. Olivia pulled the child to her breast and turned to Sam.

"We must deliver her to the physician," she said.

***

That afternoon, Dr. Isaiah McDermott, a tall man in his late forties with a sallow, clean-shaven face and glasses, arrived at the Clemenses' home. Once Sam and Olivia explained the earlier incident, he examined Jean.

"This child has a nervous disorder," he said. "Has she received some sort of harsh blow to the head?"

"Not to my knowledge," Sam said. "The sudden body jerks we witnessed today appeared out of the blue."

"Your daughter may well be a victim of epilepsy," the doctor said. "It is a nervous condition that medical science knows little about. Normally, the seizures occur when the victim is agitated or excited. In this case, the excitement of the birthday party engendered the seizures."

"What can be done?" Sam said.

Dr. McDermott shook his head sadly.

"While some medicines have been shown to slow the condition, there is no known remedy. In some cases, as a child grows older, the symptoms disappear. In other cases, they grow worse with time and the victim must be relegated to an institution."

Olivia peered at Sam, fear in her eyes.

"The best remedy is to maintain her in a calm mood," Dr. McDermott continued. "Situations that are excitable or produce extreme emotions are more likely to cause the seizures."

"We can expect more of the same?" Sam asked.

"That is correct," Dr. McDermott said. "Especially when she becomes excited."

***

That night, in the marital bed, Olivia told Sam she could never send Jean to an institution.

"The social stigma for our family would be devastating," she said. "And she would be left to her own means. I could never allow that."

"Suppose she becomes worse and we cannot control the seizures?"

"We shall cross that bridge when we arrive," Olivia said. "Until then, I intend to see that she leads as normal a life as possible. We'll tell Susy and Clara that they must help protect their sister."

***

Two weeks later, Sam received a letter from Gen. Grant.

August 13, 1884
My Dear Clemens:
In a missive from my solicitor yesterday, he informed me that I am now free and clear of any obligations to Century publishing with regard to the publication of my memoirs.
This means I can now commit my efforts to your publishing

house.

Can you kindly pay me a visit at my home so we can sign all of the necessary documents?

Further, could you bring along your oldest daughter Susy? I have heard you speak of her so often that I would be honored to meet her.

Please respond to inform me what date you can visit and bring along all of the necessary documents for my signature.

I look forward to seeing you and your daughter in the near future.

Sincerely,

Ulysses S. Grant

***

That night, at the dinner table, Sam announced that, the following week, he and Susy were making the journey to Illinois to meet with General Grant.

"Why can't I accompany you?" Clara, who was now ten, said.

"He specifically asked for Susy," Sam replied. "He didn't ask for you. This man saved our nation and I must respect his wishes."

Clara slammed her fork on the table.

"Susy gets everything and I get nothing," she said. "I am always left out."

"Young lady, you will not display such outbursts at this table," Olivia said. "Leave this table and go to your room."

Clara glared at her mother.

"Now!" Olivia said.

Clara looked away, then got up and stalked out of the dining room.

***

The following morning, while Sam was reading in the drawing room, Jean entered and took a seat beside him. For a long moment, she remained quiet until he turned his attention to her.

"Papa, may I ask you a question?" she said.

"You may ask me anything."

"Will you buy me a goat?"

"A goat?" Sam said. "Where would we keep it?"

"It could live in my room with me."

"Oh, darling, we couldn't abide a goat in the house. We'd have to keep it in the stables with the horses."

Sam studied her for a moment.

"What inspired the notion to get a goat?"

"Emily Warner has one," Jean said. "It is such fun. I love to feed it and play with it."

Sam studied her for a moment.

"Let me see what I can do."

Thirty minutes later, Sam was at the stables speaking with Patrick Mcleer, the family coachman.

"I want you to buy a goat for Jean," he said.

"What kind?"

"A pet goat. A small one, a male. Something that Jean can play with."

"Give me a couple days," the coachman said.

"Fetch me when you have it," Sam said. "And say nothing to Jean until I have seen it. I want it to be a surprise."

***

A week later, on the afternoon of August 22, Sam and Susy arrived at the train station in Galena, Illinois. The moment they stepped off the train, they were greeted by Grant's personal assistant, who helped them gather their luggage and provided transportation to the general's home on the city's trendy West Side.

When Sam and Susy were ushered into Grant's office, Sam saw instantly that the great general was in poor health. His face was drawn; his movements were slow and strained; he smiled little and he was wrapped in a heavy, woolen blanket to prevent catching a draft.

Once the documents were signed, Grant showed Sam the outline for his memoirs. For several minutes, Clemens studied the pages.

"You should flesh out your early years more completely and explain your strategy and machinations for each and every major battle," Sam said. "Particularly Gettysburg."

"When I delve too deeply into my exploits on the battlefield, it appears that I am bragging."

"Never has there been a more appropriate time for bragging than now," Sam said. "You will write one and only one autobiography. You must put everything out there for the world to see."

A smile crossed Grant's face.

"Do you think it will sell?"

"Absolutely!" Clemens said. "A two-volume set should sell at least 300,000 copies. I predict it will be the biggest royalty check in the history of publishing."

"I trust your prognostications are correct," Grant said.

Over the next twenty minutes, Grant made small talk with Susy about her life and her plans to become an author like her father, then Sam announced they were about to leave.

"One more thing," Grant said.

"What might that be?"

"Can you advance me $1,000 on the royalties?"

"I certainly can," Sam said.

Sam took out a book of bank drafts, wrote Grant a check for the requested amount and handed it to him.

"I'm grateful."

"This scoundrel that swindled you out of your money," Sam said. "When will he be released from his incarceration?"

"Another ten years."

"The day he gets out, I'm going to give him a good horse-whipping," Sam said.

Grant smiled again.

"The damage has already been done," he said.

***

In the carriage back to the train station, twelve-year-old Susy was lost in thought. Finally, she spoke.

"Papa, what is a biography?"

"A biography is a record of the events of someone's life."

"Is it difficult to write a biography?"

"Not overly difficult. The biographer must research the life of the person who is the subject."

For a long moment, Susy was silent.

"I'm going to write a biography of your life," she said finally.

Startled, Sam drew back at her words.

"Me? I'm not all that interesting."

"Papa, you're the most interesting person I know."

"Oh, sweetheart, you don't have to do that," Sam said. "I know already how much you love me."

"But I want to do it, Papa," Susy said. "It will be loads of fun and I'll learn so much about you."

Sam turned and kissed her on the forehead.

"My darling, I would be absolutely honored."

***

The following day, when Sam and Susy arrived back at the Hartford home, Olivia told Sam that Patrick wanted to see him.

"Where is Jean?" he asked.

"She's in the conservatory drawing pictures of flowers."

"Keep her there while I talk with Patrick."

At the stables, Patrick showed Clemens the goat he had purchased, a brown and white dappled male.

"The previous owner says he's very gentle."

"That's what I wanted," Sam said. "Let me get Jean."

Ten minutes later, Jean was at the stables and saw the goat for the first time.

"Oh, Papa," Jean said as she hugged and petted the animal. "He's just what I wanted. What shall we call him?"

"His name is Abner," Sam said. "All goats should be named Abner."

"Thank you, Papa!" she said. "I love you."

"I love you too, baby."

***

Now that he had the Grant memoirs under his belt, Sam pulled out the manuscript for *The Adventures of Huckleberry Finn*, dusted it off and began to prepare it for publication. It was the companion piece to the Tom Sawyer book and Sam was been writing it off and on for the past three years. Since he didn't trust Osgood to publish it, the manuscript had been sitting in a desk drawer for some six months. Now that he was in control, Sam shepherded the work through the entire printing process, even personally approving each and every one of the illustrations. Once he had a proof copy in hand, he instructed Webster to start sending out canvassers from the subscription houses to sell it.

***

One morning in early September, when Sam and Olivia came down for breakfast, Katy was waiting for them at the bottom of the stairs.

"Mrs. Clemens, I have some bad news," she said.

"What is it, Katy?"

"Jean's goat escaped its stall last night and ate three of Mr. Clemens' silk shirts that were drying on the clothesline."

"Damnation!" Sam said. "I should have expected this."

"Also," Katy continued, "he ate most of the zinnias in the greenhouse."

"Oh, no!" Olivia said.

"I'm going to kill that goat and barbecue it."

"We can't do that," Olivia said. "That animal provides so much pleasure to Jean. It helps keep her calm."

"I'm going to have it removed," Sam said. "I can't have some critter on these premises eating my clothing. Those silk shirts cost $5 each."

"No!" Olivia said. "We're going to keep the goat. And mention nothing to Jean about removing it. I fear it might engender seizures. We'll buy more shirts. You must tell Patrick to be more careful about keeping the animal in its stall."

Sam shrugged.

"Do as you wish," he said. "I must have some coffee."

***

In early October, Clemens received a new letter from Grant.

October 3, 1884
My Dear Samuel:
I am pleased to announce that our project is progressing with swift accomplishment and is slightly more than half complete as I write this.
I must tell you that, only a month ago, my physician informed me I have a cancer in my throat, which I am being treated for.
Consequently, I have lost my ability to speak or to stand and I am forced to communicate with written notes.
Despite this malady, I have every intention of completing our project, although the disease has rendered my work to be abundantly slower.
I promise, with the grace of God, my life shall continue until I have seen our project to fruition.
I trust you and little Susan are healthy and thriving and I hereby wish you and her the best of fortunes.
On my current schedule, our project should be finished by the summer of next year.
Sincerely,
Ulysses S. Grant.

***

February 3, 1885 As individuals, each of my three daughters are singular within themselves, each representing an artist in their own right. Susy is the author; she loves words, books, plays and libraries. Clara, on the other hand, is the musician, and her energies gravitate to rhythm, melody, tempo, the piano, the French harp and the works of Brahms, Beethoven and Strauss. This morning, I caught Jean, at age six, painting an image of her pet goat Abner and, in all honesty, the form she sketched was quite realistic with the tawny brown spots on its back and the snow-white of its legs speaking forth with loud clarity. This nervous disorder living within her is greatly worrisome and, while its influence shows no outward manifestations at the moment, I fear it could presage dire problems for the future. At this juncture, I have the notion it would be wise to keep the goat.

***

The following morning, Susy was in the library quizzing Sam about his life for the biography she was writing.

"Why couldn't Grandmother send you to college?"

"College? My dear, I hated school. As fate would have it, I was fortunate to escape the seventh grade."

"How did you become so intelligent?"

"I read books."

"Which authors had the most influence on you?"

"Aristotle, Plato, Rousseau, William Cullen Bryant, Shakespeare. There was no greater author in the English language than Shakespeare."

Sam waited while she furiously jotted down the notes.

"How did you meet Mama?"

Sam explained that he had met her brother Charles first, then later, after visiting her brother and writing a long series of love letters, they fell in love.

"I'll need to see your love letters to Mama," Susy said. "A biographer cannot write a complete biography without access to their love letters."

"I'm afraid that won't be possible, darling," Sam said.

Susy looked to her father, a miffed expression on her face.

"Let it suffice to say," he said, "that although I wooed your mother for almost two years, it was ultimately a bump on my head that won her heart."

"How do you mean?"

Sam explained the incident about the carriage accident.

"Well, I'm happy the accident occurred," Susy said. "If it had not, I would not be here today doing this interview."

***

Five months passed. On July 10, 1885, Grant finished corrections to the final page proofs for his memoirs. Once Sam received it, he personally edited the manuscript, then instructed Webster to rush the book through to publication and send out subscription agents to sell it.

Thirteen days later, Sam received the sad news of Grant's death.

July 23, 1885 During his final days, General Grant wrought heroically with his pen while his disease made steady inroads into his health. As he did not retreat from battle, he did not retreat from the task at hand. Toward the end, he was not able to speak, but used a pencil and small slips of paper when he needed to say something, I went to visit him near the end and he asked me with his pencil if there was a prospect that his book would provide income for his family. I replied that subscription orders and the money was coming in fast and his family could expect a handsome sum from its profits. He expressed his gratification with his pencil.

Five days later, Sam attended Grant's funeral in New York City.

July 28, 1885 Today, as I watched the six-hour funeral procession coursing up Broadway to deliver the great general to his final resting place, a deep sadness crept into my soul. Although it pains me to say this, his death could not have arrived at a more propitious time, thirteen days after completion of his manuscript. As I watched the coffin and mourners file past the offices of Charles Webster and Company at Union Square, I knew the orders were pouring in in sheer avalanches to buy his book.

***

By Thanksgiving of 1885, the *Personal Memoirs of Ulysses S. Grant* and *The Adventures of Huckleberry Finn* were recording record sales. The following summer, Clemens gave Grant's widow Julia a royalty check for $450,000, the equivalent of $11 million in today's dollars. After seeing how wildly successful the *Huckleberry Finn* book was, Clemens reprinted its companion piece, *The Adventures of Tom Sawyer*. Amazingly, over the next six months, the *Tom Sawyer* book would outsell the Huck Finn book by a 2-1 margin.

***

In early December of 1885, flush with the publishing house profits, Sam signed a contract with Paige promising to not only finance the completion of his machine, but agreeing to capitalize and promote it in exchange for half of the profits. In the agreement, Clemens pledged another $30,000 to complete the machine.

"Such a move could bankrupt you," Webster warned. "The project has become an endless money pit."

"Hogwash!" Sam replied. "I can get a thousand men worth a million apiece to go in with me, then I can get a perfect machine."

Already, Sam had been doing some back-of-the-envelope calculations and determined that Paige's machine could be worth millions, perhaps hundreds of millions of dollars. He told Webster it would take ten men just to count his profits.

"Why, he thought he could buy all of New York with the money he was going to make," Katy O'Leary wrote to a friend. *"He kept asking how much would it cost to buy all the railroads in New York and all the newspapers too. He thought he would make millions and own the world because he had such faith in the contraption Paige was building. That was Mr. Clemens' way."*

***

One morning in mid-December, Sam and Olivia were having breakfast alone in the dining room when Jean suddenly burst into the room.

"Papa! Mama!" she shouted. "Come quick! Susy and Clara are fighting in the conservatory."

Instantly, Sam and Olivia sprang from their chairs and

hurriedly followed Jean to the conservatory. There they found Susy and Clara tangled up together, each with a handful of the other's hair, screaming and kicking on the conservatory floor.

"Girls! Girls!" Olivia shouted.

Quickly, she untangled the two and faced them.

"What's going on?"

"Susy says Papa loves her more than me," Clara said. "But it's not true. Papa loves me more."

"Whoa!" Sam said. "I love both of you equally."

"You always give Susy everything she wants!" Clara said.

"That doesn't mean I don't love you."

"It does too. If you loved me, you would give things to me." Olivia interrupted.

"Enough! Enough!" she said. "You two are performing like cats and dogs and I'll have no more of it."

Olivia looked from one sister to the other.

"Clara!" she said. "Apologize to your sister!"

Clara hesitated, then meekly turned to Susy.

"I'm sorry."

Olivia turned to Susy.

"Susan, apologize to Clara."

Susy turned to Clara.

"I'm sorry."

A pause.

"All right! Peace has been made," Sam said. "If this happens again, I shall spank both of you. Is that understood?"

"Yes, Papa," Susy said.

"All right, Papa," Clara replied.

***

That night in the marital bed, Sam and Olivia discussed the skirmish.

"Clara is so jealous of Susy," Olivia said.

"I'm well aware," Sam replied. "That has been the case for some time."

"You do tend to show favor to Susy."

"I reckon I do, but Susy is more to my liking. Her essential personality is more akin to my own. Nothing I do seems to

335

please Clara. On many occasions, I am unable to camouflage my feelings for Susy. She is the child I've always dreamed of."

"My heart inclines to Susy also," Olivia said. "She is a child among children, but I would never permit Clara to have that knowledge. We must strive to show both girls that we love them equally."

"I shall attempt to show more favor to Clara."

"So shall I," Olivia said. "Jealousy does not come from without; it grows from within. To destroy it, you must reach inside her and snatch it away."

"How shall I accomplish that?"

"I have no notion," Olivia said. "Both of us should strive to show further affection for Clara."

"That is the best course," Sam said.

He turned to his wife.

"I love you, Livy."

"I love you too, Samuel."

***

December 22, 1885 *One year has passed since the birthday event when Jean experienced the gut-wrenching epileptic seizures. Since then, everything about her life appears natural. She reads, she writes, she laughs at my silly jokes and her table dialogue has become quite profound. Her life is filled with painting, spending time with her mother in the greenhouse, listening to my stories and entertaining herself with her pet goat Abner. The total of all this seems to render her quite satisfied with herself and the world around her. Perhaps providence shall grant my and Livy's wishes that she is finished with these hellish seizures and neither she nor we shall suffer again as a result of their occurrence.*

***

On Christmas day of 1885, at age 50, Samuel Langhorne Clemens was on top of the world. Not only was he the most famous author in America, but by far the richest, rich enough for him and his family to live like millionaires. At Christmas of 1885, Sam's total net worth, including his wife's inheritance, stood a $1.8 million.

Now that he was suddenly swimming in money, Sam began throwing massive amounts of money into risky start-up schemes, stock investments and improvements to the Hartford home. First, he put $12,500 into an engineering firm in New Haven, $10,600 into the Crown Point Iron Company, $10,500 in Consolidated Coal Mining, $6,000 into Kaolatype printing plates and $8,000 in a Hartford Insurance Company.

When a neighbor announced plans to buy the property next door to Sam and build a home, Sam, fearing the new home would block his view of the Park River, promptly bought the property and paid the owner the outlandish price of $12,000. Only days later, Sam and Olivia began renovations on their home, which included the library walls and ceiling to be covered in gold leaf designed by Louis Tiffany for $7,000; then came a rebuild and twenty-foot extension to the kitchen, which was another $6,000, a driveway extension for another $2,500, black walnut paneling for the drawing room and sitting room for $8,000 and new fireplace tiles at a cost of $3,000. Finally, the Clemens ordered a new carriage built to Sam's own specifications to the tune of $6,000.

Over the course of the year 1885, Sam's domestic, business and investment outlays were in excess of $125,000 or, in early 21st century dollars, more than $2 million.

On New Year's Day of 1886, in a letter to Howells, Clemens wrote: "I am frightened at the proportions of my prosperity. It seems that whatever I touch turns to gold."

Little did Sam suspect the financial calamity that was awaiting him.

21
Sagebrush Revisited

Eighteen months passed. The year was 1887. Susy was fifteen, Clara, thirteen, and Jean was seven; Sam was putting the finishing touches on a new book, *Recollections of Joan of Arc,* and his publishing company was a huge success. In early October of that year, Sam saw an advertisement in the *Hartford Courant* for Buffalo Bill Cody's Wild West show in New York and proposed to Olivia that they take the girls to witness the spectacle. At the event, the girls were mesmerized as they witnessed a reenactment of the Pony Express, Sitting Bull parading with his braves, the amazing shooting skills of Annie Oakley, and an authentic Indian war dance. At the finale, they watched reenactments of an Indian attack on a wagon train, a stagecoach robbery and Custer's last stand.

On the train back to Hartford, Clemens explained to Olivia that the show had inspired in him a yearning to revisit the Old West.

"My mind is flooded with memories of my days on the frontier," Sam said. "Seeing the show struck a yearning deep within me to see my old stomping grounds. I want to smell sagebrush again."

Olivia studied him for a long moment.

"What do you propose, Samuel?" she said finally.

"I want to make a family trip out west," he said. "The girls will enjoy it and it's high time we started spending some of this money that's been piling up in the bank."

"Let's talk to the girls."

***

The following morning, at the breakfast table, Sam and Olivia broached the subject to their daughters.

"I want to see San Francisco," Susy said. "The bay, the harbor, the fishermen, the cable cars, the Presidio… All the books I have read proclaim it is a truly beautiful city."

"I want to see a rodeo," Clara said. "With bronco riding and calf-roping and real cowboys."

"I want to see an Indian house with smoke coming out the top," Jean said.

"You mean a teepee," Susy said. "Indians live in teepees."

"Yes," Jean said. "A teepee with dogs and little Indian children playing in the front yard and animal skins drying in the sun."

Olivia turned to Sam.

"There is your answer," Olivia said. "When do you want to make the trip?"

"We'll leave at the beginning of November and return by the first day of the new year. We'll make a two-month trip out of it."

***

A month later, the trip had been planned, tickets had been purchased and the Clemens family were packed and prepared for their great adventure. The itinerary called for stops in San Francisco, Sacramento and Angels camp in Calaveras County as well as stops in Nevada, which included Virginia City and Carson City. Other sights, which would be determined later, would be in Arizona, Colorado and Montana. Sam especially wanted to see Little Big Horn in southern Montana where Custer was massacred.

For the journey, Susy had packed a box of books that included Jane Austen's *Pride and Prejudice*, a travel book on San Francisco and a volume of Charles Darwin's *On the Origin of Species*. Clara had brought along her French harp, several popular board games of the day and a small book of Irish folk songs. Jean took along her painting and sketching equipment and, before leaving, gave Patrick the coachman strict instructions on caring for her pet goat Abner. Sam had strict orders for Webster.

"Keep me apprised of Paige's machine," he said "Monitor the books for the publishing business. In an emergency, you can send me a wire."

"How will I know where you are?"

"When I arrive at each new destination, I'll apprise you of the next one."

***

On November 6, 1887, the Clemens family, along with fourteen pieces of luggage, left New York Harbor aboard the SS *California* bound for San Francisco. Over the next twelve days, their journey would not only be long but tiresome. For much of the trip, Jean was seasick and spent most of the time in her cabin. Clara complained about everything. The meat was too salty. The cabin was cold and crowded. The crew had to be called to remove small insects from her bed. The captain was less than cordial. Susy, who was happy as long as she had a book, spent most of the time reading and playing parlor games with Sam and Olivia in the ship's recreation room. Many days, Susy would spend on deck with Sam, and they would while away the time discussing Aristotle, the works of Lewis Carroll and Plato's shadows on the cave wall.

Once the SS *California* arrived in Panama, the family crossed the isthmus by stagecoach, then boarded a new ship, the SS *Calpurnia*, and the vessel headed northward across the Pacific Ocean to San Francisco. Three days later, a violent storm blew the vessel off course and Jean was so seasick, she was unable to eat.

Finally, on the afternoon of November 18, 1887, the SS *Calpurnia* dropped anchor in San Francisco. Upon arrival, the Clemens family and their luggage were loaded into a cab carriage and delivered to the Queen Anne Hotel, high atop Knob Hill. Once the family was settled into separate rooms, one for Sam and Olivia and an adjacent one for the girls, Sam took Susy to the window overlooking San Francisco.

"There she is," he said. "San Francisco in all of its raging glory."

"Oh, Papa," she said. "It's so beautiful. It's everything I dreamed."

***

The following morning, the Clemens family took a cab carriage across town to the offices of the Overland Express. When they arrived, Sam led the family inside where they were greeted with a secretary. In an office behind her, Sam could see Bret Harte sitting at a desk, his head down reading.

"I'd like to see Bret Harte," Sam said.

"I'm sorry, but he can't be disturbed."

"Tell him Samuel Clemens is here to see him."

The secretary peered more closely at Clemens.

"THE Samuel Clemens?"

"That is correct."

"Oh yes. I've heard him speak of you," she said. "One moment."

Quickly, she turned and went into the office and spoke to Harte. Instantly, Harte looked up and saw Sam. A big smile crossed his face and he charged out of the office.

"Sam!" Harte said.

He shook Sam's hand and hugged him. Later that night, Sam and his family had dinner with Harte at the hotel restaurant. Harte said Bliss was still publishing his books, he had plans to get married, and he was now half-owner of the Overland Express. After recalling their glory days at Angels Camp and later in San Francisco, they called it an evening.

Back at the hotel that night, once Olivia was asleep, Sam slipped out of bed and went to the hotel's gentlemen's room on the third floor, where he and Ambrose Bierce had engaged in a fist fight. His memories satisfied, he then ventured down to the hotel lobby, where he saw the giant mirror, exactly as it was twenty-two years ago, that he and Bret Harte had used to check out their new "city clothes."

***

Over the next five days, the Clemens family visited the principal tourist attractions in San Francisco, including Market Street, Fisherman's Wharf, Old St. Mary's Cathedral, the cable cars and the Presidio. On the afternoon of the sixth day, they boarded a small sailboat which would take them across the bay to Sausalito.

"Where are we going, Papa?" Susy asked.

"I want to show you a fish cannery," he said.

An hour later, the family was standing in front of a massive block-long building with a big sign on top that read "Consolidated Canneries." At the time, the company was one of the largest and most famous fish canneries on the California coast. Once inside the building, Sam saw a sign that read "visitor entrance" where a long line was already waiting to witness the canning operation. Ahead of them, they could see a guide and a narrow viewing platform from which visitors could view the operation.

When the Clemens family reached the head of the line, the guide turned to Sam.

"Only ten people at a time on the viewing platform," he said. "I have room for two more."

"I want to go, Papa," Clara said.

Instantly, Sam turned to Susy, took her hand and together they crowded onto the small platform.

"I want to go with Papa," Clara said.

"Wait!" Olivia said. "The platform is full. You, Jean and I will all go together."

Over the next twenty minutes, Sam and Susy witnessed the intricacies of a fish-canning operation. First, thousands of fish were dumped out of a massive holding tank onto a conveyor line where workers, mostly Chinese, quickly removed the entrails and the carcasses were washed. Next, the fish were cooked for five minutes with steam, then allowed to cool. Once cooled, workers removed the heads, fins and bones, then the meat was cut up, oil, brine, and sauce were added and then placed into tin cans. Moments later, after a lid was added to the can, it was sealed shut and then the cans, one hundred at a time, were placed in a sterilization chamber.

Finally, once Sam and Susy stepped off the viewing

platform, Olivia, Clara and Jean joined the new crowd of viewers. Some twenty minutes later, Olivia and the other girls had finished viewing the operation. As Olivia and the others rejoined Sam and Susy, Olivia took Sam aside.

"You promised to do better with Clara," she whispered.

"There are times when I am unable to control myself," he said.

"Clara is your daughter too."

"I'm well aware," Sam replied. "Come on! Let's go!"

***

The following morning, the Clemenses boarded a train which would take them ninety miles due northeast to Sacramento and the foothills of the Sierra Nevada. Over the next four days, the family visited the major sights in Sacramento, including Sutter's Mill, the abandoned fortress nearby, the statehouse, the Eagle Theater and its storied ghosts and took a four-hour cruise up the Sacramento River.

On the fifth day, Sam decided he wanted to revisit Angels Camp in Calaveras County where he and Bret Harte had struck it rich when they discovered Portuguese Joe's sardine cans. For the trip, Sam hired a buckboard for a day and, after a two-hour ride, which drew endless complaints from Clara, the family arrived at Angels Camp.

"There's not much left down there anymore," the driver said when the buckboard pulled up within sight of Angels Creek.

"I wish to see it anyway," Sam said, exiting the buckboard.

From his vantage point, he could see both sides of Angels Creek where he had been a gold prospector more than twenty years earlier. For a long moment, Sam drew in the scenery, the abandoned mines, the rusting sluice boxes, rotting wooden shacks with caved-in roofs and the tangled vines and bushes which were blocking the mine entrances. Having had enough, he turned back to the girls.

"When me and Bret Harte left Jackass Hill, this is the place where we brought our mining operation."

Olivia interrupted.

"Samuel!" she said. "Don't use that word in front of the girls. It's crude and vulgar."

"What else can I say? That's the name of the place."

"Either find a euphemism or don't use the word."

"Papa!" Susy said. "What's a jackass?"

"I'll tell you later."

"What is that stinky smell?" Susy said.

"That's sage," Sam said. "The most wonderful smell in the world."

"Papa, sometimes you seem so strange," Susy said. "Very strange."

Interruptions finished, Sam launched into the story of how he and Harte, after working their mine for four months, struck it rich while trying to find a place to bury a cat. Once the story was finished, he turned to the buckboard driver.

"Can you wait while I walk to the bottom of the hill?"

"As you wish, sir," the driver said.

Sam started walking down the muddy, weed-choked trail leading to the bottom of the hill. After walking some twenty feet, he could see his patent leather shoes were becoming caked with mud. Quickly, he returned to the buckboard.

"There was once a day when patent leather shoes would not have stopped me," he said. "I reckon I'm just getting old... or civilized."

***

That afternoon, the Clemens family returned to Sacramento and spent the night in a hotel. The following morning, they boarded a train bound for Tucson, Arizona. As the train streaked through the high, green mountains of the Sierra Nevada and into the sandy wastelands of the Mojave Desert, Susy turned to him.

"Papa, how could you live in a place like this?" she said. "It's nothing but sand, cactus and sagebrush."

"Sweetheart, you cannot know the beauty of the desert until you've witnessed its majesty at night."

***

Three days later, in the early morning, the Clemens family arrived at the train depot in Tucson. Once they retrieved their baggage, the first thing Sam did was go to the telegraph office and notify Webster of his whereabouts. After breakfast, Sam hired a carriage and the family loaded up for their next adventure.

The San Xavier Mission, a four-story, Moorish-inspired white church and so-called "dove of the desert," was located ten miles south of Tucson on the banks of the Santa Cruz River. Built in 1692 by Padre Eusebio Kino, the building was one of the oldest and most ornate Catholic missions built in the United States. Crafted from limestone and featuring a Spanish roof, courtyard and Moorish spires, the mission was named for Francis Xavier, a Christian missionary and co-founder of the Society of Jesus in Europe.

When the carriage carrying the Clemens family pulled up in front of the old mission, Olivia and the girls waited while Sam went inside. Once inside, in front of him, he saw an expansive worship hall with coffered ceilings, ornate stained-glass windows depicting Biblical scenes, a statue of the Virgin Mary and the Christ child, and high above it all, a choir section with a massive pipe organ. In the wooden pews, some fifteen to twenty worshippers were kneeling for mass. As Sam studied the surroundings, an acolyte, dressed in a white robe and cinched with a red rope, stepped forward. In his early twenties, he had long blonde hair, a peaceful face and gave his name as Jonathan.

"May I be of assistance?" he said.

"My family wishes to view the interior of your mission," Sam said.

"How many people?"

"Five."

Jonathan hesitated.

"We're exceedingly busy this morning with mass and two communions," he said. "Can you return this afternoon?"

"My family is scheduled to board a train bound for Denver tonight."

The acolyte studied Sam for a long moment.

"In that case," he said finally, "the best view of the mission interior is on the third floor. I will escort you there, but you must remain quiet."

Ten minutes later, the acolyte was escorting the Clemens family up the stairs to the third floor. At each landing, he stopped to explain the history of the each of the stained-glass windows.

"This window was designed and created by Garibaldi Petrino, the great Italian glass artisan who lived from 1565-1604. It was imported from Rome."

Finally, when the acolyte and the Clemens family reached the third floor, they were directly behind the pipe organ and above the church's choir section.

"Please follow me!" Jonathan said.

Moments later, the acolyte and the Clemens family were standing behind the organ, peering down on the church's interior.

"Below, you can see the planning that went into the mission's architecture," Jonathan said. "To the left are the pews. Extending down the center aisle is the transept, and you will notice it forms a cross as it meets…"

Suddenly, the quiet of the mission was interrupted with the sound of organ music.

Jonathan, startled at the sound, jerked his head around.

"Why is the organ playing?"

Quickly, he turned and went around the side of the organ assembly. There he saw Clara sitting at the keyboard, playing away.

"Isn't she a member of your family?" he said.

"She is!" Sam said.

"This must be halted at once," the acolyte said.

He immediately went to the front of the organ, grabbed Clara by the shoulders and pulled her from the seat.

"Young lady!" Jonathan said. "Why are you disturbing mass? This is the house of the Lord and you must respect it as such."

Jonathan turned to Sam.

"The viewing is at an end," he said. "You and your family must leave the mission at once. Follow me to the exit."

"I'm sorry," Sam said.

He stepped forward and grasped Clara's arm.

"What are you doing?" he said. "Can't you behave yourself?"

Sam, still holding Clara's arm, muscled her down the stairs with the acolyte and other family members close behind. Once they were at the mission entrance, the churchman held the door open.

"Good bye and good day!" he said.

Once outside, Sam turned angrily to Clara.

"What in tarnation were you doing?" he said. "The organ doesn't belong to you and you had no right to play it."

"I've never played an organ before," she said. "It's like a piano, but it has foot pedals."

"Come along, young lady!" Sam said. "I've had a bellyful of you for today."

***

That afternoon, the family returned to Tucson, checked out of their hotel and boarded a train bound for Denver, Colorado. In the train car, Sam and Olivia sat on one side while the three girls were seated on the opposite side.

Susy was reading, Clara was preoccupied with a board game and Jean was staring out the window as the train passed through the rolling foothills of the Rocky Mountains.

For a brief moment, Olivia peered at Susan.

"What's the book you're reading?" she said.

Susy held up the front of the book.

"*On the Origin of Species* by Charles Darwin."

Olivia's face screwed up in disapproval.

"Why are you reading that?"

"Lewis Carroll said it was a book that would revolutionize thinking about the origins of man. It explains how human beings were transmuted from primates into modern man."

"Where did you get it?"

"Papa bought it for me."

"Let me have it."

"Mama, I'm not finished."

"Give it to me," Olivia said firmly.

"Let me mark my place," Susy said, dog-earing the page she was reading.

She handed the book to her mother.

Olivia examined the book, then put it in her purse.

"What are you going to do with it?"

"I want to read it myself," Olivia said.

***

That night, in their sleeping car berth, Olivia wasted no time venting her anger about the Darwin book.

"I shall not allow my children to read such rubbish," she said. "In every manner, in every way, I have striven to teach my children to hold a strong faith in God. I will not have them introduced to the notion that man somehow grew from apes into human beings. Mankind and womankind were created by God and I intend to have that notion firmly embedded in their minds by the time they are adults. Is that understood?"

"You cannot withhold information from a curious mind," Sam said.

"No, but I can delay it," Olivia said. "If Susy wants to read such garbage as an adult, she may do so, but I will not be a party to it at this point."

"You said you wanted the children to develop a broad spectrum of knowledge across many subjects."

"Not some rubbish that is directly opposed to the teachings of the Holy Bible."

In their entire relationship, Olivia had never spoken to him in that tone before. There was a long silence.

"Yes, dear," he said finally.

Suddenly, Olivia, her face red with anger, arose from the bed.

"Where are you going?"

"Tonight, I'm sleeping with the girls in their berth."

***

The following morning, Susy asked her father about the

Darwin book.

"Your mother is reading it," Sam said. "You must talk to her about its whereabouts."

Susy turned to her mother.

"When can I have the Darwin book back?"

"When you're an adult."

Susy turned to her father.

"What does that mean?" she asked.

Sam shrugged.

From that moment forward, the Darwin book was never mentioned again.

***

Two days later, the Clemens family arrived at the train station in Denver, Colorado. In late November of 1888, Denver was a sprawling, lawless cowboy of a town which offered all of the services required for gamblers, speculators, pimps, drifters, prostitutes and other unmentionable riff-raff. After gold was discovered at Pike's Peak in 1858, the sleepy little mountain hamlet of 8,000 souls, which had sustained itself on farming and timber operations, suddenly mushroomed to over 50,000 residents. Successful prospectors bought ranches, then cattle and this brought in thousands of cowboys from Texas, Oklahoma and Wyoming. On any Saturday night, it was not unusual to see two or three gunfights on Main Street.

In the carriage, en route to the hotel, Susy turned to Sam.

"Tomorrow is your birthday, Papa," she said. "You'll be fifty-three years old."

Sam smiled.

"I don't think I've ever been happier," he said.

***

Once Clemens had checked his family into a hotel, he went to the telegraph office to notify Webster of his whereabouts. Upon arrival, the telegraph office clerk told him he had a wire waiting. Sam wondered what it was. He took the note and read it.

November 29, 1887
Mr. Clemens:
Bad news. Paige machine a calamity. Mounting financial problems at the publishing house. Your presence requested soonest. Charles.

Over the next thirty minutes, Sam composed and transmitted a reply.

Charles:
Possibly another month before I return to Hartford. Apprise me of Paige machine and publishing house problems.

An hour later, he received Webster's reply.

Mr. Clemens:
Paige rebuilding his entire machine from scratch. Publishing house creditors anxious to receive their money. Threatening legal action.

After reading the wire, Sam left the telegraph office and returned to the hotel. He had been gone for two hours.

When he returned to the hotel and opened the door, the room had been decorated with garlands and festooned with colorful decorations.

"Happy birthday!" Olivia and the girls shouted in unison.

On the table, there were wrapped presents, greeting cards and a huge chocolate birthday cake replete with fifty-three lighted candles.

"My! My! Look at all this!" Sam said. "I didn't suspect it. I have the most wonderful family on this earth."

Then, all of the family members joined in to sing the happy birthday song. Once finished, Jean turned to her father.

"Papa, you have to blow out all the candles," she said.

"I'm not sure I can," Sam said with a sly smile. "I'm old and I don't have the air I had as a young man."

"Oh, yes," said Jean. "You can do it, Papa."

Then, as family members watched, Sam blew out all of the

candles, which drew loud applause.

"Time for presents!" Susy said, holding a large box wrapped in gaily-colored paper.

Sam smiled, took the box and shook it.

"What is it?"

"You have to open it," Susy said.

Quickly, Sam tore away the wrapping paper and opened the box.

Inside was a sheaf of typed pages. The top one was the title page for a manuscript. It read: *"Papa: An Intimate Biography of Mark Twain."*

"You finished your biography of me," he said.

"Yes, I did," Susy said.

Sam peered proudly at her.

"Oh, sweetheart! I'm obliged from the bottom of my heart," he said, hugging Susy and kissing her on the forehead. "It's the greatest gift I could have received. I'll talk to Charles about getting it published when we return to Hartford."

"Papa! Papa!" said Jean excitedly. "Open my present next."

Sam took Jean's gift and opened it. Inside was a portrait Jean had drawn of Sam with her pet goat Abner peeking over his shoulder.

At first, upon seeing the image, Sam burst out in raucous laughter.

Then he held the portrait at arm's length and examined it.

"A reasonable likeness," he said. "I shall hang it on our bedroom wall so it will always remind me of you."

"Thank you, Papa!" Jean said.

"What about my present, Papa?" Clara said, handing him a small box.

"It's a small box," Sam said.

"The best gifts come in small boxes," Clara said.

Sam took the box and opened it.

As he withdrew the object from the box, he peered curiously at it.

"What is it?"

"It's a watch fob, Papa," Clara said. "You use it to keep your pocket watch safe."

"But I don't have a pocket watch."

"It was all I could think of to buy you," Clara said. "You don't like it?"

"I had expected a gift similar to the ones I received from Susy and Jean. Something you had put your heart into. Something that would have great significance."

For a moment, Clara turned to her mother. Her eyes began to fill with tears.

"It's all right, baby," Olivia said, going to Clara and embracing her.

Suddenly, livid anger flashed across Clara's face as she broke away from her mother and, with fingernails flared, she rushed at Sam.

"No! It's not all right!" she screamed. "I hate you! I hate you! You have never loved me. You have always loved Susan."

As Clara tried to reach Sam's face with her fingernails, Sam grasped her wrists and held her at bay.

Olivia limped forward and grabbed Clara's shoulders.

"Clara! Clara!" Olivia shouted. "Stop this! Stop this now!"

Instantly, she pulled Clara away from her father.

"Calm yourself down!" she shouted. "You should be ashamed."

Clara pulled away from her mother, her eyes filled with hot, angry tears.

"Clara!" Olivia said. "Let's have a talk. Please!"

"No! No!" Clara shouted.

Then she turned to face Sam.

"I hate you! I despise you!"

Then she turned and burst out of the room, slamming the door behind her.

***

November 30, 1887 *Today, at age fifteen, my darling Susy, a slender little maid with plaited tails of copper-tinged brown hair down her back and perhaps the busiest bee in the Clemens household hive, by reason of her manifold studies, health exercises and creations she daily attends to, she secretly and of her own motion and out of love provided me with the completed task to her labors—the writing of a biography of me. I have had compliments before, but nothing that touched me quite like this; nothing else that could approach it in my eyes; it shall forever keep that place.*

***

The next day, the family was up early. Clara was calmer now and, after breakfast in the hotel restaurant, the family boarded a cab carriage that would take them across town to an arena where a rodeo was being held. Upon arrival, a huge crowd of spectators had already filled the stands and the show was about to start. After purchasing tickets, the Clemens family took their seats on the first row directly behind the chutes where the bucking horses were housed. The first event was a contest between cowboys to determine which could rope and a tie up a calf the fastest from a galloping horse. Next came barrel racing where riders competed to determine which cowboy could complete a course around a triangle of barrels. The third event was the bronco-busting competition to determine how long a rider could remain on a bucking horse.

"This is what I came to see," Jean said excitedly.

Moments later, the first bronco and rider were ready to be released from the chute. The instant the chute door opened, the horse and rider shot out into the arena and the horse was bucking violently to remove the rider from its back. Bravely, the cowboy hung on to the strap around the horse's belly for several seconds, then was thrown to the ground. Rodeo personnel tried to herd the bucking horse back into its stall, but it continued to kick up its heels as if a rider was still on its back.

Finally, rodeo personnel managed to get the horse back into its stall, but the animal continued to kick its heels violently into the air. Suddenly, the animal's heels slammed into the top railing at the rear of the stall, which sent the large timber railing into the crowd. Olivia and Susy screamed as the hurtling timber first struck a man and his wife who were sitting at the end of the first row. Jean, who was seated between her father and the man's wife was struck in the forehead by the hurtling piece of wood and was knocked to the ground.

Instantly, the rodeo was stopped and medical personnel rushed to the scene. Both the man sitting on the end of the row and Jean were lying unconscious among the seats. Sam kneeled over Jean, examining the bloody wound on her forehead.

"Jean! Jean!" he said frantically. "Can you hear me?"

No response.

"Oh, God!" Olivia said. "Please don't take my child!"

"We'll have to get her to a hospital," one attendant said. "That's a nasty wound."

***

Two hours later, Sam and Olivia were at a Denver hospital at Jean's bedside. She was awake and talking, but still frightened. Her forehead was bandaged and the doctor was present.

"She suffered a mild concussion," the doctor said. "She was lucky the damage was not more severe. She should remain at the hospital for a day for observation, then she can be released. You say you have been traveling?"

"We were on vacation," Sam said. "We live in Hartford, Connecticut."

"I would advise you to return home with her as soon as possible. Monitor her closely during the return trip."

Sam turned to Olivia.

"We'll return by train," he said. "You know how sick she becomes on a ship."

***

Two days later, The Clemens family was on a train bound for Hartford. Sam, Olivia and Jean were in a compartment by themselves. Jean, her head still bandaged, was asleep on the seat across from them.

"I trust the accident doesn't affect her nervous condition," he said.

"Let's not talk about it," Olivia said. "God, in his infinite mercy, will help us with her."

They were quiet for several moments.

"Susy matriculates at Bryn Mawr next month," Olivia said.

"Have all of the arrangements for enrollment been completed?"

"She is due to be on campus January 15."

"I'll miss her," Sam said.

"So will I."

They were quiet again.

"I had a long talk with Clara last night," Olivia said.

"What decisions were made?"

"She wants to go to Elmira and live with my mother at Quarry Farm."

"From whence did this originate?"

"Mother has been asking her to come live at Quarry Farm for some time. Clara is her favorite grandchild."

"Is this the result of the fracas we had at the birthday party?"

"That's a contributor," Olivia said. "What happened at the party has been brewing for some time."

"If she was gone from home, I'd be free of her infernal piano playing."

"My opinion is that it would be beneficial for both of you. At Quarry Farm, she'd have the run of the house and Mother would give her anything she wanted."

"Perhaps it would be best."

22
Bankruptcy

Five days later, when the Clemens family arrived back in Hartford, Sam and Olivia's first order of business was to attend to Jean's medical condition. Once their luggage had been delivered to their home, Sam, Olivia and Jean remained in the cab carriage and the driver was instructed to take them to the local hospital. Upon arrival, they met Dr. McDermott and related the details of the accident. Afterward, he removed the bandages and gave Jean a thorough examination.

"The wound has healed nicely," he said, "but there will be a small scar. There appears to be no internal damage. Actually, she was quite fortunate the injury was not more severe."

"Will the accident aggravate her nervous condition?" Sam asked.

"It's quite difficult to say," the doctor said. "It certainly didn't help. We'll have to see what the future holds. The important consideration is to maintain her in a calm, serene state. If she becomes overly excited or subjected to highly emotional situations, the seizures are more likely to occur."

***

Thirty minutes later, when the carriage arrived back at the family home, Jean was instantly out of the carriage and en route to the stables. It was the first time she had seen Abner in over a month. She squealed with delight at the sight of the animal, then hugged and petted him and, after attaching a halter around his neck, led him into the small pasture behind the stables to graze. Afterward, she went into the house, retrieved her painting supplies, returned to the stables and proceeded to paint still another picture of the goat.

***

The following morning, Clara was packed and ready to travel to Elmira to live with her grandmother at Quarry Farm. Plans called for Olivia to accompany her and visit with the Langdon family for a day before returning to Hartford. While a cab carriage waited at the street, the entire family gathered in the foyer of the home to say their good-byes. As always, Olivia was in charge.

She turned to Sam first.

"Good-bye, dear!" Olivia said. "I shall return in two days."

"Good-bye!" Sam said, kissing his wife on the lips. "I love you."

"And I love you, Samuel."

With that, Olivia hugged Susy and Jean, then turned to Clara.

"Say good-bye to your sisters," Olivia said.

Clara obediently hugged Jean, then Susy.

"Good-bye!" Jean said. "I promise to visit this summer."

"Say good-bye to your father," Olivia said.

Clara embraced her father.

"Good-bye, Clara," Sam said. "I love you."

Clara looked curiously at her father.

"Good-bye, Father," she said.

Then she turned to her mother.

"I'm ready."

Then Sam, Susy and Jean watched as Clara and her mother strode down the walkway to the waiting cab carriage. As the carriage pulled away, Sam, Susy and Jean waved one final time. Clara didn't look back.

***

That afternoon, Sam was in the publishing house offices with Webster inquiring about the "calamity" with the typesetting machine.

357

"Paige has destroyed the prototype and is rebuilding the machine from scratch," Webster said.

"For what reason?"

"He says the machine will not be complete until it has a multi-column line justification function."

"He couldn't shoehorn a justification apparatus on the prototype?"

Webster shook his head.

"You know what a perfectionist he is," Webster said.

"I'm well aware."

"He has already spent the $30,000 you provided last year," Webster continued. "Currently, he is asking for another $4,000 a month to continue work on the new one."

"That infernal fool!" Sam said. "I'm going to give him a piece of my mind."

Sam stood up and prepared to leave.

"There is another matter we should discuss," Webster said.

"What might that be?"

"On Thursday past, the accountant presented his annual financial report on the publishing company. The picture he painted was far from rosy."

"We shall discuss it tomorrow," Sam said.

***

An hour later, Sam arrived at the Colt Arms factory. When the secretary told him her boss could not be disturbed, Sam, in no mood to be put off, skirted the secretary's desk and began banging on the door. Moments later, Paige unlocked and opened the door.

"Hello, Mr. Clemens!" he said.

Once inside, Sam wasted no time with amenities.

"Webster tells me you have destroyed the original prototype."

"That is correct," Paige said calmly. "I want a perfect machine."

"Do you realize I have already put more than $50,000 into the original?"

"I will not release this machine upon the world until it has

358

an efficient justification feature."

"Why couldn't you shoehorn the justification apparatus on the existing machine?"

"It's not practical," Paige said. "Will you leave the design and manufacture of my machine to me? I'm the expert."

"But it's my money," Sam said. "This is in absolute violation of our contract."

"No, Mr. Clemens. Nothing in our contract states that I cannot redesign the machine from scratch. It is MY machine."

"You fail to understand the difference between the dream and the reality. To you, they are one and the same."

"As designer, I shall do as I see fit."

Sam's first instinct was to strike Paige with his fist, but he restrained himself.

"You're frittering away my money," Sam said.

"You have the wrong attitude, Mr. Clemens," Paige said calmly. "This machine will make you millions once it's completed."

"When will that be?"

Paige shrugged.

"I'm uncertain. At some point in the future."

For a long moment, Sam stared angrily at Paige, then, without another word, left the office and strode out of the building.

***

The following morning, Sam was back in Webster's office reviewing the company's financial report for the year.

"In conclusion," Webster said. "Over the past year, the company had profits of $13,567 and incurred debts of $156,522. That means we are $142,955 in the red. That does not include a loss of $69,641 from last year."

"What happened?" Sam said.

"Of the twenty-three books we published, only three made a profit. Sales of the others did not exceed the cost of printing and sales overhead."

"Show me the list," Sam said.

Webster took a sheaf of papers from his desk.

Over the next hour, he went through the list of books the firm had published the previous year, noting expenses and profits for each one. Once he was finished, Sam turned to him.

"It appears that, since the publication of Grant's memoirs and the *Huckleberry Finn* and *Tom Sawyer* books, the company's finances have gone downhill."

"That is correct."

"I shall take $200,000 from my wife's inheritance." Sam said. "That should put the company's coffers back in the black."

***

Jean's favorite time of the year was Christmas and the yuletide of 1887, when she was seven years old, was no different. Over the past year, with Clara's help, she had learned to sing "Away in a Manger" and, during the annual Christmas pageant at the church, Jean sang the song for the congregation while Sam and Olivia proudly looked on. In her letter to Santa, she asked for new dresses, a life-size doll, a rolling hoop toy and a collar for Abner with his name on it.

On Christmas morning, Jean squealed with delight when she opened the package containing the goat collar.

"Susy!" Jean said. "Come with me! I'm going to put the collar on Abner."

Susy accompanied Jean to the stables, where she fastened the collar around the animal's neck, then tied a small rope to the collar and led him out into the pasture to graze.

"Do you think Abner likes his Christmas gift?" Jean asked.

"Oh, yes," Susy said. "He loves it."

***

Four days later, Sam and Olivia were having breakfast in the dining room when Patrick the coachman suddenly burst into the room.

"Mr. Clemens," he said. "Something terrible has happened to Jean. She is lying on the ground with her tongue lolling out and her eyes rolled back into her head. She's not moving! You better hurry!"

Quickly, Sam and Olivia were out of the house and at the stables.

There they found Jean lying unconscious on the ground. Nearby they saw the pet goat hanging from the fence. Apparently, the animal attempted to jump the fence and, as it did, the small rope attached to the collar became entangled in the barbed wire. While struggling to free itself, the animal had hanged itself.

"Jean had a seizure when she realized her goat was dead," Sam said.

Sam gathered Jean into his arms and ordered Patrick to bring around a carriage.

Forty minutes later, they were at the hospital.

"Our worst fears are confirmed," Dr. McDermott said. "She has suffered a grand mal seizure of massive proportions The accident in Colorado aggravated her condition and now I fear to tell you she will have to be institutionalized so she can receive twenty-four-hour medical care."

"Oh, we could never do that," Olivia said. "We'll hire a nurse."

"If she has another seizure of this magnitude, she may well die," Dr. McDermott continued. "I would highly recommend she been taken to the Craig Colony for epileptics."

"What can they do for her?" Sam said.

"She will be part of a self-sufficient community," the doctor continued. "She will attend school, have chores to perform and be part of a 'society,' so to speak. If she suffers another grand mal seizure, qualified medical care will be immediately available."

"She's only seven years old," Olivia said

"There are other seven-year-olds in the colony," Dr. McDermott said. "In fact, they have children as young as six. The colony will give her a goal in life, something to give her a sense of self-worth."

Olivia turned to Sam.

"We couldn't do that to our daughter," Olivia said.

"I fear we have no other choice," Sam said.

***

Three days later, Sam, Olivia and seven-year-old Jean arrived at The Craig Colony for Epileptics in Livingston County in western New York State. Upon arrival, they met the administrator and, during a tour of the facility, were shown the children's ward where Jean was introduced to the other children. Once the tour was finished, Sam and Olivia tried to prepare Jean for their parting.

"This will be your new home," Olivia said. "You'll be among other children with the same condition as yours. You will be happy here."

"I know, Mama," Jean said calmly. "Can I have another pet goat?"

"We'll talk to the administrators about it," Sam said.

Jean looked sadly at her mother.

"I love you, Mama," she said.

"And I love you, baby," Olivia replied, hugging the child.

Jean turned to her father and embraced him.

"I love you, Papa!"

"I love you too," Sam said.

***

An hour later, Sam and Olivia were in the cab carriage returning to the train depot.

"Oh, Samuel," Olivia said. "What have we done?"

"Darling Livy, we had no choice. We did this for Jean's sake. We may very well have saved her life."

"There are times when I feel God has no mercy," Olivia said. "First, Jean is afflicted with this great malady, then she must be separated from her family as a result."

She peered at Sam for a long moment, then put a small handkerchief to her face and began to sob. Sam took her in his arms and held her tightly as the carriage rumbled along the country road back to the train station.

***

Six months passed. Before making the trip out West, Sam had been furiously working on a new novel with the working title of *A Connecticut Yankee in King Arthur's Court.* He had fallen upon the idea two years earlier when Susy gave him a copy of *Sir Thomas Malory's Le Morte d'Arthur*, a late medieval collection of Arthurian legends. Even before he finished reading it, Sam was making notes for his own book.

It was the story of a common-sense New England Yankee who is carried back in time to Britain in the Dark Ages and celebrates homespun ingenuity and democratic values in contrast to the superstitious ineptitudes of sixth century England. Over the course of writing the book, Olivia played editor while Susy served as proofreader. Now, Sam was hurrying to finish the book before Susy went off to college at Bryn Mawr.

Finally, in late August, the *Connecticut Yankee* book was finished and rushed into production. After dispatching subscription agents to sell the book door-to-door and sending advance notices to book stores, Sam rushed it through publication at his company.

"Pull out all the stops on this one," Sam told Webster. "I want to see a proof copy in one week. Not a minute longer."

***

On the morning of September 4, 1888, Susy, at age sixteen, was packed and ready for her great adventure in college. Over the past two weeks, she had been packing personal belongings, writing letters to the college registrars and notifying friends and relatives she was about to become a college student. On that morning, Susy, accompanied by Sam and Olivia, were in a cab carriage en route to the train station where she would board a train bound for Bryn Mawr, Pennsylvania.

In the late 1880s, Bryn Mawr was an exclusive liberal arts college for women which catered to the offspring of wealthy, elitist parents. Founded as a Quaker institution in 1885, it was one of the so-called Seven Sisters colleges in the Northeast noted for turning out sophisticated, well-mannered young women for roles in high society.

At the station, Sam and Olivia helped their daughter through the boarding process and, on the boarding platform, prepared to say their good-byes.

"Be sure to write," Olivia said, embracing her daughter.

"I promise, Mother," Susy said. "I love you."

"And I love you," Olivia said.

Sam hugged Susy and kissed her on the forehead.

"I love you," he said.

"And I love you, Papa."

Thirty minutes later, Sam and Olivia were in a cab carriage rumbling through downtown Hartford to their home.

"We're alone again, Samuel," Olivia said. "Just us two."

Clemens smiled.

"I already miss her," Olivia said.

"So do I."

***

The following morning, Sam was in the publishing house's offices. On his desk was a legal letter from a paper company demanding $18,422 in payment. Sam went straight to Webster.

"Why hasn't this bill been paid?" he said.

"There were other bills more pressing," Webster said. "You're aware that the company is paying out almost $6,000 a month to subscription houses to sell books? Another $2,000 a month is paid out for promotional flyers to book stores, not to mention another $2,800 a month for employee salaries."

"The longer we're in business, the more indebtedness we are incurring," Sam said.

"I realize that only too well," Webster said.

"I shall transfer another $25,000 from my wife's inheritance to the company coffers," Sam said. "That should keep the company afloat for another six months."

***

The following March, Sam and Olivia received a letter from Susy.

March 3, 1889
Dearest Mama and Papa:
I am dissatisfied beyond all measure with my college experience.

All activities are done in reverse. Courses which have the least significance receive more time than those with deep intellectual meaning. I would rather spend three hours studying Shakespeare's plays than half a day with demonstrations on how to curtsy, becoming a competent ballroom dancer and delivering a speech at a women's social club.

Most of the classes I'm being exposed to are subjects I'm already well-versed in. I am fraught with an extreme ennui which defies words.

Every afternoon, students are required to attend assemblies which are little more than promotional activities for the institution. The food is extraordinarily bland and meat is served only three nights a week.

The professors are primarily stiff, stodgy old maids who are incapable of smiling and are forever instructing me regarding the "proper" way to lead my life. There is no freedom of space or thought.

I'm not sure how much longer I can endure this monotonous, ennui-filled environment.

I miss you and Papa so much!
All my love,
Susan

***

In mid-April, *The Connecticut Yankee in King Arthur's Court* was published and distributed to bookstores and subscription purchasers. While sales were brisk at first, they leveled off quickly and, while Sam had hoped for a quick infusion of cash, profits after the first three months amounted to slightly more than $8,000, nowhere near the figure Sam had hoped for.

***

In early May, Sam and his wife received a brief letter from Susy.

May 4, 1889
Dearest Mother and Father:
As of yesterday afternoon, I notified the administration here that I was abandoning my studies at Bryn Mawr.
When the dean of students asked my reason, I replied that I didn't feel I was receiving the education I had paid for.
I failed to tell them that I was heart-sick and lonely for my family home and my parents.
I miss you and Papa so much!
I shall arrive back in Hartford on the afternoon of March 6 at 2 p.m.
All my love,
Susan

***

Three days later, Sam and Olivia were at the train station to meet Susy after her eight-month stay at college. The moment they saw her step off the train, they waved. Upon seeing her parents, Susy, lugging a heavy bag, ran to them.

"Oh, Mama! Oh, Papa!" she said, embracing her mother. "I'm so happy to be home."

There were tears of joy in her eyes.

Sam hugged her and kissed her on the forehead. Then he took her bag and they began walking to the cab carriage.

"I missed you and Mama so much," Susy said. "College life is so hum-drum and artificial. The professors are stiff. The classes are boring. I didn't like the food. Further, I discovered something about myself."

"What might that be?" Sam said.

"I start to get sick if I'm away from you and Mama for too long."

"Well, you're safe now," Sam said. "You're back at home and your mother and I are happy to have you back. Come along! I want you to read my new manuscript. Also, I have a new Lewis Carroll book for you."

***

Later that month, Sam, Olivia and Susy went to Craig's Colony to visit Jean. Now, at age nine, Jean had been at the institution for eighteen months. Upon arrival, a staff member escorted the family to Jean's quarters where they found her painting a picture of a sunset. When Jean saw Susy, she ran to her and hugged her, then her parents. Over the next hour, the family asked Jean about her situation. Jean explained that she had made new friends, had chores to do, was getting schooled and had become accustomed to the new lifestyle. Once Sam and Olivia were satisfied that Jean was doing well, their daughter asked a question.

"Can I come back home?" she said.

Dumbfounded at the question, Sam looked at Olivia.

Neither knew how to respond.

Then Susy spoke.

"Mother! Father!" she said. "Can we have a word alone?"

Moments later, Sam, Olivia and Susy were outside Jean's quarters.

"You must remove Jean from this place," Susy said. "It's not fair to keep a nine-year-old away from her family."

"She says she happy here," Sam said.

"If she's so happy, why is she asking to go home? In her heart, she wants to be with her family."

Sam turned to Olivia. She didn't have an answer.

"You owe it to Jean to remove her from this place," Susy continued. "She's your daughter and she deserves more than this."

"But the doctor said…" Sam said.

"The doctor be damned," Susy said. "It's unfair to the entire family to allow this. If she were at home with her family, you would see improvements in her health."

A long silence.

"Susy is right," Olivia said. "We should take her home. I regretted this from the very moment we brought her here. Now I want to change that."

"What about the doctor?"

"The doctor can go to hell," Olivia shot back. "I want my daughter out of here."

Sam took a deep breath.

"Very well," Sam said. "We shall take her back home."

***

Two days later, Jean was living once again in the Hartford home. Her room on the second floor was exactly as it had been the day she left, complete with all her toys, personal mementos and pictures she had painted of Abner. A part-time nurse was hired and Jean quickly fell back into her old routine. Olivia started her home-schooling again and mother and daughter began spending time in the greenhouse once more. After Jean had been back for a week, she asked her father to buy another pet goat.

Several days later, when Patrick delivered another goat, both Sam and Olivia were present. Jean squealed with delight upon seeing the animal.

"I'm going to call him Abner," Jean announced. "Don't you think that's a good name?"

Sam peered knowingly at Olivia.

"Oh yes, darling," Olivia said. "That's a good name."

"A magnificent name," Sam said.

***

Four years passed. Now, in late February of 1893, the financial fortunes of Sam's publishing house were bleaker than ever. As of January, the company's books showed a total of $8,567 in assets and $365,467 in debts. Over the past three years, thirteen of the books published, including memoirs of General Phillip Sheridan and Pope Leo XIII, failed to recoup their printing costs. The previous summer, Sam discovered a bookkeeper had embezzled $25,000. A month later. Clemens provided a $5,000 advance to Henry Ward Beecher for his memoirs, only to have him drop dead three weeks later. Although he had realized some profits from the *Connecticut*

Yankee book, it fell far short of saving the company from financial ruin.

Over the next few months, Sam spent night after night trying to understand the financial quagmire he was in, trying to balance the losses of his far-flung investments, the constant outflow of $4,000 a month to Paige's machine and the rising cost of printing paper, editing and sales commissions for his publishing house against his assets. Olivia's inheritance, which was originally at $1.5 million, had dwindled down to less than $300,000.

In early May, at his wit's end, Sam fired Webster, and the following morning, after being presented with a lawsuit demanding $17,000 the company owed for printing paper, Sam dismissed the employees and locked the office doors.

"I'm not sure how I can extricate myself from this mess," he told Olivia. "At every turn, I can see no light at the end of the tunnel."

***

In mid-August, there was more bad news for Clemens when the Panic of 1893 struck. The stock market crashed, and with it, the great economic boom, which had begun with the end of the Civil War, abruptly ended. Throughout the nation, businesses, service industries and factories closed their doors. In less than six months, more than eighty-three railroads slipped into bankruptcy. Almost three million men were out of work and bread lines were a common sight in most large cities across America. New investors and low-interest loans were virtually impossible to come by. Now the publishing house creditors were clamoring for their money.

At night, Sam paced the floor, seeking some solution to his dilemma. In the margins of his Joan of Arc manuscript, he made notes about how much his debts and expenses were and tried in vain to balance the two. Finally, he decided to seek gainful employment, but after applying to two newspapers, a legal firm and a magazine, all turned him down for jobs.

"The billows of hell have been rolling over me," Sam told Livy. "These days, a body forgets pretty much everything except for visions of the poorhouse."

***

In early September, Sam paid a visit to the Knickerbocker bookstore in Manhattan to see which of his works they were stocking. While browsing the shelves, he was approached by a distinguished-looking middle-aged man with a hatchet face, gentle eyes and a drooping silver mustache.

"Aren't you Mark Twain?" the man said.

"That I am."

"My name is Henry Huddleston Rogers," the man said, offering his hand. "I've been reading your books to my children for more than ten years now. I would be honored to have dinner with you."

Sam peered at the man for a long moment.

"Aren't you affiliated with Standard Oil?"

"I'm one of the founders."

"I've read about you," Sam said. "I'd be obliged to break bread with you."

***

That night, Clemens had dinner with Rogers in the restaurant at the Cosmopolitan Hotel in New York. Instantly, the two men struck up a friendship and, over a sumptuous meal of roast duck, mashed potatoes and boiled cauliflower, they discussed their families, their businesses and their world views. Finally, the conversation turned to financial matters.

"I assume that, with all the books you have published over the years," Rogers said, "your financial outlook is quite bright."

"Frankly, no," Sam replied. "In fact, I'm in a financial quandary from which I am unable to extricate myself."

"Perhaps I could help," Rogers said.

"How could you do that?"

"As a board member of Standard Oil, I am charged with overseeing the organization's financial fortunes and making the necessary changes. In that capacity, I have an extensive understanding of monies owed and monies owned."

Sam studied Rogers for a long moment.

"You may well be a Godsend," Sam said. "Will you come to my offices on Monday and allow me to show you my books?"

"I would be happy to do that."

***

Three days later, Clemens spent six hours laying out his financial puzzle to Rogers. He provided a catalog of his far-flung investments, his list of debts at the publishing company, his ongoing expenses to maintain the Hartford home and the Paige machine that had become an endlessly-deep money pit. All the while, Rogers made notes in an effort to gather a birds-eye view of Sam's finances.

"Allow me a few weeks to assimilate all of this information," Rogers said at the end of the meeting. "I will approve a loan for $8,000 to the publishing company which will provide some breathing room. Then, I will make recommendations."

"I'm obliged," Sam said.

When Rogers left Sam's office that afternoon, Clemens felt like an angel had touched his shoulder.

***

In the late 1880s, Henry Huddleston Rogers was one of the wealthiest men in America. An industrialist and financier, Rogers made his fortune in oil refining and later became a leader in numerous corporations and business enterprises, which included gas, copper, coal and railroads. In an 1885 interview with the *New York Tribune*, Rogers reported his occupation as "capitalist" and claimed his wealth was in excess of $100 million. Rogers was exactly the sort of man whom Clemens had viciously skewered in *The Gilded Age*, about the corrupting power of big money.

"Rogers is not only the best friend I ever had," Clemens would write later, "but the best man I have ever known. He's a pirate all right, but he owns up to it and he enjoys being a pirate. That's the reason I like him."

***

After a month of probing, analyzing and searching through Clemens' extensive financial puzzle, Rogers concluded the only escape was voluntary bankruptcy.

"Bankruptcy is the only alternative," he said. "Your debts exceed your assets by more than $83,000 and I see no way to satisfy that difference without declaring bankruptcy."

"Can you save our home?"

"The Hartford home was built with Livy's inheritance and is therefore immune from the bankruptcy auction. Also, since the inheritance loaned the publishing firm $60,000 for its operations, your wife Olivia will be declared a preferred creditor, thereby retaining the invaluable copyrights to your books."

***

A week later, Rogers offered another glimmer of hope when he convinced the publishers of the *Chicago Herald* to test Paige's compositor and, if it performed according to their standards, perhaps Sam and his family would be wealthy again. A few days later, testing began and Rogers reported that the machine was setting type at amazing speed.

"The possibility of success at long last," Sam told Rogers upon hearing the news. "It affects me like the sight of land to Columbus."

Then, after only a week, new problems started when the machine began to break down.

"The machine was the nearest approach to a human being I had ever known," Sam wrote to Howells. "But that was just the trouble; it was too much of a human being and not enough of a machine."

Finally, after a month of testing, the *Chicago Herald* publishers decided the machine was impractical because of the constant breakdowns and could never be sold commercially.

October 20, 1893 *The news today hit me like a thunderclap and knocked every rag of sense out of my head. During all the days of dreaming of the riches it could bring, the Paige compositor has disappointed him many times, but I couldn't shake off the confidence of a lifetime in my luck. All my life, I have stumbled upon lucky chances of large size and, whenever they were wasted, I always blamed it on my own carelessness and stupidity. Now I need to teach myself to endure a way of life which I was familiar with during the first half of my years but whose sordidness and hatefulness and humiliation long ago faded from my memory.*

***

At Christmas, in a letter to her foster sister Susan Crane, Olivia wrote: *"Somehow, in my soul, I had been expecting this, but I had great hope that, in some way, it could be averted. Mr. Rogers was so sure there was no way out but bankruptcy and, despite my wishful thinking, I must accept his decision. Now I have a perfect horror and heartsickness of its truth. I cannot evade the feeling that business failure is disgrace. I suppose it has always meant that to me. Most of the time I want to lie down and cry. Everything to me seems so impossible and I feel my life is an absolute and irretrievable failure. Perhaps I am thankless, but I also often feel that I should like to give up and die."*

***

Sam's bankruptcy was officially filed in Federal Court in Hartford on April 16, 1894. That afternoon, Sam and Olivia sat down with Susy and told her the bad news.

"The high-flying life style we have enjoyed all these years is coming to an end," Sam said. "We must trim back our expenses at every turn."

"I shall help in every way possible," Susy said. "I wish to see us pull through this calamity."

23
Susy

Over the next few months, Clemens' friendship with Rogers grew ever closer and Sam found himself a frequent guest at Rogers' home in Fairhaven, Massachusetts, where they would spend weekends on his 227-foot steam-powered yacht, the *Kanawha*. One weekend in late April of 1895, Sam joined Rogers and a group of friends for a coastal cruise from Fairhaven to Maine when Clemens explained that he intended to repay every penny he owed from the bankruptcy.

"Why?" Rogers said. "You're legally free of all obligations."

"I'm not morally free. The right thing is to pay off every penny."

Rogers studied Sam for a moment.

"You're the most honest man I've ever known," he said. "Just how do you propose to do that?"

"I'm not certain."

"You were a first-class public speaker during your earlier years. Why don't you do a lecture tour?"

Sam peered at Rogers, then took a deep breath.

"I despise public speaking," he said. "I feel it cheapens me."

"Do you have a better resource for earning money to make the repayments?"

"No!"

"You should speak with my friend Robert Sparrow Smythe," Rogers said. "He has quite a reputation as a manager for platform speakers. He'll be a guest tomorrow night at my home."

***

The following night, during a house party at Rogers' elegant Fairhaven mansion, the host introduced Sam to Robert Sparrow Smythe during a game of billiards. A smallish, round-faced man in his early fifties, Smythe had a balding forehead, piercing eyes and a drooping mustache. Born in London, he had emigrated to Australia as a young man, where he became a journalist, a newspaper publisher and renowned theatrical manager. By the late 1890s, he had gained a reputation as a manager for popular platform speakers including a Shakespearean scholar, a Holy Land expert and a noted astronomer.

"I've heard about you, Clemens," Smythe began. "Henry tells me you are interested in conducting a lecture tour. With your reputation, you could bring down the house with audiences around the world."

"Ten years ago, I swore I would never go back to the podium."

"It could be quite profitable."

"How profitable?"

"You could easily reap $100,000 from a year-long tour, but time would be required to organize the trip. Lecture halls would have to be engaged and advance notices of appearances would be necessary, but my staff could attend to those matters."

Sam studied Smythe for a long moment.

"What would be the details of such an undertaking?"

"With a personage such as yourself, I could plan out a year-long tour with a schedule of stops around the world. I have contacts through which I could hire lecture halls in London, Amsterdam, Bombay, Rio de Janeiro, Singapore… all around the world."

"When could you do it?"

"At the beginning of July," Smythe said. "Would you like to sign a contract?"

"I would."

"Then come to my hotel room tomorrow and we shall sign

the necessary papers."

***

Four days later, back in Hartford, Clemens told his family of his new venture.

"It would be a year-long undertaking and represent the most ambitious lecture tour of my life," he said. "It would begin with a tour across North America, then take me around the world with more than 150 appearances on five continents."

Susy was aghast.

"Oh, how I hate the name Mark Twain," she said. "I should like to never hear it again. You are so much more than a mere humorist who gives funny talks."

"It's a heart-torturing decision," Sam said. "I swore I would never do it again, but now I either take to the platform or starve."

"We must do as your father sees fit," Olivia said. "Perhaps a lecture tour would awaken interest in his books. Who is going on the trip?"

"I'll need you to come along to watch after my health," Sam said.

"Do you wish that I go?" Susy said.

"It would mean the expense of another ticket at a time when we should be watchful of our spending," Sam said. "Further, someone should remain behind with the home and servants."

"And I get so seasick," Susy said. "I shall always remember the journey to San Francisco."

"What about Jean?" Olivia said.

"She's far too delicate for lengthy travel," Sam said. "That's just another reason for Susy to remain here. If they get lonely, they can go live at Quarry Farm."

"Yes, Papa," Susy said. "I wish to help every way I can."

***

On the morning of July 15, 1895, Sam and Olivia boarded the Great Lakes steamer, the *Northland*, on their way to Cleveland for the first stop on the tour. During the first leg—a grueling succession of fifteen cities from Cleveland to Vancouver in thirty days—Sam proved he was up to the task although he was suffering from fatigue, lack of sleep and a huge carbuncle on his left thigh. At every stop, crowds were enthusiastic.

"Everywhere there is constant adulation of Samuel," Olivia wrote to her foster sister. "Most audiences seem to know his work by heart. I must say he is a masterful performer, employing the deadpan drawl his mother called "Sammy's slow talk" with well-timed pauses. For one audience, the pause will be short, for another a little longer and for another still a shade longer. Samuel plays with pauses like a little child with a toy."

Lectures during the first leg included the subjects "The Jumping Frog," "The Awful German Language," "Decay of the Art of Lying" and "Learning to Love Politicians."

"There is but one Mark Twain," said the *Seattle Post Intelligencer*. "His talks are strange, engaging medleys of humor and philosophy which makes for a great literary improvisation."

***

On August 18, as Sam's troupe set sail across the Pacific with scheduled stops in Hawaii, the Fiji Islands and Australia, he realized platform work had more of a positive effect on him than he expected.

August 22, 1895 *Lecturing is a gymnastic, chest-expander, medicine, mind-healer and blues-destroyer all rolled into one. I am twice as well as when I started. I have gained nine pounds in twenty-eight days and expect to weigh 600 before January. I haven't had a blue day in all of the past twenty-eight. My wife is accumulating health and strength and flesh nearly as fast as I am. When we reach home one year hence, I think we can exhibit as freaks."*

Further, the tour had proven even more profitable than Sam had expected. The North American leg had generated $8,000 in cash and Sam had sent $5,000 back to Rogers as the initial payment for retiring his debt.

***

In late September, when Clemens and his entourage arrived in Melbourne, Australia, he received a letter from Susy.

August 29, 1895
Dearest Papa:
Both Jean and I have been safely ensconced here at Quarry Farm with Uncle Theodore, Aunt Susan, Grandma Langdon and Clara since Thursday last.

From the day you and Mama boarded ship, Grandma Langdon has been clamoring for me to bring Jean and myself to Elmira to "be with family" as she stated it. Finally, I acquiesced and we made the journey.

Jean seems to be quite happy here. She enjoys spending time with Grandma Langdon in the garden and sitting on the front lawn painting pictures of nature. She is attending school and her nervous condition has remained in abeyance. After much cajoling, Jean finally convinced Grandma to buy her another goat.

Uncle Theodore, Aunt Susan and Grandma Langdon send their love.

I have a new copy of the Collected Poems of Gerard Manley Hopkins. *I'll show it to Mama when you return home. I must tell you the poet wrote a host of lovely poems beyond* The Windhover.

Little Miss Contrary is taking piano lesson and keeps the family up all hours of the night with her incessant practicing. I am rereading Pride and Prejudice.

I trust you and Mama are enjoying your excursion and your funny talks are proceeding well.

All my love,
Susy

***

Upon arrival in the outback of Southern Australia, Olivia penned a letter to Susy.

October 17, 1895
Susy darling, dearest child:
Tuesday night, we were at Horsham, a small town in Victoria state that has an agricultural college. I think Papa never talked to a more enthusiastic audience than that night. They were entirely uproarious, taking a point almost before he had reached it. The house was packed, people sitting on the stage and standing around the sides of the lecture hall. One man traveled 75 miles, then went immediately back after the lecture. A young fellow who sat next to me began to pound his sides as if troubled by stitches, then, turning to me, he said: "If all of it is as funny as this, I shall die."
All my love,
Mama

***

After celebrating his sixtieth birthday in Ceylon, Clemens and his troupe arrived in India where Sam would spend three months crossing the subcontinent from Bombay to Rawalpindi to Darjeeling, and finally, Calcutta. Of Sam's lecture in Bombay, the *Times of India* reported:

"In addition to almost every prominent British citizen in Bombay, there was a comparatively large number of Parsee, Mahomedan and Hindu ladies and gentlemen who packed themselves into the lecture hall. It is a rugged and somewhat of a romantic figure that Mark Twain presents upon the stage, with his mass of curly hair, now nearly white, his keen, kindly eyes looking out from great shaggy brows and his strangely magnetic smile. The hour and a half during which he spoke seemed little more than ten minutes, and yet it was the most delightful hour and a half speaking that had ever been heard by the audience."

***

In early January, as Sam's troupe sailed across the Indian Ocean en route to South Africa, Sam received another letter from Susy.

December 27, 1895
Dearest Papa:
I trust you and Mama are faring well and your funny talks are successful.

Over Christmas past, Jean and I enjoyed a festive holiday with other family members at Quarry Farm. On Christmas day, there was a sumptuous repast of roast turkey and dressing, mashed potatoes and sides of cranberry. Afterward, Grandma Langdon fell ill and took to bed protesting the ambrosia tasted "slightly sour."

The entire family spent most of Christmas day playing a new parlor game called Pick up Sticks where each player tries to pick tiny wooden sticks from a pile without disturbing the others. It was so engrossing.

Little Miss Contrary spends an inordinate amount of time with Grandma, chatting away and watching her knit. Some nights, Grandma will try to sing while Clara plays the piano, but her performances are far less than satisfactory.

Jean bodes well with her painting activities, listens to Grandma while she reads her Bible and rambles on about the Book of Revelations. *Jean continues to remain free of nervous eruptions.*

Mary Ann Cord, Aunt Susan's servant who related to you the story of losing her son during the war then regaining him, passed away two weeks ago. Uncle Theodore, Aunt Susan and I attended her funeral at a small Negro church near Elmira. I had never seen so many black people gathered together in one place at one time.

I finished The Red Badge of Courage *and Henry James'* Turn of the Screw *and I must tell you I suffered nightmares upon reading the latter. At the moment, I am rereading the poems of William Cullen Bryant.*

Oh, how I wish you were here to discuss these works with me.

At best, I am a paper puzzle and, when I am not near you

and Mama, there are missing parts. Oh, how I miss our discussions about literature, poetry and the ways of the world.
   All my love,
   Susy

***

Upon arrival in South Africa in mid-March, Sam prepared himself for two months of performances in Pretoria, Johannesburg and Cape Town. In Kimberley, Sam visited the world-famous diamond mine and marveled at the operation which was yielding $45 million a year in gold and diamonds.

"I had been a gold miner myself, in my day," Sam wrote. "I knew substantially everything these people knew about mining, except how to make money at it."

Witnessing the treatment of African natives by white colonists triggered powerful and disturbing memories of the way slaves were mistreated during Sam's boyhood years. He became angry and ashamed of his own race.

March 27, 1896 *In many countries, we have chained the savage and starved him to death. In more than one country, we have hunted the savages and his little children and their mothers with dogs and guns through the woods and swamps for an afternoon's sport and filled the regions with happy laughter over their sprawling and stumbling flight and their wild supplications for mercy. In many countries, we have taken the savage's land and made him our slave, lashed him every day and ground his manhood into nothingness. There are many humorous things in the world: among them the white man's notion that he is less savage than the other savages.*

***

Upon arrival in Cape Town, the last stop of the South Africa tour, Sam received a new letter from Susy.

March 30, 1896
Dearest Papa:

Three days ago, Jean and I returned from Quarry Farm to the Hartford home. I felt being back at the Hartford home would quell the feelings of loneliness swarming about my soul. Although you and Mother are not here, being in this house represents your presence and helps ease my feelings of loneliness.

Jean was upset about leaving her goat, but I explained the railroad company didn't sell passage for goats. Although she wept profusely, she accepted my judgement, and thankfully, the incident didn't arouse another nervous eruption.

At what juncture will the tour be ended?

In every step, I see you and Mama within this house, but the real personages are not there to be seen, touched and spoken to.

Oh, how I miss my Papa and Mama!

All my love,

Susy

P.S. Relate to Mama that the poems of Gerard Manley Hopkins are awaiting her perusal. In her last letter, she reminded me that, upon her death, you had promised to read his poem The Windhover *at her graveside.*

***

On July 15, 1896, exactly a year and day since the tour began, it came to an end in Cape Town, South Africa. The following day, Clemens wrote a letter to Susy.

July 16, 1896

My darling Susy:

The tour is finished. Ended. Terminated. Dead. I delivered my final talk two nights ago and your mother and I are boarding the steamer, the Norman, tomorrow morning en route to Southampton, England.

Upon arrival, I intend to rent a home near Guilford and meet you, Clara, Jean and Katy no later than August 12. Mark your calendar at three weeks from today. More than anything on this earth, I want the Clemens family to be united once more.

I have a handsome string of tales I wish to share with you as well as a passel of souvenirs I have acquired during my travels.

Oh, sweetheart, how I long to see you once again. Never again shall I allow such a long absence to occur between us.

My mind cannot wait to pore over the poems of William Cullen Bryant with you. They are a treasure trove of beautiful words.

Your mother will provide details of your tickets and arrival dates in England.

All my love,
Papa

***

On the night of August 15, Susy fell ill. At the dinner table, she complained of a headache and, after a warm bath, went to bed early. The following morning, after she failed to get out of bed and had a fever, Katy called Dr. McDermott. When he arrived later that morning and examined her, he shook his head sadly.

"She has spinal meningitis," he said. "Medical science is aware that the disease is caused by a bacterium, but there is no known medicine to treat it. In some cases, doses of potassium bromide will relieve the symptoms, but beyond that, there is little to be done."

"What can we expect?" Katy said.

"Since the disease affects the nervous system, there is often mental confusion and a loss of the senses. The patient will go blind or lose their hearing or sense of taste. In severe cases, the victim will go into convulsions. We could take her to hospital, but there is little they could do."

"Oh, God!" Katy said. "I should contact the Cranes. How are we going to tell Mr. and Mrs. Clemens?"

***

That afternoon, Katy sent a telegram to Southampton,

England.

August 16, 1896
Dear Mr. and Mrs. Clemens:
Susy has fallen ill.
Dr. McDermott says she should fully recover.
Will keep you apprised.
Katy

***

That afternoon, the Cranes and Clara arrived in Hartford. Earlier that day, Katy had moved Susy from her own room to the master bedroom where Sam and Olivia slept, then installed a couch nearby for herself. Throughout the night, Katy remained at Susy's bedside while she slept.

On the morning of August 17, Susy awakened, sat up in bed and looked to those around her. Present were Katy, Uncle Theodore, Aunt Susan and Jean. When Katy asked if she was hungry, she didn't seem to hear.

"I hear Papa calling," Susy said, peering toward the window.

"Papa! Papa!" she said, as if she were answering a call.

Her eyes fell on her Uncle Theodore.

"Uncle Charley, do you hear Papa calling?"

"No!" Theodore answered. "I don't hear him."

"Take me to the window," Susy said. "He's in the front yard."

Theodore stepped forward, helped her out of bed and slowly moved her across the room to the window.

For a moment, her eyes searched the front yard.

Seeing no one, she turned back to Theodore.

"Uncle Charley, do you see Papa in the yard?"

Theodore peered out the window.

"I don't see him," he said. "Let's return to the bed."

Moments later, back in bed, she began to swing her arms wildly.

"The trolley for Mark Twain's daughter goes up," she said, making an upward motion with her hand. "The trolley for Mark

Twain's daughter goes down."

Then she would make a downward motion with her hand.

For a moment, she was silent. Then she raised her hand in an upward motion again.

"The trolley for Mark Twain's daughter goes up," she said again with an upward motion. "The trolly for Mark Twain's daughter goes down."

As she said it, she made another downward motion.

Then she looked around at the faces at her bedside. Then, suddenly, she covered her face with her hands and began sobbing. Katy took a seat on the bed and took Susy into her arms. Moments later, she was asleep.

***

On the following morning of August 18, family members were once again gathered at Susy's bedside. In attendance were Rev. Joe Twichell, Sam's long-time minister friend, her Uncle Theodore, his wife Susan, Patrick the coachman, Katy and Jean. When Susy awoke that morning, she was blind. Again, Katy asked if she wanted breakfast, but again, she didn't seem to hear.

"I'm blind and you are blind, Uncle Charley," Susy said in her delirium. "Tell Uncle Charley he is to care for Madame Maliban and Mrs. Warner should take note of Fitzgerald Darcy while reading *Pride and Prejudice*."

For a moment, she was quiet, then her arms began to swing wildly.

"The trolley goes up for Mark Twain's daughter," she said, making an upward motion with her hand. "The trolley goes down for Mark Twain's daughter," she said, making a downward motion with her hand.

She lolled her head around as if she were trying to view the entirety of the room. First, she looked upward at the ceiling, then toward the walls, and finally, downward to the floor. Seeing nothing, she held her open hands out in front of her as if she were reaching out to touch something.

"Mama! Mama!" she called.

Instinctively, Katy Leary, who was sitting at the bedside,

took Susy's hands, then guided them to her face.

"Mama! Oh, Mama!" Susy said as she held Katy's face in her hands. "I love you! I love you!"

Then her eyes closed back into her head and she fell back into the pillows on the bed. Those were her last words. That afternoon, she slipped into a coma and died at 4:26 p.m. She was 24.

***

That night, more than 2,000 miles away in Southampton, England, Clemens waited at the post office until it closed at midnight, hoping for some news. The following morning, he and Olivia were at the telegraph office when it opened at 7 a.m.

Just after 8 a.m., the clerk received a message. It was from Katy. Anxiously, Sam opened it.

"Susy was peacefully released today," the message said.

"Oh, God no!" Olivia said, then fainted dead away on the telegraph office floor.

***

August 20, 1896 *The greatest blow I ever suffered on this earth was the moment I fully understood that I had lost my darling Susy. I did not comprehend that she was such a large part of our life. I did not know or want to know that she could go away and take our lives with her, leaving our dull bodies behind. She was a treasure in the bank, the amount unknown, the need to examine it daily, handle it, weigh it, count it and realize it, unnecessary. Now that I would do it, it is too late. They tell me my treasure is no longer there, has vanished into the night, the bank is broken, my fortune is gone, I am a pauper. Oh, how many times I have chastised myself for mentioning the cost of an additional fare. If she had accompanied us on the trip, she would be alive today. If only I had kept my damned mouth shut. She died of loneliness. She had said she fell sick when she was away from Livy and me for extended periods. How am I to comprehend this? How am I to bear it? Why have I been robbed and who is benefitted?*

***

Susy was buried on August 24, 1896 in the Langdon family plot in Elmira, five days before Sam and Olivia arrived back in the States. Rev. Twichell officiated the service and pallbearers, including her Uncle Theodore, Patrick the coachman and Charles Warner, delivered her remains to its final resting place alongside her grandfather and her brother. As workers threw clods of fresh earth over the coffin, Katy Leary, the family's long-time servant, knelt at the graveside and wept like a little child.

***

On the afternoon of August 28, Sam and Olivia arrived back in New York Harbor. When they stepped off the boat, reporters crowded around them to get a response from Sam about his daughter's death.

"I have nothing to say," he said, brushing them aside. "Please respect my privacy."

The reporters chased after them.

"Mr. Clemens!" shouted one. "What about your fans?"

"The fans be damned," Sam shouted. "Remove yourselves from me."

An hour later, a cab carriage with Sam, Olivia and their luggage arrived at the Hartford home. The very moment the carriage stopped, Olivia turned to her husband.

"Oh, Samuel," she said, stark fear in her eyes. "I'm not sure I can do this."

"Neither am I," he said.

Then the two of them exited the carriage and, arm-in-arm, started walking to the front door.

Moments later, halfway up the walkway, Olivia glimpsed upward for a full view of the house. Suddenly, she screamed. It was the first time Clemens had ever heard his wife scream.

"Livy, darling!"

She turned to him, her face filled with horror.

"I cannot! I cannot return to that house," she shouted. "Come! Get me away from here! Now!"

Then she burst into tears, turned, and embraced her husband, sobbing uncontrollably. Moments later, she broke the embrace and raced back to the carriage.

Moments later, Sam was beside her.

"Where shall we go?" he said.

"Not here. Not in this house ever again," she said. "We shall stay tonight in a hotel. Tomorrow, we'll go to Quarry Farm and determine our future."

"What about the house? What shall we do with it?"

"Burn it! Demolish it! Then we shall be forever free of its memories."

"Livy, darling! Do you realize what you're saying?"

"I comprehend exactly what I'm saying. Get me to a hotel."

"I'll sell it!" Sam said. "I'll put it on the block tomorrow."

***

Three days later, Sam, Olivia and other family members attended a memorial service for Susy at the Langdon family plot in Elmira. Rev. Twichell officiated and commented on her passing: "Today she is at peace. She has escaped from controversies and enmities and hatreds of this earthly world. Henceforward, she will shine far above all those clouds which float over our heads, among the brightest stars in the heavens."

Olivia fainted during the tribute and had to be taken to the hospital.

At Sam's behest, the following words, adapted from Robert Richardson's poem *Annette*, were inscribed on her headstone.

Warm summer sun, shine friendly here
Warm western wind, blow kindly here;
Green sod above, rest light, rest light,
Good-night, Susy!
Sweetheart, good-night!

***

August 30, 1896 *The "forever home" where Livy and I*

believed we would live out the remaining years of our lives is no more. Its spires, its bay windows, its hallowed grounds, the roof that sheltered our heads and nurtured our souls is forever lost. Both Livy and I are incapable of returning to its chambers for fear of renewing memories of our beloved daughter. Over these past days, each of us has informed the other again and again that we could survive the horror of her death, but deep within our heart of hearts, we know it is a lie. There are times, when, at the slightest thought or memory of Susy, Livy will begin to weep and the two of us will embrace, holding tightly to one another, then sob uncontrollably. When Susy passed, she took our lives with her.

24
Nomadic Life

After the death of Susy, Sam and Olivia spent the next three months living at Quarry Farm in Elmira trying to recover from the loss of their daughter and find a new direction for their lives. Sam had somehow lost interest in his writing. Many mornings, he would seat himself at his desk, scribble a few lines and then stop. The words were not gushing forth in great torrents as they had in the past. Olivia, who had fallen into a debilitating depression, spent many days, often alone, wandering the wooded hills and valleys near Quarry Farm. There seemed to be nothing she wanted to do or was interested in. It was as if she had frozen up inside. One morning over breakfast, she told Sam, after their whirlwind experiences on the lecture tour, she wanted to go traveling again.

"England, Austria and Italy," she said. "That's what I wish to see this time. Clara wishes to take singing lessons in Vienna and we can deliver Jean to the best medical minds in Europe. A recent article in *Harper's* magazine claims that the world's foremost experts on epilepsy are in Vienna."

She handed Sam a post card.

"Take a look at this."

Clemens took the card and examined it. It was a post card of Tuscany, Italy.

"That is where I wish to finally settle," she said. "I wish to live in a yellow Italian villa surrounded with olive groves, vineyards and wineries with sheep grazing among the rolling green hills of Tuscany. Now that we can spend money again, this is what my heart desires."

"Then it shall be," Clemens said.

"Promise?"

"Promise!"

***

In late November of 1896, Sam received a letter from Rogers notifying him that, thanks to the success of the worldwide lecture tour, all of his debts connected to the publishing house bankruptcy had been paid in full. Olivia read the letter again and again, wishing to savor the joy of the moment.

"Since the death of Susy, this is the happiest day I have had," she said.

Further, Rogers had done a masterful job of managing Sam's finances. After the Hartford home was sold in late September for $31,000, Sam provided those funds to Rogers for investments, all of which paid off handsomely and, at the time of Rogers' letter, stood at over $61,500. Following the lecture tour, sales of the *Tom Sawyer* and *Huckleberry Finn* books had picked up nicely. Once again, the Clemens family had a firm financial foundation.

***

In mid-December of 1896, Sam, Olivia, Clara and Jean boarded a ship at New York harbor bound for London, England. Two weeks earlier, Sam had rented a three-bedroom cottage, sight unseen, on a London backstreet near Kensington Gardens. The eight-day voyage was a tortuous one for Jean and Olivia, who spent most of the journey in their cabins suffering from seasickness. When the family finally arrived on Christmas morning, reporters swarmed around them as they strode down the gangplank. Even before the family arrived, notices had appeared on the front pages of major London newspapers notifying the populace that Clemens was paying a visit. For the British, Sam was the foremost American celebrity and his opinions represented the voice of all Americans.

"Mr. Clemens! Mr. Clemens!" the reporters shouted, trying to get his attention.

"What is your opinion on hazing?" said one reporter.

"Can I get a comment on the hostilities between America and Spain?" said another.

"Please! Please!" Sam said. "I must deliver my family to our new home at the moment," he said. "If you'll come around in the morning, say around 10 a.m., I'll answer all your questions."

"What's the address?" asked one reporter.

"1104 Kensington Place."

***

At 10 a.m. the following morning, Sam, decked out in his signature white silk suit and black leather shoes, met with a bevy of fifteen to twenty reporters on the front porch and lawn of the cottage. As expected, Sam's answers drew frequent chuckles and outright belly laughs.

"What words of wisdom do you have on parenting?" asked one reporter.

"When I was a boy of fourteen, my father was so ignorant, I could hardly stand to have the old man around. When I got to be twenty-one, I was astonished at how much he had learned in seven years."

Polite laughter all around.

"Mr. Clemens!" said another reporter. "How does it feel to be the most famous American in the world today?"

"I reckon you can say that but, behind this mighty façade of glory and triumph lies a mischievous country lad that likes to steal apples, spy on other people's doings and wiggle my toes in Mississippi river mud."

Another round of laughs.

"Of all your travels, what's the coldest weather you ever experienced?"

"The coldest winter I ever spent was a summer in San Francisco."

More laughter.

"Do you like to exercise?"

Sam paused for a moment, then quipped:

"When I feel the urge to exercise, I go lie down until it

passes.”

More laughter as the reporters scribbled away.

“What do you have to say about gold mining?”

“A gold miner is a liar standing next to a hole in the ground.”

“Mr. Clemens!” said another reporter. “Some people say your stories are exaggerations of reality. Is that true?”

“I don’t exaggerate; I just remember big.”

Sam waited for the next question.

“Were you grief-stricken over the death of your daughter Susy?”

Suddenly, Sam stopped, then turned angrily to the errant reporter.

“Whoa! Whoa!” he said. “I shall answer no questions about my family. If anyone asks another, I will terminate the interview immediately.”

A silence rippled around the crowd of reporters.

“Do you understand?”

The reporters murmured their acceptance in unison.

“Mr. Clemens! What do you think about self-education?”

“Education begins with reading,” Sam said. “The man who does not read good books has no advantage over the man who cannot read.”

“How did Mrs. Clemens respond to the death of your daughter Susy?”

Suddenly, livid anger crossed Sam’s face.

“That’s it!” he said, standing up to go back inside. “I warned you fellows. I refuse to discuss my family. Now get off my porch!”

“Mr. Clemens! We have more questions.”

“We’re finished,” Sam said. “Get out of here! Now!”

Reluctantly, the group fell silent, unseated themselves and began to disperse. As they did, several of the other reporters turned to their errant colleague.

“You fool!” said one. “You ruined it for all of us.”

“Sod!” said another.

“Imbecile!” said still another.

***

During the late winter of 1896, the Clemens family stayed in seclusion, seeing only a handful of close friends. Jean, whose condition had worsened after Susy's death, was placed under the care of Dr. Henrik Kellgren, a Swedish physician who, using the Swedish movement cure, a daily regimen of diet, exercise and massage, claimed success in treating people with seizures. While the frequency of the seizures seemed to diminish after the treatments, Jean would never be entirely free of them for the remainder of her life.

By late March of the new year, after local newspapers had not heard from Sam, a rumor circulated that he was dying, which prompted one Fleet Street editor to send a reporter to the Clemens cottage to confirm.

When Sam himself appeared to the door, the reporter showed Sam a note he had received from his editor.

"If Mark Twain very ill, five hundred words," the note read. "If dead, send a thousand."

"You don't need as much as that," Sam said. "Just say the report of my death has been greatly exaggerated."

In later years, that would become one of Sam's most famous quotes.

***

Over the next two years, the Clemens family would remain in Europe, wandering from one city to another, travelling on trains and steamers and living in hotels and rented houses. After leaving England in May of 1897, they made stops in Paris, where Jean was fascinated by the paintings at the Louvre, Nice and Marseille in the south of France, and Berlin and Munich in Germany where Sam visited the world's largest brewery. On August 18, 1897, the first anniversary of Susy's death, they were living in the Savoy Hotel on the banks of Lake Lucerne in Switzerland.

August 19, 1897 *Yesterday will be a day I shall long remember. It has been one year to the day since the great disaster fell. Today, Livy went away to be alone. She took the steamer across the lake and spent the day solitary in a hotel. I spent the day alone under the trees on the mountain side, peering up at the Swiss Alps and intermittently choking up with grief.*

***

October 13, 1897 *Over these past ten months, Livy and I have become wanderers, vagabonds, derelicts, those who are fated to seek that which they do not know, restless, unhappy, empty souls trapped in a vast wilderness of nothingness. During that time, both Livy and I have informed one another again and again that we could survive the sorrow of Susy's death, but deep within our heart of hearts, we know it is a lie.*

***

In late January of 1898, the Clemens family found themselves in a restful little town in eastern Poland named Krakow, a thousand-year-old city famous for its museums and open-air theaters. Over breakfast one morning, Sam asked other family members where they would like to visit next.

"When are we going to Austria?" Clara asked her mother. "When we started traveling, you promised we would visit Vienna so I could take music lessons."

Olivia turned to Sam for an answer.

"We'll leave for Vienna tomorrow," he said. "I wish to see the grand old city myself."

***

On the morning of February 3, 1898, the Clemens family arrived in Vienna and took up residence in a nine-room suite at the Hotel Metropole on the Graben, a fashionable boulevard in the heart of old Vienna. The moment the family was settled, Clara beat a path to the home of world-renowned music/voice teacher Theodore Leschetizky, an Austrian-Polish pianist, composer and conductor who lived in Vienna's Wahring district. Upon meeting the great man, Clara was happy to learn he spoke perfect English and, after she reported she was Mark

Twain's daughter, the great man was quick to take her under his wing.

That night, when Clara told her parents she had been accepted, neither of them approved.

"Both Sam and I are very sorry indeed that Clara wants such a public life," Olivia wrote her foster sister in Elmira. "Women in such roles do not always turn out well."

"It is our loss," Sam said in a letter to Howells. "She will be performing for strangers. Clara must stay at least a year to study music, so I guess the rest of us must stay too, for Mrs. Clemens will not hear of the family ever being divided again."

Despite their objections, both Sam and Olivia agreed to indulge Clara, at least for a while.

***

This new venture would be the opportunity Clara, at age twenty-three, had been seeking to secure her independence. For years, she had struggled in the shadow of Susy, Sam and Olivia's obvious favorite. Now, with the older sister out of the picture, Clara began to bloom both as a musician and a woman.

Over the first six months, Clara became one of the Leschetizky's star pupils. The tutor, a smallish, bland-looking old man with a white beard, took special pains to teach Clara European techniques for playing the piano she had not seen before.

"Practice! Practice! Practice!" the great man advised. "You should become so comfortable with each piece that playing is like taking a sip of water. Each piece should become second nature to you."

After three months under his tutelage, Clara was chosen to play Beethoven's classical "Moonlight Sonata" for a recital at the Grand Music Hall in Vienna, which was attended by Austrian Emperor Franz Joseph I and his wife Empress Elisabeth. After the performance, Clara received an enthusiastic round of applause from the audience, which included Sam and Olivia.

Clara soon met another of Leschetizky's star pupils, the handsome young Russian-Jewish pianist and orchestra conductor Ossip Gabrilowitsch. At age nineteen, he was four years younger than Clara, but already a brilliant composer and deeply connected throughout the musical world. After only two months, Clara and Ossip began a tempestuous romance which brought indignant whispers from both the Austrian press and the snobbish nobles in Vienna's so-called "noble society."

***

Over the winter of 1898, Clemens, his wife and two daughters were the most eagerly sought-after visitors in Vienna. During a parade celebrating the emperor's birth, the Clemens family found themselves cut off from their hotel by a police barrier. Once a mounted officer saw their dilemma, he shouted: "For God's sake, let them pass. Don't you see it's Herr Mark Twain?"

Artists, including the world-famous portraitist Franz Cizek, requested that Sam sit for him. Sam happily obliged. Only weeks later, Viennese sculptor Theresa Fedorowna Ries shaped a marble bust image of Clemens, which he termed "a very close likeness."

One morning, when Sam went into a tobacco shop to buy a handful of cheroots, the proprietor recognized him immediately.

"Will you sign the picture card I have of you?"

"Picture card?"

Instantly, the proprietor reached under the counter and produced a colored lithograph of Sam's face printed on the front of a piece of cardboard. On the back was Clemens' biography.

"Where did you get this?"

The clerk turned to the cigarette display and took down a pack of Duke cigarettes. On the front of each pack, prominently displayed just below the company logo, was another card with Sam's likeness. Other faces featured on the cigarette packs were Buffalo Bill Cody and P.T. Barnum.

Sam smiled at the extent of his fame.

"I'll sign your card in exchange for six of those Milan cheroots," Sam said.

The proprietor happily obliged.

***

When New Year's Day of 1899 rolled around, Sam felt inspired to write again and threw himself into a collection of short stories titled *The Mysterious Stranger*. As always, Olivia was there to edit and critique the manuscript. One afternoon, while editing pages, she began to complain about the arthritic pain in her hands and fingers.

"My hands are refusing to serve me," she told Sam that night in the marital bed. "When I grasp a pencil to make an edit, a terrible pain courses up my arm. I'm not certain how much longer I can serve as your editor."

The following morning, when Sam woke up, he found Olivia in the bathroom soaking her hands in a salts bath, her face screwed up in pain.

"Livy, darling!" he said. "I didn't realize your pain was so severe."

"I'm sorry, Samuel," she said. "I can no longer do your correspondence or edit your manuscripts."

"Darling, if it bothers you so much," Sam said, "I want to make other arrangements."

"What will you do?"

"I will hire a secretary and editor."

"I'm sorry, Samuel."

"My darling," he said. "It is nothing. I will find someone."

"It shall be difficult to find a capable person in Vienna," she said. "I fear most of those who are qualified speak only German."

"Don't worry your pretty little head," Sam said. "I shall find someone up to the task."

***

Over the two weeks, Sam spent his mornings working on *The Mysterious Stranger* and afternoons interviewing for an English-speaking secretary to handle his correspondence and edit his manuscripts. The first candidate was a youngish

English teacher from Dresden, Germany, but Sam turned her down because "she had the breath of a camel." A tall, elegantly-dressed woman was dismissed after she was unable to spell the word "extemporaneous." When an older Austrian woman who wrote children's books in German and spoke perfect English interviewed, Sam asked for her opinion on "hazing in college." After the woman drew a blank, Sam turned her away.

"I'm unable to find a qualified secretary," he told Olivia that night. "I may have to return to the States to find a qualified person for the job."

"When are we going to Tuscany?" Olivia said.

"I'm in dire need of a secretary and editor," he said. "I no longer expect you to do perform those chores in your condition."

"Then engage one," she said.

"Not here in a foreign country. I'm in need an American who knows the language and is grounded in the ways of my native land. I want to return to New York long enough to hire a secretary. Once that is accomplished, we'll travel to Tuscany."

***

Eight days later, when Sam arrived back at New York Harbor decked out in his signature white silk suit, he was swarmed with reporters as he strode down the gangplank. As always, the world press kept close tabs on Sam and his wandering ways.

"Mr. Clemens!" shouted one reporter. "Just a few questions."

"Very well," Clemens said. "I'll take a few, but no questions about my family or I'll tell all of you to go to hell."

He pointed to one reporter.

"What have you learned from your wanderings?"

"I have become a self-appointed ambassador-at-large for America-without-salary."

The reporters began to scribble furiously.

"After your bankruptcy, what is your philosophy on

investing?"

"There are two times when a man should not speculate: when he can afford it and when he cannot."

A round of laughter.

"Any opinions on the ignorance of others?"

"Let us be thankful for the fools. But for them, the rest of us could not succeed."

"What thoughts do you have on the state of our nation?"

"It is by the goodness of God that in our country we have these three unspeakably precious things: freedom of speech, freedom of conscience, and the prudence never to practice either of them."

"In your work, critics claim that you have distorted the facts. Is that true?"

"Facts, or what a man believes to be facts, are always delightful. Get your facts first, then you can distort them as much as you please."

"What is your position on women's suffrage?"

"I know that since the women started out on their crusade, they have scored in every project they undertook against unjust laws. I would like to see women help make the laws and become those who enforce them. I would like to see the whiplash in women's hands, for a change."

Once again, the reporters scribbled furiously.

"Mr. Clemens, any thoughts on politicians?"

"Politicians and baby diapers should be changed regularly... and for the same reason."

"This fellow Thomas Paige, the man who drove you into bankruptcy, what's your opinion of him?"

"If I had his nuts in a steel trap, I would show no aid or succor for his pain."

Another round of belly laughs.

"Is your youngest daughter being treated for epilepsy in Europe?" asked another reporter.

Sam stared at the errant reporter with disgust.

"That's all!" he said. "We're finished!"

Without another word, Sam stepped off the loading platform, luggage in hand, and made his way to a group of waiting cab carriages nearby.

The reporters chased after him.

"Mr. Clemens!" shouted one reporter. "What are your thoughts on President McKinley?"

Sam didn't even look at the reporter. Instantly, the driver cracked his whip and the cab carriage rumbled off down the street.

***

That afternoon, Sam checked into the St. Nicholas Hotel on Broadway then went straight to the offices of the *New York Tribune* and placed an advertisement for a secretary. The following morning, he interviewed candidates in a conference room at the hotel. The first interview was with was a smallish, dark-haired woman who had been personal secretary to the president of a coal mine.

"Can you spell extemporaneous?" was Sam's first question.

"E-x-t-e-m-p-a-r-a-n-e-o-u-s."

"Sorry," he said. "There is an 'o' between the 'p' and 'r'," he said. "I'm obliged that you stopped by."

The next candidate was an older woman, poorly dressed and a recent widow, who had been personal secretary to the wife of a railroad executive.

"Can you spell the word salubrious?"

"S-e-l-u-b-r-i-o-u-s."

"Sorry," Sam said. "The second letter is 'a."

The third candidate was a tall, well-kept woman in her mid-thirties with a serious, pretty face. She gave her name as Isabel Lyon and exuded an unmistakable air of refinement. Sam explained he was an author seeking a secretary to travel the world with him and his family.

"I'm well aware of who you are, Mr. Clemens," she began. "I've read your *Tom Sawyer* book and its companion piece, *The Adventures of Huckleberry Finn*."

Sam studied the woman for a long moment. She was the first candidate who had read any of his books.

"Tell me more about yourself," Sam said.

"I grew up in Tarrytown to a well-off family," she said. "I

was educated at Saint Mary-of-the-Woods College until my father's death, then I began work as a governess for a wealthy family in Saranac Lake. For the past two years, I've been secretary to a New York state legislator, handling his personal correspondence, balancing his checkbook and serving his coffee. Also, I'm an expert typist."

"A what?" Sam said.

"I'm quite adept at using a typewriter."

"A typewriter?" Sam said. "A friend of mine showed me one years ago and I thought they were just a passing fancy."

"I'm surprised you're not making use of one," she said. "A typewriter is a portable printing press."

"Can you spell the extemporaneous?"

"E-x-t-e-m-p-o-r-a-n-e-o-u-s."

"Excellent!"

"Would you like the adverbial spelling?"

"Please!"

"E-x-t-e-m-p-o-r-a-n-e-o-u-s-l-y."

Sam was impressed.

"Do you read newspapers?"

"Mostly the *New York Tribune*. Sometimes, the *Herald*."

"What are your thoughts about President McKinley?"

"As a Republican, he is in a position of imminent power, and I feel, with the current majority in both the Senate and the House, he will render his party a dominant force in the nation for many years to come. Also, I predict William Jennings Bryan will be his opponent in the next election."

Sam waited for her comments to register.

"Any thoughts on the Spanish-American War?"

"America is rapidly expanding as a world power," she said. "I predict our armies will crush enemy forces in both Cuba and the Philippines. Spain will rue the day they sank the USS *Maine* in Havana Harbor."

Sam had heard enough.

"Are you single and free to travel?"

"I am."

"You're hired. Can you leave tomorrow afternoon for Italy?"

"I can."

25
Death of Olivia

When the Clemens family first arrived in Tuscany in early February of 1899, the first thing Sam did was rent a three-story, thirty-one-room manor on the outskirts of Florence known to locals as Villa Quatro. Complete with a coachman and carriages, it was a sprawling earth-colored, renaissance-style structure resting high atop a hillside and overlooking a lush green valley below. Only days after the family was settled, Sam outfitted an office on the top floor as a writing parlor with an adjacent work room for his new secretary. When Olivia and Jean left Vienna for Tuscany, Clara remained behind to continue her voice lessons; over the next few years, she would show up at the villa for occasional visits with her lover, pianist Ossip Gabrilowitsch. Jean, comfortable under the care of her new physician in Florence, had not had a seizure in over three years. Meanwhile, Sam was writing again while Olivia spent her days gardening and wandering the woods and hillsides of Tuscany, often alone.

***

Over the next three years, Isabel Lyon far exceeded Sam's expectations as a secretary. No only had she done an admirable job handling his correspondence and manuscript editing, she had performed well with other assignments. When a neighbor's donkey wandered onto the villa grounds, Sam instructed her to have it removed, then watched as she roped the animal then led it back to the neighbor's farm. One morning, when water to the villa suddenly stopped running,

Sam assigned her the task of discovering why. That afternoon, after Lyon went to the landlady to inquire, the home's water supply was operational once more. In the spring of 1903, Sam turned over the management of villa expenses to her with the instructions to keep track of them, provide him with a total at the end of the month, and he would provide funds for payment. As with all the other chores, Lyon fulfilled it with efficiency and aplomb.

***

Meanwhile, Clara's singing career was flourishing with leaps and bounds. In the fall of 1899, using Leschetizky's connections, she made successful concert debuts as a contralto singer in Berlin and Warsaw. The following spring, she was invited by the people of Hartford to perform at a grand concert given by the Boston Symphony Orchestra. Afterward, critics called her voice "unusually sweet and attractive" and, two days later, she was honored at a grand ball in Hartford, which included a host of celebrities, businessmen, politicians and other dignitaries.

***

Now, one morning in late November of 1903, Clara arrived at Villa Quarto with her lover to celebrate the Thanksgiving holiday. Upon meeting Ossip Gabrilowitsch, a late twenties, stockily-built man with a roman nose and a balding forehead, Clemens was quick to offer a glad hand in an effort to make the budding pianist feel welcome. Olivia, while cordial to Clara, was cold and distant toward her lover. After a traditional Thanksgiving meal of roast turkey, dressing, vegetables and cranberry sauce, Sam and Ossip retired to the veranda to smoke and chat while Clara and Olivia were together in Sam and Olivia's bedroom. Olivia began by telling her daughter she disapproved of her relationship with Gabrilowitsch.

"It's shameful," she said. "What is the public to think of your father and me as parents? Our daughter is involved in a public romance with some flighty Russian musician. If you wish to carry on in such a manner, get married, make your relationship legal and socially acceptable. What you're doing is nothing more than pure, unabashed adultery."

Clara's face flushed with livid anger.

"Mother, I'm a twenty-nine-year-old woman," she shot back. "I am perfectly capable of managing my own life."

"Let this be the last time!" Olivia said.

"What is your meaning?"

"I will not abide your returning to this house again and sleeping under this roof with a man who is not your husband. Have you forgotten decency and honor?"

"Mother, when shall you arrive in the modern age?" Clara said. "The year is now 1903. Your thinking is archaic. Your perspectives on life in today's world are horribly unprogressive and narrow."

"It's unchristian!" Olivia blurted out.

"Unchristian?" she said, glaring at her mother. "If I ever hear that word again from your lips, I shall regurgitate."

A pause.

"You heard my words," Olivia said.

Clara had fire in her eyes.

"If Ossip is not welcome here, then I also should not be here," she said. "I shall not allow you to control my life. Now… or ever!"

With that, she strode to the bedroom door.

"Ossip and I shall be leaving tomorrow!"

Then she stalked out of the room, slamming the door behind her.

***

The following morning, Sam, with Olivia noticeably absent, was on the villa's veranda trying to deliver a cordial goodbye to Clara and her lover. Once civilities were complete, Clara and Ossip boarded a carriage that would take them to the train station in Florence. From there, they would journey to the coastal town of Livorno, where they would then book passage for their return to Austria.

Sam watched as the carriage pulled out of the villa's

courtyard.

Moments later, Olivia, who had been waiting inside for goodbyes to be finished, limped out onto the veranda. For a moment, she peered into the distance as the carriage disappeared over the top of the hill.

"They're gone now," Sam said.

Without a word, Olivia turned to go back inside. Suddenly, as she opened the door, she stopped and her face screwed up in intense pain. Then, grabbing her chest, she fell to the veranda floor, gasping for breath.

"Katy! Katy!" Sam called into the house.

Moments later, Katy appeared.

"Livy has had a heart attack," Sam said. "Help me get her inside and I will go for the doctor."

Over the next ten minutes, Sam and Katy managed to get Olivia into the master bedroom on the second floor and into bed. Then Sam rushed out of the home to the doctor's office in Florence.

Two hours later, Dr. Carlo Giovanni, a smallish, fortyish man with a salt-and-pepper beard and glasses, arrived.

"The walls of her heart are as thin as paper," he said. "She must remain quiet, not become agitated and take her medicine. The slightest excitement could cause her to have another heart attack and die."

That afternoon, upset by her mother's sudden health turn, Jean had a grand mal seizure and took to bed. Her condition had been in abeyance for over two years.

***

November 30, 1903 *Our children are not dead, but lost to us all the same. They are still with us, but they have become grown women and they no longer walk with us on our level. There is now a wide gulf, a gulf as wide as the horizons between our children and ourselves. We were always having vague, dream-glimpses as they were in their long-vanished years—glimpses of them playing and romping, with short frocks and spindle legs and hair tails down their backs and we could not hear their shouts and laughter. How we longed to gather them into our arms. But they were only dainty and darling specters that faded away and vanished, and have now left us desolate.*

***

Five months passed. During that time, doctors forbade either Sam or his seizure-haunted daughter to go into Olivia's sick room for fear they might induce another heart attack. Only Katy and a private nurse were permitted in the room.

"I am afraid to even go in and see my wife," Sam wrote to Howells. "Even if the doctors permitted it, for I would surely give out some startling yarn that would make the hair of a wolf stand on end."

Although Sam and Olivia were separated from one another, they continued to write notes back and forth.

"Although they were forbidden to see one another," Katy recalled, "nothing could bring a smile to her face like a note from Mr. Clemens. Three or four times a day, when the nurse approached her bed with a little slip of paper, her face would light up with happiness. Those notes were like a rainbow during a storm, always with a new variety of colors."

One morning, Olivia laughed out loud when she learned Sam had placed notes on the trees outside her window instructing the birds not to sing too loudly for fear of disturbing his wife.

In one note in late April, Olivia noted that, despite their differences, she longed to see Clara. That afternoon Sam wrote a letter.

April 27, 1904
Dear Clara:
Herein rests my humble request that you to return to Italy and make amends with your mother.

The recent heart attack has left her bed-ridden and, upon doctor's orders, her only accompaniment is through Katy and her nurse. Occasionally, Jean and I are allowed at her bedside.

While she refuses to publicly admit to it, she yearns to see you once again. The fracas of last fall has been forgotten and, while she proves herself demanding, she yearns to have you here once more.

Can you spare a short visit without your friend? Although you and she have your differences, she remains your birth mother.

I trust you can find it in your heart to forgive and forget.
Love,
Papa

***

Two weeks later, Clara showed up at the Villa Quatro without Gabrilowitsch. Upon arrival, she announced she would be there for only a few weeks since Leschetizky was arranging a recital for her in Paris. Despite doctor's orders, Clara went straight into Olivia's sick room. Upon seeing one another, they embraced, then wept as they held one another tightly. There was no mention of the earlier fracas.

Over the next few weeks, with Clara serving as "assistant nurse," Olivia began to mend. Her breathing improved, she was eating full meals again and she announced she wanted to start walking again, asking Clara to accompany her. At the beginning of the third week, she announced that she wanted to go to Rome and see the sights.

Sam was elated with his wife's improvements and hastily put together a trip for himself, Olivia, Clara and Jean to travel to Rome. On the seven-day trip, they paid homage all of the major sightseeing destinations, the Vatican, Colosseum, Trevi fountain, and Palatine Hill.

When they returned to Florence, Olivia pulled no punches about Italian men.

"Never have I witnessed men being so forward with women." she said. "They boldly come right up to you and unabashedly make vulgar advances. I had read about the profligacy of the roman emperors, but what I witnessed was a shock to my system."

***

Three days later, Clara received a letter from Leschetizky. After reading it, she went straight to her father.

"My tutor has informed me that he has arranged a recital at the Teatro della Pergola in Florence on the night of June 4," she said. "I would like to remain at the villa with you and Mama to prepare myself for the appearance. Can you have a piano delivered to the villa?"

"As you wish, my dear."

Over the next few days, Clara threw herself in preparation for her Florence debut. Far into the night, Sam and Olivia could hear the intermittent tinkling sounds of the piano and Clara's voice ringing through the halls of the villa. Meanwhile, she continued to provide spiritual support to her mother by accompanying her on her daily walks and serving as "assistant nurse."

***

A week passed. On the morning of May 28, 1904, the stress of life at the villa, caring for her mother and simultaneously preparing for her Florence debut, became too much for Clara. When Sam awoke that morning, he heard screams and the sound of breaking glass coming from Clara's bedroom. He went to investigate.

When he opened the door, he saw Clara ripping the sheets off the bed and throwing pillows at the wall. Already she had knocked over the bureau, spilling its contents on the floor, and crashed the lamp from the bedside table through the window.

When Sam entered the room, Clara rushed at him, her fingernails poised to attack. Instantly, he stepped backward, then grasped her flailing arms.

"God damn! God damn!" Clara screamed as Sam held her arms tightly in his grasp.

"I hate my mother!" she screamed. "I hate all of you for keeping me away from the man I love."

"Clara! I had no involvement is the banishment of Ossip," Sam said. "That was totally and completely your mother's doing."

"I hate her! I hate her and I hope that she dies. If she doesn't die, I will kill her."

"Calm down! Control yourself!" Sam said. "So, what do you wish?"

"I must have Ossip here as my accompanist to practice," she said. "I cannot adequately prepare myself for the recital unless I can practice with my accompanist."

"What do you wish?" he repeated.

"That Ossip come to Italy."

"Your mother will have a conniption."

"Let her!" Clara said. "My singing career is more important than her archaic religious beliefs."

Sam studied his daughter for a moment.

"Go ahead!" he said. "Tell him to come. I'll try to make it right with your mother."

That night, Sam tried to smooth the situation over with Olivia.

"I don't approve of my daughter fornicating in my house," Olivia said.

"After the recital, they will be gone. The recital is to further Clara's career."

"I don't care! I don't approve!" she said. "I wish to remain reclusive until this sordid affair is finished."

***

Two days later, Gabrilowitsch arrived at Villa Quatro. Sam, trying to maintain peace, greeted him cordially and assisted him with his luggage up to Clara's room. When he showed Ossip the piano he had purchased, the Russian was pleased. At dinner that night, Olivia was noticeably absent and, when Ossip asked about her, Sam explained she wasn't feeling well.

When Sam went to Olivia's bedside that night, he found his wife weeping inconsolably.

"We have failed as parents," she said. "I will never understand why God sent a daughter like Clara to us."

"Darling, please show some patience," Sam said. "This will be over in another week."

"I'll have no part of it," Olivia said. "Handle it as best you can, but I shall remain indifferent."

***

Over the next two days, Villa Quatro was filled once again with the contralto refrains of Clara's voice, only this time, it was accompanied by Ossip's piano playing. Over and over, Clara sang arias from the opera classics *Lucia, Martha* and *El Capitan*. After the fourth day, Sam had heard "Song to the Moon" from *Lucia* so many times, he knew most of the words by heart.

***

On the night of June 4, Clemens, Katy, Jean and Isabel Lyon attended Clara's debut in Florence. When Clemens and his entourage appeared at the concert hall, they were instantly recognized and other attendees rushed forward to greet them with smiles and handshakes. From the first, the audiences were delighted with Clara's performance and, once it was over, Sam declared the event a "triumph."

That night, when Sam started to relate the recital's success to Olivia, she cut him short.

"Keep your words to yourself," she said. "I have no interest in hearing about the success of a harlot, especially when she is my own daughter."

"Livy, darling! I wish you would loosen your strictures."

"Right is right! Wrong is wrong."

***

The following morning, while other members of the family were having breakfast, Olivia, who had remained in her room since Ossip's arrival, came down the stairs to the dining room. When Sam saw her at the bottom of the stairs, he turned immediately to her.

"Livy, we're happy to see you," Sam said. "Come and join us."

As if she hadn't heard, Olivia went straight to Clara, who

was sitting at the end of the table beside her lover.

"Mother, do you wish to join us?" Clara said.

Olivia wasted no time in launching her attack.

"You are a shame and a disgrace to this family," Olivia shouted, wagging her finger at her daughter. "I wish to God I had never brought you into this world."

"Livy! Livy! There is no need for this!" Sam said.

Olivia wasn't finished.

"You're a whore. A harlot! A Jezebel," she said, still shaking her finger in Clara's face. "God shall smite you with his wrath to punish you for your sinful ways."

Sam arose up from the table and pleaded with his wife.

"Livy, darling! You shouldn't be carrying on like this!"

Olivia still wasn't finished.

"As punishment for your transgressions, you shall burn in the pits of a perdition where fire and brimstone rain down…"

Suddenly, she stopped. She grasped her chest.

"Where fire and brimstone…"

Then, without another word, her face turned an ashen white color, her eyes rolled back into her head and she collapsed on the dining room floor.

Instantly, Clemens was kneeling over her.

"Katy!" he said. "Let's return her to the bedroom. Tell the coachman to bring around a carriage. I'll get the doctor."

***

Two hours later, Dr. Giovanni was back at Oliva's bedside.

"She has suffered an aneurysm," he said, after an examination. "A major blood vessel has burst inside her head and she is now in a coma."

"Will she live?" Sam asked.

Dr. Giovanni shook his head sadly.

"Such an injury is not survivable," he said. "You may register her at the local hospital, but there is little they can do. Her life is now in God's hands."

***

All that afternoon, the entire family remained at Olivia's bedside. By nightfall, the only one remaining was Katy. Just after 7 p.m., Katy left the bedside to make some tea. When she returned, Olivia, still unconscious, was gasping for breath.

She turned and raced down the stairs.

"Mr. Clemens! Mr. Clemens!" she shouted. "Come quick!"

Instantly, Sam and his daughters raced up the stairs.

There they found Olivia, her mouth wide open, desperately trying to suck life-giving oxygen into her lungs. Gradually, over the next twenty minutes, her breathing became more and more labored to the point it could be heard throughout the house, then suddenly, it stopped.

Olivia was dead.

"It was a pitiful thing to see her lying there cold and unmoving," Katy wrote later. "Oh, Mr. Clemens cried all that time. Clara and Jean put their arms around their father's neck and they cried and cried, the three of them, as though their hearts would break."

Later that night, Sam assigned Isabel the task of making arrangements to have Olivia's body removed from the villa and transported back to the United States for burial. Clara, convinced her returning with Gabrilowitsch to the villa had caused her mother's death, threw herself on her mother's bed once the body was removed, then locked herself in the room and refused to move for two days. Jean, upon witnessing her mother's body being carried away, suffered another seizure and required hospitalization.

June 5, 1904 *Six hours ago, the best heart that ever beat for me and mine was carried silent out of this house and I am now as one who wanders and has lost his way. The life of this family is wrecked. My daughters and I have no plans for the future. She always made the plans; none of us are now capable. We shall take her home and bury her with her dead at Elmira. Beyond that, we have no plans. The children must decide. I have no head.*

***

On the night of June 28, 1904, Clemens and his entourage, along with Olivia's body, were on board the steamer *Prince Oscar* when it sailed out of Livorno, Italy for the trip to America. Before departure, Clara said her good-byes to Gabrilowitsch, who was returning to Vienna to prepare for the winter season. Jean, upon boarding, was assigned to the ship's medical facility while Sam tried to deal with a new sorrow, the depths of which he not felt since the death of Susy.

*****

July 3, 1904 *There is no God and no universe; there is only empty space and within it a lost and homeless and wandering and companionless and indestructible thought. I am that thought. And God and the universe and time and life and death and joy and sorrow and pain are only a brutal and grotesque dream, evolved from the frantic imagination and that same insane thought.*

*****

On the afternoon of July 14, when the *Prince Oscar* dropped anchor at New York Harbor, Isabel Lyon made arrangements to have Olivia's body transported from New York to Elmira for burial in the Langdon family plot. Sam's long-time friend Rev. Joe Twichell, who had married Sam and Olivia, and overseen the burial of both little Langdon and Susy, officiated the funeral service.

Once Olivia's coffin was removed from the church to the cemetery, mourners gathered around the graveside to pay final respects. During the service, Clara, who had suffered what Sam called "two-thirds of a nervous breakdown," had to be restrained from throwing herself into her mother's grave.

As workmen began to throw clods of fresh earth back into the open grave, Sam stepped up to the open grave. He had a copy of Gerard Manley Hopkins' *Poems* in hand and he began reading *The Windhover*.

I caught this morning morning's minion, kingdom

of daylight's dauphin, dapple-dawn-drawn Falcon, in his riding
Of the rolling level underneath him steady air, and striding
High there, how he rung upon the rein of a wimpling wing
In his ecstasy! then off, off forth on swing,
As a skate's heel sweeps smooth on a bow-bend: the hurl and gliding
Rebuffed the big wind. My heart in hiding
Stirred for a bird, – the achieve of, the mastery of the thing!
Brute beauty and valour and act, oh, air, pride, plume, here
Buckle! And the fire that breaks from thee then, a billion
Times told lovelier, more dangerous, O my Chevalier!
No wonder of it: sheer plod makes plough down sillion
Shine, and blue-bleak embers, ah, my dear,
Fall, gall themselves, and gash gold-vermilion.

By the time Clemens had finished reading the last line, workmen had heaped the grave high with fresh dirt. Sam closed the book of poems and turned away from the grave side. He had fulfilled his promise to his beloved Livy.

***

After the funeral, Clara went into a deep depression and had herself committed to a New York sanitarium. Several weeks later, when Jean was slightly injured in a carriage accident, Sam rushed to the sanitarium to tell Clara about the incident. Although doctors warned Sam to be gentle with the news, he stormed into her room and waved a newspaper in her face with a lurid headline about the accident. After hearing her father's version, Clara, distraught and crying, immediately sent him away. Before leaving, doctors insisted that Sam not try to contact his daughter for the foreseeable future. For more than seven months, Clara remained bed-ridden and disconsolate, forbidden to even read her mail.

***

August 17, 1904 *My confidence and trust in Miss Lyon's*

ability to organize, manage and execute grows with each passing day. While my head was disjointed with the sorrow of Livy's death, she did an admirable job of attending to the details of transporting the body back to the States. Over the past three years, she has edited my manuscripts and handled my correspondence, the tasks she was hired for, with both efficiency and aplomb. Adept, alert, intelligent and gentle in approach, she is a worthy editor for my prose. Olivia hated the word "stench" and would strike it out instantly, while Miss Lyon simply changes it to "odor," which is acceptable with me, then moves on. She is a secretary among secretaries and I consider myself quite fortunate to have discovered her.

26
Pining for a Seduction

In the late summer of 1904, only days after his wife's burial, Clemens moved himself and his entourage into a three-story brownstone on Fifth Avenue in New York City. They would remain there for almost four years. During that period, Sam spent mornings writing his autobiography, which was being serialized in *Century* magazine; afternoons, he spent with one Albert Bigelow Paine. In early 1906, Sam met Paine, an author, poet and member of the Pulitzer Prize committee, at the New York Public Library while researching his autobiography. The two men took an instant liking to one another and, only days after the initial meeting, Sam designated Paine his official biographer.

One afternoon in the summer of 1907, while Sam was visiting Paine at his Redding, Connecticut home, Paine pointed out to Clemens a piece of property nearby which was up for sale and suggested it would make an ideal homesite. A month later, Sam purchased the property and hired architect John Mead Howells, son of William Dean Howells, to design and build a home on the property. Clemens obviously had his late wife in mind when he explained the design he wanted.

"A home built in the style of a Tuscan villa," Sam said. "Perhaps an earthen color with a slanted tile roof, arched windows and a courtyard with a plenitude of greenery and a fountain."

***

When completed in February of 1908, including electric

lights and a new contraption called a telephone, it was every inch the home Clemens had requested. A two-story structure, it featured an almost flat terra-cotta roof and a dark yellow stucco exterior to simulate the quaint, aged look of a Tuscany home. The ground floor included a formal dining room with arched windows and French doors, which opened out onto a terrace with a fountain and dancing cherubs. While the highlight of one wing was a reading area with a lush garden filled with miniature trees and flowers, the other featured a billiards room decorated with old news clippings and caricatures of Sam.

On the day he moved in, Clemens dubbed the residence "Stormfield," a name taken from his short novel *Captain Stormfield Visits Heaven*, royalties from which helped pay for the home. To repay Miss Lyon for her years of loyalty and hard work, Sam built her a twelve-room cottage on the grounds and named it Lobster Pot since it resembled a Maine lobster pot. When he handed her the keys, he told her it "is yours as long as you are in my employ."

After her mother's death, Jean's seizures became more frequent and severe and her behavior between more and more bizarre. Some days, she would try to help Sam with his work, but, more often than not, her efforts would be interrupted with a violent seizure. Meanwhile, Sam struggled to reconcile himself to Jean's worsening condition and the fact that she was "heavily afflicted by this unearned, undeserved and hellish disease, and she is not strictly responsible for either her disposition or her acts."

Meanwhile, Clara's star as an international concert singer continued to rise. After recuperating from her mother's death, she returned to Vienna, where she was reunited with Gabrilowitsch. The following summer, however, the couple had a violent blow-up and Clara abruptly broke off the engagement. A month later in Amsterdam, at a concert for the King and Queen of the Netherlands, she met Charles Edmund Wark, a classic pianist from Cobourg, Ontario who quickly became her new accompanist.

Over the winter of 1906 and into the late summer of 1908,

Clara and Wark performed together in a series of highly-acclaimed concerts in London and Paris. After a London benefit concert to raise money for American girls to attend Oxford and Cambridge universities, several London newspapers reported that Clara was having a scandalous affair with Wark, a married man.

***

Now, in late April of 1908, Isabel Lyon was ruling the roost at Stormfield. Over the past four years, while serving as Sam's editor, secretary and research assistant, she had slowly but surely gained control of virtually every aspect of Sam's life. While living in the New York brownstone, Clemens had turned over management of the household and its finances to her. Each month, she kept tabs on expenses and, at the end of the month, Sam provided the funds necessary to pay them. Once the family moved into Stormfield, she continued in that role and, in early 1907, Sam gave her the ultimate control, power of attorney over his business affairs. This meant she had full authority over the family's purse strings and oversaw the spending of all of Sam's income.

***

On May 1, Clara, having finished a successful winter concert season in Europe, returned to the States to visit her father and sister at Stormfield for the first time. Upon arrival, she went straight to the writing parlor on the second floor to greet her father, then, after she didn't see Jean, she asked about her.

"She is in the conservatory being punished," Sam said.

"Punished?" Clara said. "For what?"

"The gardeners spent all day yesterday morning planting chrysanthemums, then, in the afternoon, Jean comes along and pulls them all out of the ground."

"Why would she do that?"

"God only knows."

Five minutes later, Clara was in the conservatory where she

419

saw Jean seated on a stool, facing into a corner.

When Clara entered, Jean turned briefly around to see her, then quickly faced back into the corner.

"Jean!" Clara said. "Aren't you going to give your sister a warm hug?"

"I can't get up," Jean said. "If I do, Miss Lyon will be angry."

"Nonsense!"

Then Clara took Jean's shoulder, swung her around, and hugged her.

Once the embrace was broken, Jean quickly returned to the stool.

Suddenly, Isabel appeared.

"I saw that!" she said, going straight to Jean. "You were told to remain seated and facing into the corner."

"She got up to give me a hug," Clara said.

"She disobeyed me!" Lyon said.

Then she turned back to Jean.

"Didn't you disobey me? Tell me that you know you disobeyed me."

Jean cowered away, turning her face back into the corner.

"Look at me when I'm talking to you," Isabel said, grasping Jean's chin and turning her face to her own. "You'll never learn anything if you don't listen."

"Clara pulled me up to…" Jean said.

Isabel interrupted.

"Don't talk back to me," she said. "You knew my orders."

Then she slapped Jean on the side of the head with her open palm.

Clara was livid with anger.

"Who in God's name do you think you are treating my sister in such a manner," she said. "She's a twenty-eight-year-old woman and you're treating her like a child."

"She doesn't have her wits about her," Isabel said. "She has to be controlled."

"You can't treat her like a seven-year-old."

"How else should I do it? Your father approves of my methods."

"Well, I don't!" Clara said.

Instantly, Clara turned to Jean and took her hand.

"Come on!" Clara said. "We'll go for a walk."

"No! No!" Jean said, pulling back her hand. "Miss Lyon will be angry."

Then, quickly, she seated herself again and returned her face to the corner.

Lyon turned to Clara and smiled triumphantly.

Five minutes later, Clara was back in the writing parlor with her father.

"I cannot believe what you have allowed Isabel to do to Jean," she said.

"Someone has to control her," Sam said. "I have neither the heart nor the patience."

Clara shook her head in disapproval.

"I never dreamed Jean's condition would come to this," she said.

"Neither did I, but we have no other choice."

Clara paused for a moment, then turned back to her father.

"I want to ask a favor," she said. "Tomorrow, I plan to go to Quarry Farm to visit Uncle Theodore and Aunt Susan. Can you allow me $200 for the trip?"

"You'll need to speak to Miss Lyon," Sam said. "She's in control of the purse strings these days."

***

The following morning, when Clara was packed and ready to leave, she went to Isabel and asked her for $200.

"That amount is unavailable," Isabel said. "There have been some unexpected expenses this month. I can only provide you $100."

Clara peered at Isabel for a moment, then returned to the writing parlor and told her father Isabel had refused the requested amount. Moments later, Sam was back downstairs with Isabel.

"Give Clara the full amount she requested," Sam said.

"We had unexpected expenses this month."

"Provide her the requested amount," Sam said. "I'll rectify

421

the shortfall from another source."

Then he turned and went back upstairs.

Isabel counted out $200 and placed it in Clara's hand.

"If I were you," Isabel said, "I would not become too high and mighty."

"What does that mean?"

"I know some secrets I could share with your father."

"Namely?"

"Namely that you have been having a sexual affair with your accompanist, a man named Charles Wark. I understand he is married."

For a moment, Clara glared at Isabel, livid anger in her eyes.

"You wouldn't do that."

"Oh, yes, I would. Just try me."

Without another word, Clara turned from Isabel, went to her father and told him she would be leaving that afternoon for Quarry Farm.

***

Two mornings later, while Katy was preparing breakfast, Jean entered the kitchen, grabbed a butcher knife and attacked her. When Katy realized what was happening, she screamed and ran out of the kitchen. When Isabel heard the scream, she rushed into the kitchen, wrestled the knife away from Jean, then locked her in an upstairs closet. Moments later, she took Katy, who had a cut on her right cheek, and reported the incident to Sam.

"Jean is beyond our control now," Isabel said. "It's time to send her back to Craig's Colony."

"Do you determine that's the only solution?"

"She's crazy," Lyon said. "We have no choice."

"Then proceed," Sam said. "Handle everything. Escort her up there, talk to the administrators, pay the necessary fees, then come back. I want to know nothing about the details. Just take care of it."

***

Now, with Jean absent, Sam, except for Katy and two other servants, was alone at Stormfield with Isabel Lyon. His mornings were spent writing *Letters from the Earth,* a series of essays collected from various times in his life. During the afternoons, Lyon would come to the writing parlor to edit his manuscript, handle correspondence, then attend to managing the servants and the household. Once Isabel had finished her work, she would retire to the Lobster Pot and her own world. One afternoon in early June, after she finished her work, she invited Sam to come to the Lobster Pot for dinner.

"I could make roast beef with mustard sauce and boiled cabbage," she said. "I make my own sauce."

"I do love roast beef and cabbage," Sam said. "What time?"

"Seven sharp."

***

That night, when Sam showed up promptly at the appointed time, Isabel had a sumptuous meal prepared. After the meal, Sam retired to the sitting room while Isabel cleared up the table and dishes, then joined him, taking a seat in a chair while Sam sat on the settee.

"Did you enjoy the dinner?" she asked.

"Quite enjoyable."

A long pause.

"Mr. Clemens, have you considered taking another wife?"

"I should have a woman in my life," Sam said. "At this juncture, however, my disposition is not ready again."

"Have you been satisfied with my work?"

"Oh, yes," Sam said. "You have made me an excellent secretary."

Isabel arose from the chair, then took a seat beside Sam. For a long moment, she didn't look at Sam. Finally, she turned to face him.

"Would you consider me as a prospect?"

"For a new wife?"

"Yes."

Sam didn't answer at first.

"You've been everything I could ask for in a secretary," Sam said. "Bringing romance into that equation would not be wise."

She was quiet for a moment.

"Can I show you a new dress I purchased?"

"Please do."

Isabel arose from her seat and went into the bedroom, then moments later, returned wearing a stylish dark blue dress. Tight-fitting, it emphasized the outline of her breasts and hips. She spun herself around for Sam to see her.

"Do you like it?"

"Quite fashionable," Sam said. "It fits your form like a hand in a glove."

"Do you think so?" she said, running her hands over her breasts and thighs.

Now Sam could see where Isabel's intentions lay.

He got up from his seat.

"I think I should be leaving," he said. "I'm much obliged for the meal."

"Did I say something unpleasant?"

"Oh, no! It's getting late and I have work to do tomorrow."

Then Sam took his hat and started to the door.

"When will you arrive at Stormfield tomorrow?"

"I hope I didn't do anything to offend you."

"You created no problems," he said.

For a moment, she studied Sam.

"I'll be there at eight tomorrow," she said finally.

***

June 5, 1908 *Over the past seventy-three years of my life on this earth, I have joined my body in carnal embracement with only three women: Laura Hawkins, Ina Coolbrith and my beloved Livy. Each occurrence was fulfilled at that particular moment due to the demands of the moment. Now, at this advanced juncture, I have absolutely no intention of making Miss Lyon the fourth. Three was enough. Although she has been pining for a seduction for several years now, I have absolutely no romantic interest in her.*

***

A week later, Clara returned from her visit at Quarry Farm. When she realized Jean was missing from the household, she went to her father. He explained that Isabel had recommended that Jean be returned to Craig's Colony.

"That foul witch!" Clara said. "Jean had her moments, but she was incapable of doing anything that couldn't be tolerated."

"She attacked Katy with a butcher knife."

"No matter! It was all for show, to release her frustrations and get attention. Jean has too kind a heart to truly hurt another person."

"She doesn't realize her actions," Sam said.

"Perhaps, but she is not dangerous."

Clara studied her father for a moment.

"Don't you see Isabel's plan?" she said finally. "She convinced you to send Jean back to Craig's Colony because she wanted you all to herself."

"What is your meaning?"

"Now that Mother is gone, she has designs on you. She wants to win you and marry you for your money."

"Rest assured that shall not happen," Sam said. "Already she has attempted that ploy and I nipped it in the bud."

"She has taken control of your life," Clara said. "Your life is no longer your own. It belongs to Isabel."

Sam didn't answer at first.

"I'm seventy-three years old," he said finally. "I need help managing my affairs. The energy, the quick step, the sly smile, the call to action, the madness of youth… It's all gone now. Old age has crept up on me."

Clara peered at her father for a long moment. She didn't reply.

***

Three days later, on a Saturday, Sam and Clara walked across the grassy hillside between Stormfield and the Lobster

Pot to view the latest work on the cottage. Over the past few months, Isabel, with Sam's approval, had been having some renovations made to the dwelling. The roof needed repairs, the kitchen was being enlarged, the bathroom ceiling needed replacement and landscaping work was needed near the entrance. To complete each project, Isabel hired the workers to do the job, then, once complete, she presented Sam a bill for their work, which he paid without question.

When they arrived, Sam and Clara could see that fresh cedar shrubs, intermingled with zinnias, roses and pansies, had been planted along the front of the home.

"The new greenery dresses up the front of your cottage," Sam said. "What was the cost?"

"A total of $722."

She reached in her pocket and withdrew a receipt.

Sam took it, then peered at it.

"That seems high," he said.

"The workers had a dig out huge stones, which meant extra work," Isabel said. "Naturally, that cost more."

Sam inhaled, then withdrew a book of bank drafts and scribbled out a check for the requested amount.

Ten minutes later, Sam and Clara were walking back along the footpath to Stormfield.

"Do you feel Isabel is being honest with you about the renovation projects?"

"Absolutely. She is one of the most honest people I've ever known."

"You did feel that the cost of the landscape work was high?"

"I did, but I have no reason to question Isabel's integrity."

***

That afternoon, when Isabel went into town to pay bills, Clara returned to the cottage. Knowing the back door was never locked, she snuck inside and went to Isabel's desk where she kept documents related to her business dealings. After several minutes of searching, she found a folder labeled "renovation receipts." Quickly, she tucked it under her arm, then retraced her steps back along the footpath to Stormfield.

That night, she made a list of the various renovation projects at the cottage and its costs. Then, after asking Sam for access to his bank draft register, she compared each worker's invoice with the amount Sam had paid to reimburse her. Finally, after two hours, she added up the totals and concluded Isabel had overcharged her father a total of $8,212. Once she had rechecked her figures, she took her findings to Sam.

"She has embezzled at least $8,212 from me," Sam said. "In all likelihood, there is more."

"What do you intend to do?"

"I'll have a word with her tomorrow."

***

The following morning, when Miss Lyon appeared at Stormfield to begin work, Sam called her into the formal dining room. There, in front of him on the table, he had all of the workers' invoices and the corresponding bank drafts spread out before him.

"I have a stone-cold case against you for embezzlement," he began.

Then he proceeded to lay out his evidence as Lyon's face slowly took on a shocked look. Finally, after twenty minutes, he was finished.

"I could go to the authorities with this," he said. "But I don't wish for the resulting publicity and idle gossip. Thus, I am relieving you of all appointed duties and dismissing you from my employ."

Isabel didn't answer at first.

"When I moved in, you said you were giving me the cottage," she said finally.

"Only as long as you were in my employ. Now that I am closing my business relationship with you, I'm retrieving it. This is a notification that you are to have yourself and all personal belongings removed from the Lobster Pot in three days.

"Do you understand?"

"Is there nothing I can do to make amends?"

"Nothing whatsoever. I cannot abide a thief."

***

A week later, Clara was ready to leave Stormfield and return to Vienna for the fall concert season. As she and her father bounced along in the cab carriage en route to the train station, Clemens asked about her itinerary.

"First, I'm going to Rome to spend a few days with Carlo," she said.

"Who is Carlo?"

"He's my agent. Once I get bored with him, then I'll continue on to Vienna."

"What happens when you arrive in Vienna?"

"I'm meeting Ossip."

Surprised, Sam turned to her.

"Has that old flame rekindled itself?"

"For the moment," she replied. "In his letters, he claims he has matured since the break-up. Now he says he wants to get married and settle down."

"What happened to the Canadian?"

"Charles? He is the accompanist to an Italian soprano now."

Long pause, then Clara continued.

"Once I arrive in Vienna, Ossip and I will attempt to work out our differences and determine if we have a future together. Then I'll decide."

Another long pause.

"I just hope you're happy," Sam said.

"If I decide to marry Ossip," Clara said, "can we hold the wedding at Stormfield?"

Sam smiled.

"Absolutely. I shall be there with bells on."

27
Halley's II

Fifteen months passed. On the morning of October 6, 1909, Clara Clemens and Ossip Salomonovich Gabrilowitsch were married on the front terrace at Stormfield surrounded by bouquets of beautiful flowers, lavish wedding gifts, invited guests, friends and family. As always, Rev. Joseph Twichell was there to officiate. Once the vows were complete, the old women sniffled into their handkerchiefs and gushed about what a beautiful bride she was. Following the ceremony, there was a wedding feast and dancing. Finally, when the festivities were finished, friends and guests threw handfuls of rice and watched as the couple, suitcases in hand, boarded the cab carriage that would take them to the Redding train station, then to New York Harbor for the return to Europe and their new lives in Berlin. As Sam waved good-bye to the newlyweds, he didn't expect to see either of them for at least another year.

***

Two months later, out of the blue, Clara suddenly showed up again at Stormfield. She was alone.

"Why aren't you with your husband?" Sam asked.

"We have been quarreling of late, so we agreed to be apart for a while. We still love one another, but we need some distance between us."

"I understand," Sam said. "Me and your mother used to get like that at times. How long will you be here?"

"Not certain," she said. "One, maybe two months."

"Then I need your help with something."

"What might that be?"

"I want to bring Jean back home," Sam said. "I can no longer abide the thought of her being in the institution."

Clara paused before answering.

"Suppose she is uncontrollable?"

"No matter," Sam said. "We'll find some way to manage her. I just want her back home."

***

Two days later, Clemens and Clara arrived at Craig's Colony, the institution for epileptics in western New York State. When Sam explained to the administrator his intentions, the man was quick to issue dire warnings.

"I must tell you your daughter is in the throes of postictal psychosis," he said. "Her attention is often absent and she is a danger not only to herself, but to those around her. She is subject to bouts of hallucination, which, at times, can be violent."

"No!" Clemens said. "We want to take her home."

Two hours later, Sam, Clara and Jean were in a cab carriage taking them from the institution grounds to the local train station. During the ride, Jean would have lucid moments during which she could carry on a social conversation, then, at other times, she was in her own world engaged in a lengthy conversion with her long-dead pet goat Abner.

"Abner, I have informed you many times the grass along the little stream is sweeter than the grass near the barn. And you should not be trying to jump over the fence. If you became entangled in the mesh, the barbed wire could cut into your neck, you would die and I would no longer have Abner as my child."

Sam and Clara looked at one another knowingly.

"Abner!" Jean started up again. "Are you listening to me? This is your mother speaking."

A long pause.

"Christmas will be approaching soon," Sam said. "I remember how much you loved Christmas as a small child."

"Oh, yes, Papa!" Jean said. "I love Christmas. It's a time when all the world is happy and at peace and filled with joy and good will."

"Have you made your list?"

"I shall have it ready tomorrow."

***

Upon arrival back at Stormfield, Sam suggested to Jean that she live in the Lobster Pot, Miss Lyon's old place, which had been sitting empty for more than a year.

"No! I want to live at Stormfield with you and Clara."

"As you wish," Sam said.

So, a part-time nurse was hired for Jean, a room was set up for her in an upstairs bedroom and, over the first week, she fell into a new daily routine. Many days, Jean, Clara and Sam would take long walks across the wooded hillsides near the home; afternoons would be spent playing croquette on the front lawn; at night, they would play whist until the wee hours. Jean seemed to be doing quite well.

***

On the morning of December 22, Clemens was reading in his study when he heard shouting voices in the front yard. When he peered out the window, he saw Clara, Katy and two other servants chasing a naked Jean across the front yard. By the time he was down the stairs to the front door, Clara and the servants had Jean in tow and were leading her back into the house.

Sam met them at the door.

"What happened?" he said.

"She appeared at the breakfast table without clothing," Katy said. "When we attempted to take her to her room to dress, she ran out of the house into the yard."

Sam turned to Jean.

"What happened?"

For a moment, Jean peered into her father's eyes, then burst into tears.

"Oh, Papa!" she said, burying her face in Sam's chest. "There are forces within me which I cannot control."

***

On December 23, two days before Christmas, the events of the previous day were forgotten. Jean and the entire Clemens family were preparing for Christmas. A huge Christmas tree had been installed in the parlor with all of the appropriate decorations and colorful lights. Sam and Clara had spent the previous two days shopping in Redding for the items on Jean's wish list. Clara, Jean's nurse and Katy had wrapped all of the gifts and placed them under the tree. There was a pile of some twenty to thirty gifts under the tree in an assortment of box sizes, all wrapped in happy holiday paper. Everything was set for Jean to have a big Christmas.

***

The following morning, Christmas Eve of 1909, Jean's tragic destiny was finally fulfilled. Katy knew it was Jean's custom to awaken promptly at 7.a.m. each morning, then go to the bathroom where Katy would assist her with a cold bath. When Jean did not appear at the bathroom that morning, Katy, sensing a problem, first went to see if she was still in bed. After she didn't find her there, Katy rushed into the bathroom to see if Jean had tried to bathe herself. There she found Jean lying lifeless in the bathtub. After spending several minutes trying to revive her, Katy ran out of the bathroom to get Sam.

"Mr. Clemens! Mr. Clemens!" Katy shouted.

Sam, who was already out of bed, met her at the bottom of the stairs.

"Katy? What's the matter?"

"Jean is dead."

Moments later, Sam was in the bathroom gazing down at his dead daughter lying on the bathroom floor.

He shook his head sadly.

"She's happy now," he said. "She's gone to be with her

mother and sister, and if I thought I could bring her back by just saying one word, I wouldn't say it."

Later that day, the examining county physician attributed Jean's death to drowning, noting "the victim, a known epileptic, suffered a seizure while bathing, passed out and drowned."

***

Three days later, Sam and Clara were on a train to Elmira, N.Y. for Jean's funeral. At the train station, they were met by Theodore Crane, husband of Olivia's adopted sister who was in charge of Langdon business and family affairs. In the carriage en route to Quarry Farm, Sam asked a favor of him.

"Regarding the burial plot beside Olivia, I want you to reserve that place for me and have Jean interred on the adjacent plot."

"You want to be buried beside your wife?" Crane said.

"That is correct."

It shall be done," Crane replied.

***

Funeral services for Jean were conducted by Rev. Joe Twichell at the Langdon family plot in Woodlawn cemetery in Elmira. In attendance were the Clemens family, the Crane family and close friends. As Jean's body was lowered into its final resting place, Rev. Twichell read solemnly from the book of common prayers.

"We therefore commit this body to the ground, earth to earth, ashes to ashes, dust to dust; in sure and certain hope of the Resurrection to eternal life."

***

The following morning, after spending the night at Quarry Farm with the Cranes, Sam and Clara took an early train from Elmira for the return trip to Redding. When they arrived at the Redding station that afternoon, father and daughter were loading their baggage into a cab carriage for the return to Stormfield. Once Sam had hoisted the last piece of luggage into the carriage, he turned and took Clara's hand to help her into the carriage.

Suddenly, he stopped, grabbed his chest and slumped to the ground.

"Papa! Papa!" Clara said.

"Driver!" Clara said. "My father has had a heart attack. Help me get him into the carriage and go straight to the Redding Hospital."

***

Sam spent the next three days in the Redding hospital undergoing treatment for a heart condition. When he was ready to be released, he was paid a visit by Dr. William Quintard, a fiftyish, graying man with a kind face and salt-and-pepper beard.

"You have angina," he said. "You're going to have to take things quietly for a while or you won't be with us."

"Fate has already decided those matters," Sam said.

"What are you saying?"

"I came in with Halley's comet and I plan to go out on it."

"How do you plan to accomplish that?"

"When I see it coming, I'm going to reach up, grab on to its tail and ride off into the heavens."

"That will be quite a feat."

"It's going to happen," Sam said.

Dr. Quintard laughed.

"You're one of a kind, Clemens," he said. "After God made you, he threw away the mold."

***

Four months passed. After his return to Stormfield, Sam's lifestyle underwent a drastic change. Dr. Quintard ordered him to avoid "all situations which could involve stressful feelings and high emotions." His meals consisted mostly of grains, fresh fruits and vegetables with little or no meat. Mornings, he spent in the writing parlor, and afternoons, with the help of a cane, he would take short walks across the nearby wooded hillsides, ruminating, philosophizing and trying to make sense of his life.

April 17, 1910. *Many times, I have ruminated over the thought of having a heart-to-heart talk with Clara relating to our family conflicts during her younger days. Some days, I feel I should apologize, make amends and attempt to arrive at some level of peace within myself in the matter. By the same token, I truly do not want to relive the sorrows of those experiences, the violent incident during the trip out west, her accusations that I loved Susy more than she; which is true and always shall be. Despite these considerations, I wish to clear the air and personally arrive at some measure of closure. Tonight, when Clara comes home, I will discuss it with her.*

***

That night, just after 9 p.m., Sam called Katy to his bedside.

"Where is Clara?" he asked.

"Oh, sir! I thought you knew," she said. "She had a gentleman caller earlier tonight. She left with him around seven."

"Who was the gentleman caller?"

"She didn't say."

"Did she say when she would return?"

"No, sir!"

Sam paused for a moment.

"The moment she arrives, tell her I wish to speak with her."

***

April 18, 1910 *The candle of my life is growing ever dimmer. These old creaky bones are feeling the depths of the tiredness and suffering and pain of these past seventy-five years. It would please me to think that, upon my passing, I might see Livy and Susan and Orion in some other world, but, in my heart, I know such notions are only a fantasy. A dream. A delusion. A hallucination. When they lay this mangy old*

435

carcass in the ground, I will welcome the rains that will come to slowly create seams in my coffin; through those seams will crawl small worms, then more small worms, then even larger ones which will finally consume my flesh, bone and sinew and endow it to the ages. I have absolutely no delusions that I shall spend eternity dancing happily around God's golden throne while I subsist on a strict diet of milk and honey.

***

That night, after Clara still had not appeared at his bedside, Sam asked Katy about her again.

"I'm sorry, Mr. Clemens," Katy replied. "Still no word from her."

"Do you have any notion where she is?"

"No, sir, I do not!"

"The moment she returns, tell her I wish to speak with her."

"It shall be done."

***

The following morning, Sam reread the thin volume *Papa: An Intimate Biography of Mark Twain,* the book Susy had written for him. By rereading its pages, it somehow brought her back to life. His eyes always filled with tears when he read the last line in the little book… "All of us are on our way to Keokuk to see Grandma Clemens, who is very feeble and wants to see all of us, particularly Jean, who is her namesake. We are going by way of the lakes, as Papa said that would be the most comfortable way. This afternoon, we arrived in Keokuk after a pleasant journey…."

April 19, 1910 *Each and every time I read the arrested sentence which ends the little volume, it seems that the little hand that traced it cannot be far-gone, but will shortly return again to finish it. But that is a dream, a creature of the heart, not of the mind—a feeling, a longing, not a mental product. I am like Aaron Burr, who lost his daughter at sea. Rereading Susy's little book provides me with the same feeling that lured*

436

Burr, old, gray, forlorn, to the harbor to stand in the gloom and the dawn gazing seaward through veiled mists and sleet and snow for the ship which he knew had gone down forever, the ship that bore all of his treasures, his daughter.

***

April 20, 1910 *The grandest, happiest, most glorious days of my life were spent out west on the frontier. Over all those years since, this fellow Mark Twain has managed to turn Samuel Langhorne Clemens, a raw-bone, unwashed country kid that likes to squish his toes in Mississippi mud, into a staid, self-satisfied, comfortably-refined Eastern gentleman that knows how to use a salad fork and to stand when woman enter a room. Such is the price of love. Yet somehow, far beyond all this comfort and finery and technological newness, my spirit still resides out there in that desert alongside Ben Coon, Scratchy Mitchell, the jackass rabbits, the mountains, the sand, the tumbleweeds, the coyotes and the sage. I reckon you could say I've got a sagebrush soul.*

***

On the evening of April 21, 1910, Sam had a dinner of vegetable soup, cornbread and milk. When he started back up the stairs to the writing parlor, he was too weak to mount the steps and asked Katy to provide some assistance. Once Katy helped him up the stairs and he was comfortably in bed, he took his copy of Rousseau's *Social Contract* from the bedside table.

"Is there anything else?" Katy said.

"Have you heard from Clara?"

"No, sir! I have not."

"Where could she be?"

"I have no idea, sir."

Katy paused before leaving the room.

"Anything else?"

"Will you hand me my glasses?"

Instantly, Katy retrieved his glasses from the bedside table. As Sam took the glasses, he peered into Katy's face for a brief

437

instant, then his face screwed up in pain and he slumped forward in the bed.

"Mr. Clemens! Mr. Clemens!" Katy shouted, going to the bed to examine him. Sitting on the side of the bed, she turned his face to hers. He was unconscious and gasping for breath. Quickly, she ran down the stairs and called Dr. Quintard.

***

Samuel Langhorne Clemens died at 6:22 p.m. that evening in his bed at Stormfield, his glasses and a copy of Rousseau's *Social Contract* resting in his lap. Some thirty minutes after Katy called, Dr. Quintard arrived, pronounced Sam dead and closed his eyes for the last time.

As he did, Katy noticed an exceptionally bright light outside in the night sky. Quickly, she turned from Sam's bedside and rushed to the bedroom window.

"There is it!" Katy said. "It's Halley's comet. He always said he would die when it passed through again."

Seconds later, Dr. Quintard and Katy were standing side-by-side at the window gazing into the heavens.

"Yes, he did," the doctor added. "I wonder how he knew."

***

Three days later, more than 5,000 people, including Clara Clemens and an unidentified male escort, showed up at the Brick Presbyterian church on New York's Fifth Avenue for Sam's funeral. There was not enough room inside for all of the mourners, so those who were unable to get inside milled around outside. There were friends, relatives, fans, politicians, celebrities, statesmen and fellow authors as well as curiosity seekers who only wanted to see Sam in his final public appearance. As always, Rev. Joseph Twichell was present to officiate. Clemens was buried two days later beside his beloved Olivia at Woodlawn Cemetery in Elmira.

***

While Sam was eulogized by thousands of celebrities, newspapers, politicians, scientists and national leaders, the most poignant, the most telling, the most unforgettable came from the man who knew his heart and soul better than any other, his long-time friend William Dean Howells.

After viewing Sam in his coffin, Howells wrote:

"I looked for a moment into the face I knew so well. And it was patient with the patience I had so often seen in it; something of a puzzle; a great silent dignity, an assent to what must be from the depths of a nature whose tragic seriousness broke into the laughter which the unwise took for the whole of the man. Emerson, Longfellow, Lowell, Holmes—I knew them all and all the rest of our sages, poets, seers, critics, humorists; they were all alike and like all other literary men; but Clemens was singular, sole, incomparable, the Lincoln of our literature."

28
Afterword

Sam died without knowing he was about to become a grandfather. When Clara arrived unannounced in November of 1909, she told her father she was estranged from her husband, but, out of shame, neglected to tell him she was also four months pregnant. On August 19, 1910, five months after Clemens' death, Clara gave birth to Nina Clemens Gabrilowitsch, a bouncing baby girl, at Stormfield.

***

As his sole survivor, Sam made Clara the executor of his literary estate. In a short, clear will, he insured that the money and rights to all of his work would forever remain in the family. At Sam's death, Clara received a lump sum payment and a regular income for life, "free from any control or interference on the part of any husband she may have."

***

Laura Hawkins, Sam's childhood sweetheart and the model for Becky Thatcher in both the *Tom Sawyer* and *Huckleberry Finn* books, married Dr. James W. Frazer in 1858, with whom she had two sons. In later years, she served as matron of the Hannibal Home for Orphans and the Indigent. She died in 1928.

***

Ina Coolbrith, poet, essayist, librarian, and Sam's lover during his San Francisco days, was named California's first poet laureate in June of 1915. For more than thirty years, she had written poetry and played mother hen to San Francisco's literary community while providing inspiration to the careers of numerous authors, including Sam, Bret Harte, novelist Jack London and poet Joaquin Miller. She died in San Francisco in 1928.

***

Author Bret Harte, after leaving the Overland Express in San Francisco, moved back to New York and, using his political connections, later served as U.S. Consul to both Germany and Scotland. He died in Camberley, England in 1902. His most enduring contributions to American literature were the short stories *The Luck of Roaring Camp* and *The Outcasts of Poker Flat*.

***

Ambrose Bierce crossed the border into Chihuahua State, Mexico in the late summer of 1913, telling fellow reporters he wanted to "gain some first-hand experience of the Mexican Revolution." He was never seen or heard from again. While many theories abound, it is believed he was captured by revolutionary Pancho Villa's troops and executed as a spy. His most famous literary works were the lexicon *The Devil's Dictionary* and the short story, *An Occurrence at Owl Creek Bridge*.

***

William Dean Howells, Sam's closest friend and literary confidante for more than forty years, died on May 11, 1920. An American realist novelist, he was best known for his long tenure as editor of the *Atlantic Monthly* and the novels *The Rise of Silas Lapham* and *A Traveler from Altruria*.

***

Isabel Lyon, after leaving Sam's employ, married Ralph Ashcroft, one of Sam's business associates, in 1909 and moved to Canada. After they were divorced in 1927, Lyon returned to New York and resumed work as a secretary. In later years, she never spoke of her association with Sam, but, in the early 1950s, she met regularly with Hal Holbrook, who was developing his one-man show *Mark Twain Tonight*. Lyon died of a heart attack in her Greenwich Village apartment on December 4, 1958, two weeks before her 95th birthday.

***

Clara's husband Ossip Gabrilowitsch served as conductor of the Detroit Symphony Orchestra from 1919 until his sudden death in 1936. In 1944, at the age of 70, Clara remarried one Jacques Samossoud, a Russian-born conductor twenty years her junior, who proceeded to loot her inheritance to finance his gambling habits. In 1951, to pay her husband's debts, she auctioned off her Hollywood home, her jewelry collection and numerous personal papers and memorabilia her father had given her. Bed-ridden and deeply depressed, Clara died in San Diego on Nov. 19, 1962.

***

Clara's daughter Nina, aged 56 and known as a heavy drinker, was found dead January 18, 1966 in a Los Angeles hotel room. Empty bottles of drugs and alcohol were found at her bedside. Nina was Sam's last direct descendant and, after her funeral, she would spend eternity alongside all of the other members of the Clemens clan at Woodlawn cemetery in Elmira, N.Y.

The End

Author's Note

This novel is a dramatization of the life of Samuel Clemens AKA Mark Twain. As such, I have taken some liberties with not only dialog and situations and the addition of some made-up characters, but also with certain events and/or the dates they occurred.

Since human beings do not live their lives in plots, I was forced to change some of the facts of Samuel Clemens' life to create a cohesive dramatic narrative. As a result, the two most glaring departures from reality is in the life-spans of his two brothers, Orion and Henry.

In real life, older brother Orion died in 1897. Since I needed a reason for Clemens to be traumatized and reconsider his life, I killed off Orion in the year 1866, a full thirty-one years before his actual death.

Regarding Henry, in real time, he was born in 1838 and died in 1858 at the age of 20. In the book, since the plot progression would not permit Henry's birth in 1838, he was born in 1840 and died in 1858 at the age of 18. Other than those two glaring discrepancies, I tried to adhere to the other facts of Clemens' life as closely as possible.

Finally, I have tried to create a dramatic narrative which blends the facts, the fictions and the history of Clemens' life such that, once the reader has finished, they have a much broader, more intimate knowledge of the man, his personal life, his works and the influences which drove him to create those specific works.

Thanks for reading!

The Author

Other books by John Isaac Jones

A Quiet Madness: A Biographical Novel of Edgar Allan Poe

The Bird of Time: A Story of Friendship

The Hand of God

Alabama Stories

The Duck Springs Affair

Thanks, PG!: Memoirs of a Tabloid Reporter

Thirteen Stories

The Angel Years

For Love of Daniel

Tembo Makaburi

Going Home

The Last Cowboy

The Agreement

Other books may be viewed at:
https://www.amazon.com/stores/John-Isaac-Jones/author/B008PR3DQ8?

Editing and Formatting by BZHercules.com
Cover design by MiblArt, Kyiv, Ukraine
Special thanks to Dr. Michael Palazzolo, M.D., for his timely and expert research assistance.